"Jae Byrd Wells has ....ıng ııovel dealing with a new race of part human/part fish beings. An evil doctor uses a rare catfish DNA to change his subjects which he has collected in many ways including kidnapping, into Human Electric Cave Catfish. Jayne Flynn and the kidnapped Marian Harrison, along with about 60 others, must learn how to survive with their new bodies. The families that were left behind must also deal with the changes to their loved one. A great read with many twists and turns."

- Margene Burnham NBCT, Public School Librarian

"A great read we are glad to recommend to anyone, can't wait to see what happens in the sequel."

- Anita Siemer and Company, Bookstore Owner

"Jae has crafted a merry romp into the creepy and slightly macabre. The relationships among people, research, and ideologies ring true. The ending leaves me wondering what will come. Happy reading!"

- Laurel Zhang, Education Manager

"Ms. Wells has a unique style of character development to her story that in part mixes a sense of melancholy and reverie. She does a great job with development of her story's characters."

– John Yates, broadcaster and writer.

The "Tail" Begins

TALES FROM SCHOOL
Book 1

Written By

Jae Byrd Wells

Illustrated By Ann Warren

iUniverse LLC
Bloomington

THE "TAIL" BEGINS
TALES FROM SCHOOL Book 1

iUniverse books may be ordered through booksellers or by contacting:

iUniverse
1663 Liberty Drive
Bloomington, IN 47403
www.iuniverse.com
1-800-Authors (1-800-288-4677)

ISBN: 978-1-4917-3023-2 (sc)
ISBN: 978-1-4917-3024-9 (hc)
ISBN: 978-1-4917-3025-6 (e)

Library of Congress Control Number: 2014905698

Printed in the United States of America.

iUniverse rev. date: 04/04/2014

Dedication

With All My Love
To My Beautiful Children and My Beloved Soul Mate.

To my Parents, Brothers, Sisters, and In-laws

In honor of all Veterans

For love and support:
Karin, Rebecca, Jessica, Joan, Jaelene, Sharon,
Melody, Anita, Lisa, Bill, Bob, & Donny,

In loving memory of Ernie & Anja

Contents

Foreword

When Jae and her family come into my bookstore, it's like a sudden flurry of happiness has swirled in the door. The kids rush to the children's books, while Jae and her hubby ask about what might have arrived since their last visit. We talk about books, life and progress on her writing. I was excited when she told me that she would let me read her manuscript.

When I first read her book, I couldn't put it down. After I finished, I wanted to know when book two would be ready to read. I have read a great deal of science fiction and fantasy in my life, finding a new "universe" that is so original and yet so "down-to-earth" was fantastic.

The new humanoid race that Jae has created in her books is faced with many challenges just to survive and realize very swiftly that they must learn new ways or die. They have great potential to help advance the sciences of health, longevity and other medical issues. They could plumb the depths of the oceans or help with great technological breakthroughs in the science of gene therapy. But first, they just have to learn how to be a new race, how to adapt to the change that overtook them, and how to get along with those who have not changed at all.

If you could choose to swim and breathe underwater like a mermaid or stay on dry land and watch friends and loved ones swim away, which would it be? If you were afraid of the water, and you weren't given a choice, could you stand the necessity of living underwater? And what do you do when a xenophobe comes banging at your door?

Introducing people to good books is my passion in life; sharing her fantasy world with readers is Jae's. Her tales spin a maelstrom of adventure in the lives of her characters, keeping her readers wanting to know more about how the challenges and conflicts of her new world can be resolved.

It is always a joy when I find a new good book to share with my friends. And, it is always a privilege to have an author friend share their new book with me. It is then, my great joy to share my friend Jae's new book with you, my friends and fellow readers.

A great read we are glad to recommend to anyone, can't wait to see what happens in the sequel.

- Anita Siemer and Company,
Bookstore Owner.

Acknowledgements

Weston Schartz, Ernie Fincher, Mark Frank, and Billy Durham each gave me opportunities to prove that there is more to a person than just their 'cover', much like a book.

Richard Mgrdechian, Alex Bodnar, Sam Fishman, Steve Padelski and Dave Bray enticed me out of my hardened shell of discouragement by reminding me to fight for the things I believe in, whether personal convictions or dreams. Thanks for treating me like a person and giving me the time of day to share my dreams with you.

Employees (including Ann, Judy & Allen) and customers alike at my favorite writing location enjoyed my presence and progress. Thank you for brightening my days of work.

The wonderful computer genius, Robert Iverson, needs to be commended for saving my book scads of times on its journey through technology.

A very special acknowledgement for help with research goes out to the kind employees of the Sedgwick County Zoo, Exploration Place, Albuquerque Public Library, Albuquerque Biological Park, Louisville Public Library, Wichita Police Department, Kansas Department of Mine Reclamation, USS Silversides Submarine Museum, and the Muskogee War Memorial. They supplied me with the proper educational resources to help provide truths for my work of fiction.

DriedRiverBottom

Out of Hope

Chapter 1

*asp*! Jayne's naturally tan hand covered his mouth. It was possible the security camera might show how his cheeks burned from the inside out. Slowly his fingers traced the corners of his chin. He secretly hoped that it would look natural and intelligent. Since the afternoon had crawled by with minimal customers, he had been flipping channels. A missing persons program caught his eye since, there, plastered across the screen was a face he saw on a daily basis. Ashen-faced, he turned the knob on the small TV on the counter to minimize the volume. The slender man's shaking fingers would not cooperate. First, the volume bounced too low, too high and then tolerably low. Jayne's throat swallowed the lump again.

Aches and pains ran up and down his body that would only stop if he bolted out the door. Oh, if only he could! Bright sun rays from the giant front windows teasingly beckoned to him. The glass begged to be broken out of the shop in the converted small marine mammal park. The entire oceanarium outside of Bodega Bay, California was once open to the public; now only 1/10th of the main commercial building was being used to house Snake's Rock: Exotic Pet Shop. It conveniently sat on a corner near several abandoned buildings and large vacant parking lots, almost perfect isolation to hide the torment inside.

Goosebumps rippled from head to toe and stung like fire ants. Jayne knew that the boss monitored the security camera focused on him. He sighed. 'Big Brother' lurked in the same building. The compounded noises from parrots, parakeets, and exotic monkeys flooded the room, confounding the hidden microphones, but brightening Jayne's soul. The combined hum of the fresh and salt-water fish tanks was overwhelming, so the reclusive boss normally muted the volume.

As he <u>watched</u>, Jayne could not believe his eyes or ears. The name or story did not hit home. Yet, the radiant face of the young woman he called 'Hope' was drawn in a black and white sketch, age progressed to what she might look like today if found. Marian Harrison's younger profile sported tom-boyishly blunt curly hair. Staring at the old picture sent chills down his spine since he loved seeing her long, curly, chestnut brown hair dance.

Leaning onto the counter with his elbows, his throat tightened and his nostrils flared as the deep voice of the male host rang in his ears.

"…Marian had a high I.Q., but she had the usual problems for someone so smart. She did not fit in well at school, being the youngest of her class having skipped a grade. She had no desire for travel and preferred routine. When she was younger, her parents thought she was possibly autistic, but she just greatly needed a regular schedule. She also had an intense fear of water."

Blood drained from Jayne's face as he thought to himself. I *had always suspected she had been kidnapped, but to see her parents beg for her safe return.* He snorted. Tears longed to well up, but stopped in their tracks. This show desperately needed to remain hidden from his boss. The back of his short black hair stood on end. Every noise in the store heightened his awareness of his surroundings. To regain emotional control, Jayne massaged his clean-shaven chin. Nerves in his brain processed every word and picture that the TV displayed.

The TV show continued with a male swimming competitor. Anthony Rodriguez grew up in Galveston, Texas. Few people from his past searched for him. The secluded surfer never dated in his pursuit of fame and fortune. The Mexican descendant bummed off his swimming coach by living in his garage. A brief home video showed Anthony bragging about a sure win at the next competition.

Several people from the swimming community expressed their loss when he never showed up to the swim meet. Anthony's manager voiced his hope for his star pupil's safe return. With no leads, the police continue to be puzzled with this mysterious disappearance.

Jayne's brown eyes widened. He pretended to sneeze so that his hands could completely cover his flushed cheeks and his gaping jaw. *Oh, my God!* His silent words rang out to the heavens. *Oh, my God! That's Jonathon! He's burly now… but that face… I know even better than Hope.* Quivering hands moved from his cheeks to his eyes before stroking his hair. His head throbbed. When he started to shake his head, the journey stopped before it could complete its return. Anthony's voice on the TV mimicked last night's memory of his friend, Jonathon. The accent, including a surfer's tongue with the rolled r's, was undeniably identical between the two men. Even though the old Anthony proudly sported a pencil mustache and short hair, Jonathon's facial features matched, including the chiseled jaw. Many times over the last few years, Jayne had cut Jonathon's bangs to eye-length and trimmed his facial hair. Pain gripped the pet shop employee's stomach and tightened its grasp, causing it to try and rotate. Acid crept up his throat like spiders crawling.

The door chimed from speakers around the 3500 square feet of retail space. Breath escaped Jayne's gut as though an invisible force had punched him. Swiftly, Jayne flipped the TV off and inwardly cursed. *Dang! A customer! The boss will turn up the speakers and listen. Aw, man! I wonder how many more people I know on tonight's program. I wish I could finish.* From the inside corner of the L shaped wooden counter, Jayne briefly stood on his tiptoes to look in the general direction of the door, getting a peek over the shelves at who was walking in. After the seventy-year old customer entered, she side stepped the vertical piles of pet food along the eastern wall. Jayne watched her pick her way through the aisles toward him. Although his body faced the counter, his head turned toward her with a forced polite smile. His mind raced. *It's gentle Dee. She won't take long. I'll be back in front of the TV before the next case.*

Dee's expressionless amber eyes used to look radiant and bright. Today, trouble traced lines across her face as if she'd aged ten years in the span of a month. Those soft hands unusually shook against her sturdy body. There was something different about her stylish snow-white bun, for it seemed to drag her down; her petite legs wavered, shortening her once aristocratic pace into a protective gait.

Jayne glanced back to the counter with silent calculations from his memory. *Let's see, she needs birdseed for her bird and wild seed for the neighborhood birds.* His fingers immediately tapped keys on the register. Jayne guessed aloud, "...and cat food for the neighborhood cats."

Click click tap tap bring click went the register as he finished ringing up her purchase.

After she handed over her cash, she uttered, "Jayne, could you please be a dear and help me out to the car today? My knees are not what they used to be."

The register opened and Jayne placed the money into the correct slots. He would normally look at her directly, but his mind raced in other paths diverting his gaze. Jayne didn't dare complain out loud. *Ah, man. I oughta help her though, her limp is getting worse. Arthritis must have finally reared its ugly head.*

"Yes", Jayne responded with a crack and a hiss in his voice. Putting his fist to his mouth, he cleared his throat. "I may have found our missing frog. Let me see if I can cough it up. You know what I mean?" Half-heartedly, he forced a giggle at his lame joke, but Dee's forced happy expression remained. He snorted and shook his head at the floor. After he handed her the change, he closed the cash drawer. In a hurry, he proceeded to pick up the bags throughout the store and place them one at a time on a flat-bed cart. Two strides at a time, Jayne pushed it over to the register where Dee stood admiring the trinkets on sale. *Oh please hurry,* he thought to himself before sighing aloud.

She picked one up, turning it over and over before repeating the process with the next small keepsake.

Clearing his throat, Jayne impatiently voiced his progress, "Mrs. Graham, I'm ready." With that, she responded by smiling and heading for the door. Little conversation occurred as he pushed the squeaking cart to her vehicle. Jayne thought to himself, *I can't believe she parked the car all the way out in the middle of the lot! There's a good handicap spot closer. Why'd she park so far away with her waning health?*

"You are Andie Flynn's son?" Dee broke the silence in a hushed tone. "Are you not, dear?" They reached her tan Jeep Wagoneer.

Dee's sweet voice soothed his nerves. With one last squeak, he brought the cart to a halt. Looking directly into her experienced eyes, Jayne noticed her face now appeared less troubled. He shifted his weight. "Yes, Ma'am."

"She was really ill before her death." Dee's pleasant voice calmly continued. "Without insurance, she did not go to the doctor unless she had to. I delivered groceries to her. Perhaps you do not remember me. Today, I ran across a picture of you and your mother and made the connection. It always bothered me why you looked so familiar these last few years."

Although she paused to let Jayne comment, he only gave her nods of his head and crossed his arms. As a mixture of unpleasant and fond memories flooded back, his arms slowly unfolded. At last, hesitantly, Jayne spoke. Choppy words choked him as he stood as rigid as a mannequin. "I worked hard instead of playing. I worked every small job I could in order to pay bills. I did home-schooling work at her bedside to help her fall asleep. She was in so much pain. I told her I had a girlfriend. My pretend adventures gave her a life to dream about. I never did have a girl. I just told her that. I worked here before I was legally old enough. I passed my G.E.D. after she died. I was finally old enough to work here full-time when I turned sixteen. I've paid off the bills. I'm 21 now. I'm still here... I've been here for eight years." Shrugging, Jayne stopped talking and sucked in his breath.

"Eight years?"

Leery-eyed, Jayne peered partially over his shoulder at the storefront while he waited for her to open the cargo door hatch.

Jayne set the bags inside. His body ached as though he felt feverish. Trembling, he took an opportunity to think, *Dee could take me away from here.* Glancing vacantly back at the door, his fingers scratched the corners of his mouth. As he turned around, he stared at the deserted strip mall across the street, avoiding Dee's face. Tears flowed down his cheeks. Only the spirits heard his angry cry. His eyes widened in fear as he thought, *But then, what about Hope, and Jonathon?*

Jayne used one hand to wipe his face while the other one slammed the door harder than he intended. He felt Dee's presence as she followed him around to the driver's door.

"Where do you live now? Do you have an apartment somewhere nearby? Do you have a car yet? It's too far away for a bicycle. I have never seen you outside of this place."

Jayne cringed. His lips felt numb while a dirty feeling nagged at his soul. He didn't utter a word.

After Jayne carefully opened her door, Dee paused and fretted, "Jayne, dear?" She made direct eye contact. "Are you in any trouble, Jayne Flynn?"

Those loving words pinned darts at the very center of Jayne's heart. His drained, troubled face was neither acted nor forced. But grimly smiling, he enunciated politely, "No, Ma'am. And you just don't need to go troubling yourself." His words sounded as weak as he felt. "Okay?"

She answered with a tender expression and handed him two books from her purse. She forced the words out as if practiced, "Your Pa said you might like these."

"Thank you." Smiling, Jayne gently accepted the books with open hands. "Um. These are…um. These are from…" Hardened emotions stopped Jayne in midsentence. He let the question linger in the air, but she didn't correct herself.

"Be careful, Jayne." She nodded. Her maternal instincts kicked into high gear. "You come from good upbringing. I like you and don't want to see anything happen to you." Dee observed sternly, but kindly before she shut the door. She started the engine and drove off hurriedly.

Jayne's throat tightened. "My so-called father..." Jayne's breathy words returned to his thoughts, *...died of an alcoholic overdose years before mom got sick. I never saw him read.* As Jayne stared after the leaving vehicle, his face changed expressions a half dozen times: quizzical, perplexed, peace, and then fear, gripped him. A fresh breeze of air whipped his eye length bangs. Mimicking the soldiers on the TV, he did an about face. Tired legs trudged to the cart that he had left at the rear of her car. Pushing it awkwardly with the books in his left hand caused him to zig when he should have zagged. As he reached the storefront, he paused and took a step back.

The door opened and out came a taller, bulkier man. He forcefully stole the books out of Jayne's hands and challenged Jayne with frightening blue eyes.

"Gimme my books back! She... she... she let me borrow them. I have to give 'em back" Jayne hollered at him. "I got to keep them nice!" His caring palms and fingers reached out as he watched the thug not so carefully flip through the pages and drop the books on the thin worn carpet. The books thumped like faith crumbling to pieces.

"Humph," protested the bully with a slight snarl. To himself, he concluded there wasn't anything unusual.

Sadly, Jayne picked up the books and lovingly straightened the slightly creased pages. His slumped shoulders voiced his inward dashed dreams. He thought, *Maybe it's stupid to hope there's a hidden message from someone who wants to rescue me. But who would rescue me? Dee is the only one who knows I am stuck here.*

Both young men cringed as the sound system squawked, "What kind of an idiot are you, Douglas Baldwin? Don't ever do that in front of the windows! Someone could be watching!"

"Ah, there ain't no one 'round for miles." Doug fixated on the closest security camera, flailed his upper limbs and growled. "All this area... It's *deserted!*" Turning around and mumbling under his breath, Doug locked the pet shop door with a key on his key chain.

Taking big steps, Jayne sauntered toward the wall covered with fish tanks. Staring at the aisle with the dog toys and collars, he quickened his gait. His hurried pace led him to the opposite side of the store, where snakes, reptiles and exotic creatures sunned under the bright lights above their cages. Two steps inside the outstretched aisle, a big hand roughly grabbed his shirt collar. Jayne choked and gagged as he was wrested away from his path.

When Doug released his grip, Jayne rubbed his throat with his right hand and caressed it. He forced his throat to swallow several times in the attempt to get it to once again feel normal.

"Nice try, dufus," growled Doug as he forced Jayne on to a direct path to the counter. "Why did it have to be snakes?"

Jayne's mischievous grin turned upside down. He pouted a little as Doug inconveniently avoided the snake aisle.

Once they reached the counter, they walked around it and through the office behind the checkout counter.

Grumbling, Doug gave Jayne an extra shove into the organized office. He sneered and spat, "Come on, fancy pants! You got chores to do."

{:-)-]~~{

Across the street from Snake's Rock: Exotic Pet Shop, an old strip mall obscured two stealthy occupants. They were using a high resolution video camera along with a pair of binoculars for their stake-out. They observed and documented the interaction of Jayne and Dee.

"Well, she got him outside," brown eyes vocalized to the green eyes in an Oklahoman drawl. Sweat droplets started to form on his forehead.

"Okay," answered his partner. "She knows the boy, knew him and his mom years ago. She doesn't think he could be involved in a smuggling ring. If she thinks he's innocent, then we should too. Remember …innocent until proven guilty." He shifted his weight from one foot to even his stance.

"I don't think this is a smuggling ring. At least… not now."

"Isn't that what I said in the first place?"

"Hmph."

"He doesn't seem to suspect that she's wired."

"Something's wrong. He's definitely afraid. We need to find out why. There she goes. Let's go meet her and get the bug." Lowering his binoculars, the slightly balding man furrowed his light brown eyebrows. Pulling the binoculars back up quickly, he gasped as he used both his eyes to witness Jayne's confrontation at the storefront. "Wow! Well, what do we have here?" His voice rose to a new level. "Did you see that?"

"So what are we looking at?"

"There's something else going on here." With sorrow building in his heart, he shook his head. "That kid hasn't set foot outside until today." His olive skin flushed as his mouth snarled. "Well, that's it, call the boss! He's being roughed up and shoved back inside by a blonde-haired, Popeye-armed, thug with a flat-top-hair cut! Man!" He emphasized each word.

"I bet."

"Geeze."

"How many people live in there?" The taller of the two men, with pale freckled skin, snatched the binoculars to peer with his green eyes. "I see him. They're in the store now. He's pushing Jayne back beyond our scope. I bet that boy is never allowed outside the premises. I bet he doesn't even know what a mall is!"

Thinking of his teenage daughters and his credit card bill, the shorter man mumbled, "Lucky bastard!"

{:-)-]~~{

Rolling and stretching his neck, Jayne looked around at the brightly-lit pet shop's office. Imitation and real wood decorated the office from ceiling to floor. A black swivel chair sat behind the heavy oak desk. An up-to-date computer, black mesh organizer tray and cup sat neatly on the nearly empty desk. The copy machine/fax and scanner stood tall and vertical on a 2 drawer file cabinet in the corner.

Jayne's lips tightened and his eyebrows knitted as he followed Doug. Inching right, Jayne stopped and stared at the door to the storage unit and bathroom.

Doug loudly cleared his throat.

Hanging his head, Jayne closed in the distance between him and Doug. Walking alongside the western wall, Jayne's fingers traced the spines of old marine biology texts and reference books packed in the ceiling to floor bookcase. He had excelled in memorizing the helpful information. The bare south wall behind the desk provided Jayne with nothing to zone in on. When they reached the southwest corner, Doug reached out his right hand to move three small books on the highest shelf. The wooden shelf unit creaked as it parted, pulling back from the rest.

Doug barreled through, followed by Jayne. Once more the mechanical whirring and creaking echoed through the small claustrophobic room as the hidden passage closed. Cringing, Jayne sighed and lowered his head into his collarbone. Before the light from the office disappeared, Doug reached for the ceiling. His fingers wrapped around the metal chain hanging from the middle of the chilly metal room. *Boof* went the door and immediately a click sounded from the light as Doug switched it on.

Glaring at the opposite door resembling a bank vault, Jayne muttered under his breath. No one could exit either direction without the key and combination code that unlocked it. After Doug unlocked it, Jayne's feet automatically followed Doug through the heavy metal door. He yanked on the cord for the light switch, turning it off. "Well, there goes another piece of my soul. I swear! Every time! Every time I leave the shop."

The door locked on its own causing Jayne and Doug to scrunch up their shoulders. Old concrete walls and floors soaked up the dim lights from overhead. Straightening up, Jayne tucked Dee's books into the back pockets of his pants. Trudging loudly down the extended, dank hallway, he thought to himself, *Even Doug is dragging.*

When they reached the supply room, Jayne shifted his weight several times back and forth. Listening to the jingling heavy keychain, Jayne rolled his eyes and silently grumbled. *This place is full of locked doors.* Once the metal door swung open, Jayne turned on the industrial wall switch. Man-made brightness and warmth flooded his senses in the windowless room. He hastily, but precisely grabbed testing equipment off the shelves. Completely filling his lungs and exhaling, his frown softly turned upside down. A shuffled footstep caused him to look up. Once his eyes met Doug's, he averted them. "Jerk. Hmph. Some friend!" His grumbling stopped short because of the movement out of the corner of his eye. *Poor Doug*, Jayne thought as he watched Doug leave the doorway for a small lecture from the old man. Discreetly observing, Jayne scrutinized the boss's normal appearance, which always included a surgical mask and cap. Wiry tufts of fake silver and black hair drooped onto his shoulders.

"Idiot... pay you good money... keep... under check... you come...go as you please...can leave..." The boss's loud lecture died down to where Jayne could hear no substantial raised words.

When he stopped straining, he conversed with his soul. *Man, what did I get myself into? Every time...the more I learn about this place, the more I... I should have just gotten into Mrs. Graham's car today. What other way could I ever escape? There's nothing. Nothing!* His eyes widened. *Oh, how selfish can I get? What would happen to Jonathon? If I left, I'd be abandoning him.* Without conscious thought, Jayne gave a nod of acknowledgement as Doug entered the room.

Doug averted his gaze with a scowl.

What about Doug? Jayne silently questioned reality. *What would Doc do to him, if I left on his watch?* His arms full and his hand awkwardly holding a clipboard, Jayne followed Doug out of the supply room. He placed everything on a waiting cart and started pushing. On his way down the hall, he unconsciously paused every few feet as he followed Doug and Doc. With a thousand yard stare, he continued mulling over the facts. *I couldn't even turn Doc over to the law if I wanted to. No one I know has seen that horrid doctor's face. His ancestors could be Mexican,*

Arab, Persian or even from India. All we can ever see is his skin color. He doesn't seem to have any detectable accent and speaks good English so... he had to have grown up in America.

All three walked through another locked door. All personal escape plans went down a mind drain when Jayne looked up and saw her face through the glass barrier. Jayne played the daydream in his mind of her awake and chatting with him. *Oh, Hope. No wait, I found out your real name. It's Marian, isn't it? I swear I will not leave without you.*

Observing her closed eyes, he became enticed with her full lips. The curves of her cheeks forged a memory and her full eyelashes never left his thoughts as he strode around the room collecting water samples.

The access hoses, which allowed water to be drained for testing purposes, soaked up the dim blue lights in the room. The abundant moisture and high humidity gave the room a thick atmosphere. Constant humming made for an oppressive din. Huge shadows cast across the room with the loneliness of a cemetery. *Well, I still haven't earned enough trust. The tanks' main blue lights are never on when I'm in here. It would sure be easier. Doug's warden-like attitude is getting old.* Jayne paused briefly in his thoughts to change emotional gears. *We never play cards anymore. He's gotten cranky. We at least used to be friends when the boss wasn't watching.*

Doug's watchful eyes burned into Jayne's soul as he darted from one tube to the next.

An hour and a half passed by. Jayne's feet would not keep up with his knees. *Is this day ever going to end? My feet hurt. First an eight hour shift in the store and then another couple hours here.* When Jayne tugged at his jeans to hug his waist better, he felt the books in his back pockets. *Dee. The books. I wonder what they are? Maybe there is something special about them... Maybe there are pages taped together with a message inside! I wish I could go to my room right now. But no! I have to wait for my neighborhood 'friendly' thug."* His thoughts surfaced aloud. "I'm done testing for ph imbalances. There's nothing wrong with the water today. Hmmm. The filtering systems are all functioning. I've replaced filters." Flipping roughly through the papers on his clipboard, Jayne mentally checked everything off. "Whew. Done."

"Hey, lil' punk," Doug's booming voice caused Jayne to jump and turn around. "Ain't you done yet?" He was standing behind Jayne with his huge forearms folded.

"You know, you seem to enjoy your little job here," Jayne taunted as his face reddened. He spat, "Don't you? Bouncing at bars wasn't good enough? You had to answer the ad! You had to get the job and come ruin mine? You know what I mean?"

"Now, listen here, cage-cleaner," Doug's in-charge sneer faded as he became testy. He unfolded his arms. "Yes! Note! I *did* answer the ad, which means that I'm not the one who's in charge here! Weren't *you* already here when I got here? You waltzed in here as a kid and begged to be paid under the table to clean cages. *You* needed the money bad enough to *beg* for it! So don't blame *me* for your choices!" Doug pointed his forefinger menacingly at Jayne. "When your mom died, Doc paid the bills and let you move in so that you didn't have to go into the system! Sure, I was hired to monitor you and the other employees, but what if some other guy was hired?" Doug flailed his arms. "Would he be as nice as me? Would he hang out with you? If I leave, who would Doc hire in my place? I'm not the one who brought you in here!" Doug ran his hand through his hair before throwing both hands in Jayne's direction. "You are! Doc paid your mom's medical bills so it's your job to pay him back with your time! You're not a slave here, you have a past! You stopped getting cash here the day that Doc paid the bills for you!" His blue eyes scowled. "I got my own bills to pay and Doc won't give me an upfront!"

Although each sentence knifed him in the gut, Jayne silently stared without flinching.

"Why'd you have to make contact with that old lady? Why didya have to take books from her? Now the boss is breathing down my neck! You're supposed to stay in the store! It's your job to call me to help someone out to their vehicle! You're gonna get me in trouble! I'm sorry I roughed you up too much, but… Gawd, loser! My neck is on the line here too! The boss is always watching! Ain't he? The cameras are always watching! You're getting too brave for your own britches! Now, hurry up and put your stuff away! It's time for my shift to be over!"

Jayne's lips parted to counter, but doubled back. They both walked as fast as they could. When they got to the supply room, Jayne parked the cart, put the remaining supplies up and threw away the trash. Conversation was non-existent while Doug escorted Jayne to his small one-room apartment. Jayne played the waiting game again while Doug unlocked his door. He walked through, turned around and faced Doug. When the door slammed in his face, Jayne sighed. "Well, I guess I can't blame him." Jayne threw up his arms and planted them hard onto the door and allowed his head to fall onto the door too. He stood there a few minutes with dark clouds welling in his mind.

Counting the meals in the last week on one hand, Jayne realized that he had only eaten the dried jerky and fruits he usually had for lunch. He had totally skipped morning and evening meals for days. He hadn't really felt like eating hardly anything lately, after all what was the point?

But a bitter-sweet scent tickled Jayne's nose, causing him to eventually stir and follow the aroma to the kitchen. The plump vegetables bobbed in the tomato soup base. He tasted the air and feasted on it. His favorite soup contained limited spices: basil and cinnamon. Licking his lips, he grabbed a bowl out of the mostly barren cupboards. Even they seemed useless with so few dishes to store. There were three each of cups, plates, bowls, silverware and mugs. Flashbacks of his mother's full cupboards made his hand reach into his back pocket. *Mom. Dee.*

Vacancy camped out in Jayne's eyes as he stared at the big crock-pot containing only two servings. A lonely tear slowly made its way down his cheek with the pull of gravity. Blank white walls closed in around him. The refrigerator displayed four trophies: a score-sheet of Doug and Jayne's last Texas Hold 'em game, Jayne's poorly drawn picture of Hope on a paper towel, a picture of his mother and a letter from his mom's chemo doctor saying that all the bills had been paid for. Turning back to the task at hand, Jayne picked up the pace and filled his bowl. He placed the hot bowl on a plate, grabbed a spoon, and a glass of water.

Instead of slowly walking, he energetically carried his supper toward the blue couch. When he spilled it all over his hand and the blue carpet, he yelped. "Ouch!" He loudly sucked air through his mouth, "Shhhhhh." He growled, "Rrrr... Hhot!" Rapidly, he set it on the coffee table to allow the soup to cool a bit while he rinsed his hand in cold water. After he cooled his burn down in the kitchen sink, Jayne wondered aloud, "I wonder what's gotten into me?" It was safe to talk aloud for Jayne knew there were no speakers, microphones, or cameras in his room. The satellite TV service provided noise but no true form of communication.

Pondering his actions, Jayne looked around for a clue. He shook his head. "Hope! And not the person!" An incandescent smile spread across his lips. One foot at a time, he tossed his black Crocs off and settled onto the couch. The steaming soup stole a glance from him. *It really is too hot. I've got time,* he thought as he pulled the books out of his pockets and scrutinized them. The book of poetry and the fairy tale disappointed him. *Well, so much for hope. Ah well, it's more enjoyable reading than I've had in a while.* Flipping through for anything hidden, Jayne lost time as he skimmed a few poems. Setting the poetry book down with one hand, he picked up the fairy tale with his other. His slouched body jerked to a more upright position when he scanned through the fairytale book. A cartoon figure drawn in the bottom left hand corner of the pages moved slightly when he turned them. Playing with the cartoon, he chuckled. As Jayne scanned it again, he noticed a break in the pattern. Finding the page, his eyes widened when he saw a picture that didn't fit the moving story. Discovering another page with a misfit 'toon and holding it in between his fingers, Jayne examined it closer. On the previous page, blue ink underlined several words. Pencil or black ink marked the rest of the book.

Jayne dropped the book on the couch and leapt over the back. His toned but lean legs carried him into the kitchen. His greedy hands yanked open drawer after empty drawer until he found a pencil. Next, he fumbled with the paper-towel roll and nearly dropped it several times. Determinately tearing off a towel, he dropped the roll on the kitchen floor. His arms pumped carelessly as he ran back to the couch. Putting the pencil hand on the back of the couch, he hurdled and landed sideways beside the book.

It's a message! Flipping through the book, Jayne found and wrote down each blue underlined word. Staring at the words, he couldn't even read the mumbo-jumbo. He rechecked his work and wrote the page numbers under the words. He originally wrote it starting from the beginning of the book. At a second glance, he read the words as if he wrote them from back to front. Jayne swore and then exclaimed, "Hot-diggity-dog!" He bounced with his knees up and down on the couch. "Whoohooo," he hollered aloud and then whispered, "A message!" Jayne stood up with his treasure and took his bowl of soup to the kitchen. He dumped the cold soup back into the pot to warm it up again. Concentration caused his eyebrows to lower. Staring at the message to pound it into his brain, he absentmindedly grabbed a small cast-iron pan and placed it on the hotplate. Taking a match from a drawer, he lit the paper-towel, dropped it in the pan, and watched it burn. As soon as it turned to ash, he washed the ashes out of the pan and placed it into the drainer. Jayne filled his bowl again while he stared wide-eyed. '*Know you're in trouble. Ready to help. Tell us how. What are we up against?*' Hmm. *Short, but sweet.* He blew on his spoon and wolfed down his first bite of food since his beef jerky at noon. *But, the question is, how do I answer?*

Getting ready to take a second bite, he heard a key rattling in his door. Startled, he closed his mouth around his spoon before he finished blowing on it. Spitting his hot bite back into his bowl, he dropped his spoon on the counter. Life in his veins drained to his feet. A drum pounded in his ears. Jayne faced the door and held the counter.

"You look like you've seen a ghost!" Doug's eyebrows furrowed as he briefly looked around the room. Turning to stare at Jayne, Doug's eyes penetrated as though he could read Jayne's soul from looking into his eyes. His nose and lips twitched before he inquired, "What are you up to?"

"Nothing, Dougie," Life flooded back into Jayne and he deeply inhaled. "I drifted off on the couch and was just getting ready to eat my supper. I guess I'm really tired out." His hands trembled.

Doug lowered his voice. "No hard feelings about earlier? You know I got to keep up the act."

Jayne cocked his head and eyes at an angle as if he considered it. "Hmmm." He curled his nose. "So that means I get to make trouble for you!"

Doug snorted. "Let's go! Get your shoes!" After Jayne complied, Doug closed Jayne's door, and shoved him past the other apartments. "It's going to be a long night."

The two faced each other. Jayne's crooked grin flattened and at the same time Doug's face soured. Jayne watched Doug's bulky shoulders slouch. "You're as tired as me," he muttered.

Doug responded by turning to face the elongated walk beyond the door.

He's becoming as much as a prisoner as I am, thought Jayne. *Doug's putting in extra hours, but not getting paid.* He rolled his eyes. Going through the doors after Doug, Jayne forced his feet to drag him along. Doug turned around to find the wayward soul. He huffed as he clomped around and behind Jayne. Roughly, he pushed him along past the storage room and the tank room. A bitter, deathly tasting stench wafted from the next room. As he passed the open doorway, he thought, Ew! *It still looks like something from Roswell...an alien trophy room.* Shaking his head, Jayne turned his face away and quickened his pace. Heavy footsteps behind told him that Doug followed his lead. The two slowed down as they approached lights flooding the hallway from two open doors. Jayne glanced into the first lighted room. *When will this maniac be finished?* The procedure room lay in shambles. Blood painted the floor. Fumes from cleaning solutions and chemicals infiltrated Jayne's mind. Flashbacks of his mother's frequent hospital visits caused Jayne to miss a step and trip, crashing to the floor.

"Come on, move it," ordered Jayne's arrogant guardian. He roughly helped Jayne to his feet.

"Ow!" Jayne grabbed his throbbing bicep after Doug released it. Opening his mouth to protest, Jayne saw movement in the doorway. It was Doc. He stared hard at Doug and Jayne.

Doug grabbed Jayne's hand and pulled him past the doctor. "Your 'friend' is singing again and his voice is carrying over the still night air. If you don't get him to settle down, the boss is gonna box our ears and then hang 'em like trophies!"

As promptly as Doug jerked Jayne down the hallway, he released his hand.

Here's my favorite doorway! *But I'm so tired.* Jayne thought as he slipped through the door and up the steps. He pleaded, "Jonathon, where are you?" After he noticed that Doug didn't follow, he grinned from ear to ear. He sang at the top of his lungs, "Jonathon?" Once he reached the watery holding pens in the locker room, he focused his eyes to stare under the surface of the dark water. Only the vibrations of the giant air pump and filter could be heard. Giving up, he turned around to find his unlocked locker. With a complete lack of care for the material that clothed him, he stretched his clothes as he pulled them off. Throwing open the door of his locker, he grabbed his blue swim trunks and yanked them up one leg at a time. Leaving his clothing scattered on the concrete floor, Jayne hurried into the old oceanarium show arena.

"Come on, Jon! I've got some news! It's not fun when you hide!" Taking a deep breath in, he dove under. Searching high and low became a chore. Panic set in as he surfaced. "Come… on… Jon…" Jonathon loved this game, but Jayne was in no mood for it tonight. After diving and surfacing several times without any results, he angrily shouted, "Dang it, Jon, where are you? I *want* to talk to you! It's important!" Out of breath and tired, he dog-paddled over to the demo stage and crawled out. Breathing deeply, he kicked his feet, angrily splashing water and stared after its landing. Giving up, he admired the sliver of beautiful stars in between the canopy and the concrete wall. As he gained control of his breathing, Jayne daydreamed about new possibilities of being elsewhere.

"Aaaaaaah," yelped Jayne as a light coffee-skinned hand grasped his foot and pulled him in. After struggling to release the grip, he raced up to the night air. Jayne reached the surface out of breath from the surprise attack. Skimming the surface of the water, Jayne saw a head pop up. The distinct long black and silver streaked hair hung over Jonathon's forehead and in his eyes. Jayne could only imagine the ornery sparkle in his friend's eyes and the smirk on his lips. Water flew through the air as Jonathon hurled a splash over Jayne's face.

The young males were soon engaged in water games like a pair of young kids. They swam, splashed each other, and played tag. Fun, buffoonery, and adrenaline soon crashed; Jayne shook his head and wearily waved his hand. He swayed toward the stage, completely exhausted. The last bit of energy in his body wasn't enough to get him out of the pool.

With knitted eyebrows, Jonathon followed and gave Jayne a gentle boost over the edge. Elbow over elbow, Jayne slowly crawled out of the pool. His body haltingly obeyed his nervous system's commands as he struggled to sit up. One by one, his feet unwillingly crept over the edge to dangle. The ocean waves thundered from the distance inside Jayne's head. The strip of bright stars in between the canopy and the concrete wall tossed and turned as if imprisoned in a universal kaleidoscope. Gravity increased its pull. His head and shoulders rhythmically teetered forward and backward like the waves he heard in the distance. A roaring rush of nothing sucked the sound waves away from his ear-drums. Jayne's tongue slowly licked over his parched lips while fairy-like dust sparkled in his peripheral vision. Dizzy, weak, and light-headed, Jayne reached his hand toward the sky as blackness gobbled him whole.

{:-)-]~~{

Chapter 2

Clad in non-faded jeans and a navy blue t-shirt, Tyler Sharp breathed heavily as he climbed the extended stairway. The western part of the structure included two circular stairwells; Tyler had chosen the northern one. "Whew," he panted as he reached the second floor. "Boy, am I out of shape. Geeze. 36 and out of shape." He sighed. "Too much sitting." Light usually flooded the room from the curtain framed windows strategically placed around the foyer, but now the blinds were all closed. He peeked through the window on the South wall and sighed. Concrete obscured the beautiful view but allowed for parking above the enclosed ground level garage. The unoccupied spaces briefly reminded Tyler how alone he felt. Reaching out with his hands, Tyler located the wooden bench and rested momentarily. Checking his collar with his right hand, the corners of his mouth saluted the heavens. His favorite black ink pen lodged securely clipped onto his shirt collar, he hadn't lost it.

Tyler pleasantly smiled at the recollection of when his large extended family collaborated to build their 190 by 100 feet rectangular Tudor style house with its front door facing west. What could pass as a ski lodge, started with seed money from a deceased relative. The vacation retreat, designed for all seasons and holidays, conveniently brought together the huge family in comfort instead of trying to cram into each other's houses. It was strategically located in northern New Mexico since they were spread over the Southwest United States. Pinion, juniper, white fur and Ponderosa pine trees loved the climate south of Taos near the Rio Grande. The plot the family had purchased even had a small orchard of apple trees.

His clean-shaven mouth parted as he snickered. *I can just see the small house that we grew up in*, he thought.

A flashback stole his thoughts away to when his older sisters Marcy, Beverly, Kelly, and Bonnie were running through the house. They opened the door for the neighbor girl, Gabriella Cook who was four years older than him. They all screamed with overenthusiastic delight. Jack, his long-limbed father, ignored them as he sat in his favorite black recliner reading the business section of the newspaper. Gangly young Tyler sprawled with his stomach on the floor reading the Sunday Comics. "Would you girls cut it out?" Tyler yelled at them before intensely looking at his dad. "Girls are such a bother!" Jack smiled, but never gave Tyler eye contact or verbally agreed. Young Tyler never understood his father's affection for his sisters until surprise sister, Melista, later ensnared Tyler into the role of protective big brother.

Standing up, Tyler stretched the tight muscles in his legs. With a quick step, he started east down the enlarged dim hallway. It sometimes felt like 'hide and seek' while searching for his daughter and wife. He passed the open door to the huge girls' bunk room on the left and the boys' bunk on the right. Not even glancing at the three master suites on the right, Tyler inched his steps on down the left side of the hall.

"Gabby, where are you?" he worriedly challenged at just slightly above a soft whisper. His eyebrows bunched up as he gazed into the large nursery west of his master suite. The afternoon light trickled in enough for Tyler to see the room. Softly, his eyebrows lifted and a wide grin spread across his face as Tyler peered in at the two rocking chairs, toddler beds, bunk bed, cribs, and bathroom. Mary enjoyed her bottom bunk and one could see she kept the nursery nice. One wall framed a huge locker style dresser and closet. The bookshelves attached to the bunk beds remained tidy.

A chuckle escaped through Tyler's pursed lips. One of Mary's many dolls lay abandoned on the real changing table with the diaper unsecured. Flipping his hand in the doll's direction, he shook his head, turned around and padded toward his bedroom. Stopping at the end of the hallway, Tyler glanced up at the 8ft ceiling knowing he would find the same number of empty rooms on the third floor. Tyler's tenderness contorted to a longing frown.

After stepping through the doorway, the painting of he and his beautiful wife on the wall above the bed caught his eye. Tyler slyly smiled at his mother's signature in the lower right-hand corner. *Hmm,* he thought to himself. *I wonder what project mom is working on right now. Wonder if she's still painting brides and grooms?*

Below the headboard, face down on the pillow, lay his beloved. Creeping up silently, he came to a halt. If she was asleep, he didn't wish to disturb her. Carefully, he positioned his foot to prepare for an about-face.

"Why on earth?" Gabriella Sharp leaped to seat herself upright causing Tyler to flail his arms and back up a foot. "Why *did* you arrange for Mary to go to Mom's?" Glaring at him, she waved her arms around the empty room and squawked, "Isn't it quiet enough around here without our daughter being gone for a week? We live in a ghost town! A dark haunted house! This place was for visiting, not *living in!*" Her yelling softened to where each word exploded with sarcasm. "The bathrooms are stupidly placed on the outer walls in each room. *Sure,* the bathrooms have sunlight, but the bedrooms are dark without the aid of candles or light bulbs."

"Honey, now you know how you get this time of year," Tyler scoffed and then continued. "I thought it would be best for Mary and you."

Gabriella's jaw dropped. "What do you mean 'how I get this time of year'?" Her full, dry lips quivered, her eyes shimmered with tears, and her small fists tightened.

Tyler briefly and silently prayed that his choice of words would not get him thrown into the doghouse. "We're coming up on seven years together. We were childhood friends and then didn't see each other for 18 years before our parents contrived to get us together." Tyler inched toward the door. "We spoke *countless times* on the phone during my business trips for dad's company before we stood *together* at the altar!" Gabriella lowered her gaze. Tyler's voice trembled, desperate to reach her. "You agreed to marry me because you needed someone in your life that you felt safe with and our parents knew I always had a crush on you. No one forced you to marry me! But your first marriage left you with baggage and, I'm sorry, but you take it out on Mary and me! Especially during this week!"

Narrowing her eyebrows, Gabriella jumped off the bed and pointed her shaking forefinger at Tyler. She wailed, "You ...you take that back! I do not take it out on you two."

There was no way he could look away from those ferret-like eyes. When his brave loving smile couldn't wipe the anger off her face, he stood his ground and lifted his voice. "Gabriella, honey, you have been sulking and hiding around this huge house for the last week! You snap at me and Mary every August while you live in the past. You spend day and night weeping over a daughter who has been missing for 8 years; since before you and Marshall divorced. You don't talk about her with Mary or with me. Mary doesn't even know she had a sister! But she is smart and will figure it out; wouldn't it be better if it was from you?"

Gabriella opened her mouth several times, but whatever she craved to say stayed closed up in her chest. Tears flooded over her already reddened cheeks. Sniffles started and increased in volume.

"Honey," Tyler's expression softened as he begged. "Please... live in the here and now. Live in the present with me and Mary. You've grieved long enough. Let Marian be a precious memory and not a hurtful one, for all of us." Tyler emphasized his words with his hands by simultaneously reaching and pulling. "Let Mary be free to be Mary. To take swimming lessons or at least let me teach her. She's old enough to start learning how!" Tyler waved his hands in the air. "I can't control that Marshall's sister left your daughter, Marian, unattended as a toddler and she almost drowned! Marshall and his sister are not in our lives. Mary is not Marian. She is not afraid of water! In fact, she has an unhealthy attraction to the unknown. Our daughter needs to learn how to swim and I need you to be happy! Mary's old enough take baths and not always have to take a shower! To enjoy a walk in the rain and splash in the puddles if she wants to."

Gently, Tyler reached out with open arms. Gabriella cringed away.

"Gabriella Samantha Cook-Sharp! Now, that's not fair! I never hurt you when we were children! Even after we were reunited and married, I have never once laid a hand on you in anger! You treat me as though I have!" She timidly crept into his open arms. Tyler encircled her as he softened his voice. "I thirst for you to look at me with that sparkle in your eye just like you did when we were neighbors! Remember the fun we had?" Tenderly, he cupped her chin in his hand and lifted her face to meet his gaze.

Allowing herself to grin softly, Gabriella inched closer and relaxed her muscles.

Tyler affirmed with a bigger smile.

Suddenly, her reluctant smile faded and she jerked her way out of his loving embrace, leaving Tyler to blankly stare.

Her shrill voice rang in Tyler's ears. "You accused me of cheating on you! I have always been faithful!" Turning her back, her arms flailed and her shoulder length brown hair whipped about. "One minute, you told me I was the reason you had a sweet tooth and the next…" She paced beside the bed with her hands rhythmically pumping back and forth.

"You yelled, screamed, and accused me of things that I never did!" Silence filled the room except for her heavy steps that stopped before she twirled around and faced him with her body. Cheeks reddened, she leaned forward. Her piercing blood-shot eyes made full one on one contact. "I *was* faithful! I never *once* betrayed you!" Scowling, she pointed with her finger and an icy stare.

Gravity pulled at Tyler's baby face. He lowered his voice and sweetened it. "I know, honey. I know. I did think so, but I don't anymore. When she was born, I thought she had Dad's Mexican heritage. Well… when her skin color didn't lighten up like the doctor said… I'm sorry," he lamented. Momentarily, he dropped his jaw with closed lips. His eyes were stricken. After he swallowed the huge lump in his throat, he apologized, "I should have never accused you. You might have been married before and had a child… but you're *my* first marriage. I didn't know how to handle things." He slowly shrugged his shoulders. "It's a learning experience."

Tension clung to Gabriella's muscles. Shifting her weight from right to left, she stood upright and defiantly folded her arms.

Tyler's shoulders dropped and his hands hung to his sides. He shook his head back and forth. "I never expected the blood test to show that I was the father. I was so embarrassed." Looking down, Tyler ran his fingers through his neatly trimmed slightly curly black hair. "When further tests revealed that I had a recessive gene from an African ancestor, I didn't know what was going on! I mean my own mother didn't even know! Grandma never told anyone that she met mom's real father when she lived that short time in Africa."

Unfolding her arms, Gabriella softened her icy facial features.

Tyler emphasized each word with a higher octave. "Even Grandpa let Mom think that he was her biological father when he walked her down the aisle to marry Dad. Robert Jr. never knew anything either." Caught up in his own world, he threw his hands up into the air before he paused.

Gabriella softened completely, reaching out her arms. She knew he was hurting even though they had hardly discussed anything until today. Maybe it was best for Mary to be gone this week, it was too hard to yell and work anything out when she was around.

Dejected, he shook his head. "I'm sorry I fought with you to name our daughter after my grandma. It was a mistake." His almond-shaped emerald eyes stared blankly without their normal sparkle.

"That name was so close sounding to my lost daughter, Marian. Marshall and I broke up after Marian went missing. You were my new start in life. It was like she was dead and no one was left to care except me. I didn't need such a reminder." Timidly, Gabriella moved closer to Tyler. "What was your biological grandpa's name again? Did you ever make connection with his relatives?" Her brown eyes softened as she reached to touch his arm.

Tyler straightened his shoulders and stood taller. She had never really shown any interest before. It surprised and pleased him. "It was Amari. Amari Borano." Quickly, he whirled away from her, threw his hands, and let them fall without warning. "It's been three years of searching and still no word from any family there." Turning toward Gabriella, he lifted his booming voice. "Can you believe it? Three years."

"Even with the knowledge," Gabriella revealed in a breathy tone. "It didn't do our daughter any good. Mary's jet-black frizzy hair and dark skin are like a beacon. She has always been teased by her peers that she's adopted. It didn't matter where we lived." Trembling, her throat constricted. "I can't work anymore. I have to home school her..." Her voice drifted off and ended in a croak.

Slowly, Tyler inched closer so he could hear her better. After an awkward pause, he soothed her. "At least, dad and mom have let us live here this last year. We ought to start looking for a place to move to so that my family can be more willing to use this for a retreat again. We need to find a community where such differences don't matter. I can do web design anywhere."

Shifting his weight closer to her, Tyler wrapped his arms around her slender body. "Honey, I'm going to go down to the den, you just rest for a while. Think about what we could do to help Mary, she needs to know." As soon as he finished talking, he cupped her cheek in his hand and kissed her forehead. Slowly, he released his hand and turned to the door. Without hesitation, Tyler ignored the small elevator and strode down the connected square stairs to the main level. Blank thoughts consumed him while static controlled his mind. He was emotionally adrift, but somehow hopeful. Tyler's sudden halt in the enlarged hallway caused him to sway before he caught his balance. He stumbled, but rose immediately. Staring east, Tyler hesitated. His eyes darted west toward the conservatory and wooden room. Loneliness limited his choices. Ghosts of the past nibbled at him until he strode past the kitchen. He welcomed the comforts of the den into his soul.

Once Tyler reached the den, his somber attitude didn't change. Feeling numb, Tyler walked around the spacious room. It could be considered quiet, but he could not find solitude. Slowly, he navigated his way through the black furniture before he thoughtlessly dropped on the leather couch. He concluded that he should keep thinking to a minimum, but his thoughts raced anyway.

Mindless escape became a goal so he sat up and reached for the remote laying on the polished walnut coffee table. The TV flashed as channels flipped by, pausing occasionally on a program. He was searching for anything to do with football for it was full of order and chaos. Right now, Tyler needed things to converge into order.

Surfing channels, Tyler chanced on a show featuring missing persons. He laid the remote next to him on the armrest. Becoming engrossed in the show, he accidentally knocked the remote off. His lean but square shoulders sagged while he sat slightly mesmerized.

The start of the fourth story built tension in his muscles and bones. Panic set in when he frantically searched for the remote and could not find it. Forgetting his increasing age, he used his hands to hurdle over the table. In that one adrenaline powered flight, he landed crossed-legged semi-close to the TV and manually turned it down. Details of a missing person's story unfolded. Leaning in, he intently soaked up every word.

"Marian Harrison, being an avid reader, often traveled on her favorite shortcut from the local library back to her home. Her quiet Philadelphia neighborhood gave her a false sense of security. There were no witnesses to her abduction. Her parents both had solid alibis and were clearly never suspects. Gabriella Harrison, her mother, was at an interior design conference in Hawaii. Math teacher, Marshall Harrison, was in Vegas." The story continued, telling how the parents returned to find only an emptiness that continues to haunt them. The Harrison's old neighbor appeared on screen talking in great length about the time and circumstances of the disappearance.

"Turn it back up." Gabriella choked on her words and startled Tyler as she entered the room.

Tyler's eyes widened.

The missing persons show continued. "...Marian had a high I.Q., but she had the usual problems for someone so smart. She did not fit in well at school, being the youngest of her class having skipped a grade. She had no desire for travel and preferred routine. When she was younger, her parents thought she was possibly autistic, but she just greatly needed a regular schedule. She also had an intense fear of water."

They showed an interview clip of Marshall Harrison, her father, as he spoke to the audience. His slick black bowl cut hairstyle stood out against the light blue background. Confidence leaked from the pores of his bronze skin tone. Nicely tailored clothes matched his clean-shaven face. "Marian was the easiest teenager anyone could have. Primping in the bathroom was not her style like so many girls of her age. Even the sound of running water actually gave her motion sickness. Since Marian was an honor student, her teachers even excused her on days that had a high probability of rain."

Slightly quivering, Tyler obliged by turning it back up. Mental fog slowed his movements. *She hadn't wanted to talk about it all week long and here she is watching it?* Tyler shook his head. *She has hardly mentioned it in the last seven years. Shoot, this program is the only way I am getting any details after all this time.* His beloved wife hiccupped. Tyler watched helplessly as her whole body shook. Tyler's cheeks stung as he watched her start to openly cry.

Gabriella's arms flailed as she plopped on the couch. "My baby! Oh, my sweet baby!" She hid her face behind her hands and snorted a couple times. Trying to control herself, she took a deep breath and held it. Loud coughs escaped her tight lips as her emotions reached a boiling point. "I want my baby back!" Gabriella reached out for her husband. "What's happened to her? Why has there been no word all these years? She was 15! Fifteen! I want answers! Is she dead lying in a ditch or is she a prisoner in some psycho's backyard or basement?"

Walking around the couch, Tyler's shoulders dropped. Carefully, he sat next to her. His comforting arm went behind her to rest on the back of the couch; however, she flew into his chest and snuggled up. Changing directions, Tyler put his arms around her instead. "Sorry about earlier."

Looking bewildered at Tyler, Gabriella uttered, "Huh... what?" Her sorrowful eyes darted back to the TV. Every word grabbed her heart keeping her from focusing on her husband.

The background showed pictures of Marian's happy childhood and of what she might look like today. "She hated the idea of all that water surrounding that tiny bit of land, so she begged to stay home while her mother went on that 'awful journey' to Hawaii. Marian's father later split up with her mother because of how distraught she was over the loss of their daughter."

Gabriella jerked her legs and arms as if poked by pins and needles.

"Gabriella moved on, remarried and had another daughter with her current husband Tyler Sharp. Since no body has ever been produced, both parents continue to hope for her safe return. Marshall Harrison has diligently worked to raise awareness, by offering a reward and money to fund efforts to locate her. Tyler and Gabriella Sharp also seek Marian Harrison's safe return. This show will be airing on Marian's twenty-third birthday, August 7th. If you have seen this young woman, please contact..." The missing persons host continued and started another interesting tale.

{:-)-]~~{

Chapter 3

The beautiful mountains displayed their glorious scenery through the large kitchen windows. Dolores Cook, pleasantly plump and halfway in between 5 and 6 feet, sighed as she paced back and forth in her kitchen. A burning pain crept from her heels to her ankles from being on her feet all day. She sighed as she thought to herself, *Better go check on Mary.* Gazing out the window, she beamed as she saw her granddaughter, Mary Sharp, run around inside the high fenced-in backyard with her playmates from the nearby town.

The last of their blood line ran through Mary's veins for Gabriella was their only child. Mary, a bold and beautiful but thin child, carried a recessive gene for the darkest mocha skin color in all the family including the Sharp's. Curly dark hair bounced as she ran around the yard. Her doll face and high cheek bones framed a huge laughing smile. The girl was as thin as a rail in Dolores' opinion so she fed Mary every chance she could with large meals.

If only she knew. Dolores glanced at the counters where a half-eaten German chocolate cake still lay. She licked her lips. Her diabetic husband had already exceeded his limit. The sweet flavor lingered on her taste buds, but the number of calories created an invisible shield. Eating rich and fatty foods would not force the emptiness in her soul to evaporate.

Empty ice cream cartons, disposable dishes, and napkins piled high in the trash can. It had been a regular party all day long, complete with the cleanup. Over the years, Dolores listened to Gabriella's wishes. She never told Mary about her half-sister; but celebrated the best she could under the circumstances. Dolores had originally planned to honor her missing granddaughter by having no water balloons. Even so, she sent her husband on a last minute trip into town because the children insisted that they needed water balloons to appreciate the unusually hot weather. Hazel eyes blinked, allowing two tears to escape down her cheeks. Under her breath, she uttered, "Marian, I miss you, child." Slowly, she wiped her cheeks with her hands. Walking through the kitchen into the living room, she paused at the window. "Oh, please hurry, Jer," she begged. The leaves on the trees in the distance blurred as bounteous tears fell. A few tears trickled past the mole on her right cheek. She adjusted her bifocals. Whirling about, she rushed over to the television and turned on the satellite box. She opened the DVR menu. Finding the missing person's program, Dolores became mesmerized as she pressed play. Although she was uncomfortable, she stood in the middle of the room. Images of her granddaughter playing with dolls engulfed her mind during the commercials.

A gentle, but firm hand on Mrs. Cook's right shoulder brought her back to reality. The first thing she saw was her husband's thin body and his slightly protruding belly. Next, she saw his square face with a few experienced wrinkles. Looking into her husband's sparkling blue eyes, she saw his dazzling smile fade as he dropped the three sacks of groceries on the fluffy carpet. Warmth filled Dolores' soul as he wrapped his arms around her. The mention of Marian's name from the speakers caused Dolores to spin around in his embrace where she could watch the program. The two became lost in the story and unaware of the world around them. Not only did the deep voice of the host echo in her ears, but his words rang true from her mind's eye.

"...Marian had a high I.Q., but she had the usual problems for someone so smart. She did not fit in well at school, being the youngest of her class having skipped a grade. She had no desire for travel and preferred routine. When she was younger, her parents thought she was possibly autistic, but she just greatly needed a regular schedule. She also had an intense fear of water."

"Is that whose birthday we're celebrating?"

Jeremiah jumped at the small intuitive voice behind him and clutched his racing heart with a clenched fist. It felt like with another jolt that it would jump out of his body. Dolores' gentle eyes sharply changed to the 'deer in the headlight look' with absolute consumed fear. They both turned slowly around to face the small voice directly.

A small hand sharply pointed at the screen of the TV where a slightly younger picture of Gabriella and Tyler Sharp stood staring back. Mary cautiously looked from one grandparent to the next and back again. Her fear instantly disappeared as her rigid arm relaxed down to her side. She spoke up with excitement mingled with curiosity and a side of anguish. "Those are my parents! Wait! Who is Marian?"

Another small voice broke the silence. "When is Marian coming to her party?" sought the curly blonde haired eight-year-old standing next to Mary.

The curt auburn-haired ten-year-old declared with the haughtiness of being older than her. "We're not celebrating a birthday of a long lost friend of your grandparents. We're celebrating Marian's birthday. *Duh*. Marian is your sister, Mary."

Color drained out of Dolores' cheeks and her mouth dropped. She didn't know what to say, do or feel. The contents of her stomach churned. She hopefully stared at Jeremiah for answers and strength. When he answered her eyes with a stare of his own, she panicked, but her words never left her mind. *Oh my. Oh my. I didn't break my promise to Gabby. Surely she'll understand that Mary overheard the TV report.* Her eyes widened, her mouth closed, and her hands trembled as she reached for Jeremiah.

Love slowed Jeremiah's movements as he took her hand. She responded by gripping it tight. "Gabby said that it was okay to have the party. Mary is old enough to understand. She is smart, but let her parents explain things." He turned to their granddaughter and lovingly smiled. Placing his hand gently on her shoulder, he suggested, "Mary, how about we take your mom a piece of cake later and she can tell you all about Marian?"

Mary's eyes jumped as well as her feet. "Sure, Grandpa," she replied with enthusiasm. Grabbing the sack that her grandfather had dropped, Mary faced her playmates and grabbed their hands. "We've got the balloons! Let's go fill 'em up."

Still wide-eyed, Dolores stared after the three girls as they headed back to the stairway door where they had 'snuck in'. Mary's gregarious nature caused her to pause at the doorway to whisper with her friends. Giggling ensued and they retreated down the stairs two at a time. Dolores cringed as she heard them shouting about their new find. Mary was obviously the last one out. "Guess what, you all, I got a sister!"

Numbed, Dolores tightened her lips, mindlessly following Jeremiah as he searched for their cordless phone. Picking it up off the marble kitchen counter, he proceeded with the dreaded phone call.

{:-)-]~~{

Tyler turned off the TV's power and the two sat holding each other. Gabriella's legs seemed to disappear into the couch with her black jeans, apart from her bare feet. Her white shirt collar was soaked from her tears. The spirit of grief lingered in the air like a lost soul in Purgatory.

Since his pocket watch was hard to get to, he checked the wall clock every few minutes. Fifteen awkward minutes passed and Tyler's neck was screaming. A crick was forming. Turning his head slowly, Tyler soaked up the beauty of his wife, tear-stained cheeks and all. Nodding, Gabriella drifted into a deep emotionally drained sleep. Carefully, he laid her on the couch and covered her with his football team's throw blanket. Rolling his head around, Tyler attempted to force the crick out. When trial became error, he reached up with both hands to snap the nagging feeling out. With hushed movements, he turned the TV on and muted it while he tuned it to a channel that played peaceful music. Flipping off the mute, beautiful soft music filled the room. Tyler checked on his wife and saw a soft peaceful expression forming on her face. Satisfied that she was safe, Tyler plodded up the undersized stairway trekking into the gloomy hallway.

Right as he shuffled into the kitchen, the telephone rang. Startled, he jumped and then sprinted toward the phone. *Oh, please don't wake up Gabriella.* Picking it up, Tyler inquired, "Hello?"

After the other end's quick response, Tyler's spirits dive-bombed. His body jerked. Tyler's numb fingers lost their grip on the phone. The phone's stretched curly cord did not catch the phone before it clunked to the floor. Scrambling, he scooped it up and placed it back to his ear upside down. Tyler's shaking hands fumbled with the phone until he held the receiver right side up. Once he could clearly hear his father-in-law, Tyler shrieked with a rasp. "I'm sorry, Dad… I… I dropped the phone."

Crestfallen, Tyler teetered back and forth ever so slightly. *Oh, man. Oh, boy. Oh, no.* Gathering his wits about him, he let his breathing even out. He softly answered, "No, no, no… we don't blame you. I understand." Tyler grimaced and closed his eyes. "Mary walked in while you were watching it. Don't worry." Briefly, Tyler paused as he ran his hand through his hair. "So, you're packing up and heading this way?" His masculine voice churned with turmoil as his last word ended in a squeak. He opened his glassy eyes and sighed. "Okay. I'll be seeing you. Have a safe drive." He waited until Jeremiah hung up.

The phone jiggled when Tyler slammed the phone onto the receiver.

Grunting, Tyler put his hands on his temples and his elbows on the kitchen counter. Caressing his temples, he inhaled and exhaled deeply. Jerking to attention, Tyler tiptoed back to the dimly lit den to peer into it. *Oh good, she's still asleep.* Padding back to the kitchen, Tyler hastily grabbed the phone as soon as he was within reach of it. Pressing a speed dial, Tyler tapped his foot. It rang and rang, finally going to voicemail and he could hear his mother's pleasant voice asking for a message. He tried her cell phone and when she picked up, he didn't wait for her to answer. "Hey, mom, can you come over? I'm sure that Gabby would appreciate the distraction and company. Oh, and the Cooks called. Gabriella's going to have to explain things to Mary. She walked in when the Cooks were watching a missing persons' program about Marian." He paused. "Yeah. So I will see you in a couple hours? Cool. Thanks."

{:-)-]~~{

Chapter 4

Leaving the kitchen, Tyler ignored the doors on the north wall leading into the dining room and tea room. His fogged gaze never glanced at the library, office, or wooden room on the south side. Walking in a zigzag pattern down the hallway, Tyler thoughtlessly made his way toward the front room. A barrier of emotions kept his eyes from functioning.

Stumbling into the wall, he placed both hands above his head. The thick sound-proof wall braced Tyler's weight as his mind tumbled, *How is she going to handle it? Mary has always longed for a sister. Is she old enough to understand that Marian was kidnapped? Gabby is going to have to stop moping before we have another child.* Tyler dropped his hands and turned his head to stare down the dim hallway. Aloud, he pondered. "At least our moms will be here to help her explain things." Unconsciously, he whispered, "Ohhhh."

Fear closed his mouth before he declared anything else aloud. Instead, he thought, *I could sure use some support myself.* Tyler spun around and trekked on. He didn't bother to turn on the lights in the hallway. Picking up his pace, he reached the sun-lit room within several strides. A warm carefree smile snuck onto his lips as his lungs filled with a rich inhale of fresh air. Instead of a living room, the Sharp's had made the front room tiled and full of chest-high and knee-bumping potted plant life surrounding several small and large fish ponds. Two circular benches framed fountains which sat in between the front door and the two stairways that led to the upper floors. One needed to wend their way behind the fountains to see the stairs and slides leading down to the basement activity center.

Tyler sat on the bench in front of the fountain with the statue of a child and a mother breastfeeding an infant. He soaked up the warmth radiating down from the skylight. Staring at the fountain with the statue of the father teaching his son how to ride a bike, his cheeks glowed with admiration. An hour passed with minimal movement or orderly thought. Tyler cleared his mind from the upcoming task by being grateful that he hadn't had to come up with all the money to pay for this residence. Many windows, candlesticks, and skylights helped keep the electricity bills down while wood stoves and fireplaces helped with heating and cooking. Ah, the months of planning, construction and finish work that the family had put in to keep costs down, considering both short-term construction and finished, long-term operations. He got up and spent another hour doing chores, which included checking on the small concrete building across the yard that contained huge batteries for the wind and solar generators. These powered the house, the stables, and an enclosed chicken pen north of the house. The small gardens were lit at night with solar power. After finishing his outside work, he carried the eggs inside the house. He rinsed them in the kitchen and left them to dry on a towel. Tyler went back into the front conservatory to wait again.

The salt and fresh water filled concrete aquariums and Victorian bathtubs filled the air with moisture. Tall plants and potted trees enticed Tyler's nose with fresh oxygen. The slightly humid air always left Tyler having to occasionally move around to keep from stiffening up. Still waiting for company, Tyler jumped when he thought he heard a vehicle. *Gabby's folks are on the way, but they have a longer drive. Couldn't be them. Mom should have been here almost an hour ago. Hope her and dad didn't have car trouble.* Perplexed, Tyler started for the door. *But they didn't park in the garage. Would someone be dumb enough to try and sell something out here?* Before he could get to the door, it swung open. Barreling in, the short, deeply tanned, plump woman bunched up her doll-face with a set jaw. Both smooth hands tightly gripped brown leather luggage, causing her to try to kick the door shut. She missed and huffed. Tyler's glazed eyes shone when he saw the two silver streaks that broke the straight thick black hair above her ears. His voice started at a high flute note before ending deep. "Mother, let me get your bags!"

"No." Mildred shook her head. She walked across the length of the staged front entrance and shuffled down the two steps. "Don't bother, dear! Your father dropped me off and went to park in the garage. He said he would come in through the office so he could drop something off on his desk." Noticing his worried expression, she gently sang. "Sorry we're a bit late, Ty. Dad and I had a last minute dinner guest. We were at a restaurant when you called. We knew it would be a bad week for Gabriella and we had planned to come and liven up the house tomorrow anyhow. You know...try to get her mind off her sorrows a little sooner this year. I had already invited your sisters… We've been planning for weeks. Jack and I both took a few minutes to phone the girls and tell them to move a little quicker." She paused, searching for a disapproving look. "… They should be here soon. Hope you don't mind. I figured asking for pardon would be easier than asking for permission." Mildred's eyes narrowed over emerald irises that could penetrate souls. She stepped away from the door before she let her bags plunk to the floor. "Whew."

The slightly opened door burst open again. In bounced a long limbed figure sporting a black leather jacket and purple helmet.

"Hey, if it isn't silly-Milly, all grown up," Tyler grinned from ear to ear as he teased his eighteen year old sister. "Sueprise! Sueprise!"

Her black-gloved hands pulled off her helmet. She threw her head around to let her rumpled brown hair loosen its sweaty grip on her neck. "Yes siree, big brother and you're just going to have to get used to it! I might have been a surprise, but you know you love me!" Melista's cocky wide grin never left her face as she gave him a bear hug with her helmet still tightly gripped in her hand.

Tyler sniffed at Melista. "Well, at least you don't stink."

"Of course I don't stink! I never have."

"I *did* change your diapers you know."

Melista lovingly punched him. She and Tyler held each other, but then, Tyler backed away so he could slightly look up into her eyes. "Hey! Why weren't you a brother? I mean out of all my sisters, you're the one that inherited dad's height! Why," he spun her around with his left hand and continued, "you have grown up overnight! It's just been a year." Tyler barely finished his spin with her when his four older sisters elbowed their way through the open door.

Hello, little brother! You hogging the summer house all to yourself?" Bonnie teased her brother. Her emerald eyes beamed. She might have been trim, but with gentle strength, she pushed her shorter sisters aside to reach him.

"Tyler, it's about time you let us visit!" Plump Marcy flailed her arms when she almost lost her balance at Bonnie's nudge. Her button-nose turned up. "It's our house too."

Trying to catch herself, Marcy had grabbed at her shorter and leaner sisters, Kelly and Beverly. They held Marcy up and helped her to release her grip on their nice but now wrinkled shirts. Marcy wore a muumuu style dress. Beverly sported a white shirt and black skirt while Kelly and Bonnie wore colored jeans and shirts.

"Hey, there! Good to see you, too! We never said that you had to stay away." Tyler opened his arms graciously. "So glad you could all make it!"

The shorter, older sisters crowded the taller Melista out of the way for a giant group hug on their baby brother. All Tyler could do was grin and bear it. He didn't let it bother him like it used to. Although the Sharp ladies all lived within a four-and-a-half hour radius of the summer house, they had not seen each other in a year. They all filled the room with high pitched voices, talking a mile a minute about everything in general. Tyler let the hen house be. He knew better than to try and get a word in when six women were all talking at once. Carefully, he weaseled his way out of the middle of the circle. Melista and Mildred inched their way inside the circle and the gossiping climbed to new decibel levels.

Feeling a bit left out, Tyler scanned the room and puckered his lips. His heart and feet jumped for joy as he saw a parade coming down the hallway. Straight away, his smile returned as he admired his tanned nephews, nieces and noticeably average brothers-in-law. They were all meandering toward him, conversing and back slapping each other in greeting. It was good to have noise in the summer house again.

The cousins were all talking rapidly until they reached him. They excitedly spread their hugs onto Tyler, Grandma Sharp and the aunts. The commotion was almost too overwhelming for Tyler as he picked his way through the procession. He beamed as his parents attempted to sneak a kiss. With Mildred's small slightly plump stature at 4'9, it was still funny to see his 6'2 father bend over to kiss her. After their lips parted, Jack's blade like nose gently bumped against her small bunny one.

A knock at the door stunned the assembly into silence. Everyone looked around the room with quizzical eyes. Many whispered, "Isn't everyone in the family here?" Tyler shrugged his shoulders.

Mildred and Jack exchanged roguish grins as they worked their way to the door to open it. Jack announced, "We have a surprise addition to the Sharp family."

"Uh, Grandma, aren't you too old to be a mother again?" a teasing voice piped up in the crowd. No one knew who made the comment, but all enjoyed a chuckle anyway. The amused few snorted in their failed attempt to hide their energetic laughter. Mildred scrunched her nose, but left a brilliant smile plastered on her cheeks.

Jack opened the door while Mildred eagerly waited. A shapely older woman traipsed in finding all eyes staring at her. Slowly, she closed the door. Gorgeous for her age, her round brown eyes put everyone at ease. Small black braids were gathered into a pony tail in the back, while she wore a brown camo scarf covering the top.

"Jambo. Hello, big family," greeted Zola, a darker African, emphasizing the word big.

"This is Zola Kipsigi. As you all know, Tyler and I uncovered that Robert Davis Sr. is my stepfather. My real father's name was Amari Borano and Zola, here, is his other daughter, my younger half-sister. We are ten years apart. So please welcome your Aunt Zola into our wonderful family!"

Everyone showered her into the family with literal open arms. The elder nephews then helped Zola with her bags and guided her to a bedroom. The leftover children zoomed to the hidden stairways to the basement. Mildred pulled Tyler aside. "Ty, where's Gabby?"

Tyler whispered to her, "In the den."

"Marcy, come with me. You others get started in the kitchen," their mother ordered. "I'm sure everyone could handle a late snack."

"Yes, Mamma," Beverly, Kelly, Bonnie, and Melista all simultaneously blurted.

The two ladies strolled down the hall and silently slipped through the heavy curtains to the den doorway. As noise tried to follow them in, Marcy loosened a second set of heavy curtains behind her. Mildred gingerly sat down next to a sleeping Gabriella while Marcy sat in a black, leather covered rocking chair. Tired, Marcy closed her eyes for a spell. Mildred helplessly watched as her daughter-in-law's face tightened, lost in a never-ending nightmare.

{:-)-]~~{

Jack and Tyler led the rest of the men into the wooden room. The manly room, filled with handmade treasures, gave the room the air of accomplishment. Unlike the rest of the modern house, the walls were fabricated to look like a log cabin. One wall was lined with two wooden church pews. Two chairs, constructed from bones that they had gathered from the woods and other hunters, sat side by side. An antler chandelier hung from the 10 ft ceiling complete with bayberry candles. Cushions on the benches and chairs were covered with rabbit fur. Mounted stuffed animals with a natural looking background filled one corner. Though the men rarely went on hunting trips, deer and fish trophies hung on the wall. Thin dyed leather hand stitched curtains hung in front of the window.

"I haven't even been in here since the last time we got together," Tyler admitted as he found and sat in the bony chair that he had made.

Jack sat in the tallest widest bony chair and pleasantly sighed as his weight settled comfortably.

Angular framed, Jerome Burgess' ferret-like blue eyes peered at Tyler through his small saddle bridged glasses. "It's not like you haven't had the opportunity." Massaging his square-cut beard, he stood deep in thought as he stared at the mantel. His sandy buzz cut hair stood in the shadow of his prick ears. Peaceful meditation covered his brain as he meandered over to sit in his medieval-style throne. "Bonnie has been chomping at the bit for us to come to the summer house."

"We never said you all had to stay away. It's just not the same being in here by myself," muttered Tyler. "Too quiet."

"Sorry, Tyler." Jack shifted his weight. Sorrow glazed over his eyes. "We weren't trying to neglect you. You all just needed some time to heal. That last town you lived in…" His voice trailed off as his eyes stared into space.

Tyler picked up where his father had left off. "Those people were so mean to us. Mary and Gabby were both traumatized. Mary is just a child. How can people be so cruel in this day and age?"

Jack shrugged his shoulders. Love and compassion stretched out from his soul through his kind eyes to boost Tyler's spirits.

Tyler smiled and calmly sighed. His family was safe and so was he!

"Wow," Kelly Shaw exclaimed. "It looks and feels like old times." Blond haired and blue eyed, he remained somewhat fit from his surfing days, but had put on a few happily married pounds thanks to his wife Kelly's cooking. His hair no longer hung at chin length, now featuring a shortened professional cut. However, he had kept his goatee. He sat on his bamboo chair under his surf board mounted on the wall.

"Oh, I remember the day I made this." Marvin Hart, barrel-chested, ran his fingers over his unique chair. Structures from around the world were carved in the arm rests and supports of his wooden chair. The only strawberry blond hair he allowed to show was his imperial beard for he regularly maintained a completely shaved shiny head. Freckles covered his skin. "You guys waited for me to finish it, before we moved all the furniture in. Bev was due any day. You all stayed up with me in that cold workshop while I finished it. And then you stayed awake because she delivered the following day." Everyone simultaneously groaned with the recollection.

Clean-shaven with brown hair and eyes, Clifford Clark smiled, highlighting his high cheekbones. "I got to take a nap with the little ones since Marcy and I had your kids!" Tall and raw-boned, his diaphragm shook with his deep ornery laugh. The others waved him off. Slow and precise movements guided him as he went to sit in his rustic Southwestern chair.

"So, how long are you guys staying?" Tyler made eye contact with each of them in the time it took for them to answer.

Jack spoke up. "Marvin and I brought along a building project we are working on. Cliff can safely access his accounting with our firm over the net."

Marvin encouragingly nodded. "Bev still has several acupuncturist clients in the neighborhood. If she can't find enough, she's still a full time homemaker."

Clifford lit a pipe. In between breaths, he announced, "Marcy too, she can ship her naturalist products from anywhere." He played with the smoke bellowing out from his lips. "What about your landscaping business, Kelly-He? What have you and Kelly-She got going on?"

"There's nothing huge right now for me. I hired help a couple of years ago. I spend most of my time these days designing yards on paper for them to install. I brought two projects to work on. They'll keep me busy for a few weeks." He stood up and borrowed a light for his own pipe. "Kell can find odds and ends of work nearby too.

The massage industry is thriving with all the stress people put on themselves these days."

"I can make some calls while I'm here. My insurance venture has been pretty stable the last ten years, my staff can handle most things." Jerome stood up and lit his handmade pipe. "Bonnie might find a few jobs, but when she took up being a beautician, we all knew it was more of a hobby for her anyway. The children are her life."

"You guys still haven't answered my question." Tyler stood up and paced.

Jack's eyes beckoned to his sons-in-law as he explained to Tyler, "I think we can be here for as long as you need us." Turning to Tyler, his knowing eyes were soothing. "Besides, we have at least a month of vacation time to make up for."

The men exchanged warm laughter; a few back slaps and verbally expressed their agreement.

The door hesitantly creaked open. A tea cart appeared with chipper Melista behind it. Crude metal cups, saucers, and pot that they had pounded out in the small blacksmith shop sat on the tray.

"Hmmmm." Jack popped the question, "What do you have here for us?"

"Gunpowder tea." Melista pulled off the large metal bowl lid so the men could see the pastries, crackers, and jerkies neatly organized.

"Melista?" Clifford stood up. "We've got it here. Thanks. Could you check on the children?"

Clinking the lid down, Melista grinned and nodded. She scuttled out, closing the door behind her. She hurried to check on her nephews and nieces. Her tomboyish gait softened after pausing at the coat closet to hang her jacket. Her steps quickened as she neared the basement stairs. The young woman walked down a few steps with innate feminine grace. She paused. Although Melista considered herself too old for childish games, she scooted onto the slide that paralleled the stairway, and slid to the bottom.

Opening her eyes, her muscles froze. Melista grimaced thinking she had been caught. Blinking, she saw that darkness covered the room except for the occasional flash of the disco balls. The room sparkled like a prom dance and bumped with the music blaring. Checking to her right and left, she found not a soul nearby. The corners of her mouth twitched upward settling into a deep mischievous smirk. Melista inched next to the wall and positioned both hands over the stretch of light switches. After she tightly closed her eyes, she used both hands to flip all the light switches on. Rows of bright lights instantly flooded the basement causing all the unsuspecting occupants to wince, cringe, or drop to the floor with agony.

"Hey!"

"What?"

"Hey, who did that?"

"Nooo!"

Melista flipped the main lights off again, not only to appease them, but also to keep her secret crooked grin hidden. There were other switches strategically planted around the room. Her accusers might assume the flash of lights was an accident, but only she would know the shady intentions of flooding the room with brilliant light. She had been instructed to check on them. Momentarily blinding her nephews and nieces and causing them to unsuspectingly yell their check in made her day. Opening her eyes, she quickly scoped out the room. Four empty pool tables framed a lonely square patch of carpet, except for the one nearby which was lit with a hanging light above it. The niece, Willetta, closest in age to Melista motioned for her to join her. Four more pool tables separated the area with eight card tables with hanging lights turned off. The farthest lit table still had two occupants howling about being blinded. Melista sauntered toward her niece as she racked up a game and gave her aunt a strained wink in between flutters of both eyes. Melista nonchalantly returned the wink before shrugging off her gentle accuser with an innocent face and a shrug.

{:-)-]~~{

On the couch in the den, Gabriella lay curled up under a throw blanket. Her golden brown hair hung next to her chin. Her eyes darted under her eyelids. She slept, trapped in a dream.

The airport was hectic. Flights delayed. Gabriella desperately shouted, "I need to get home." Her shaking hands clawed past multiple expressionless people. "Please let me through!"

The zombies refused to acknowledge her presence or budge from their overbearing rigid paths. The maniacs mocked her death defying push to the goal. Some crossed her path from the right while others zigged in from the left. Beyond the bobbing heads, she could barely make out Tyler standing at the gate, peering at his watch. The twenty foot distance blurred to fifty. Still, hot air cracked the atmosphere with a cruel drought. The people between Gabriella and the gate towered as motionless as old trees. Long minutes trudged slowly into hours before she arrived unmistakably at the gate. Waving her arms frantically around, she searched the gloomy shadows. Where was Tyler? There! No, wait. At second glance, Marshall stood with arms crossed. Marshall? When she closed her eyes and opened them, Tyler stood there with open arms. Sprinting into his arms, Gabriella cried. He hugged her into a REM-like peace.

As the arms on her tightened, Gabriella stared dumbfound at his eyes. Tyler wasn't Tyler. Marshall's hand reached around and firmly grasped her wrist. Wrinkles formed from the strap-like bondage. Without a word, he dragged her down the boarding walkway. Entering the plane, she and Marshall switched places. Now, he pulled as if he was gravity and she was falling off a cliff. Drained from fighting, Gabriella used the seats beside her to aide in her struggle to walk down the aisle. Once Gabriella ignored Marshall's dead weight, she gained strength in counting the rows as she passed.

...forty-eight, forty-nine... fifty. Gabriella's hands flailed as Marshall yanked her back into the forty-ninth row. They sat down with Gabriella next to the window seat. Knowing the entire ocean rocked around below, Gabriella did not dare look out the window. Smoke drifted from the engine of the plane and formed into leering rumba dancers.

Shrieking, Gabriella's eyes furtively darted about. The rows upon rows of empty seats mocked her maniacally. When she zoned in on a chair, it moved back and forth as if in a focusing lens. Gabriella jumped up, only to scream as a sharp pain gripped her pelvis. A seatbelt restrained her. Her fingers fumbled with the broken buckle. Its brass arms tightened with a ratchet lock. No matter how hard Gabriella struggled, she could not escape her chair. Her pleading eyes stared as her tight closed fist beat on the window. "Someone help me!" she yelled in anguish.

When no hero came, Gabriella let her eyes focus on the window and beyond.

The vast ocean parted like clouds and she could see Marian picking her path down an old brick alley. Gabriella looked at her hands and watched the airplane pass through her body like she was a ghost. She floated in the air.

Marian awkwardly danced around puddle after puddle of water as though they were made of boiling acid.

Gabriella's voice cracked as she soothed her daughter. "It's okay baby. I'm here! Mamma's here. Everything is going to be okay." The longing mother stretched out her inviting arms, but could not reach her daughter. An invisible force field held Gabriella in the air above Marian, unseen and unheard. She felt as though she could just reach out and touch those wavy curls and that soft skin. With a tear stained smile, Gabriella admired that determined chin. She yearned to hold her daughter. Warmth crept into her arms as though she were holding a warm body. Alas, she could only watch as Marian struggled to avoid the puddles.

Marian occasionally stopped and searched her environment. When she looked in Gabriella's direction, Marian's eyes were blank and defensive as she stared straight through Gabriella. Marian jumped into a run for her life, but the whole scene appeared as if in slow motion.

The clouds broke wide open and giant drops of rain fell to the ground. Before the droplets reached eye level, they formed into daggers. The gladiate droplets sustained their shape, but rippled as the atmosphere slowed them down.

Gabriella's glistening eyes opened as wide as humanly possible.

The lively, malevolent droplets drove their way in and out of Marian as they struck her again and again. Blood oozed and dripped off of her, leaving gaping red wounds.

"Baby, run!" Gabriella's legs kicked and thrashed. She wanted to help. "Run, Marian, come home to me!" The cold liquid knives paused in midair, turning at a 90 degree angle. They glared at her with icy eyes and followed her movements with the snake-like movements of cobras. Immediately, several launched an attack on Gabriella, jabbing and tearing at her skin. A watery cloud descended and wrapped around Gabriella. Trapped in an invisible bubble, water filled in and up around her. With both hands, Gabriella pushed it away, but with little success. Her hands burned as she pushed through the steel-forged droplets of water. Forming their assault, they danced around under their own power. Eyeing their targets, they coiled up, hissed and darted to and fro with an unwarranted vengeance.

Gabriella shook. She crossed her arms and caressed them with stiff fingers. Her lips trembled from cold and/or fear.

The puddles increased in size and volume. Water-made gnarly hands and blubbery arms reached out for Marian, snatching at her ankles. A bloodcurdling scream sang out from her open mouth. Tears poured down her face. "Mom! Help Me! I want to be home in your arms. Why aren't you home? You should be here to help me!"

Out of a huge puddle, a big wave of water mounted high. Half-way down, it parted. A large gaping shadow mouth grinned with snaggle-teeth. Licking its lips, a hoarse shrill chuckle cut the air as the watery tongue raced from side to corner-lifted side. Opening wider, the H20 beast swallowed Marian whole. Rushing whooshing winds echoed as they tunneled through the alley and pushed the beast back into the drains. Loud sucking and slurping sounds ended in a gurgle of water and Marian's fading screams.

A lasting drawn out "No" pitched forth from Gabriella's slack jaw. Gabriella, screaming, clawed at the cloud that imprisoned her from her daughter.

A very concerned mother-in-law ordered Marcy to get a damp cloth while she hovered over Gabriella. Determined, Mildred attempted with both hands to help free the tortured soul from her blanket-wrapped nightmare. Her pained eyes watched helplessly as Gabriella continued to thrash about.

Marcy dove into the room with a cool wet cloth and applied it to Gabriella's forehead. Water trickled down Gabriella's face. She fought the air with her fingers imitating stiff open claws.

"Shhh, baby." Mildred raised her voice. "It's me, Mildred. I'm here. It's Tyler's mamma." Mildred raised her voice louder. "Marcy is right here, too." Her apprehensive eyes pleaded with Marcy.

A frightened gasp and then a blood-curdling scream broke the silence as Gabriella's frantic eyes popped open. She jumped up.

Backing up, Gabriella's sister-in-law stood rigid with open arms. Her body trembled with fear.

Mildred shook in her heart, but her outward appearance remained strong. She sat down on the couch next to her daughter-in-law.

Searching for familiarity as she stared at each face, Gabriella slowly relaxed her once rigid body. In a football-like tackle, Gabriella jumped into Mildred's open arms and planted her bottom right next to Mildred. "Mom! It was horrible. Marian! She was in the alley where the cops said she was kidnapped! Marshall! Tyler turned into Marshall! The plane… the plane to Hawaii! Marshall hurt me." Gabriella briefly broke away to rub her arms. She focused on one face and then the other. "He… he turned into Tyler." Sobbing buckets of tears, Gabriella only confused her relatives. "A giant puddle ate her up. She said I should have been there." Two sets of loving eyes melted Gabriella's rigid limbs into the comforts of the couch. "Mildred?" She reached a hand out to both her in-laws. "Marcy… Where did you all come from?"

Mildred shifted her position with dissolving tension.

Marcy followed suit. After inhaling deep, she whispered, "Your folks are on their way."

Gabriella grimaced. "Did… did something happen to Mary?" Her hands flew to her burning cheeks. Sharp pains stabbed at her flesh.

Gastric acid ignited fire in her guts. Her face soured as she disposed of her juicy burp. With her right hand still clutching her cheek, her left fist dropped to cover her belly.

Inching toward Gabriella, Mildred's hand cupped her chin in her hand. "Everything's fine. But… Mary has found out about Marian. We are all here for you as you explain everything to her."

"How?"

"A disappearance program."

Tears poured down Gabriella's frightened face. Mildred and Marcy cried too. Her pain was their pain.

A few female heads poked through the den curtains and Marcy shooed them away with a sharp shake of her head.

Finally, Gabriella seemed to be all cried out and released from the pain she felt so deeply, at least for a while. Her lips twitched into a gentle cautious smile as she sat back and listened to Marcy and Mildred visiting, sharing humorous tales of home life. After several minutes, she followed their enchanting conversation into the kitchen. With raised eyebrows, Gabriella greeted the rest of the women.

The house was again noisy and filled Tyler's heart with joy. *This house is way too big for just the three of us to live here*, he thought to himself while smiling merrily. He walked to the kitchen and saw his beautiful wife smiling and genuinely laughing. However, the closer he examined her face, the clearer he could see the tear stains. He looked at her quizzically.

Gabriella mouthed, *Thank you*, in return. Her firm lips stretched into a big grin. The hustle and bustle in the kitchen ceased right before Gabriella felt a tug on her arm. It was Mary. They had arrived.

"Hiya, mom. We brought you a slice of *birthday* cake." Mary shouted to be heard.

"You did, baby girl? Well, where is it?" Her mother lovingly answered with her hands on her daughter's shoulders.

"Grandma's got it." Mary responded innocently like her mother should know better. Little Mary looked so excited and energized.

Gabriella peered at the entrance to the kitchen. "Mmmom," declared Gabriella before she rushed over to give Dolores a hug. "You're here!"

Marcy grabbed the dessert out of Dolores' hands just before Gabriella reached her.

Mother and daughter embraced softly.

Mary interrupted them. "Hey, Mamma, can you tell me about my sister now?"

"Sure darling," Gabriella answered with a calmness that was only on the surface. She took her daughter's hand in her own. "Let's go upstairs." The two held hands as they walked through the kitchen. They reached the two doorways in the far corner. One led to the hallway. The other opened into an old style fenced-in elevator that reached all floors. They didn't use it as Mary was impatient so instead, they took the stairwell framing the elevator shaft. Mary eagerly took the lead as she and Gabriella hurried upstairs. The mother could tell her daughter was very excited. They reached the room a bit out of breath, for Mary would not slow down. In the bedroom, furnished with precious antique furniture, was a locked corner dresser. Gabriella opened it with a key on a chain around her neck and revealed a big picture of Marian. In the drawers were stuffed animals and clothes. Gabriella took time to show everything to her daughter. Picture albums captured brief merry moments of Marian's life. There were trinkets and pretties that belonged to her first born. The two sat on the floor and talked with everything spread out.

"Who's that?" Mary pointed at a picture.

Gabriella started to shy away, but held her ground. "That's Marshall, Marian's dad. He was my husband a long time ago."

"He was your ex-boyfriend?"

"No, honey, he is my ex-husband."

"Do we get to meet him?"

"No, we don't."

"Is Marian staying with him? Did he get married again?"

"We can't find Marian. She disappeared. The police think she was kidnapped. Here, Mary, look at this picture."

"How'd you marry daddy?" Mary's eyes focused on the picture even though her curiosity didn't miss a beat. "Was he friends with your ex?"

"No, honey." Gabriella paused. "We were friends and neighbors when we were kids. After I divorced Marshall, Gramma Cook and Grandma Sharp thought that we needed... they arranged for our marr..."

"The TV said she was scared of water. Is that true?"

"No, honey." Gabriella paused. "We were friends and neighbors when we were kids. After I divorced Marshall, Gramma Cook and Grandma Sharp thought that we needed... they arranged for our marr...for us to meet again."

"The TV said she was scared of water. Is that true?"

"Y-y-yes," stuttered Gabriella as she straightened her posture. The interruption had stolen her thoughts. "Yes..." Gabriella's despondent eyes stared into a distant blank world. Pain beat her heart with an irregular note. Air pushed on her head and gut. She heaved out, "Yes, she was."

"How could she take a shower if she was scared of water? Did she drink water?"

Gabriella timidly smiled before a soft chuckle escaped her lips. Placing a hand on her daughter's shoulder, she kindly volunteered, "Marian still drank water. She was just scared of baths and..."

Mary interrupted, "Is that why you won't let me take baths?"

Pulling her hand away, Gabriella deeply sighed. "No... no." She shook her head to control the burning sensation in her eyes. "We were letting you get older and daddy and I have decided that you are finally old enough." Brightening her face and forcing a plastic happy expression, Gabriella continued. "When you got back from your trip, we were going to let you."

"I'm back tonight! Can I have one tonight?"

"Yes," Gabriella said with a hiss not meaning to sound annoyed.

The opening door produced Dolores and Mildred. Gabriella gladly welcomed them in with a wave of her hand. They joined the mother-daughter fest, adding a third generation to the party. Mildred pushed a snack cart over to the table. Dolores helped Gabriella pick the treasures up off the floor. Mary jumped over to the small oak table and took a seat. There were four wooden chairs, so there was room for everyone. Mildred set the table with fresh fruit and the chocolate delicacy that Dolores brought. It turned into a regular female bonding party. Gabriella enjoyed watching her daughter explode with personality. As of tonight, they <u>became</u> closer as a family than ever before. The loss of Marian had restrained Gabriella, forcing everyone to stay at arm's length. The tide had, once and for all, turned.

Time of the Polliwogs

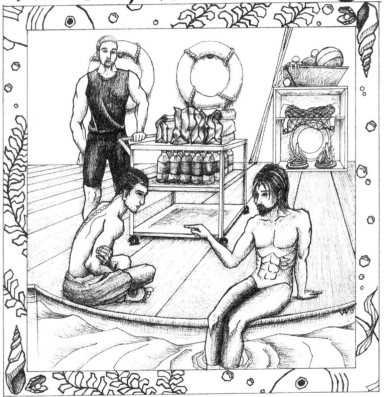

Learning to Swim

Chapter 5

he black binoculars were traded back and forth in between two sets of restless eyes.

First sight was the street, the parking lot and then, lastly, Peter was able to focus on the pet shop's windows. Little to no movement could be seen. Shaking his head, he disturbed the clear angle of the binoculars. Fear shook his guts and made his words stammer. "The store doesn't look right with Jayne missing from view. It's been more than a week since that woman gave him our books with the hidden code. He didn't even show up for work the morning after." His shaky voice ended slightly hoarse. "The thug's been running the store. He's not sporting his ornery smile, he even looks worried. Something's gone wrong!" Turning around, he tightly gripped the binoculars as he let his arm drop to its side. His troubled face and eyes darted about the room before landing fearfully on his partner. Articulating every word, Peter's voice escalated, "Something's gone very wrong."

Kenneth's green eyes widened and his eyebrows rose. "You think they were smart enough to find the code?" Taking a step back, his firm jaw dropped. "I hope we didn't cause the young man's death." Sadness seeped into his eyes. His eyebrows contracted and his lips trembled leaving only his body to stand its ground. "What started off as an investigation into potential exotic animal smuggling has shown that Jayne is probably being held against his will."

"Well, something fishy is going on in there. What was that strange noise we heard the other night coming from the entertainment area? It didn't sound like any creature I've ever heard." Peter's thick eyebrows ruffled with concern. He looked over at Kenneth observing the fear on his friend's face. "Don't worry, Kenneth. He's probably all right. Your idea for the underlined code was good and well-hidden." He ran his hand through his thinning brown hair. Worry tightened his jaw as he voiced his own concern. "We've got to get in there somehow and have a good look around." Peter wanted to hide his own fears and tried to reassure himself and his friend. Recalling a past hostage crisis which ended in disaster sent shivers up his spine. *I can't lose another hostage.* His mind switched gears to do what he did best: focusing on the job at hand. "Well, we know something's up with Jayne, but... what?" His question only reached the ears of his partner. Kenneth lingered, trapped in his own world as he calculated possible outcomes.

Silence filled the air as both men racked their brains for a plan. Special Agent Peter Austin backed away and set his heavy binoculars down on his black duffle bag. The cogs in his brain creaked on; his eyes rolled and darted about, unnoticing. His unvoiced concerns hovered around him, they shot persistently into his brain from every angle.

Special Agent Kenneth Hershkin shook his fist at the building across the street. "We sure need to get in there without raising any flags." He paced. "Jayne has got to still be in that large building somewhere. I mean, we have been watching the delivery trucks and nothing big enough to hide him in has left the building! Yet..."

"Agreed. Hey, maybe I have an idea."

{:-)-]~~{

Chapter 6

Startled awake, Jayne slowly moved his head as though it would fall off at a sudden jolt. Batting his heavy eyelashes, Jayne's eyes rolled with vertigo, and then he forced his pupils to focus straight ahead. The cold bare ceiling of a hospital room taunted him. Not recognizing the timeline in which he woke, he briefly thought he was with his dying mother. "Mmmmahhh," he mumbled. The far-off word hammered his head. Jayne grimaced. The gentle bass drum of his heartbeat encouraged his brain into action. As his senses broadened their horizons, he realized that he was older and his mother passed away years ago. Jayne's head rocked back and forth. Alone in the cruel world, Jayne almost begged for death.

Moist air tickled at his nostrils. Reality pulled at his limbs like an ancient torture device. Deep in the heart of the oceanarium, Jayne realized he lay on a hospital bed. His eyes cautiously darted around before his head thrashed with his search. An intense, ear-piercing scream mounted from his diaphragm, traveled up his throat and out where it echoed in his ears and in the room.

"Ahhh! You *slime ball*! You *dirty* corrupt *bastard*," he hollered as loud as his weak vocal cords could manage. The asthmatic sounding words that came wheezing out of his mouth could not strike fear into the dead of the room. Anger curled his fingers. He growled, "Where are you, you snake? You'd better show yourself!" By the time he finished ranting, his squeaky voice had neared its limit. When he could not completely vocalize his anger, he thrashed his arms, legs and hips, only to find himself restrained. Fear fueled the fire of anger to a boiling point. Furious, he tried to pound the table, but froze when the lights around him flickered. Holding his breath, Jayne waited, not sure what to expect next.

A delicately sculptured face appeared. Dangling, chin length, black dyed hair hung from a blue nurse's cap. Pale skin was highlighted by flushed cheeks. Her long arms reaching over his body intimidated him. The two had never before walked within arm's length. Jayne stared into her unreadable close-set blue eyes. He inhaled, exhaled, and then sneered.

Crestfallen, she spoke with a shaky voice. "Jayne, everythang's gonna be okay, darlin'." With desperation, her articulated words flowed in a calmer tone. "It's Billi Joe Sparks carin' for ya…"

"How can you say that?" Jayne's malevolent voice interrupted her, increasing his icy stare.

Smoothness guided her words, but concern haunted her facial features. "Darlin', your friend saved your life. You blacked out… so your friend dragged himself by his arms down the hall to get you some help. Boy, was he exhausted!"

Jayne's defensive hatred eased as his ache for self-preservation was put on hold. Sudden concern for Jonathon overwhelmed him.

Noticing Jayne's limbs relaxing, his caregiver carefully continued, "…by the time Doug got there, you had rolled into the water and drowned. It was Doug who pulled ya out. You were colder than a well digger's ass." She tossed her hair. "I know the doc ain't all kosher in his methods and all, but…"

"I bet he put drugs in my groceries," interrupted Jayne.

"Ah, horse squeeze! You were dyin' and he brought you back," replied Billi with cheeky displeasure. With slow hesitant movements, she checked his vitals. In case he showed any aggression, her muscles remained alert and ready to jump back.

"Yeah, sure. He just needed another experiment." Jayne coughed out his inimical words.

When her wary eyes panicked and her cheeks reddened, Jayne put aside his anger. He inwardly pondered, *Why is she so scared? Is she as much of a prisoner as I am?* He shoved his thoughts away to ask, "So am I a freak now?"

"Sit up and see for yourself," she ordered with maternal instincts. Without losing direct eye contact, she finished unstrapping him.

Slowly, Jayne sat up with his bold eyes staring at his body.

"Well? You're still you... ain't ya?"

Rubbing his thighs and shins, a grin pulled on the right corner of his mouth. About to take a deep breath to exhale a sigh of relief, Jayne paused. His chest rattled. Scratching the itch on the back of his neck, Jayne shot up from his slouching posture. What his fingers touched, fermented the saliva in his throat and stomach. He lifted his rigid hand in mid-air to the right of his ear.

Billi Joe stood up and placed a hand mirror in his outstretched fingers.

Oblivious to the sliver of silver under his cuticles, he brought the mirror in front of his face. A five o'clock shadow speckled his chin. In an instant, his face paled. Funny curvy vertical ridges framed his once smooth forehead. Sharp eyes grew wide while his body ached to lie down, pass out, and hopefully wake up from this living nightmare. His free hand touched his cheek. Hardened leathery skin covered his muscles, which did not please Jayne one bit. All the things that Jayne had tried not to pay close attention to about Jonathon, stared at him in the mirror. Blind spots lifted an ugly veil and harsh truth flashed bright. Touching his spine, Jayne concluded that he did indeed have that funny strip of bumps exactly like Jonathon. Jayne switched hands holding the mirror. Caution, shock, and fear guided his right hand as he felt his back. At once, he threw his head back in disgust. Looking at the ceiling, a strange feeling, growing hot and fuzzy, trickled its way all over his body. It left just as sharply and quickly as it had crept over him.

Noticing that her self-control helped calm Jayne, the gentle nurse touched Jayne's hand. When he threw his eyes to meet hers, hastily she withdrew her hand and cowered a bit. She busied herself by taking out his I.V. Ankle braces jingled as he rotated his feet. "Can you get these next?"

She shook her head and her eyes grew with fear.

A scuffle of feet startled her. She jumped aside. The doctor stood behind her.

"Well, I think it's high time you woke up!" His cheerful voice and wink disgusted Jayne. "You won't be mad for very long, will you, now? You well enough to get back to your duties?"

Jayne took a deep breath in and enunciated. "Not until you explain your actions. What is going on here? I think I have a right to know, especially now!"

The doctor played with his signature surgical mask that covered his mouth and chin. "All right, young lad. We'll get to that in a few hours. You still have things to do to finish up with the nurse here." He scuttled away while he threw his voice back toward them. "And make sure you improve your eating habits. Don't I buy enough food?"

Gulp. Jayne thought, *does that mean he knows I wasn't eating? I was depressed!*

The nurse hastily pushed a tray of food forward, glancing over her shoulder at the back of the disappearing doctor.

After devouring a cup of vanilla pudding, cubed cheese, and a cup of salmon broth, Jayne felt increasingly like himself. With his blood sugar stabilized and his stomach full, the nurse switched ankle irons. Although the new ones were mobile with no cords attached to the bed, there was a cord connecting the braces. Each sported a key lock so Jayne couldn't remove the shackles himself. That got an eye roll out of him.

When the efficient nurse finished, she helped him to his feet. Jayne stood steady enough to take a few steps. A few fresh steps would prove that he was stable enough on his own. *I'm so glad I can still walk.* His concentration went from his feet to his hips. He noticed he still wore swimming shorts.

"Let's go… Sparky."

Jayne recognized the deep bass voice. Turning around, a weak tenderness spread over his lips when he saw the familiar crossed Popeye-arms and bulky shoulders. Doug wore his black tank top and tight knee length shorts. His precise cropped blonde mustache and thin goatee fashionably framed his lips and chin. For the first time, Jayne liked the familiar sight of Doug's military style haircut.

"Thanks a lot, runt! I've had to work the shop for more than a week. I hate cleaning those tanks. They're slimy. How you force yourself to deal with all that algae, I'll never know." Doug shuddered, releasing his arms to dangle at his sides. "Doc had to hire someone before I let those mangy snakes starve! I couldn't even feed the turtles because they were in the snake aisle." He was almost his usual annoying brash self, but he seemed to be distracted and keeping his distance. His nervous pace back and forth in front of Jayne caused Jayne's head to have to follow Doug's movements to keep up with his conversation.

Jayne shook his head and shrugged. He'd been out for more than a week. Pausing, he cross-examined Doug about the monkeys, ferrets, and the parrots. Satisfied with Doug's assurances, he walked out the hospital room and moseyed down the hall. The crook in his smile turned smug and his chin reached higher: he wasn't dead yet! Doug didn't have a hands-on escort either! Chipper as ever, Jayne strutted; he might still have hope, after all.

The darkened doorway of the conference room loomed ahead with only a small light fighting the darkness. The tunnel effect vacuumed Jayne in pulling him away from what little righteousness and justice there was left in his reality. There was no turning back. Every time Jayne earned trust, he was a shove deeper into Hell. This time, there was no running away. Beyond the menacing door lay a snake ready to gulp Jayne into the next uncelebrated step in his life. Jayne's shoulders drooped and his feet dragged behind him. His spirits plunged to the floor when he heard the doctor clear his throat.

Sighing, Jayne lurched one step toward the door when someone pierced the gloomy hallway with heels. When he whirled about, he saw Billi meant no harm. When her stroll landed her directly in front of him, his eyes widened. Billi's four inch heels added to her already 6'1 height towering above Jayne's 5'8.

Politely smiling, she helped him into the vest she carried. Duty increased Jayne's feelings of being a child in her presence. Quizzing her with his eyes, Jayne willingly put his arms into it.

Tossing her head, Billi whipped around. She then marched down the hallway in pure haste.

The outside of the vest was dry to the touch, but against his chest, its innards felt cold and wet. Shivering from his head to his toes, Jayne acclimated to the temperature. Leery, he hobbled into the room. Immediately, the far wall flashed with pictures from a projector.

Vacation travel slides? Jayne thought as the doctor cheerfully explained them, but left out details of the locations. Enthusiastically, he verbally drew vivid pictures of the whole experience. Slides of mountains and caves from his vacations unhesitatingly flashed one after the other. *The pictures show the 'good' doctor taking samples on multiple trips. Not one photo shows his face or his true hair color. That stupid cap always covers it.*

Numerous pictures flashed by showing a major excavation of plant and marine life.

Jayne, frustrated, was nevertheless curious as to where this was going. Sarcasm reached a boiling point, but he restrained his tongue. Only his mind could hear the rage that struck the ground from the heavens. *And this affects me, how?* His right hand gestured in the air toward the brightly lit wall.

The doctor grew excited when he started giving details of a particular cave from deep within the journey. Many passages were lit by flashlights and floodlights. A natural skylight brightened the cave in the last picture. The water was crystal clear. Extra pictures portrayed the doctor breeding and dissecting the unique fish. The doctor did not share his discreet discovery of the rare fish with anyone nor did he trust anyone inside the oceanarium with their caretaking.

Doc bragged, "Like its cousin, the cave catfish, it can withstand colder temperatures. This unique electric cave catfish is capable of producing and controlling up to 450 volts of electricity like its more distant relative, the electric catfish. Its current is used for defense and against prey. The electric source is an organ composed of mutated muscle tissue. This rare breed is hardy and was found in a coastal cave. Each has a unique rainbow tail. Since it's so rare, it should be on the endangered list, but because I'm the only one who has them, I will devote some of my time to stabilize their population. I found them just in the nick of time!"

Jayne sat up, the information no longer bouncing off his tormented mind. He started to understand what the doctor was trying to get to...

The doctor noted, "Its flesh and organs are closely related to a pig. Its habitat is most peculiar. The surface water remains fresh while the bottom channel holds salt water. This causes the middle stream to mix. The fish thrive in *all three* environments! The cave is an area where the salt and fresh water mix before moving on. Its entrance once had only a small opening allowing in air and light, but it has eroded wider. That's how we got in. What a discovery! This breed of fish is amazing. Their DNA is something to be admired."

Jayne's stomach turned inside out. Fogginess crept over his mind. His emotions were heating up his insides. Had the doctor truly used fish DNA in him?

The doctor switched off the projector. "Come on, Jayne. Let's take a walk."

Doug, still standing outside the door, followed Jayne and the doctor. They quickened their pace down the hall toward the giant, smelly room. This would be the first time Jayne received full, authorized access instead of just a stolen glance. Grateful to not be needed, Doug held back, giving the doctor and Jayne space.

With green lights attached to the tall rectangular tanks, Jayne's nerves tingled. Enclosed in the reservoirs were the failed attempts of the doctor's experimentation. Jayne swallowed at a stubborn lump alienating his throat from the rest of his body. The air reeked with the strong stink and taste of formaldehyde preservation. Faces, cold and hard, stared ahead. A disturbing panic sickened Jayne. He did not prefer to look, but morbid curiosity pinched him like a bear trap. No matter where he turned, the dead alien-looking figures were everywhere. The ceiling seemed to be collapsing, pressing his soul into a pancake. A weight pulled at his knees. Full-blooded, partially morphed, and human shapes were bound about the hips, making them mostly genderless. When Jayne realized the women's chests were bare, he respectfully glanced away. His feet dragged as though his ankles were weighted with bowling balls instead of light shackles.

Eleven-by-fourteen picture frames labeled each glass casket with the names, ages when kidnapped, pictures and complications. The non-prejudicial, evil scientist incarcerated the young and old alike. The tour included every ethnic background. Jayne stopped briefly at a 'tomb' of a young child. He put his hands on the glass and laid his forehead against it. The doctor did not notice and continued to bounce from one topic to another. Doc lost Jayne while enlightening him with the procedures, surgeries and new capabilities. "Soft vertical ridges on the forehead are unique to the individual subject. The frontal suture on the skull mutated with cartilage to protect the sonar organ. The organ is connected to the sinus cavity and brain through a quarter-sized opening… the two hemispheres of the brain work together as one…"

As Jayne faded in and out, he could hear technical jargon, but he just didn't care. Closing his eyes, he concentrated on building emotional walls around his heart, soul and mind.

"…Eyes have nictating membranes… living subjects are able to control the dilation of the pupils to control the intake of visionary perception at lower depths…. inner ears and the spleen mutated to tolerate higher pressures at lower depths… outer ears are pointed because of the difference in sound reception under the surface. The heart has increased in size resulting in a lower heart rate, but they are able to pump more efficiently. Blood vessels increased in numbers to maintain heat and tolerate the colder temperatures. The body fat has also increased. You might notice that you gained a pound or two, but since it's all spread out evenly, you don't look overweight…"

Tears formed in Jayne's eyes. His thoughts thundered in his mind, *So many dead… so many lives messed up… So many loved ones who miss them… Oh God! Forgive mankind's sin against you!* It was all Jayne could do to keep his cool. *Oh, what have I become? What have I done to help this maniac?* Weary from the drastic changes in his world, his shoulders slumped. The floor beckoned to his knees, begging for him to collapse and wake up from this nightmare. He hid his face from the creepy looking faces that towered above him.

"Jayne? Jayne? Where are you?" The doctor's urgent voice fretted, "Come on, Jayne. Quit gawking. We need to finish. I have other things to do."

"Um… here!" Jayne's voice's cracked. Straightening his shoulders and back, he dodged through the eerie containers to catch up. "I'm coming," he said as the doc threw his voice so Jayne could still hear it. Jayne could not understand the doctor's calm explanations about the pain a subject had gone through when he died during experimental I.V. therapy. *Did Doc have no compassion for his test subjects?* It became somewhat clearer when the old man stated that the victim had completely paid for his crimes against humanity. *Pretty sure he would have preferred jail time…* Jayne wondered what made the doctor think he was judge, jury and executioner. It frustrated Jayne that no one knew the doctor's real name. He'd turn him in, in a heartbeat, if it weren't for the disguise he wore.

Silence overcame the doctor while the two walked out into the hallway and crossed to tour the main lab where the successful subjects were imprisoned. Jayne breathed the fresh air deeply as he strolled inside the huge moist lab. Peace blanketed Jayne after they left the freaky museum of failures behind. Now Jayne's eyes willingly opened to his surroundings. The blue lights were turned up brighter than usual. The same vertical glass columns stood like giant rook chess pieces creating an alien effect, but now the occupants were alive! These were the tanks that Jayne had been responsible to test for PH balance and water quality, finally fully revealed under the brighter lighting.

Jayne recalled seeing a science fiction movie with a unique fluid hospital bed. Remembering the scene, Jayne daydreamed about being the hero. *Too bad I don't have a laser sword to cut this doctor in two!* Jayne continued his observations. There were a number of 'fluid hospital beds'. Unlike the movie, these were slightly tinted. Tubes and cords were hooked up to each individual for nutrition I.V.'s and monitoring patches. The bundled lines leading out of each tank were connected to multiple types of medical equipment placed alongside. Feeling physically uncomfortable, Jayne's eyes widened. Their faces were without oxygen masks. His intestines gurgled. The males flaunted silver streaked stringy pony tails while the females each wore a pair of floating pigtails. Jayne counted twenty-nine males and thirty females.

The doctor explained the trials and errors on a case-by-case basis while Jayne soaked it in. "I have transformed these humans into their current state without excessive surgeries. My initial experiments were in regenerative medicine that caused great pain and all the subjects died. At first, I had grown DNA altered organs outside the body and surgically used them for transplants. After those experiments, I tried injecting cells into the abdominal cavity where they naturally migrated to the lymph nodes, growing marvelous organs for transplant surgeries." He briefly chuckled at his success.

"One host would grow many of the same organs. It took weeks with transplant complications and the surgeries spun-out over a day. All these subjects have the chromosome for fins, but I purposely left out that gene in your I.V. solution. Surgeries were easy, but the subjects kept rejecting the transplants. Finally, my procedures evolved into an augmented common sense approach. I pulled vials of spinal fluid from individuals and mixed it with some of the electric cave catfish DNA in a regenerative cell nutritional solution. I re-injected the mutated spinal fluid back into the host. Then they received mutating IV therapies to increase and encourage growth. Since it was accelerated, if not sedated, some of the subjects had heart failure from the physical strain. Around the same time the cartilage softened for the sonar organ to grow and the neural connections connecting both sides of the brain was too much. I lost a few before learning to keep them all heavily sedated what with the intense splitting headaches."

Jayne shuddered.

"Three months ago, I finally perfected a formula which supercharges the growth process. Subjects can now progress through the procedure in six days which originally took six months. Yours only took three days, no tails." The doctor eyed Jayne from head to toe and smiled proudly. "Never underestimate the power of science and technology. I brought you back from the dead." Haughtiness filled the doctor's voice. His god-complex reached the surface of his skin with a malicious laugh.

The scientist's deep grating guffaws drowned out Jayne's low toned growl. Listening to the doctor made Jayne grateful for being under heavy sedation. His lips tightened into a mirthless smile as he watched the doctor promenade around the giant room. It irritated Jayne the way the doctor treated him like a valuable buddy, almost like a middleman in this horror movie he was trapped in. No matter how many times Jayne pinched his arm, he knew the nightmare was indeed reality. A recent, yet somehow remote memory of the coded message flashed in his mind. Considering that brief outside contact as a possible savior, Jayne played up his part with new enthusiasm. Staring again at the individuals enclosed in their personal tanks, he felt a complete connection with the subjects in this evil prison. Jayne momentarily relaxed. He was at least partially like those who floated in those glass cells.

The doctor's explanation continued. "If you'll notice, a silver bumpy stripe runs along your spine like those in the tanks. The line sticks out a bit like the top fin on the electric cave catfish. All of your organs are attached to it through your nervous and circulatory systems. Now moving on to your respiratory system... like the ones before you, you also have unique lungs. During the mutation of the lungs, I lost a few subjects."

Jayne's face froze with fear. How could he trust this arrogant doctor?

With complete disregard for the emotions of his employee, the doctor continued, "When water enters the sinus cavity through the nose, it signals an organ attached to the trachea to produce mucus which coats the inside of the lungs." His voice commanded attention while his hand beckoned to Jayne as though he were a prominent hypnotist. "Under the protection of the mucus, they function as gills in either salt or fresh water. When you come above the water's surface, you will spit out and possibly cough out the remaining water and mucus, so that your lungs can function mostly like a normal human." His swaggering ceased. Doc turned to face Jayne. "You will breathe above and below the water like the Queensland lungfish. You will quickly adapt to your environment as the alligator gar. Your sinuses will never be the same, but on the bright side..." He chuckled. "You'll never have use for a nasal rinse. In a sense, I have simultaneously cured your hay fever and found the missing link in evolution. Those in the tanks and you are alike; however unlike those in the tanks, you, Jayne-boy have both of your feet and legs." Doc slapped him on the shoulder like they were old chums and he had done him a favor.

"Will I ever wake up one day..." Jayne gulped and his eyes widened. Pointing at his feet, he continued, "and find tails?" He was clearly concerned. "Does the I.V. solution mutate over time?"

"No." Doc snorted, "You don't even have the chromosome that produces tails. When I spliced your DNA in the Petri dish..."

As the doctor explained it, Jayne realized how immeasurably he loved his lower limbs. Unconsciously, he bent over and rubbed his kneecaps while he stared at his feet planted firmly on the floor. He enjoyed running up and down the stairs in the seating of the oceanarium. It was the only jogging he was allowed. Many times, he had peered over the horizon, closed his eyes and imagined running down the beach. A hand waving in front of his face caused him to find who cut his thoughts in half. "Huh?"

"I said swim bladder." Doc's cheek bones moved the mask as though he smiled a toothy grin. "You don't really have a true functioning one. Your lungs fill up with water, which lessens the relative pressure on them."

Doc again motioned to Jayne to follow him. Sarcasm dripped from his mouth. "Now that you're back from dreamland-"

Jayne froze before his thoughts could betray him. *Dreamland? If only this could be a dream! Am I dreaming? Hah. A really, really bad dream?* Jayne's inner voice broke free to tumble out. "Hah." He covertly used his right hand to pinch his left arm one more time. *Ouch, rats!* Scratching his chin, Jayne's mind churned. His chin dropped and his mouth stood ajar momentarily before wild laughter escaped. Jayne laughed. "Dreamland." He laughed. "La La land." He clutched his sides and leaned against the tank next to him, hysterical.

Horrified, Doc stared with quizzical concerned eyes and crept several feet back.

Inhaling loudly, Jayne tried to control his insane laughter down to a giggle.

"Are you going to be all right?"

"Yeah, Yeah." Jayne straightened his shoulders and lifted his head. "Sorry. Ummm... You were saying?"

Giving Jayne a second glance, Doc decided that Jayne had had his moment and was ready to continue. He pranced on. "I want to go over your breathing habits again. The mucus that coats your lungs also coats your mutated vocal cords. That is why your voice has decreased in decibel level." His words and gait stopped at the same time. Turning to the tank before him, the doctor changed topics and called Marian Harrison by her experiment number posted on the tank. Articulating each word, he stood taller. "I learned to forsake names so that I can stay unattached to my 'miracle projects'."

Jayne's muscles lost their tension as he gazed lovingly upon Marian, his Hope. He leaned forward, slightly parting his legs. Daydreaming engulfed Jayne again as he imagined her awake, diving, jumping in a pool or flying through the ocean. Subconsciously, he thrust out his chest. Scenes swept through his mind of her anywhere but in the prison that she unconsciously floated in. He imagined dancing in the pool with her.

The doctor moved to gain Jayne's eye contact. Doc thought, Is Jayne going to have a fainting spell? The now quiet doctor scratched where his mask met his chin, analyzing the situation. Suddenly, it clicked. Jayne was not about to have a fainting spell. He was in love. The doctor's peculiar face morphed into a wide evil grin. Standing taller, he threw out an enticement,. "You can now swim in the water like her without drowning."

Startled from his daydreaming, Jayne threw his shoulders back and lifted his chin high. He looked directly at the doctor's face. The doctor smirked behind his mask and continued through the room. Naturally pumping his fists, Jayne remained alert as the two hurried along.

"You are going to need to swim exceedingly often to keep your new anatomy running at maximum capacity. You will have to keep the gills wet or you could die. You are now one of them whether you look completely like them or not. You are not predominately human or fish. We will have to change your schedule so that a balance of swimming and landlubbing will keep you strong and healthy. You will only work in the store occasionally, as extensive dry hours will not be tolerable for your new health requirements."

"If most of them in the tanks are capable of living without life support, then…"

Pausing at the next enterprise, the doctor whirled around and directly faced Jayne.

Grimacing, Jayne hesitated, "Why… I mean…" Jayne hurried through his plea, "why not let them go? Like Jonathon?"

"We did let one wake up and take a swim, but he refused to go back into the tank for monitoring. Your friend liked his freedom so abundantly that he was willing to kill a staff member to stay out there. I'm afraid Jon, as you call him, will use his organic electrical charge against me any chance he gets. I ordered the staff to starve him, but they disobeyed. I would have eliminated him, but then again, I do like seeing my trophy alive and swimming." He tilted his head back slightly. "*That* in *itself* is a big accomplishment. Besides, you have been his kryptonite and he will do just about anything, including letting the nurses attend him, just so he can see you. I suggest you continue keeping him under control. You've done a better job than *Doug* ever did."

"Unlike them," Doc mockingly spat toward the nearest exhibit. "Your services are needed. You work here, Jayne. You still have a debt to pay." The doctor paused for full effect, while Jayne dropped his gaze and stared at the floor. Brightening his voice and his face, Doc stated, "Like them, you too need to have the biological electricity to keep your gills functioning. The ankle braces are acting as a ground wire to keep you from shocking others. I'm sure you don't want to go around shocking people!" Staring deep into Jayne's eyes, he lowered his voice. "What would your *mother* say?"

Jayne swallowed, but the huge lump in his throat persisted.

Cold contempt entered Doc's eyes. He stiffened his posture and sneered, "Now that you are aware of the necessity to control the problem, I will allow your grounding shackles to be taken off. As to the others, I don't trust them. I do not want my staff injured by uncontrolled mobile electroshock therapy." The doctor dryly laughed at his own joke, then turned somber. "If you even have an inkling of a desire to harm someone who works for me, I will make sure you join in the fun… in either the tank room… or the room of the doomed." After abruptly turning on his heal, Doc strode to the nearest tank. He stroked the glass, admiring his handiwork.

Jayne bounced back. Placing his hands behind him, he gripped them tightly together to maintain overall control. It truly was tempting just to zap the smug devil, but of course, he was still grounded at the moment. *Besides,* thought Jayne. *I don't even know how to conjure it up to electrocute him.*

Devilish pride induced a simper so strong that it could prevent an earthquake. "The medical industry will honor me with what I have proven. I will have DNA researchers kissing my very toes!" The doctor laughed, wickedly rubbing his hands.

The high pitch in the doctor's laugh forced Jayne's hair to stand on end.

When the doctor found his voice again, it mounted with enthusiasm. "This opens new doors for human-kind! Life-saving surgeries will make me famous. I wasn't really interested in bringing about a new species, but now that I have…" His voice lowered a notch as he mentally counted his chickens before they hatched. "Well, when the time is right, I will be rich." Doc waved his hands as though he retained an admiring audience.

Jayne's happiness, fear and anger were all spinning around in his head. It was all too overwhelming to take in the change in his personal universe. *If I can escape to the outside world, I could very well be treated like a walking plague. Science Fiction is supposed to remain Fiction. Can there ever be peace for me? Will I ever have the adventure of a normal life? I never had one before.* Jayne's toes curled. *What will happen if I fall asleep? Could I wake up a non-consenting full experiment? Maybe a failed one, at that? Someone could slip something into my food! I would be drugged… go to sleep… and never know it!* Entertainment whether from books or movies, hardly ever reflected his reality, but now, even his thoughts had joined in the confusion. He swallowed hard, fighting off the panic as he stared at his prison warden. "So what are my duties now, Doc?"

The doctor looked at the glass enclosure from top to bottom. He traced the corner with a finger. "Well, for starters, keep up the excellent work with the tanks." The doctor watched Jayne lick his parched lips. "Second, you ought to start learning how to take care of your new abilities. Why don't you go get a drink of water and go for a swim? Take the rest of the week off and recover fully. It wouldn't hurt for you to regain more of your strength, as well."

Thirst had indeed become his weakness. Jayne licked his dry lips again.

"You may venture about as you please." He said before lifting his voice. "Doug, why don't you escort the young lad to the pool? Please deliver some drinking water to him as well."

"Yes, sir," Doug answered.

Lumbering toward the oceanarium's watery theatre, the two remained silent. Doug opened his mouth a few times, but never uttered a word. When they reached the first maintenance door, Doug paused, but Jayne, lost in thought, continued on. Doug watched Jayne, then picked up his pace and caught up. When they reached the stage prop door, Doug collided with Jayne who had suddenly stopped and was just standing there.

Carefully, Doug helped Jayne out of his vest while Jayne continued to stare straight ahead opening and closing his fists. Slowly and cautiously, Doug watched Jayne's face as he unshackled Jayne's ankle bracelets. "Hey, Jayne. I'll get you some water." When Jayne didn't answer, Doug waved his hand by Jayne's shoulder. He knew that it wouldn't kill Jayne to swallow a little sea or salt water, but even Jonathon preferred to glug fresh water. When Jayne looked at him, Doug repeated, "Jayne, I'll bring you some bottled water, okay?" He nudged Jayne. "How about something to eat too?"

"Yeah, okay," spouted Jayne with a nod and a shrug. Then he looked at the retreating Doug. "Wait! Did you call me by my name?" Too late: he uttered it after Doug left earshot. He wondered what was taking flight through Doug's head. Something had mysteriously switched in his mannerisms.

{:-)-]~~{

Chapter 7

Jayne heard a splash from the pool and turned to head toward the noise. He saw Jonathon's big grin, but could only manage a twitch in the corner of his mouth.

Wiping his hair out of his eyes, Jonathon proudly welcomed Jayne to have a full on view of his forehead. He waved Jayne to the pool again, but his disarming smile wavered as Jayne took his time.

Moping, Jayne inwardly murmured. *Why does everyone have a take on my life, but me?* Sitting at the side of the pool, he dangled his legs in the water. The last time he dangled his legs, he almost lost his life. A deep frown froze on his face.

Jonathon moved through the water without splashing. Lifting his body with the strength of his arms, Jonathon plopped down beside Jayne. The two sat while an uncomfortable silence drug on. Jayne's feet played in the water, starting ripples that enticed his meaningless focus. Jonathon's head darted around like a bird. First, he looked at the water and then at Jayne's feet. He looked at Jayne's face, all the while being ignored by Jayne. The cycle of glances rotated.

Clearly uncomfortable, Jayne looked at Jonathon and focused on his forehead. "You look like an alien." During the span of their relationship, Jayne never stared. The fact that Jayne's forehead now mimicked Jonathon's gave Jayne's careless thoughts voice. He didn't care what Jonathon thought. Jayne sighed when he realized that his lonely hours had included way too many hours TV surfing. "You look like an alien off the Sci-Fi Channel."

"Duuuude! Wouldn't know. Never really had a mirror and it's not like I've had an opportunity to watch any TV." Jonathon beamed, running his fingers through his hair. "Now… that it doesn't bother you anymore, I'm thinking about making an appointment with a real barber." He flung his hair from side to side. "I'm thinking I need a trim."

Jonathon's chipper response startled Jayne. Looking down, Jayne fretted, "So, why did you save my life? Is this life any better than the life I had? I mean, what has changed? We are *still* under lock and key! We're *still* in a tank… a cage! We are *still* robbed of freedom to *go* where we *want* to go *when* we want to *go*! We *are not* free! Why the optimism? We are *prisoners*! I'm *still* a bondservant! And you… *you* are still stuck here *chasing* your tail in this pit!" His angry words died when he saw his friend's saddening face. Immediately he changed his tone and demeanor. If Jayne had been a dog, his tail would have been tucked between his legs. "Sorry, Jon, I'm still kind of shocked, you know…"

Like a flash, Jonathon interrupted his friend. "Nah fish. I've been thinking about an escape plan. So what do you say? Dude, you with me?" His eyes reflected a dangerous daring.

"Escape?" Jayne gave him the third degree. "How is there even a remote possibility of an escape… from here?"

"Ah, quit being a gory parasite. We can ditch this sand."

A change of thoughts triggered ideas that danced around in Jayne's head. They could take over the security room and walk right out the front door, except Jonathon couldn't walk. They could get Doug to cause a distraction while Jayne made an exit through the front door, but that could leave Doug in trouble. *Where would I go? Who is left to turn to?* He did not care. He would dart, sprint, and run until he found a cave on the coast to spend the night. He could stay there and come up with a plan to rescue everyone. They could all live in the underwater caverns along the coast. The feeling of being the hero strengthened Jayne. Daydreaming grabbed hold of his mind as he fantasized living in a wide-mouth cave with Hope and the others. He concluded the others should find other caves while he and Hope would live happily ever after. Thoughts of Hope brought back a brief, jumbled recollection of the missing persons program. Image after image lit up his memory, causing excitement to fill his every cell.

"Oh! Jonathon, have I got news for you! Your real name is... oh... I had it before I blacked out."

"And almost drowned? Doug said you were malnourished. *Why* did *you* stop eating?"

"Don't interrupt my thoughts!" Jayne threw his hands in the air and shook his head away from Jonathon. "It's... um... oh it started with an 'A'."

Jonathon leaned back and used his hands to prop him up. "Sick."

"Antoine? No... Andrew... no that's not it... Oh, oh! Anthony! Yes, Anthony." Jayne brightened before disappearing among the boulders in his brain. "Anthony Rogers?" He closed his eyes tight. "No. That's not it." Jayne slouched and his saddened lips tightened. "Anyway," he said as he sat up straight and made eye contact. "Your name is Anthony and you were a professional swimmer. You were just as competitive then as you are now. Hey, your swimming manager still hopes to find you. They spoke of no family, but your real name is Anthony."

"Duuuude. My real name," Jonathon gasped as his eyes widened. "Totally tubes, bro!" Silence cut his thoughts in half. "Anthony. Hmmm...Anthony..." His quizzical eyes stared blankly ahead. Tiny flames lit large candles in his eyes as if a wish was cast. "Rod...riguez. Cha brah! Rodriguez!" Jonathon almost shouted as he deeply exhaled. Impressions of the past thundered over him causing him to shiver.

"Yeah that's it! Anthony Rodriquez!" Excitement fueled Jayne with optimism. "So Anthony, that will be hard getting used to. Anthony, what should we..."

Jonathon interrupted. "Wow. Wow, dude. How did you find out my name?"

"A missing persons program."

"Naw fish, I think you better keep up calling me Jonathon." Jonathon's deep eyes focused on Jayne's soul before they darted around. He lowered his voice. "If you didn't hear my name from that dumbass...if...if...iffen you start calling me by my *legal* name without doc tellin' you...who knows what he would do to you...or us...for that matter."

"Yea...Yeah, I think you're right." Jayne sat upright, stretched his back, and shifted his weight on his butt. The concrete was starting to feel extra hard. "Good thing too, because it would be hard getting used to calling you anything but what I named you." It was Jayne's turn to search his surroundings. He motioned Jonathon closer. "Speaking of the missing person's program..."

"Yeah."

"Hope!" He laughed through his first sentence. "Oh my, I forgot. Hope! You know the one I told you was pretty?"

"That hot bunny you talk about all the time?"

"Heck, Yeah! The one that's been here for almost as long as me. Remember when I found her drugged up and crawling in the hallway... and...and... I held her until Doug rushed me to my room before Doc found out?"

Jonathon nodded and inched closer.

"Doug used to tell me all kinds of stories about how the doctor had so many problems with her." Jayne briefly paused and leaned in. "I know why!" His memories before surgery instantaneously flooded back. He chatted with an infinite source of fuel. "Her parents miss her so much. Her real name is Marian Harrison. She hates water!" He shrieked, "She was aqua phobic!"

Jonathon snorted before he lifted his voice. "That crippler chick is aqua phobic?"

"Aqua phobic?" The two men marveled in union. They rolled their eyes, belly laughed, and held their sides.

"Aqua phobic," Jonathon's voice oozed sarcasm. "Water?" Loud echoing laughter escaped his open mouth.

"Scared of water," laughed Jayne.

Using their hands, Jonathon and Jayne splashed water at each other. When the sarcastic carefree laughter died down, silence hung in the air. Then a hollow guffaw cut the air like a sonic boom.

Jonathon and Jayne cringed and momentarily froze, staring at each other. They whirled around. It was Doug. Horrified looks swept over both Jonathon and Jayne.

Doug's brittle laughter faded into a polite smile. The expression vanished as a deep frown checkered Doug's lips. Shrugging his shoulders, he strode over to the two and handed Jayne a big canteen of water. "I'm sorry I took so long. I brought you guys something. Here. It's full of sea water from the coast."

Jayne hesitated as he accepted the peace offering. As soon as Jayne supported its full weight, Doug turned and sprinted to the door. Jonathon and Jayne exchanged glances. They shrugged their shoulders and stared at the jug. Jayne opened it, sniffed at the contents, and passed it to Jonathon. After Jonathon followed his friends' example, they took turns splashing their faces with the salty-sweet taste of freedom.

Squeak. Squeak. A wheeled metal cart appeared, pushed by Doug. On it was a variety of fast food. Doug took the tray, filled with food, drinks, and desserts. He placed it down in the middle of the three. Folding his legs, he helped himself to a drink and a sandwich. There was plenty for all three of them.

Jayne sniffed the air and noticed that his sense of smell was heightened. He maliciously grinned. Different bags offered different fragrances and he could distinguish them. It was as if he had passed out human and woke up canine.

Jonathon's facial features twitched as homesickness for his past distracted him.

Pure excitement filled Jayne's face as he had missed out on fast food for several years. Although his hand crept slowly toward the food, his eyes never left contact with Doug's. He watched every movement. It was hard to trust Doug sometimes.

Loudly chewing and swallowing his food, Doug said between bites, "Don't worry, dude, your secret's safe with me. I think I can help you guys out. Even the help around here isn't safe anymore. I'm splitting too." His excitement turned like a tornado through a mobile home park. "Next time Doc leaves, I can lock the nurses in their apartments and I can handle the ogre who assists Doc." Dropping his double bacon cheeseburger on its paper, Doug clenched his fists and shook one toward the door. "I can catch him with his knife down."

"Dougie," Jayne jeered. "Don't you mean with his pants down?" He snorted. Doug's confidence was going to get him killed. One doesn't bring fists to a knife fight. The fact that Doug was ready to leave filled Jayne more or less with comfort, but his evolving fears kept him silent. He took a bite of a fish sandwich and savored it. When he took another, he noticed his taste buds were heightened as well. He stole a minute to sniff toward the coast. The moist, salty sea air smelled sweet compared to the bitter filtered salt water sitting around him.

Looking nervously about, Doug opened a new topic. "Hey, I could get in big trouble telling you guys this, but I have been warned about your 'talents'. Jonathon, if you could tone down your anger, you could control the amount of electricity that you generate. Instead of killing someone, you can make them just pass out."

Jayne watched Jonathon snap back into reality and pay close attention. This seemed to be information that Doug was openly giving. It was new to Jonathon and it was new to him. Jayne turned to face Doug. "Can I use mine? How?"

Explaining what he retained, Doug sounded like a closet genius. "It isn't learned, it's just instinct. An unconscious nerve triggers it. I can't really tell you how to use it. They tried removing the electrical generation organ from several patients because of the danger to others. They died because the gills somehow need the electrical energy to work. The nerves must be joined with the fish DNA that was fused through your human spinal fluid."

Jayne sat deep in thought. He did not remember ever hearing intelligent conversation from Doug. But at least the information sounded reasonably useful.

"Even if you did escape this maniac, you won't ever be able to live like a normal human again. Doc already tried attempting reversal on some. They had no lungs…" He grimaced and then stared at his feet. "I'm sorry about that." Doug heard a splash. Jonathon scooped up handfuls of water.

"Hey," Jayne griped as Jonathon poured a substantial amount of water on his neck and back. Lifting his food high in the air, Jayne barely saved it from getting soggy. He shot Jonathon an icy stare.

Doug covered the food and moved it to safer ground. When the drenching was over, Doug's eyes emanated trouble. "Couple years ago, Doc took out a newspaper ad and promised a free experimental cure for spina bifida in exchange for work as a volunteer nurse. Several nurses came in with children that suffered from MD. By the time they found out the doctor's crazy cure, it was too late. The children had already gone through the genetic I.V. therapies and had been transformed into the human lungfish. The nurses, Mrs. Goldblum and Ms. Luhrman both live under the doctor's thumb because their children are in forced comas in those tanks. They fear one wrong move and the doctor will make sure they never hold those kids again."

"Which ones?" Jayne pried. "How old are they? Are they cured?"

"There's Harvey Goldblum. He's 13 and Juliet Luhrman. She's 14. They know their spines have straightened and according to MRI's, their brains are functioning normally, but…"

"Their mothers haven't seen them awake… yet." Jayne stopped talking and gulped the last two bites of his meal. "Why are the tanks tinted?"

Doug slapped Jayne on the back. "Modesty, bro! The fish/humanoids have all the parts of human anatomy needed to reproduce. You probably notice that Jonathon always keeps his thighs together, a natural reflex that protects his privates while swimming and gives outstanding force to his swim kick. However, the ones in the comas have to have their thighs wrapped and tied up to help them protect the private areas. Since they can't do it out of instinct, they have to be bound."

For the first time, Jayne gave in completely to his curiosity. Without shame, he stared hopelessly at Jonathon's lack of human legs. He noticed that although he was considered naked as a human, his fishy thighs hid his private parts. The silvery cat-fish skin stopped in a lip around his waist. It almost looked like a fish devoured him up to the top of his hips. The lip ended in a v shape of fish flesh that stopped under Jonathon's navel. Then he stared into Jonathon's eyes. "You have separate leg limbs, but I've never seen you walk. You don't have a single tail like the mermen of legend."

Like a bat out of hell, Doug quickly answered so that Jonathon didn't have to. "Jon's legs are part fish and part human. He still has bones for ankles and feet but he can't walk on them. He is a Hecc now. The ankles now function like tails. They might look like a scuba suit with split fins, but they're designed to work together - to help him swim faster. He was pretty scratched up and bloody when he went to find help for you, Jayne. While screaming for help, he military crawled over the concrete all the way to the hallway and beat on the wall with his fists." Looking from Jayne to Jonathan, Doug talked to both of them, yet somewhat ignored them, since they were both still staring at each other.

Jayne continued staring at Jonathon's fins, whose toes disappeared beyond recognition. Now the flesh came on down in ripples or ridges flowing from the metatarsals and the phalanges to make fins. The fascinating ripples in the silvery tinted flesh ended right before a split, which was between the now transformed second and third toes. It almost looked as though the skin had mutated into a tail. The fish flesh covered the whole lower half of Jonathon's body. Jayne shivered at the thought of how painful the procedure must have been. His gaze suddenly broke and he exclaimed, "Wait! Stop! What is a Hecc?" Jayne stared at Doug with a very confused face. Jonathon turned and faced Doug as well.

"H.E.C.C. stands for Human Electric Cave Catfish. The Heccan is a male and the Heccwan is a female in the Doc's terminology. They really can't be named Mermen and Merwomen. Those legends had only one fish tail. The H.E.C.C.'s have two separate limbs and tails."

"Ooooookay." Deep in thought, Jayne's left side of his face squinted up. He was determined to not miss a beat. Puzzled and shocked, he stared at Doug.

"Hmm…" Jonathon brushed his bangs aside.

Doug gazed into the distance as if trying to recall things he heard. "They can use their two tails separately or they can hold them together for greater power. All Heccs have the spinal bumps and flesh from the electric cave catfish. The small bumps are covered with silver and blue. All the Heccs' hips and legs have a silver tint added to their natural skin color. Each one has unique rainbow colors on their tails." He beamed at Jayne and Jonathon. "Those are awesome!" Doug looked away from them. He blankly stared at the water again to gather and puzzle together his firsthand account. "Everyone's DNA seems to affect their individual color patterns like fingerprints. Their hips and legs are covered with fishy flesh like a catfish, with no scales. Their legs are now shaped so they fit together tightly. They can kick from their knees separately or cooperatively in perfect rhythm. The fins covering their toes stick out like divers' flippers. They can still wiggle their toes, to flex their fins, but they have stronger muscles in them than regular humans do."

Doug paused and finished off his pop with a slurp. After he grabbed a bottle of water on the bottom of the cart, he opened and tasted the water. Acknowledging Jayne and Jon's undivided attention, he continued. "The Heccs still have a hankerin' for sunlight and air exposure. The doctor has had a lot of problems having to drain tanks twice a week to let their skin breath. Since he keeps them indoors, he shines a sun lamp on them too. He usually has the tanks completely full to give them a good soak though. I think they've been in comas long enough. He should let them all loose like Jonathon here. He seems to be doing okay." He gave a wink and a slight grin to Jonathon. Doug exhaled sharply before he inhaled and exhaled slow. There had been a lot to remember and explain.

Jonathon glowered. "Yeah, but this canopy is no fun." He pointed at the canopy covering the stadium. "I'm ready for a real sunbath instead of a shadow bath." He rolled his eyes and pouted complete with folded arms.

Doug and Jayne chuckled.

"Sorry," fretted Jonathon. "Doug, go on. This is the first time anyone has explained… this much to me." Jonathon's eyes intently focused on Doug's eyes.

Doug meekly smiled and nodded. He directed his attention simultaneously between Jonathon and Jayne. "The DNA in a Human Electric Cave Catfish is very different. I heard the doctor talking about how the mutated DNA slows down the aging process. Ol' Doc can't guess their lifespan, but he has an idea that they will live longer than humans. Also, when they get hurt, they heal faster. That was discovered when Jon, here, got scraped up." Doug turned directly to Jonathon to make sure he personally heard him. "By the way, thanks Jon. I've kinda grown to like this guy." He winked at Jonathon. The nightmare flooded back. *Jayne, cold and limp…laying on that hospital bed. Big tough me standing there pleading with tears all over my face. Doc's threatening words that he wasn't going to save him unless Jonathon quit protesting being hooked up to an I.V. and give up blood samples.* Clearing his throat and squashing his emotions, Doug didn't explain his wink.

Jonathon understood. He thought, *I hope Doug doesn't tell Jayne.*

After a few minutes of silence, Doug sighed and took a lingering drink. All this talking taxed the strength out of him. Noticing that they had stopped eating, the three men ambidextrously grabbed the rest of their side items and desserts.

In awkward silence, Jayne stared at Jonathan's legs while he ate. Jayne and Jonathon both looked alike with the spinal bump, forehead ridge and ears, but Jayne differed with human legs and feet. Unconsciously, he stretched his feet and played with the range of motion with his ankles. "I'll have to start wearing a handkerchief to cover my ears and forehead."

"Never thought about having to do that." Jonathon placed his weight on his hands behind him. His somber facial features suddenly twitched causing his lips to curl with mischievous pleasure while excitement sparkled in his eyes. "You'll love the kiff nictitating membranes that move horizontally across your eyes."

"Why?" Jayne lifted a brow.

"They're not just for safety."

"Do you see better than you did when you were human?" Looking at the water, Jayne shivered.

Taking his cue to let the two have an uninterrupted conversation, Doug forced himself to just chew and swallow leftover food.

"I can see details on the bleachers under water just as well as above the water. Man, my sight is totally righteous!" Jonathon sat up and glanced around at the bleachers.

"Hmm," Jayne hesitated. "What else? How else am I alike and different? When I looked in the mirror, I noticed silver streaks in my roots starting." Glancing at his legs, he noted, "Shoot, you can see the silver hair starting in my leg hairs!" Jayne snorted softly. "You look like an old man."

"Isn't this just my color?" Jonathon pitched his voice with a playful lisp. Masking his masculine fingers, he wiggled them as effeminately as he could. His nails were the shade of shiny polished silver.

Doug shuddered at Jonathon's perfect performance.

When Jonathon saw Jayne's long face, his mischievous snigger faded. "Don't worry. When you grow into yours, you'll get used to it."

The awkward moment ceased as sea creatures called from the ocean.

Doug shot Jonathon a warning look.

"Ah, come on, Dougie," Jonathon protested. "Can I answer them? Please?" Jonathon attempted batting his eyes, but did not master a smooth flicker.

With an exaggerated shake of his head, Doug nixed that thought. Jonathon flashed puppy dog eyes in Doug's direction, but was ignored. Quietly, they finished eating.

Jonathon hesitantly spoke. "I know Doc ordered you to starve me after I fought to not go back into a tank. You snuck food and water bottles to me."

Doug shrugged as if it were no big deal. He nodded and then he gave a sly grin.

Jonathon mocked, "Duuuude, when I wouldn't die or go back calmly, that 'Dr. Moreau wannabee' looked like he was having a coronary. It was my *duty* to give him shock therapy...pronto." Lickety-split, his jeer turned somber. "Nah fish... I wasn't trying to hurt the nurse. How's she doin'? Haven't seen her 'round."

Rubbing his chin, Doug scrutinized Jonathon. "After you shocked her, she almost didn't make it. She was resuscitated, but she couldn't survive on her own. The doctor tried to help her by making her one of his patients like he did to Jayne. She had improved and was ready to wake up, but the doctor removed her electric organ. She was one of the ones that didn't survive because he tried to eliminate the electrical generation. She didn't make it because of the doctor, not because of what you did." Jonathon looked grim in spite of Doug's reassurance.

The constant emergencies following the nurse's accident had worn Doug out. The sights and sounds pulsed in his memory. "She was one of the nurses that had brought in a child. She had no family except for the child she had fostered and adopted. That one also didn't live because of the 'Electric Organ Crisis'. Really Jon, this is all the Doc's fault, not yours."

They sat for a few minutes, letting their full bellies, and Doug's information settle.

Finally, Doug broke the silence. "Hey, Jayne, you might have started out as a just a job description to me, but remember the laughs we had?" His emotions caused him to stumble through his words. "And remember the nights we played cards? What about the Sci-Fi marathons?" Words failed him as he choked up.

"Gorram it! Why did they cancel that Sci-Fi Western? None will compare." Jayne placed his hand on Doug's shoulder.

Rubbing the back of his neck, Doug found the courage to continue. "We were always together. I had spent so many hours with you that, well, I hated to lose you. When I chose to spend extra time off the clock with you... well... we have had some fun... betting on sports with our candy. We've had some good times." The memory of carrying a limp Jayne after attempting CPR filled him with uncontrollable grief. He fought the stubborn lump in his throat, failing to move it. A tear welled up in his left eye. He shivered and curled his toes. Doug cleared his throat quietly and then loudly. Controlling his emotions, he straightened up. "At least before you became buddies with Jon. Then you spent a lot of time with him and I never saw you except when I had to keep you in line. You almost died and I didn't care about losing you as my job, because I had already lost you as a friend." He ended with a remorseful sigh.

Jonathon and Jayne exchanged a knowing glance. Jayne rubbed his chest with his left fist. Jonathon winced and stared at his empty hands.

Looking down, Doug hesitated. "You think I can join you both *this time* for a swim?" He was laying his full trust on the table, for this huge risk. It could end in them drowning him easily. Patiently, he waited for them to show their emotional cards.

Scratching his ear, Jonathon contemplated. His face brightened with a mischievous snicker. "Sure, brah, as long as you go get the kiff toys!" A short chuckle escaped his lips as Doug stood up. The doctor had Doug take his toys away for discipline on the nights that Jonathon sang lonely songs to the ocean. Many times, he feared not the consequences of the doctor's wrath, until Jayne's life received a threat. The doctor's highest priority consisted of keeping unwanted attention at bay. The unknown whims of a madman kept the scientist from crying crocodile tears for the loss of any employee or experiment if it meant protecting his identity. Still speaking to Doug, Jonathon patted Jayne on the back. "Jayne here needs a warm up and I think I've been disciplined enough. I want toys again!" Turning, he faced Jayne as he exclaimed, "Brohein, you ready for some awesomeness? You ready for a totally rad experience?"

Doug took his cue, stood up, and then disappeared through the doorway.

Jonathon watched for Doug to return and whispered, "Cowabunga."

Kicking his foot in the water, Jayne decided, "Alright. Let's go."

Jonathon screeched, "I'm so rapt!" Then noticing Jayne's leery expression, he soothed. "Come on, brohein. I'm here."

Jayne eased into the water but paused at his waist, holding his weight with his arms. Eagerness and confidence fell when shadows on the surface of the water mimicked a fictional time portal. Scrambling for the side, Jayne's anxiety surpassed his nerves. He crawled out and away from the new world. "I...I passed out!"

"So?"

"I drowned!"

"You did, but now you're a Hecc like me. That's sick, duuuude."

"I don't look like it!"

"No problemo. You don't need fins! You already got what you need! Gills, man, gills!"

Jayne inched his way to the edge. He eased into the water up to his neck. Fear of drowning haunted his movements. He had been born a human and still expected to die like one. He passed out a human and woke up a H.E.C.C. His thought processes computed based on human experience. Being a Heccan was still a foreign concept. Floating with his head above water gave him a chance to deal with part of the phobia. His thoughts haunted him. *How can I let go under water?*

Jonathon respected Jayne's time and dove under. Becoming impatient, he came up and floated beside Jayne. Once he acquired Jayne's attention, he gave him a reassuring grin. "Okay, brah, there's nothing to be scared of. Just do the opposite of what you were taught. Exhale... and dive under."

After watching Jonathon walk the talk, Jayne obeyed. Taking a deep breath, Jayne paused and blew it out. Diving underwater, bubbles floated up from his mouth. He shut his mouth, shook his head and tried to stop water from entering his nose. Profanity and cries screamed in his brain because his nose disobeyed him. Bubbles escaped as the water entering tickled and burned. He shook his head. Clamping his hands over his mouth and nose, Jayne swam for the surface.

Jonathon grabbed Jayne's hands away from his face. Staring into Jayne's panic stricken face, he detained Jayne's wrists. Jonathon's powerful fins pulled them deeper. Jayne stopped struggling and stared back. A sloggy feeling cooled his chest while his lungs filled with water. Instead of passing out, Jayne felt the fresh oxygen filling his mind with energy as his gills filtered the water. Jonathon let go as he saw relief form on his friend's face. Jayne drifted, but then his body went rigid as he focused on the tickling sensation. Jayne's eyelashes blinked rapidly as the tendons in his neck stood out. Then fear tightened its grasp on Jayne again, causing him to dart toward the surface.

Jonathon stopped him with a tight hold on his ankle. Shaking his head dramatically, Jonathon wagged his finger with his free hand. With his head, he motioned for Jayne to follow him deeper. This was no regular human swimming pool; this was deep enough to show off killer whales and dolphins to an oceanarium audience. Jayne shivered as the temperature in his body instinctively adjusted. Life suddenly filled his body as he defeated that old mind killer, fear. Shooting off like a rocket, Jayne felt fresh oxygen surge in his muscles. Grinning, he spun. He dove. For the fun of it, he made an algae angel on the underwater viewer's window. Jayne thought, *I can't believe the two remora suckerfish cannot keep up with all the algae in this tank. I will have to order a few more in.* The algae didn't feel as slimy as when he had touched it as a human. It soothed his nerves with a glimmer of Heaven.

Jonathon grinned from ear to ear as if mocking Jayne.

Situating himself in a reclining position on the window's ledge, Jayne thought, *Ah, I see why Jon likes to sleep here...especially since no one comes into the visitors lobby in the basement... what with all the boxes blocking the stairway and the outside entrance boarded up.*

"Oh! Gnarly," Jayne mouthed the words to Jonathon, who stayed close by his side.

This was an old game for Jonathon, but watching Jayne was like watching a child ride a bike for the first time. A noise on the surface of the water froze Jayne and Jonathon in their routes. They looked at each other before racing to the surface. Jayne traveled slower than Jonathon did. Jayne stared from behind using the full swim to the top to study his friend's swimming motions. The excellent vision through the water satisfied Jayne, heightening the adventure. The force of the water rushing past his eyes didn't hurt or sting. His fearful human desire for blinking faded.

Jayne's hands broke the surface before his head and upper body, as he broached the surface like a submarine doing an emergency blow. Until today, Jayne had lacked the ability to hit the surface with that superb force without a fear of drowning pushing him upwards. The old desire to inhale air from burning lungs disappeared from Jayne's memory. The water called to him to dive back under. Out of the corner of his eye, Jayne's awesome feeling faded as he watched Jonathon still in the air. He had reached a greater height with his body completely out of the water. Ah, *no fair*, Jayne thought. Coughing, he spit out a portion of water and shook his head. Air no longer felt like a familiar old friend. Each inhale triggered a slightly stinging burning sensation in his chest. He coughed again. Jayne felt an unusual ache to dive down again, but obligation forced him to the edge of the water to meet Doug.

With greater strength from his tails, Jonathon again made a fifteen foot leap, a dolphin's jump. He rotated three hundred and sixty degrees before his body hit the water again.

Jayne blinked his eyes and admiringly took a second glance. His lips formed the word 'wow', but his vocal chords never pushed the word above a butterfly's whisper.

Stopping in mid toss of a toy, Doug stood rigid and mesmerized.

With a wide grin on his face, Jonathon dove under only to resurface with yet another jumping trick, flipping his tails high.

Without deep consideration, Doug ran to the hoops for the seals and dolphins. Grabbing one, he race to the edge and dangled the ring over the surface of the water to see if Jonathon would jump through it. Doug laughed with sharp snorts when Jonathon did. "Show off!" he yelled as he dropped the giant hoop in the water. He skipped back to the cart. Filling his arms to his chest, he carried the toys to the water's edge. Three colorful beach balls floated in the water after Doug tossed them. Four bright balls of different sizes thudded when they hit the water before sinking from their weight.

After hearing another couple of splashes, Jayne put his head under the water to watch as diving rings sank to the bottom. Butterflies fluttered in his stomach. The gentle rhythm of his heart skipped a beat, pounding faster. His forehead honed in on the instinctive signal being sonared to him. First the purple ring sank, and then the pink one. His thoughts caressed his very soul. *You elude me, my pearl.* After he watched the yellow one sink, he could no longer contain himself, no longer fight his instinct. A shiver ran from head to toe as he raced after the red one sinking a few feet away from him. His gut ordered him to chase and fetch like a Labrador retriever would for a master.

Doug was unnerved as he stared at Jayne, concern wrinkling his facial features. The first time Jayne did not surface quickly caused Doug to hold his breath. Putting his hand over his mouth, he gasped.

Jonathon saw Doug. He swam as close as he dared to the edge, used all the strength in his lower limbs and splashed Doug back into reality.

After Doug sputtered water out of his face, he yelled. "Hey!" The corners of his mouth lifted into a mammoth smile. "I don't have gills!"

"Brah, he's good to go after the rings alone," said Jonathon. With deep eyes, he held onto the side of the pool with both his hands.

Doug stood in his everyday clothes, dripping wet with Jonathon's reminder. Sitting down, Doug proceeded to undress to his boxers. Doug heard Jonathon laughing hysterically. Searching the water's surface for Jayne, Doug stood up for a more useful scan.

With ease, Jayne surfaced and swam to the edge. Coughing, he almost lost the yellow ring under his right elbow and the red ring under his left elbow. Both his hands were occupied with large seal rings. Jayne scooped up the purple hand-sized diving ring he had dropped when he coughed. One by one, Jayne handed Jonathon everything stowed on him, including two rings hooked on his feet.

A short bark-like laugh escaped from Doug's tightened lips. Within seconds, he doubled over noisily laughing, holding his ribs with crossed arms.

Bright-eyed, Jonathon joined Doug laughing, but followed with several sharp coughs.

Shrugging his shoulders, Jayne sheepishly looked from one to the other. "What?"

Fighting to regain lost dignity, Doug composed himself. Lifting his hands above his head, he dove in, hands and head first.

Full of glee and energy, Jonathon dove under the surface.

Jayne shrugged his shoulders, placed both hands palms up under the surface pulling himself under. All three swam up to the surface with Jayne breaking through last. After several laps around the gigantic swimming pool, they grinned as they tossed a ball. The two H.E.C.C.s carefully engaged Doug, not wanting to drown their only favorable human friend.

{:-)-]~~{

Chapter 8

The sun played its image on the decrepit street and parking lot. Its blazing anger chased away small daring clouds. Moisture licked at the coast and fought against the sun. Spotted foliage begged for that moisture, dancing their individual rain dances in the slight breeze. Snake's Rock: Exotic Pet Shop's sign sported a hissing cobra whose eyes seemingly scoped the movements of the lonely late afternoon customers. Agents Peter Austin and Kenneth Hershkin drove up and parked in the miserably hot lot.

Sweat tickled Kenneth under his shirt as he slowly exited the vehicle. The gigantic lump in his throat refused to budge under the natural pressure for releasing it. He glanced up at the cobra's menacing eyes noticing that they cleverly concealed security cameras. *Talk about hiding in plain sight. What is going on here?* He sharply inhaled as he focused on the front door. Dressed in a long-sleeve plaid shirt, old ragged trousers, white shin-length socks and scuffed up black shoes, he appeared twenty years older than his real age. His makeup artist's excellent job featured a white wig. Fake wrinkles on his face, as well as the translucent skin tone made him feel old on the outside. Kenneth displayed the persona of an old man dragging a wheeled oxygen tank. Only the agents knew of the vessel's modification to carry surveillance equipment.

Since the FBI lacked actual concrete evidence of something afoul, the two now acted solely on their own. Peter's confiscated badge and his suspension made the situation dangerous and illegal. Kenneth's flashback of Peter's argument with their boss tightened his muscles as he cringed. The boss's words thundered in his inner ear. *We've not seen enough evidence of smuggling or human trafficking to obtain a search warrant. Quit wasting FBI resources and move on to the next case.* Peter's persistent arguing led to a heated exchange, resulting in a pissing contest and Peter being accused of insubordination. Self-control silenced Kenneth's rebellion. *Stupid bean counters.* Taking vacation time, Kenneth joined Peter, his longtime partner, in their close-up investigation.

Scanning the shop with deep interest, Peter sought for an attendant. A few days ago, Peter had finally caught sight of Jayne through his binoculars. So he knew he was alive. Strangely, Jayne was dressing differently with a bright life jacket, headband and swim shorts. Only Jayne's black Croc's remained the same. A new employee lurked in the pet shop, and even the parking lot, without restriction. Peter's face wrinkled on its own. After the first few days, the thug had completely disappeared from the pet shop.

The new employee, owner of a red Porsche, emerged from the office. His hardened face and mannerisms manifested a lack of respect for anyone. Money, his idol, drove the hard working young man to extra effort to afford his pricey pleasures. Hired with the promise of commission bonuses, he sang like a professional salesman.

With a blank stare, Kenneth half-heartedly listened as the employee raved about rare expensive fish. Nodding his head with pretend enthusiasm, he picked the man's brain with polite questions.

Peter reeled in the conversation with a son's interest. His hounding questions emphasized his worry over maintenance issues.

Kenneth interrupted the two men, asking for the nearest restroom.

Without breaking eye contact with Peter, the young man waved Kenneth to the office. He said, "Just head straight into the office. It's in the back." Directing the conversation to his main attraction, he sold the pros of low maintenance pets to the old man's 'son'.

Kenneth searched around cautiously to locate all of the cameras in the store. He proudly sported a few hidden cameras of his own, strategically placed on himself and his portable oxygen tank. The careful and tedious task made for a difficult journey for the 'old' man. Slow and awkward movements led Kenneth behind the counter to arrive at the office. The cylinder, stumped by boxes and supplies, left a trail of tumbled goods behind it. Acting like a grumpy old man, Kenneth performed in solid character. In reality, he didn't mind; he wanted to make thorough observations and have increased video exposure from his pocket pen camera. An empty feeling poured into the pit of his stomach. When he reached the office door, he entered cautiously and walked purposefully to the storage room. However, to any hidden onlooker, the old man fought the wheels carrying his oxygen with his head down. To the spectator, Kenneth's face genuinely lost his direction as he gazed around the storage room. He went back through the door and searched around until he found the bathroom door. Shutting the door, he went inside and peered around. After he was sure no hidden cameras spied on him, he turned on a tape recorder in his left pocket. He breathed a sigh of relief. The sounds of an old man having diarrhea clearly would disturb any listener. Agent Hershkin then went about finding a perfect place to make a peephole.

Next to the toilet paper holder, Kenneth found a set of old holes from a previous toilet paper unit. With skillful quiet movements, he unscrewed the top on his tank and pulled out a snakelike camera. He placed it carefully next to him on the ground. Like a magician, he reached into the tank and pulled out a neat wad of coat hanger wire. After unraveling it, Kenneth used both hands to manipulate the sharp ended wire to extend the hole through the outer layer of sheetrock on the far side of the wall. With a quick twist of his wrist, he wrapped up the wire and tucked it away. Carefully, he pushed the lens of the camera into the hole. He reached his right hand around himself, untucked his shirt and pulled out the netbook tucked into his waistband. As

Kenneth flipped open the small monitor, his left hand plugged in the camera. Several seconds passed before a scene from beyond the wall flickered on his screen. When he turned the camera to and fro to have a wider scan around the adjoining room, he gasped. His whole body lost control and shook. Kenneth feared another earthquake in his gut would dislodge his soul from his bones. The scene before him was straight out of a sci-fi movie lot without need of a green screen. Real, dead, mutated humans drifted in green-lit rectangular aquarium tanks. Losing his vision, Kenneth blinked his unbelieving eyes and focused on the tank closest to him. The plaque read, Zupid Lawz Zuckez.

The sound Kenneth heard next petrified him. Honing in on its source went no further than his taut stomach. Both of his hands flew up to his mouth as if the physical action would stop the mental dam from bursting. Darting over the toilet, he took a couple of deep breaths and swallows. The spasms from his stomach crept up his throat causing the chain reaction of removing his hands. Hotdog, oatmeal chunks, and a pasty liquid spewed out of his mouth. Acid burned his nose as the liquid dripped from his nostrils. The bitter funk and taste made him snort, wrinkle his nose and shudder. Staring at the toilet, Kenneth clung to his frozen spot. Images from his spy eye popped into his head. Feeling like he could now appropriately control his emotions and nerves, he snatched a wad of toilet paper. With a shaky hand, he wiped his mouth and nose with the paper and flushed it.

Shuddering all the way to the sink, Kenneth gathered his wits. Quickly, he rinsed his face and mouth. He was about to remove the spy equipment, when movement on the monitor showed three men. Invisible nails shackled him to the spot in which he knelt. Without question, he recognized the thug. He didn't recognize the other two. One wore a surgical mask, gown and cap. Without warning, a rough looking lanky cowboy reached around the throat of the thug. The glint of metal and the cringing reaction of the thug suggested approximately an 8 inch blade. Their missed conversation could be blamed on the lack of funding for audio equipment. Kenneth knew previous assumptions about who was the real thug would have to be dismissed. The task of understanding the motives and sorting the innocent from the criminals around here just intensified. Kenneth waited until the men left the room so that he could remove the camera. Once they left, he prepared his equipment to leave and placed a clump of putty into the far end of the hole. After he turned off the tape recorder, he flushed the toilet again. With a quick wash of his hands, Kenneth flipped the faucet off. Awkwardly, he left the restroom like he had found it...well, sort of. His nerves shook every joint in his body. The taut grip on the handle of the oxygen tank forced the blood to leave Kenneth's knuckles. When he opened the door, he found the two men in the office waiting for his return from his drawn out absence. Kenneth gasped and patted a clearly weakened hand over his racing heart.

"You okay?" Peter blurted with genuine concern. "Um... Dad?" Straightening his posture, he carefully approached his partner.

"Yeah, uh, no." Kenneth reported honestly. His face twitched with queasy horror. Holding his troubled stomach, he swallowed the acid in his throat. The foul burp of regurgitated all beef hot dogs lingered on his tongue. Inhaling and exhaling labored his breathing.

Impatience pushed Peter to excuse himself and his 'father'. He explained to the clerk they would be back after preparing for the upcoming fish purchase. The two men trudged for the door in character. A faint smiled etched one corner of Kenneth's lips as Peter let him lean a bit on him. The survey of the saddened clerk considered the old man's difficulty in walking, no sale today. Peter knew that something amiss had bothered his partner and he would get the full details of it when they entered the rented Lincoln. The elongated aisle grew even longer for Kenneth. At this point, Kenneth silently wished the tubes in his nose actually delivered oxygen. The door loomed far away. Fog weighed on his mind. Kenneth sighed as soon as he waddled through the door. Aching heat burned Kenneth's feet even through his shoes. Every thump of his heartbeat sounded like bullets firing from behind his eardrums.

Once Kenneth reached the car door, he dropped heavily into the seat of the vehicle. The engine roaring to life pleased his ears and his shaking limbs. The whole time they elusively drove around the block, Peter entreated Kenneth to deliver the details. Kenneth, still beyond disgusted, shook his head. He would not utter a word, no matter how efficiently Peter annoyed him. After they parked behind the mall, the two made their way to the observation hideout opposite the pet shop.

Kenneth, first to walk through the door, wore a disturbed frown on his face. His distressed eyes zoned out the world around him. After taking off his shirt, he came to a halt, snorted and loudly used bad language.

Peter lingered outside the door, but rushed in to find the reason for his partner's hostility. They left the room in almost perfect organization, but now they found dismay and disorder spread throughout the room. One of the two green folding cots lay tipped upside down while the other contained the entire disheveled contents of Peter's and Kenneth's duffle bags. Their camp cooking gear lay dumped on the floor next to their portable propane stove. The red and white water cooler stood atop a gray crate untouched.

The Supervisory Special Agent, dressed in a black suit, sat on a crate in the middle of the room with his arms folded. Confiscated large makeup bags and suitcases rested by his black shiny shoes.

His sharp jaw set menacingly to kill. His brown eyes would have neutralized the two men if he were anything but mortal. In his early thirties, intimidation did not come from his lanky limbs, trimmed eyebrows, manicured nails, blunt black hair style and pointed nose. His rank and ability to cut off the agents' retirement, shot cutting edges of fear into any agent's mind whether they were older than him or not.

In raised tones, Peter and his younger boss argued about policies and procedures.

With a weary heart, Kenneth knelt down on his numb knees. He opened up his laptop. Promptly, he fiddled with the buttons and cued up the footage. Two pairs of feet marched up and hovered over Kenneth's back. He wasn't classified as claustrophobic, but started to feel a touch uneasy with his boss's two bookends. With annoyance that soon turned into despair, they were pressing against his back, crowding him, watching the footage he had captured.

The young athletic black man jabbed Kenneth and told him to rewind it before he loudly whistled in the direction of the SSA.

Quickly, Kenneth cued the evidence to the beginning and paused it.

The two bickering men paused and wandered over. Recognizing Peter's footstep, Kenneth pressed play. This time, he stepped out of the way to let the others watch. Feeling his stomach churn, he knew he didn't desire a repeat performance. The taste in his mouth made him reach for a bottle of water to sip on.

"Crazy...That's just insane." The boss shook his head. He fairly convincingly apologized in a roundabout way that didn't sound truly full of remorse. With an obligation for justice firming his steps, he immediately got on his cell phone and requested permission to get a raid team organized.

Relieved, Peter crossed his arms.

"You're lucky this video turned up grounds for a search warrant. You now have a real case," the boss hissed at Peter when he ended his phone call.

Engrossed in the replay, Peter hadn't heard him, for he continued to stare with morbid curiosity. His eyes watched the footage again and again, as the two coworkers unbelievingly replayed the video. They simultaneously manned the controls. Peter's mind was reeling like an old-fashioned filmstrip as he stared, frozen in place.

Kenneth picked up the upside down cot, straightened it and sat down on it. Relief spread over his body when he took off his tight shoes. Caressing his slightly blistered heal with one hand, he deeply inhaled and exhaled. A hand appeared with a container of makeup removal wipes. It was Peter. Kenneth mustered a forced smile and gratefully accepted the offering.

Hours passed with intense planning and discussion. Phone calls were made to obtain search warrants. Both Kenneth and Peter were relieved when the boss and his aides left and they were alone. The cot invited Kenneth like the hypnotic gaze of a cobra. It pulled him into its cold and careless grasp, then constricted its arms deceptively around him. Attempting to fight the hypnotism only drained his muscles of any remaining strength. Every time he closed his eyes, he startled awake with wide eyes. The footage of the carefully preserved altered human corpses replayed in his subconscious. Not knowing and not wanting to care, Kenneth pleaded with his brain to forget the images. Menacing dreams caressed him. Faces of the people that Kenneth loved and cared for kept showing up, floating behind the glass. He fought the images mentally and physically. Kenneth suddenly shot off the cot like it and he were on fire. Shaking off the disturbing visions, Kenneth sat down. A sixth sense told Kenneth that a presence stirred. Peter was sitting up, staring at the paint spotted floor.

Startled back into reality, Peter acknowledged Kenneth. "The team will be here and ready for us to manage in the morning."

"Yeah, I bet." Holding his head as if it would self-destruct, thoughts still hovered in Kenneth's mind like a puppeteer above his theater. Kenneth had recognized one of the faces. It was from a missing person's case that he had been on almost ten years ago when he worked for a police department. That memorable case had solved itself today. He knew he needed sleep, but knowing that he could tell the old and frail parents that their child's end both tortured and relieved him. Kenneth laid back and closed his eyes. Deliverance and finality etched a faint smile on his lips since he now saw the back of his eyelids without horrible images. After tomorrow, many past cases would no longer haunt him like evil spirits. A heavenly peace calmed his aching and jittery bones.

Both men were physically drained from the effort and stress of their spying expedition. Final plans and preparations for infiltration could wait for a much needed full night's rest. Exhaustion won the battle of thoughts and the two drifted to sleep. Simultaneously, they both peacefully smiled in their sleep as they mutually dreamed of rescuing Jayne Raye Flynn and delivering him into Dee Graham's hopeful arms.

{:-)-]~~{

Fishing for Worms

Could They Get
Away With It?

Chapter 9

lanet Earth remained unaware that at 10:30 in the evening on August 31, the unveiling of life inside the pet store would affect all. Two teams dressed in black crept like predators into the depths of the building. The boogey man danced in every shadow and in everyone's blind spot. They hadn't exerted huge amounts of energy, but fear caressed their brows, causing sweat to gather in inconvenient places. The entire FBI crew had taken two full days to arrive, prepare, and get briefed. The outdated, county registered blueprints remained heavily guarded in the mind palaces of each agent. Vast amounts of cloud cover cast huge shadows, but the FBI needed to hurry before the bright moon peeked through to reveal their operation. The black asphalt might slightly hide the front door team, but the sand behind the store would expose the other team instantly if moonlight shined through. Only darkness meant a stealthy advance.

The posse had avoided the few street lights that were working as they slithered down the street from the abandoned strip mall. Once they reached the huge parking lot for the oceanarium, they went their separate ways. Kenneth took a crew of five while Peter commandeered the other four. With all the uncertainty of the evening and the need to use non-lethal force, the teams had prepared goodbye videos to loved ones just in case. If they didn't make it out, their final requests would be properly settled. They were keenly aware that people were being harmed, even tortured, in that building. By whom and to what extent were the questions that haunted the minds of all who saw the briefing pictures. "Shoot 'em first and sort 'em out later," Peter had told them when he armed the sheep-in-wolves'-clothing with tear gas and tranquilizer darts. Pride barked in every move that Peter made, having received his promotion.

After having been there once, Kenneth refused to invade through the bathroom, so he led his team behind the fence that would take them to the waterfront. The savor of salt tickled his nose and kept the haunting memory of formaldehyde preserved bodies at bay. However, every crunch on the sand made Kenneth's heart leap. The hardest part of this mission was the lack of information concerning what they were up against. The unknown collection of weapons and cameras being used by the undocumented villains made the whole operation increasingly dangerous for everyone inside and outside of the building. It could easily go either way. Everyone prowled cautiously, pausing several times to conceal themselves under various breaks in the deteriorating wooden fence. They took each step to heart as if they traveled over a forgotten mine field. Kenneth's job depended on his crew reaching their target before Peter's team advanced to the storefront from the parking lot. Lacking a small army to surround the entire building, they hoped to quickly advance to a spot where they could easily break in.

Meanwhile, a third team disguised as noisy teenagers, arrived with revving engines. Peter's team hid momentarily behind a hippies' van as it neared the building. A green street rod zoomed up and stomped on their brakes right beside a broken street lamp. The woman driver sprang out of the van and screamed at the two men and one woman in the car.

The 'hoodlums' ignored the van and increased the stereo and turned on the hydraulics. The lady got back into her vehicle and slowly drove around before finding a working light in the shop's parking lot. The street rod's occupants called out to the passengers in the van and they got together to party. Whiskey bottles were full of non-alcoholic drinks for sobriety, but appeared otherwise. Beating music kept the two advancing teams in timely coordination. Female agents danced in their shorts and seductive tops, while the men put on a show with adolescent posturing, rough-housing and playing hacky sack. Some of the agents were a little rusty with their game. It was hoped that any guard watching from inside the storefront would be preoccupied with the entertainment. One jeep, occupied by two male passengers, arrived and made donuts in the parking lot hoping to drown out any harsh sounds that escaped from any careless agent. No one but the teams knew that after two songs, the donuts would stop.

Peter's team advanced between the five abandoned vehicles before disappearing into the brush. They planned on popping up right next to the building.

The two nervous uniformed teams advanced according to plan, timed to the music. Peter had planned extra time to allow for unexpected problems and deviations. Still if two delays on top of three happened with Kenneth's team, the schedule would be completely spoiled.

The path to Kenneth's goal included a steep climb up the concrete wall leading to the outdoor water theater. He needed to get inside before Peter crashed through the front door. Worried about Kenneth's fear of heights, Peter shivered and moved on.

{:-)-]~~{

Mounted next to a light in the arena room, a security camera softly hummed. By now, "Big Brother" didn't bother Jayne, for he had grown used to constant surveillance. The light, however, annoyed him tonight. He shaded his hand from it. Jayne focused on the small sliver of sky in between the shade and the concrete wall. Admiring the stars disappearing and reappearing from drifting clouds, Jayne casually floated in the pool. Once he drifted out of the light, his bright smile turned upside down. The moon hid behind storm clouds and he never realized how much he loved seeing it. His nostrils flared with the different smells on the wind tonight. Making no sense of the new sweet and bitter scents, he closed his eyes. "Star light, star bright, come back to me and take me far from here." His arms left his sides to drift over his head where his two first fingers clasped each other. Jayne forced a happy expression to return with his bouncing eyebrows. *Buoyancy's fun.* Having conquered his natural fears of drowning, he thought, *there might be some advantages to being a biracial Hecc. I get to walk on land and breathe under water.* When he froze his limbs in the water, vibrations came alive against his skin, only his feet danced back and forth in the water.

Without warning, strong hands grasped around Jayne's left ankle roughly yanking him under the surface and down to the darkest depth. Jonathon had been at this game for a few days now. His forms of harassment branched to new levels now that his playmate echoed the same abilities. A month ago, Jayne would have panicked and thrashed out, but he let his body relax with the flow. Without an instinctive desire to struggle, he patiently waited until he found an upper hand. In the brief moment that Jonathon released his grip, Jayne pounced, creating a rough tumble. The two Heccans wrestled <u>and</u> fought full strength. Neither male desired air, for their gills worked wonders. Their bodies tussled about, smashed against the walls, windows, and the floor. They flew up and broke the surface noisily several times. Both escaped each other's grasp and headed deeper and deeper. The only advantage they needed was a split-second chance to gain control over the other. Neither knew the goal, only the journey.

{:-)-]~~{

The team Kenneth led, reached the northern wall and were preparing to climb. When he paused briefly, his team stopped behind him without questioning his actions. Kenneth listened before he tossed his rope. He secretly wished he could avoid the vertical assignment, but then he shook his head with the memory of the floating, mutated dead. Not necessarily a religious man, Kenneth grew up believing in a higher power. Tonight he shot up a prayer and a climbing hook toward the heavens. After checking the mount, he was first to climb. Without his team climbing behind him, he would have sunk into the ground. Kenneth loudly struggled over the top only to discover that they were not alone. His eyes widened as he recognized the voice from Dee's wire. He signaled to the others the okay, but they would be greeted by an unexpected host.

Instinctively, Kenneth reached his hands out with concern when he saw Jayne being pulled under the water. Although Jayne did not promptly return to the surface in the time allotted to a human, Kenneth did not want to give away their location. There was more to this story than Jayne being held against his will. The man they came to rescue would have to be left to his fate momentarily. Kenneth motioned to pick up the pace. He helped his teammates climb over the last hurdle just before the 'thug' walked in. The shadows hid the agents in the open air. They retarded their breathing and watched the 'thug' throw one end of the bug net into the water, stirring the still surface of the water.

Kenneth's worry disappeared when he saw Jayne resurface unharmed. Relief turned to an alien invading fear when he realized that Jayne resurfaced in excellent health despite his coughing. Diving without equipment seemed unnatural for the length of time he had been under. Kenneth shook the questions aside. *Maybe my mind is playing tricks on me.*

The team froze, avoiding even the slightest movement as they watched the scene before them play out.

{:-)-]~~{

Jayne disappeared under again. The surface of the water shook as if two angry sea lions tussled. *That was totally choof. Jon knew I had just finished coughing and he had the nerve to pull me under again!*

Jayne dove to the depths to escape Jonathon's grip. With acquired arrogance, Jonathon proved his superior swimming skills and the two twirled, tumbled and grappled. The thrill of the cat and mouse game only heightened the adrenaline powered match. At one point while they were grappling, Jonathon rolled Jayne like an alligator. Jayne increased in determination to find a way to beat this Heccan at his own game.

The wrestling match ended when a bell chimed above the surface. Pausing in their physical debate, they looked at each other knowing that Doug sounded the dolphin bell on the pole. While they raced to the surface, they playfully pulled each other back to skillfully cheat.

There stood Doug on the concrete stage tapping his foot, waiting with a wheel chair. His fingers angrily drummed the back of the chair. "Hello?"

Jayne and Jonathon simultaneously coughed and dog paddled. When they caught their breath, they swam to the edge.

"That was hella savage, brah. Hella savage!" Jonathon grinned.

Jayne nodded and continued to paddle.

Doug sang his annoyance, "Helllooo?"

The two Heccs' heads danced in obnoxious humor as they sang, "Helllooo, nurse."

"First, I signaled you with a net and you ignore me. Then you answer to a dolphin bell!" Doug snorted. "I should just use stink bait next time, you'll come quicker." Doug mocked, rolling his eyes and his head. "Come on, guys! Do I look like a nurse with long skinny shaved legs and a nice chest?"

With a smirk, Jayne said, "I knew I saw you standing by my side when I was incoherent." He and Jonathon lifted themselves up with the power of their arms and waited on the edge momentarily. Their lower limbs still freely dangled underwater.

"Cha brah. I *know* I saw him in a tight shirt that made his kiff chest spill over," Jonathon mocked with a smirk as he turned to face Doug. "Hey, French nurse *Dougie*, do you have a *bra and corset* to *help* maintain your sleek *figure*?"

Faking a hearty laugh, Doug sneered. He stammered. "They're not boobs! They're muscles!" His pecs simultaneously popped to show his sinewy strength.

"And," teased Jonathon. "You do manscape, don't you? Duuuude?" He blew over exaggerated kisses in Doug's general direction.

Awkwardly, Doug strutted like a woman until he positioned himself neatly behind Jonathon. His modeling ended as he roughly used his foot to push Jonathon back into the water.

Jonathon went under with his arms flailing. When he resurfaced, he stuck out his tongue to show Doug his annoyance at having to cough out the water again. "That was totally choof, *(cough) (cough)* Duuuude. *(cough)* Totally choof."

Jayne responded by dropping over the edge. With a tightened jaw and lips, he kicked and splashed Doug to the best of his ability.

Cowering behind the wheelchair, Doug complained. "Ack! Guys! You're getting me and the wheelchair wet! I know you like water, but I'm not wearing trunks!"

Jayne and Jonathon lifted themselves completely out of the water and sat along the edge. "Okay, okay, you win. They're *man* boobs." Jayne teased Doug as he nudged Jonathon with his elbow. Despite his best efforts, Jonathon laughed. His face soured as he rubbed his left lower rib. Dizzy, Jayne stumbled as he gathered his feet under him while he simultaneously laughed and coughed.

"Come on, guys!" Doug howled. "We need to get moving. Big night, you know!"

Nodding, Jayne grimaced. Tonight was progressing toward being a never-ending night. Jonathon had received permission to join Jayne for his chores. They both beamed at each other with pure ornery delight. Doug, too, grinned from ear to ear, for he would be able to have extra time conversing with his new friend. With Jayne's transformation, Jonathon now proved willing to safely interact with the staff. Doug, still considered a trusted bodyguard by the boss, dared not let on about his own escape plans. Jayne had been the one to talk the boss into giving Jonathon additional freedom. Unknown to the boss, Doug and Jonathon were searching all available angles for a massive escape. Filled with enthusiasm, Doug talked a mile a minute about everything, forgetting his introverted personality. Holding the wheelchair stable, Jayne watched as Doug lifted Jonathon from the edge of the pool. Without considerable straining, Doug carried Jonathon and dumped him in a reclining position in the chair.

Jayne threw a damp beach towel over Jonathon's lower limbs.

Jonathon shivered as his body temperature readjusted. "Thanx, bro," whispered Jonathon as he flashed a toothy grin.

"Are you ready?" Jayne's eyebrows danced as he teased his friend. He sang as loud as he could without cracking, "Are you ready to rumble?"

"Shyau!" Jonathon hunched down ready for a race. "Let's rumble!" His face focused on the adventure that lay in store for them.

Unknown shadows sent shivers up and down Doug's spine. The wind blew in unfamiliar spirits which stabbed his sixth sense with uncertainty. Something, somewhere was not right with the world tonight. He glanced warily up at the sliver of scenery on the distant horizon unaware that Jayne had already skidded off. When he lowered his chin, Doug hollered, "Wait up, Jayne!" With a jump start, he dashed to the door.

{:-)-]~~{

Kenneth and his party held their breaths and froze as one lingered, staring in their direction. They relaxed as they watched the three disappear down the corridor. Kenneth didn't get a satisfactory look at the third figure in the wheel chair for the three had been between the flood lights in the shadows. He shook himself free of questions and thoughts. He continued his job as team leader. Kenneth waved at the man on ground level keeping track of their whereabouts. As soon as he waved, the lookout ran to signal Peter. Kenneth hand signaled his men to follow him. They forgot about watching out for cameras as they walked down the steps to follow Jayne.

{:-)-]~~{

Gosh. This is slower than watching diamonds form, Peter thought. His team continued to be alert for security cameras as they strategically dodged toward the building. They waited for their cue.

{:-)-]~~{

Jayne and Doug's boss planned on staying the night. There were twelve apartments in the old oceanarium and his was furthest southwest. Walking in, he closed the door and locked the three padlocks. Looking around the cluttered room, he sighed under his mask. Heading straight for the bathroom, he scratched his left butt cheek. Staring in the mirror, he roughly pulled off his surgical mask. His gloves snapped as he peeled them off, too. Holding them in his left hand, his fine surgically attuned right fingers eased the uncomfortable itching. Twitching his nose and mouth, his once clean shaven chin spattered with a 5 o'clock shadow. His pencil stash also itched. He hated that mask and threw it and the gloves into the trash. Blinking his eyes, he popped out his brown colored contacts with his finger to reveal steely blue eyes. With his free hand, the doctor pulled out a contact case from his pants pocket. He carefully hid his contacts in it before tucking the container back in. Reaching into his right pocket, he pulled out a match. His left hand snatched the bottle of high potency rubbing alcohol off the sink. After he poured the flammable liquid in, he lit the match and dropped it into the metal trash can. Dark stinky smoke filled the room.

After closing the door behind him, the doctor dragged his aching body from the bathroom to the kitchen. Too many twenty hour days had exhausted him. Last he checked, it was at least twenty days of all work and no play. Pausing briefly in front of the sink, he quickly filled up and greedily gulped down a glass of water. After gruffly wiping his mouth with the back of his hand, old secretive habits won out. Pulling two blue gloves out of his pocket, he snapped them on. Gloved hands in blue picked up, opened and poured Clorox over the faucet and glass. With a flick or two of his wrist, the doctor used a cloth to wipe off the prints and DNA.

Drudging to the bedroom, the doctor let his dragging limbs slog along. Instead of a bed, he stared at a converted office space. Popping and stretching his aching back, he wished for the comforts of his three-story domed estate. This fleabag of a bedroom lacked any bed, much less a comfortable king-sized bed with red silk sheets.

Sighing, the doctor snorted at the oak desk and black leather chair. Facing the wall, he bent over and pulled his sleeping bag out of a black gym bag. Popping his neck, the scientist arched his head to the ceiling. The wall in front of him framed two huge flat screen TVs. He wrinkled his nose at the rambunctious trespassing teens in the parking lot. Shrugging his shoulders, he let the weight of that matter drop, it was nothing unusual this time of night. Swiftly, the middle-aged man hopped up and walked back into the living room and plopped his sleeping bag on the couch.

Heading back for the pillow, a buzz in his shirt pocket stopped him in his tracks. Viewing the inner screen, he read the text, *Operation stunted. Loading dock clear. Boat out back.* Rereading it did not magically alter the words. When he stood in front of his security system, he stared wide-eyed. Each TV portrayed four separate camera angles. The camera overlooking the pool required a second deeper steadfast search of its shadows. A lump formed in the doctor's throat. Rubbing them with his rough gloves, he focused his weary eyes. Men clothed in black and carrying weapons were entering his property through the arena. Placing his left hand over his shocked mouth, he backed up until his posterior touched his desk. Darting eyes watched each camera angle while his right hand fumbled around his desk. "Bloody maggots," he spat at the camera. "Stinking selfish leeches!"

Whirling about, he punctually gathered papers off his cluttered desk and stuffed them in his open briefcase. It clicked when he slammed it shut. Glancing at the camera, he muttered, "Need to give my inside man a bonus." Another team was walking alongside the pet shop walls. He grabbed his keys off the hook next to the door, and opening it, raced down the hall and unlocked a storage room. He closed the door while puffing and panting. There was no time to catch his breath.

{:-)-]~~{

The filters on the tanks sang an eerie tune. Jayne didn't know whether or not Jonathon and Doug would get caught scheming. He was feeling uncomfortable and perhaps a bit edgy. It was in the air. The aura circulated and stood his hair on end. A low voltage of electricity pumped through Jayne's limbs from the churning thoughts. *How are we going to get everyone out of the tanks… let alone… out of the building? Are they going to wake up and immediately know how to use their electric organs? Are they going to use them on me? How are they going to cope? Are they going to blame me? I wasn't the one who turned them into a bunch of mermaids!* He knew he wasn't responsible for their condition, but he felt like an unwilling accomplice.

Doug and Jonathon cautiously crept down hallways checking out possible escape routes. When they had exhausted their minds, they joined Jayne back in the 'tank room'.

There still seemed to be another cause for the uneasy mood as he exchanged the water in each rectangular chamber one by one. Jayne couldn't accuse the full moon since darkness loomed outside. Shadows waved the unrecognized in his face. Frustrated, Jayne couldn't figure out the source bothering him. He disciplined his mind and occupied his body with the chore of checking the Ph levels. New tasks made Jayne's work last a lot longer than his old job. Indeed, Jayne had been entrusted with several additional jobs as well as expanded access to the equipment. Tonight took longer than it should have since he was trying to study the machines, to find a way of waking up the prisoners for escape. Playfully bantering, Doug and Jonathon discreetly blocked Jayne from the view of the cameras.

Taking a break, Jayne walked over to the circular metal station in the middle of the room and grabbed a cup of water from one of the sinks. He doused himself over the 5 foot grated floor drain. Shaking his head, he played with the water on his face. *Brrrrraaaaahh.* When the last of the water dripped down his bare shoulders, he took a white fluffy towel and dried his face, hands and arms. Jayne cringed as the towel touched the prominent strip of fishy flesh on his back. The short dry fibers on the towel poked him. Deep bodies of water called to him. Absentmindedly, he lifted his wet vest from the adjoining sink and pulled it on.

{:-)-]~~{

Inhaling deeply, Peter winced and stood ready for action. It was the calm before the huge rumble of an eager tornado. He drew all the positive strength into his body and exhaled all the bad possibilities. Sweat dripped down the back of his neck causing his hair to stand on end. Fear stole the saliva in his mouth as well as the umption in his gumption. Goosebumps rippled up and down his spine. The blood in his veins refused to flow into his toes from his knees as he stood frozen in time.

Signal acquired. Peter nodded. The time was now. Instinct fused with rehearsal as the team used a window cutter to enter the pet shop. With precision they flew through the shop and skillfully used a masonry saw to open a path into the room of horrors behind the bathroom.

{:-)-]~~{

With the remote, the misanthropic scientist opened the garage door high enough to army crawl out. He glanced at the sidewalk directly in front of the pet shop. *Clear.* One foot at a time, he patiently paused in his movements to make sure the teens didn't spot him. The door closed behind him with a click of a button. Closing his mouth, but not holding his breath, the masked doctor with hands of blue pursued his escape to freedom.

The creator of the Human Electric Cave Catfish disappeared around the corner. Carefully, he picked his steps down the stony path to the dock where he boarded his unregistered sailboat. His companion in the shadow nodded. With little effort, the skilled doctor piloted the boat out to drift quietly into the darkness. The steady crash of the waves could be heard in its place.

{:-)-]~~{

Jayne danced back over to the workstation, refreshed from his water break. Bright red lights suddenly flashed. Jayne and Jonathon's shrill tone mimicked the sirens. Both he and Doug covered their ears.

Flashing lights blurred Doug's vision. The sirens echoed. Fear gripped Doug as he scanned the room. Did they touch something they weren't supposed to? Panic climbed to the top of the hairs on his head. No one had ever heard the loud intimidating alarms before. All three males stared at each other, petrified with fear. The alarm stopped, but the warning lights continued to flash. Doug, Jonathon and Jayne froze in place fearing movement could cause an disaster. Doug inhaled deeply as he left Jonathon and began pacing the floor.

A swift movement caught Jayne's eyes. A man covered in black slipped into the room. The stranger pointed a menacing-looking gun in all directions. Death beamed its thieving eyes around the room. The man pointed the gun at Jayne, but switched targets. He signaled to the others to proceed down the hall. Two men came in behind him and they casually approached Jayne with their weapons pointed at the ground.

When Doug saw the three men, he went berserk tackling the lead man.

All three intruders were startled and fumbled with their weapons and posts. As a unit, they hollered for cooperation. The lead man dropped his weapon as he struggled in his attempt to fend off Doug. The other two men pointed their weapons at Doug asking for permission to fire.

Jayne rushed into battle. Jonathon threw off his cover with a war cry. He pushed the wheels on his wheelchair to give him enough speed to ram into one of the attackers.

"Ow! Hey, quit it. Stop!"

Two of the tanks were knocked over and momentarily stopped all residents in their tracks.

"Stop! Don't move! I said, stop!" was yelled at Doug, Jayne, and Jonathon who ignored the intruders' commands. Jonathon's strange appearance warranted a shot into his chest by the agent he had attacked. Jonathon quickly backed up, yanked out the needle and dove out of the chair.

Two of the three attackers aimed their weapons, but missed their shots because of the shock of what had come out of the aquariums. Jayne and Doug lurched toward the destruction.

Two tranquilizer darts burrowed into Jayne, but he did not feel them. Adrenaline propelled him onward.

Despite the pain and emptiness conquering his chest, Jonathon continued on his challenging journey toward the black Heccan.

"You maniacs!" Jayne lamented, staring at the remains of the other tank, as he reached out for her. "Blasting and smashing around here! Help me! Please!" He knelt by a Heccwan's broken tank.

Doug shouted at Jonathon. "Stay there, Jon! I've got him! Don't move! You'll hurt yourself!" He raced to help him.

Jonathon's slow journey damaged his lower limbs. Blood trickled down, smudging up the floor with his flippers dragging behind him as he turned the corner. Almost to his goal, fog rolled over the brain waves in his mind. Scents in the air mingled beyond recognition.

Jonathon managed to touch the flipper of the black Heccan before he collapsed into a world of darkened dreams.

Catching up to Jonathon, Doug didn't quite make it. *Ziiip. Sting. Pain. Pressure.* Fog rolled in his mind as his legs went limp under him.

Kenneth stopped in his tracks. "Dang it! He was not to be shot!" He definitely felt less than pleased with his incoming agents. "Bogey," Kenneth roared several times as he turned to and fro. He saw his right hand man, Agent Ned 'Bogey' Maxwell enter the room. "Do something!"

Throwing his hands up, Bogey waited for detailed instructions. His square jaw tightened and his pecks flexed on his barrel chest. Every black hair on his body hankered to fearfully shed. All the muscles he had acquired in life were no match for this alien portal that he had staggered into. All the training that he ever went through was sucked down a mental drain. He didn't know what to do. Shifting his weight from one long muscular leg to the other, Bogey stayed in place, stymied by the unforeseen complication of broken tanks.

Searching the room, Jayne turned to see who they were talking about. His shaking knees struggled to buckle when he saw Doug's slumped figure. He yelled a drawn out, "No!"

Kenneth shook caution to the wind and picked up his pace toward Jayne. "Mr. Flynn, it's me. I'm your outside contact. Jayne, everything will be okay."

Jayne could not hear the comforting words from the outsider, as his familiar environment collapsed around him. Jonathon and Doug both lay still. Jayne kneeled and scooped up the female Heccwan whose cell had crashed in the domino effect. When he flipped her over, his blood turned cold. There was no mistaking her long curly chestnut brown hair or her hourglass figure. The silver streaks in her hair reeled him in. Although his eyes burned, few tears welled up. Grabbing and yanking the tubes from the machines, he disconnected them while he steadied his balance. Next, he stripped Hope's broken I.V. from her veins so that no air would reach her heart. Her head bobbed around and she coughed. Jayne's eyes pierced the air around him as he gawked at the agents.

Kenneth shrugged his shoulders and bent over Jonathon, checking his pulse. Having seen Jayne work on Hope, Bogey tended to the black Heccan's I.V.

In a daze, Jayne turned his head to where his eyes couldn't see the limp forms of Jonathon and Doug. The room teetered as if gravity had disappeared. A loud nothing echoed in his ears. Jayne's head tipped forward and then backward. Staring at the ceiling, his hand burdensomely lifted until his fingers felt the back of his shoulder. Tracing their way up his neck, his fingers found two small darts protruding from his flesh. His thoughts blurred. *They must have... shot me... before...*

Jayne's hand buckled under its weight and collapsed to his side. With great effort, he focused again on Hope. Tears fell onto her face while he stroked her hair with his other hand. An undiscovered force zipped his lips together. Jayne could not even form the words beyond his mind. *Am I dying? Will she?* Gingerly, he wiped his tears off her cheeks. When his fingers traced her forehead ridges, he noticed the unique sparkling rainbow jewel. It intrigued him how the pretty spot of flesh reeled his lips to hers. Tenderly, his dry lips parted and pecked her lips. Jayne's eyes noticed Hope's eyelids flutter open. "Hope, oh, Marian," he managed to wheeze out before he gasped. *Not ag...* Jayne collapsed to the floor still holding her.

Hope timidly peered around. When she realized the young man with the familiar voice holding her was still alive, she felt safe. She violently coughed. The warmth of his lips pulsed on her mind as she clawed at the unfamiliar people dressed in black reaching out for her. Their soothing words blurred in her mind as they pulled her from his arms. When Hope moved her lower limbs to stand up, she saw rainbow tipped flippers. Water was all over, under, and around her. Her worst nightmare was upon her. Hope's lips parted and quavered with a shrill ear-piercing scream. She shook her head. Her scream ended in a gurgle and a cough and she fainted away.

{:-)-]~~{

Chapter 10

The FBI teams carefully and politely rounded up everyone who walked inside the oceanarium. They used Doug's keys or broke down doors. No one threatened the agents' lives or projected hostility. Instead of the waiting vans, the inhabitants were secured in the formaldehyde room for careful monitoring. The original and agent-made exits were easy to guard. No one wanted to escape even though they waited in their least favorite location. The bitter stench of the preserved dead caused everyone to step lightly with their noses in the air and mouths clamped shut. The few agents working in the room, with faces turning green, pressed their stomachs with a hand as they refrained from looking at the horrors directly. The nurses placed a hand in front of their face or sat with their heads bowed between their knees. The agents in charge of guarding them chose to stand right outside the door. They were not worried about escape artists so they daydreamed or concentrated on the blissful ignorance of life before the pet shop. One agent loudly lost the contents of his stomach after staring at the alien looking figures. The woman agent standing next to him caught a whiff or two of the funky vomit and followed his lead.

One by one, agents escorted the trembling nurses to the conference room for questioning by Peter and Kenneth. After the agents finished, a heavy burden weighed on their shoulders. Saddened, Peter called his SSA and hesitantly reported that the psycho responsible for all this had slipped through their fingers. The missing, unidentified criminal would not be around for questioning. Peter's boss verbally expressed his anger and gave orders to shut off the doctor's office so their ERT team could sweep it for prints and DNA. After the call concluded, Peter hung up and loudly relayed the message. Turning to Kenneth, he muttered, "I still don't know which nurses to trust."

"Let's wait for Jayne. He might know."

"Are you sure we can trust him?"

Peter nodded. "We've got to."

Kenneth opened the door and gave Bogey both orders. Closing the door, Kenneth conferred with Peter briefly on their next step. Both used their cell phones to call for aide. Ambulances, doctors, specialists, and scientists were all interrupted from their rest. The agents hoped their expertise could assist in helping save the victims of this awful nightmare. In short order, government vehicles and helicopters dropped them off at the front door of the pet shop to be politely escorted in. They arrived in the midst of the confusion and predictably added to it. They insisted Peter order the mutated individuals wakened and immediately taken to local hospitals. All the Hecc nurses argued and complained. Explaining everything they could, the nurses still could not fill in all the missing pieces. The outside doctors and scientists eventually agreed and rescinded their orders. Peter and Kenneth went to the tank room.

I.V.'s were removed from each living experimental victim before they were lifted out of their watery cells and placed on gurneys. They were wheeled over to the exam room in the building where they were awakened from their induced comas. None had any recollection of the surgeries performed on them and were shocked to see the current state of their body's. Realization of their incredible transformation included all stages of shock and grief. Freely displaying their emotions, they screamed, cried, or blamed anyone who attended them. With helplessness, Peter and Kenneth gawked as Mrs. Goldblum and Ms. Luhrman bolted out the room with tears flowing down their cheeks. Others hovered or worked to finish the difficult duty of safely awakening them all.

The last victim to be awakened was a strapping young Heccan. He flexed his pearly skin covered biceps as his eyelids fluttered. "Where am I?" Inquisitive gooseberry-green eyes scanned the environment. His jaw dropped as he saw the unusual occupants in the room staring directly at him. When he tried to stand, his cherubic face hit the white-tiled floor. Glaring up at the hospital bed, his perfect fingers traced his face. The small traces of blood didn't seem to bother or worry him. He fretted, "I boarded the plane without a beard!" Straight away, he sat up.

When Peter and Kenneth offered to help him up, their hands were roughly slapped away.

"I got the job! This was supposed to be a career booster! My modeling career was supposed to really take off! How long have I been out? Did we crash?"

Peter took the Heccan's file from the nurse and held it within six inches of his face. A photocopy of his driver's license stared back at him. "Do you know your name?"

The well sculpted male sat slightly back against the wheel on the wheelchair. His eyes filled with intense hatred. "Do you?" He scoffed. "I *am* Val Lee *Hawley!*" After tugging at his brunette and silver beard, he played with the muscles in his toes. The silvery rainbow fins rippled. Slowly, he extended his left hand toward his lower limbs. When he touched them, he cringed.

"Val, your plane never reached Russia. It went down just off the coast of California." Kenneth swallowed as he remembered the missing pictures splashed all over the news. He knelt to make eye contact, but Val refused to meet his gaze. Carefully, he explained, "You're still here… in America. You've been a victim of human experimentation."

Wide-eyed, with a lifted unibrow, Val shouted vulgar threats. "Experimentation? …Is there an *antidote?*" His tenor voice ended in a squeak.

Kenneth inhaled as though he was about to drown. His sharp exhale let an unintended whistle escape his tightened lips. "I… I… I don't know."

"Nooo! You… you change me back! Find someone who can change me back!"

"I'm just here with the FBI. They didn't… We didn't… I… if we had known…" Peter stumbled over his words. "Maybe… we could have caught him… we… we… were here because of a… possible enslavement… and… human trafficking."

Uneasy silence took hold of the assembly. When no one budged, Caucasian Nathan Mal Hawk used his smooth tapered hands to cumbersomely inch his wheel chair closer to the action. Leadership and confidence filled his veins. The oldest H.E.C.C. tapped on the agents' backs causing them to startle. Kind eyes stared at him as they made a path for Nathan to ease closer to Val. His shoulder length hair pulled in a pony-tail bounced as he nodded. "You might find some advantages, Val. I did." Running his fingers through his shoulder length hair, he admired the sandy blonde silver striped colors framing his face. He said, "I'm not balding anymore and my carpal tunnel is gone!" A broad mischievous smirk widened causing his bushy mustache to twitch over his poufy beard. Animation and excitement danced in his chirpy hazel eyes as he inched even closer to Val.

"Your life is halfway *gone*, old *man*," taunted Val as he shook his fist. "My life was just *starting*!"

"You think if I walk back into the stock brokerage, that they will *let* me have my old job back after I have been *gone* for who knows how *long*?" Nathan's wry face vanished. "Do you think I can waltz up to my old ski club in Utah and take up skiing again like nothing happened in my life? My favorite hobby was biking!" His knuckles turned ash-white as his fists alternatively tightened and loosened around the arms of his chair. "Wake up and smell it, boy. We all had lives that were cut out of us. We each will have to find positive things about this life if we are going to live through it. We can't fight each other… we now have the same probl…"

"I bet," interrupted Val. "…you have a wife and kid, don't you? I bet you think that makes you special!" Val spat in Nathan's direction.

Kenneth and Peter shifted their weight.

Nathan pushed out of his chair as though he attempted a standing position. He stopped and sat on the edge. "I don't even know if my wife lives or not! The last memory I have... the last *memory* is watching my son as the male lead in the ballet and then I was called outside..." He choked on his words. "She was late... They told me my wife crashed my Jaguar into a building! The brakes had malfunctioned. She...she had just found out that she had cancer. I don't even know if my wife is still alive...and if she is...how is she doing? ...did she wait for me?" Nathan's hands frantically pushed at the wheels on his chair to back it up. Pausing, he closed his eyelids tight. "Let's just get through today! Find something *positive* about being *alive*!" Staring hard at Val, he lifted his voice. "You have the three most important things there are: life, health, and *freedom*."

Before Val could answer, another heated voice cracked through the air. "You think you're the only one whose career was about to take off?" The anger reddening in his cheeks burned, but could not show its true color in his chocolate skin. The well-favored trim, but muscular city boy shook his own fist in Val's direction. "Me..." Bruce John Viesel thumped his heart with a strong fist. "Bruce... just got my college scholarship... right before I was going to be the starting quarterback at the top college in Kansas... fans would have been shouting, go Viesel!" Bushy eyebrows furrowed over his brown eyes. Sitting back in his wheelchair, his biceps quivered while the muscles in his neck danced. "I... I... was at my bachelor party in Cancun..." Bruce's hollow eyes focused on the agents present and pleaded. "How long have I been gone?"

"We're going to do everything we can to locate all of your families." Kenneth's hands bounced as he leapt into the conversation.

"So what, Diesel! You weren't going to be in high society. You were going be just some dumb jock... Jaha..." Val paused.

"He said his name was Viesel, not Diesel!" Roland Logan McGregor skillfully maneuvered his chair closer to Val, Nathan and Bruce. He ran his hand through his shoulder-length sandy-blonde hair. "I... was in high society..." The body-builder used his strong fingers to twirl a silver strand of hair against his broad shoulders. "My bald head became who I was known for as an actor! I was at the height of my career. I owned homes and rental property in 5 states." He shot Nathan a plastic grin. "I *am* grateful for my new hairdo." Roland's firm jaw tightened as he released the strand to gawk at his silver fingernails. "But, how are my action-loving fans going to accept me now?" Tapping his fishy thighs, Roland's voice cracked. "I can't do cop and action movies anymore. My adoptive parents in New York have already passed away, but I was in a beautiful marriage of 6 years… is my famous wife going to accept me or did she move on and marry someone else?"

Bruce's eyes twinkled. "Hey, welcome to the party, pal. You'll just have to *Try Harder.*"

Roland's eyes shot darts in Bruce's direction.

Bogey entered the room with uncertainty. "Boss?" Humans and H.E.C.C.s alike startled.

Peter and Kenneth turned around and met Bogey halfway.

"What's up?" Kenneth asked. Worry already etched his face. He cringed as Val forced the wheelchair next to him to fall on its side.

Bogey made a face. "The local EMS tried to wake Jayne and his friend."

"And?" Peter shifted his weight from both legs to primarily one.

"They insisted a H.E.C.C. nurse take over."

"Okay." With a drawn out voice, Peter was slowly losing his patience.

"The nurse Billi was able to get Jonathon, to wake up, but-"

"Wait, who is Jonathon?"

"According to his file, his legal name is Anthony Rodriguez, but… the nurses call him Jonathon."

"Okay, so now what is the problem?"

"Sir, he's being difficult. He won't cooperate until Jayne wakes up."

"Oh, he was the one with Jayne. Okay. So… where is he now?" Kenneth's eyes diverted to see what Val was up to. Val sat erect, staring at his fins. Without hesitation, Kenneth returned his attention to Bogey.

"Sir, he is refusing to leave Jayne's side."

Kenneth and Peter deeply sighed. Their postures slouched as if yokes weighed them down. Frustrated and overwhelmed, they wearily followed Bogey.

Bogey trotted at an even pace. "Hey, Pete, wasn't that Roland McGregor, the star actor in the Try Hard trilogy?"

"I knew I recognized his face and his voice." Peter smacked his forehead. "I don't know how my wife will take this news."

"Didn't his boat go down off the coast?"

"That was a Christmas to remember." Bogey rolled his eyes.

"Yippy-ki-yay," sang Peter.

When they found Jonathon, Kenneth explained to him they were waiting on Jayne before making decisions, partly to placate him and partly stalling while they figured things out. The agents secretly staked everybody's lives on Dee's judgment of character. With Jonathon being difficult, Peter lost his charming personality and loudly ordered Jonathon to go help settle the newly awakened H.E.C.C.s. Jonathon turned his head, ignoring him and stared at Jayne. Passionately, Kenneth pleaded with Jonathon that this was a 'Hecc matter' and the agents didn't know how to handle it. He also convinced Jonathon that Jayne would want him to. Reluctantly, Jonathon agreed to help. Kenneth and Peter accompanied Jonathon as he was wheeled into the overcrowded hospital room.

Jonathon helplessly observed the room. A few agents were pleading with the aggressive H.E.C.C.s while the nurses stood against the wall. Guilt, sorrow and love reddened their tear stained cheeks. Lower level cupboard doors stood ajar, their contents scattered onto the floor.

Kenneth whistled loudly with his two fingers and requested silence. When he gained attention, he calmly ordered, "Agents! Step outside in the hall! As soon as Jayne wakes up from both tranquilizers, we will finalize plans." He pointed at the nurses. "In the meantime, escort them to their rooms to refresh themselves and gather their possessions so that when we are ready to leave…they are ready too." Kenneth muttered under his breath that he hoped this would allow the nurses a chance to compose themselves. The agents complied and directed the nurses into the hallway. Turning to the remaining occupants, Kenneth calmly raised his voice for all to hear. "I understand this is scary and a huge adjustment, but we feel the necessity to move on to the next step. Jonathon here has several months awake and living as a Hecc. He can answer many of your questions. His friend Jayne should have more answers as soon as he wakes up."

The H.E.C.C.s relaxed a little. Tension eased from their faces for they were given a glimmer of hope.

Jonathon wheeled himself to the middle of the room. "Agent Austin, we'll wrap this up in a hurry. We've got to get them to the water… pronto."

Kenneth and Peter nodded and closed the door behind them.

Bogey disappeared for his rounds.

{:-)-]~~{

A well-favored, tall Caucasian man with chiseled features stood guard in front of the door of the make-shift apartment. The slim fingers on his right hand ran through his teased cropped black hair before settling behind his sturdy back. His left hand rested on the wall behind him. Crisp new blue jeans fit his hips and cheeks as snug as a glove. He didn't mind strange women, sometimes with boyfriends in tow, begging to caress his athletic biceps and pecks. Muscles on his sculptured face throbbed and tightened with agony. Instead of his usual appearance of being bright-eyed and bushy tailed, his alert green eyes nervously scanned around the empty hallway in which he stood.

The door behind him creaked open slightly.

The agent took two half steps away from the door, signaling the all clear to the one behind him.

The clean-shaven, Latino man in his early fifties crept out. Wearing a black suit, white shirt, and loud tie, he hurried down the hall without giving the agent a second glance. Rings on his fingers glinted when the dim lights tickled the metal and stones.

The agent's jaw tightened as he watched the man's silken dark brown hair bounce with each hurried step. Holding his breath, he waited for the gentleman to turn left and ease around the corner.

The agent cringed as he saw the man stop dead in his tracks right smack in the intersection of the 'T' shaped hallway. The bright light illuminated the small pocket sized datebook that the businessman flipped through.

Footsteps echoed in the hall coming from the left before the agent recognized Bogey's voice thundering.

"Hey," said Bogey. "You're that Cancer specialist, right? The one… that takes… only celebrities as patients?"

Doctor Malo Susantivo cleared his throat without looking up. His eyebrows narrowed and his nostrils flared. Malo's left cheek twitched.

Bogey stepped closer to the doctor and politely waited until he had his full attention.

Tucking his datebook away, Doctor Susantivo peered up and tucked his hand neatly behind him. Standing tall and mighty, he looked down his nose at Bogey. "Now, then what can I do for you, agent…"

"Maxwell."

"Sir, uh…I mean Doctor?"

"Susantivo."

"Dr. Susantivo, we deeply regret having you come all the way out here. We apologize for taking up your time…" Bogey paused. His words failed him.

"Agent Maxwell, I don't know if I can take any *more* apologies." Doctor Susantivo huffed. "What is it that you covet now? I have done as you asked. I have looked at their lab work, the uninformative files you provided, and have looked into their eyes. Their muscles are atrophied from extended inactivity. Their stamina is reduced, both should improve with time and exercise. No amount of feeling sorry for them is going to change the facts. They will remain as they are. There is nothing I can do for them…and there is nothing *more* I can try to do… either by commands or begging from any governmental agency. And how do I know the government wasn't behind these experiments in the first place! For all I *know*, you guys want us *civilians* to clean up *your* mess. This is not my specialty. I need to be heading back to my office. I have my own duties to return to."

Bogey growled. "Speaking of which, what are you doing in this hallway?"

The guard in the shadows placed his hand on the grip of his sidearm. Lifting the Glock in the shadows, he pointed in Bogey's direction.

"I needed a quiet place to look over my schedule and cancel my appointments unless you will be releasing us soon." The doctor paused for a response.

Bogey fought the lump in his throat. He side-stepped the question. "Sooo… there's no hope for them returning to their families as normal humans?"

"Not likely." Dr. Susantivo boldly straightened his posture, shook his head and walked away.

With slouching shoulders, Bogey sighed. His eyes followed the doctor until he stepped out of view.

Quietly holstering the weapon, the grimacing agent inhaled silently. He gathered his wits before Bogey turned and scuttled toward him. He held his position as Bogey neared him. His right arm crossed protectively over his churning stomach as his left hand rested on his waist above his weapon.

"Hey, Ace."

The handsome agent scrutinized him. When Bogey's frown turned upside down, 'Ace' straightened his shoulders and stood respectfully.

"I'm here for the report."

'Ace' swallowed. He stretched his stiff muscles from head to toe. "Oh…yea…The ERT team hasn't even started on this room, yet. They said they had orders to start from the shop and work their way back here."

"What?" Bogey roared at the top of his lungs. "I can't believe this! Orders from who? What good is planning when we are just overruled by desk jockeys that aren't even here on site?" His arms flailed about before his right fist landed hard in his left hand. He paced back and forth. "How did they get orders to work the other rooms first? This room was supposed to have been top priority! Oh, man, Ken and Pete will have my hide!"

'Ace' cringed until Bogey disappeared down the hall toward the pet shop. He had cursed and ranted all the way.

{:-)-]~~{

Peter ordered all scientists, local doctors and nurses to leave the premises. They were handed gag orders before they left, not that non-disclosure agreements ever really prevented leaks. But he could hope…

Kenneth excused himself to check on Doug who slept off his two tranquilizers strapped in an ambulance under guard. Leaning against the hall, Peter called the SSA and argued for the safety of the H.E.C.C.s. The SSA added the Special Agent in Charge to the conference call. The SAC gave Peter permission for extended time to stay at the facility to allow all investigations of the premises to be finished, carefully, with all evidence being put through a fine tooth comb.

Within seconds after Peter hung up his cell phone, Jonathon opened the door.

"Okay… We're ready to go to for a swim! They need the water time to air out their baggage. In here, we are handicapped…and trapped." A rascally grin crept across Jonathon's face. "Water is a freedom that they have never known."

Relieved, Peter advised his team to assist. Wheelchairs aided in making trips down the hall to the show pool. Some H.E.C.C.s doubled up on the wheel chairs to speed up the process. As they passed through the hall, mug shots were taken of the freed prisoners, H.E.C.C.s and nurses alike.

Kenneth arrived as the last wheelchair with two Heccans was being pushed down the hall. Kenneth took over for an exhausted agent. He and Bogey exchanged glances as they saw a grinning Jonathon sitting on the edge, waiting.

As soon as all the H.E.C.C.s entered the water, Jonathon insisted Kenneth stand at the door personally. Standing tall with pride, Kenneth relieved the current guard, a gangly agent who gladly left his post at the door. Kenneth briefly inquired of Bogey about Peter's whereabouts. Bogey explained that Peter was researching in the conference room. With a knowing expression, Kenneth shooed several congregating agents away from the doorway. He stood alone and pondered recent events.

{:-)-]~~{

Plenty of surveillance pictures froze the action at the facility, but Peter's interest fixated on the victim's mug shots. The digital camera provided pictures for the laptop computer. Peter used the portable printer to print off the mug shots to study further. He settled into a comfortable location in the conference room and compared them with the missing person's database. The list would be officially and significantly shortened as of today. It was a rare event to check off so many individuals found safe and alive in one operation. Twenty women and twenty men ranging from the age of sixteen to fifty were found along with seven girls and eight boys ranging from fourteen to sixteen.

Just four weeks ago, the disappearance of triplet girls, Debbie Renee, Katia Amanda, and Peggy Linda Rodgers, caused a big uproar at their school because of the lack of security. At first, officials reported them as a prank kidnapping, so the investigation lacked intensity. Speculation turned to runaways when the girls were not returned to their foster parents. In the last month, the girls were allegedly sighted roaming two states away from home.

The twin fifteen year old boys, Patrick Ray and Paul Robert Armstrong, went missing almost two years ago. Reported as runaways, no one suspected foul play. Letters from the twins explained their desire to live their own lives and make their own choices. As Peter's eyes continued spilling over the case file, he frowned and tightened his jaw. He flagged the file, requesting further investigation for kidnapping. The horrific thought crossed the agents' mind as to whether or not the parents had sold the boys to the maniac. Peter choked on a frustrated tear.

The count totaled up sixty healthy, breathing, completed H.E.C.C.s. Peter now turned to other pictures. Acid in his disturbed stomach crept up his throat and burned near his heart. "Ack," Peter mumbled as he numbly glanced at the pictures of the deceased. Snapshots of the human experiments in the formaldehyde caskets rattled Peter from the inside out.

Noisily, Bogey entered with three stacked filing crates. He wandered back and lurked in Peter's peripheral vision. The agents, especially Bogey, knew better than to startle a fellow agent.

"Ah, Special Agent Maxwell. So glad you could join me." Peter stared straight ahead, refusing to take even a brief moment to look up. "Bogey, you are just in time. I have finished going over the ones who survived. Now, I get to look over the ones that didn't make it." Looking up at his agent/friend, he ordered, "Well, sit down. Sit down." He placed the pictures to his left, sharing the view with his co-worker. "These were the first human experiments, according to the plaques next to them." Turning to his laptop and searching around, Peter exclaimed, "Look, Bogey, a number of them are on the wanted list!" Peter showed them to Bogey and they both nodded in morbid agreement. While Bogey stared at pictures of the entombed, Peter delved into the Fed files on the laptop. He pointed and declared, "They weren't very nice men."

A loud, prejudicial snort escaped Bogey's lips as he lowered himself heavily into a chair. A second glance told them the experiments didn't look even remotely successful. Several individuals lacked lower limbs while ugly lumps protruded from the chests or spines in others. Excruciating pain shaped their facial features. "They don't look like they had a peaceful passing."

"Lucifer Israel Badde, a known serial killer, targeted blond-haired and blue-eyed women. Seems like he came to a fine end since he escaped during a prison transfer." Peter tightened the muscles in his throat. "He killed the guards on duty with no mercy. It was assumed that he was causing further problems while on the run, but I'm sure this evidence will prove that he's been dead for a while. At least he's not still out there killing anymore. Some of the cases we thought were linked to him will have to be reopened." Pointing to the next picture, Peter announced with venom. "Hamaan Dydeby Ropbourne was wanted for the horrific murder of his family. He found out his family didn't share his 'peaceful' beliefs." Bogey and Peter stared at the next set of pictures.

"That Bonnie and Clyde incarnate?"

Peter's eyes filled with reproach as he stared at the modern villains. The only pictures in the custody of the Feds showed the criminals escaping a few banks. Sarcasm dripped and mixed with truth from his lips. "Yes, but their legal names were Festar Ing and Yetchy Fungu Wounde. They're an undocumented Asian couple that pulled off seven bank heists in five states in less than fifteen days. Like the historical Bonnie and Clyde, they wore body armour and were brutal and thuggish in their dealings. They never hired the same crew twice. There's no telling how the psycho got hold of this wandering dangerous couple."

"Uh, boss? Shouldn't we call off the resources that are still on those cases?"

Letting an expletive loudly slip, Peter hurried to make a few phone calls to put a hold on the, now, unnecessary goose chases. Quietly, Bogey waited for his boss to end his conversation.

When Peter finished his calls, he returned to the task at hand. He put away the first collection of pictures before he placed the next two in front of him. Comparing the pictures against the profiles on the laptop, he made a spitting noise. "Juzte Donnet Tuche and Otto Hake Dick were pedophiles that had been seen hanging around schools."

Bogey heaved a sigh, relieved the awful men were beyond a doubt off the street. His niece attended one of those schools, causing his family considerable amounts of worry. Bogey refused to share his thoughts with Peter, but mocked, "You mean no more getting out early for good behavior?"

"Yeah, especially since each man was a repeat offender." Peter cursed again as he put away the pictures and pulled out another. As he went back to his laptop, Peter hit his fist on the table.

The whack startled Bogey into a slight jump. He reached to his side for his weapon, but eased off.

"Zupid Lawz Zuckez was a man that did not deserve this psycho's wrath!"

"Huh?"

"His rap sheet marked him as a sex offender, but that's not the whole story. The law doesn't differentiate between peeing on the side of the road and indecent exposure. So they slapped him with charges of a sex crime!" Peter lifted his voice. His eyebrows narrowed. "After Zupid had worked exhausting hours, he thought he could sneak a relief, but was caught. The local government made an example out of the traveling construction worker. Then, marked as a sex offender, Mr. Zuckez was harassed countless times for just trying to live as an honest hardworking citizen. It's too bad that the neighborhoods he chose to live in turned out to be as friendly as a lynch mob." Peter's shoulders dropped. "No one cared to look up what really happened." Peter shook his head from side to side. "They just wrecked his home time and time again. They even put him in the hospital a time or two before he moved on again. Evidently, the *doctor* didn't look carefully into his subject's credentials either."

Bogey's crew would have been shocked to see his appearance weaken to sadness. His tough persona distanced most of his co-workers, thus hiding his soft side. The workaholic always kept work and home separate. Bogey stood up and stretched his aching muscles. Moving farther away from Peter, he swung a chair around and used it for a foot rest. He pulled an energy drink out of his jacket pocket. Chugging it gave an excuse to hide his crestfallen face from Peter.

Losing his last bit of enthusiasm, Peter pulled out innumerable pictures and cases. Since Bogey seemed to have lost interest, he placed the pictures directly in front of his laptop. A tear formed in his eye. Peter flipped through the pictures of adolescents who had no one looking for them. "Screw this." Peter huffed. "These minors have police records way too long for me to look at tonight. Their rap sheets include known gang membership, drug use, and/or prostitution. These police cases were not high priority since they were not on the disappearance list. Most of these are botched experiments, too." Peter silently read through the names and studied the pictures.

Overwhelmed with his own deep thoughts, Bogey did not verbally or physically acknowledge his words.

Peter mulled over the list aloud. "The deceased ranged from sixteen to twenty-two at the time they disappeared... I mean... they were just young adults..."

Bogey shifted his weight and scowled at the ceiling. Anger boiled in his muscles causing his knee to bounce with a fidgety twitch.

A tear slipped down the side of Peter's cheek. "It doesn't matter whether or not they were a menace to society. The 'breath of life' leaving any body still leaves behind a corpse. Every homicide detective is taught to treat all investigations equal no matter what." Switching gears, Peter pulled out experiments where evidently, the doctor attempted to improve the lives of several senior citizens. The experiments had originally gone well, yet had failed for unseen physical reasons. He spoke up. "These ten adults range from sixty-five to seventy-five. In these missing cases, they were known to have medical conditions. They wandered off with Alzheimer's or Dementia. No one would have ever thought that they had been kidnapped… let alone found entombed by a psycho's handiwork. Hmmmm…" Peter's voice trailed off as his lips formed the phonics without pronouncing the names aloud.

Bogey crushed the can on his forehead to make himself appear manly from the inside out.

After Peter cringed at yet another victim on the lists, he lifted his head. Blankness crept over his eyes as he stared at the files. He didn't want to look anymore, but his job entailed the responsibility. With a heavy heart, Peter continued rummaging through file after file with the subjects marked by name and number. Sparking to life, he scrutinized the files which were not found in the missing person's database. Then, sadly, Peter shook his head. "These completed Human Electric Cave Catfish were encased in the preservation tanks because they did not live after the scientist removed their electric organ, which by the way, the subjects can evidently use as a weapon."

"You mean the ones out there…" said Bogey with a shaky voice. He pointed in the direction of the live H.E.C.C.s. "They have the electric organs that can zap people?" Bogey's head snapped into his shoulders and his eyebrows lowered. "Jayne out there is a walking tazer?"

Nodding, Peter continued without verbally acknowledging his agent. "There were a few adults that had their electric organ removed: Monique Angelica Schwaben (age 45), Misti Kiera Cooper (age 31), and Patricia Madeline Woodworth (age 48)." Lifting his voice in anger, Peter cursed. "There are three children that had spinal diseases that were supposedly improved by the doctor. According to his well-kept records, the changes had improved Theresa Marian Frye (age 6), Deborah Nanna Green (age 4), and Lilly Sandye Chessher (age 9), but with the removal of the electric organ, they did not survive. It looks as though Lilly's two sisters and brother did not survive either. Their mother was a nurse here…" Peter's voice cracked. "…before she too… wow… a whole family… gone…"

Agent Maxwell reached his limit. His chair crashed as he bolted up. "I'm gonna go make rounds." With an exaggerated basketball dunk, Bogey tossed his can in the trash on the way out.

Peter flashed him an understanding glance. After Bogey disappeared around the corner, Peter responded with hurt disgust. "I wish I could just walk away, too." Bleary-eyed, he looked back at his computer. After a minute or two passed, his fingers tapped the keys filling the atmosphere with a rhythm. The wall clock ticked loudly. Emptiness and a loss of humanity filled the room with a creepy loneliness. Agitation built in his bones and glimmered in his eyes as he glared at the screen. "There are so many...." Peter vented his emotions into the cold empty room.

The sandman blew deceptively in Peter's ears and eyes. Fog rolled in over his weary brain. His aching hands scrolled through the names of the missing people, dead and alive. Pounding drums echoed in Peter's head. No one could have seen this widespread operation as connected kidnappings. The number of missing people found together in the same building amazed the agent. Although many of the missing people were abducted in broad daylight, Peter found their final destination the only common denominator. A few Hecc's shared vivid stories about some dreams when they were awakened, but no clues emerged that would help to bring their kidnappers to immediate justice.

The whole matter had taken a toll on the rescuers. They were tired, confused, disgusted and emotionally drained, so Peter ordered shifts to be taken for rest. He himself downed cup after cup of coffee while he pored over the reports, photos and the FBI database. Extended paperwork would have to wait. He wrote down names and addresses on the mug shots so he could return them to their loved ones. When he completed his work, he saved most of the files and exited out of the remaining. As he waited for the computer to shut down, he silently prayed that resolving the mess would fall under somebody else's command. The FBI had just cracked the biggest missing persons case in history. Yawning, Peter stretched before collapsing into a deep sleep in his chair.

{:-)-]~~{

Chapter 11

The wheelchair Kenneth fell asleep in throbbed and cramped his legs. Vulnerability snapped him to attention when he noticed two co-workers outstretched on the floor. His eyes widened as he sucked his breath in and held it. But a loud snore rumbled from one man and the other's chest lifted and lowered naturally. Kenneth realized nothing ill threatened the safety of he and his men. Blinking the sleep out of his eyes, he regarded his old Timex watch. It read sixteen past eleven in the morning. While darting his eyes back and forth, he also focused his hearing. Happy whoops and hollers beat-boxed from the room behind him. With several nudges from his boots, he awakened the men. Both hands were swinging at his sides as he strode down the hall.

With a shuffle of his heel as he turned the corner, Kenneth scrutinized the conference room. Peter sat in front of his computer with his head down. Two disheveled stacks of pictures lay on each side of the laptop under Peter's outstretched arms. With robotic, slow movements, Kenneth sat on the heavy table. A mischievous grin stretched his lips and showed coffee stained teeth. With his forefinger, he poked his partner.

Peter shot up, but sat back down when he recognized his partner. He wearily blinked his bleary eyes at Kenneth, key marks impressed on his cheek. A blank sour look revealed frayed nerves as his eyes darted back to his laptop.

Forcefully, Kenneth bit his lower lip to stop a snicker from escaping. "You party all night? Hey… Sounds like the Heccs are in good humor."

CA Peter Austin stretched, yawned, and stood up. "Why would they be in good humor? They just found their *world* turned upside down!"

"Pete, they can't be angry and mope around forever! I remember my friend telling me about his father's funeral in his childhood. When his mother got caught with an extra slip from the laundry clinging to her skirt, even she had a worthy chuckle." He watched one corner of Peter's mouth twitch. "Just be glad they are starting the cycle of acceptance." Kenneth placed a caring hand on his comrade's shoulder. "You look as though you could use some fresh air. Let's go for rounds together."

Peter nodded as he grabbed a folder. The two exchanged exhausted looks as they shrugged their shoulders. With wide strides, they carried on in silence. Most of the three teams sleepily nodded their greeting as their bosses passed them by. The H.E.C.C. nurses stirred on their blankets in the formaldehyde room. Kenneth and Peter continued on to find Jayne.

In the 'tank room', a short, heavyset nurse stood by Jayne's side as he still slept. Broken glass from the two tanks littered the disheveled room as though a tornado had ripped through it.

Recognizing concern in Peter and Kenneth's eyes, she realized the government men actually were there to help them. Openly, she cried and latched a scared hug onto Peter. Her bubbly personality always made people overlook her roly-poly body. After her red bun fell out in her excitement, her hair uncurled, framing her round creamy face.

Momentarily and distressingly, Peter held her. He used only his eyes to plead with Kenneth to save him. As soon as the nurse released him, Peter backed away, uncomfortable with her anxious tears.

"Thank you! Oh, Hallelujah. Oh, thank you for saving us," she sang between sniffles. Her thick arms wiped her sunken green eyes. Cowering away from the men, she used her hand to clear her throat. Once she had regained composure, she projected a business-like attitude and posture. Turning back to the agents, she hesitated, "He has been stirring. He should wake up soon. He slept off the tranquilizers and then fell into a tired and deep sleep. I didn't want to disturb him."

Peter's radio squawked, "Peter, come in."

"Go ahead," Peter answered with authority.

"The special visitor you ordered just arrived."

"Bring her in."

Kenneth glanced at Peter and nodded. "Good and just in time, too."

The startled three scampered back as Jayne loudly gasped. He jumped up into a frightened sitting position. When he completely processed the view of the empty aquariums, horror sculpted wrinkles all over his face. Expletives slipped off Jayne's tongue as he swung his right hook at Kenneth.

"It's alright. Calm down, Mr. Flynn," comforted Peter. With palms facing up and open, he raised his voice in anguish. "We're here to help! I'm Peter and this is Kenneth."

An anger-fueled flush painted Jayne's cheeks.

"Jayne!" soothed the nurse with a shaky voice. "Calm down. It's okay." Her hand flew to her head as her hair stood on end.

Jayne energized the gurney he sat on.

"Everybody back," yelled the nurse as she tackled Kenneth and Peter. Her weight gave her the advantage as she used her momentum to knock Kenneth and Peter off balance.

"Jayne Raye Flynn!" The feminine voice shocked everyone into silence. Escorted by an agent, Dee Graham put one determined foot in after another.

Hearing her voice and seeing her, shocked Jayne. Surprised that his middle name echoed in his ear for the first time in a decade, Jayne sat taller.

Without fear, Dee marched right up to him, stretched out her arms and gave him a hug like a mother bear reunited with a prodigal cub.

At first, Jayne' arms dangled by his sides under her arms, but then he returned Dee's hug while the agents helped the nurse up.

They approached Jayne and Dee with uncertainty in their eyes and footsteps.

Tears flowed down Dee's cheeks. "Oh, Jayne. You're free."

"Free?"

"Yes. You can walk out the door and never look back."

"You came for me." Jayne's heart dropped into his toes and returned to his chest. His eyes burned as he softly exhaled the foreign words, "Free. I can leave…" Peace flooded his shoulders.

"Come on, Jayne. Let's go. I can take you home now."

Jayne's feet tiptoed, following his arm being led toward the door, but a piercing pain wrapped its cords tightly around his heart. His lips felt numb. *Hope.* Jayne recalled how soft Hope's enticing lips felt when he kissed her awake. Drums beat in his head as his heart picked up its rhythm from his breathing and blood pressure increasing. A light flush covered his cheeks as the brief but strong image of beautiful Hope dazed him. Jayne's pupils dilated while the skin on his chest hardened.

As promptly as his blood had warmed, it cooled down causing a chain reaction in his body. The memory of Jonathon and Doug's laughter, so well known over most of these last few years, tickled Jayne's inner ear. Their broad smiles filled Jayne with a longing for his friends. *Doug,* thought Jayne. Pain ripped open his chest as he re-witnessed his rescue in his mind. The last images of his two buddies were of their limp bodies. The shadowy mind killer, fear, caressed and tightened all of Jayne's muscles. His innocent gait halted as he stood frozen. Jayne's knees itched to knock together as his elbows shook against his body. A bitter taste formed in Jayne's mouth causing his stomach to turn inside out.

Dee babied Jayne's arm and tried to encourage him to keep walking. Her pleasant smile faded as she realized the intensity of the matter. Something was wrong. Her own heart raced as she second guessed herself.

Acid churned in Jayne's restless stomach. Nervous tension fed his bowels. Jayne's fists tightened as he shuffled away from Dee.

"But… are my friends… *free* to leave…*too*? Can they go back to their loved ones?" His eyes turned away from Dee to stare icily at the agents. "Have the nurses, Mrs. Goldblum and Ms. Luhrman been reunited with their children?"

Peter inhaled deeply before he touched the iffy subject with a ten foot pole. "Yes, All the victims are free to go…And even though Mrs. Goldblum and Ms. Luhrman have some explaining to do in front of a judge, they have been reunited with their children. The unorthodox treatments have given Harvey Goldblum and Juliet Luhrman increased freedom of movement and improved health, so they do not seem to hate their mothers. They are adjusting to their different, but less severe limitations."

"That true, Mrs. Goldblum?" Jayne turned to the nurse.

"Yes, Jayne. I have seen my son."

"And he is alright?"

"Yes. His health has greatly improved and, in the water at least, he has much more freedom of movement than ever before." Rebecca's troubled face brightened with a semi-smile.

Kenneth interjected, "I wouldn't suggest it as a cure for all physically handicapped children…" He left his thoughts hanging and switched subjects. "Speaking of being reunited… when you're ready, Jayne, Jonathon needs you," suggested Kenneth with caution. "The nurses say that he has been asking for you since his first coherent words after he woke up." He continued to be wary of the young male who stood before him, even if Dee danced about him as a doe in a quiet meadow. "Special Agent Maxwell said to give you a message from Jonathon."

Jayne's voice cracked. "A message?"

Peter shot Kenneth a puzzled look, begging for clarification. The returned shrug remained as his only answer.

"Cavemen."

Jayne paused, froze, and begged for the word to be repeated. After Kenneth repeated with a hesitant crack in his voice, he cleared his throat. "Any idea what he was talking about?"

"That's our code word for 'safe'." Overcome with happiness, Jayne flew into Dee's arms again. "He's alright, Dee! He's all right! I'm alright! I'm free! Jon's free!"

The two agents exchanged glances with a sigh of relief.

"And safe," sang Dee. Leaning close to his ear, she whispered, "You're safe now, Jayne, with people who care." Taking a step back, Dee looked him over from head to toe. Her voice shook with nervous fulfillment. "I'm here. I promised your mother before she passed on. I promised I would check on you. I'm sorry it took so long." A tear rolled down her left cheek.

Melting in Dee's motherly embrace, Jayne relaxed further as the last drop of tension left his body. He let go and a peaceful smile slowly painted his face, followed by his own sigh of relief.

Smiling, Kenneth introduced himself and Peter. "We have been waiting for you to wake up and help us sort this mess out. What can you tell us?"

Jayne gave a brief description of how he came to be incarcerated in the never ending nightmare. When he included finding the secret code in Dee's book, the agents interrupted with joy as they admitted their involvement.

After Jayne willingly shook their hands and thanked them, Peter immediately showed him head shot after head shot from his folder. "Here, …take at look at these!" His enthusiasm ended in hesitation. "These… are the people that we have… here… in our custody."

Peter and Kenneth nodded. Kenneth inched to the side of Jayne so he could also look at the pictures that Jayne concentrated on, while Peter closely watched Jayne's face.

Jayne examined the pictures and searched his memory as he looked at each face several times. "There were people that worked here that weren't even here. They were off duty."

"You mean these?" Peter reached into his folder and produced seven sketches. Several names dotted each page.

Looking up from the colored pictures in his hands, Jayne studied each black and white face Peter held. "Yeah, those are the ones."

"I've checked on them." Peter's eyebrows lowered. "Do you have any new names to add to these? So far these are all aliases."

Jayne shook his head. Lowering his chin, Jayne flipped though each picture with both hands. The last black and white picture had one alias below it; Doc. Jayne's jaw dropped. "You let the 'I.V. Scissor King' escape," Jayne growled as he verbally bashed them. His fists twisted against each other to control his underlying hostile desires. "He was here!" His heart raced while his ears pounded. Anger mounted in his soul and he clenched his fists. "Out of all the people that needed to be behind bars! He was *here!*"

"Yeah," Kenneth muttered.

A weak smile spread onto Peter's face. Jayne's spunky answer increased Peter's trust in him.

Consumed with a heightened awareness, Kenneth's body jerked. He stared quizzically. "Wait, 'the I.V. Scissor King'... you mean the doctor responsible, right?"

Jayne nodded with a tightened jaw. The muscles in his neck danced.

"Don't worry. We won't rest until we find him," soothed Kenneth. He placed a reassuring hand on Jayne's shoulder.

Worry did not leave Jayne's face. Dreams of running on the beach haunted his thoughts. The middle of his chest hurt as his breathing increased and his limbs quivered. He needed to confirm his ticket for passage on the 'Underground Railroad' to the 'Promised Land'. "Are all the Heccs as free as Jonathon?"

"Jonathon?" Peter scratched his chin.

"Antw...I mean...Anthony! ... Ah... You know what I mean."

"Yes, Anthony, he ..." Peter paused. His mind raced. *I need Jayne to trust me.* Peter lifted his chin and corrected himself. "I mean... yes, Jonathon is free. He needs your help with the other Heccs. They are in the performance room."

"They are free? They are all awake and swimming?"

"Yes, every one of them" said Kenneth with a growing smile.

"Good. That is how it should be. Free. And we can all leave this place?" When Jayne received an affirmative from both agents, he stood taller. Looking around, he stretched his upper limbs and back. "When can we leave?"

"Let's wrap up a few things first." Peter stated as gently as he could. The numb feeling of wandering blindly through a mine field still troubled him.

Jayne stared at his abdomen when a low growl rumbled from his gut. Covering his stomach with one hand, Jayne asked, "What time is it, or, what day is it?"

"12:20 pm. It's lunch time. You've only been out for hours. You haven't lost any days." Kenneth replied, peering at his watch.

"Has everybody eaten anytime lately?"

When the nurse and agents shook their heads, wheels turned in Jayne's head. "Rebecca?" Jayne looked the heavyset nurse in the eye. "Can you stretch mine and Jon's meal out into a stew?"

"Why yes, I think so."

"When it's done, take it to the conference room. Please and thank you." After a sharp nod, Jayne turned toward the door of the performance arena only to abruptly sit down in a nearby wheel chair. His head throbbed.

Rebecca disappeared with a brave face. The nurses would start afresh and finally be able to return to the outside world, despite all the previous bumps.

"Where's Doug?" A lump formed in Jayne's throat. "He's my friend, too."

An emotional punch tightened Kenneth's and Peter's guts. They had discussed Kenneth's version of the raid where Doug and Jayne seemed to be getting along. Peter mulled over the development in his mind. *I did not expect to hear the word 'friend' and 'Doug' in the same sentence.* Peter swallowed as he considered his limited options. *Jayne's cooperation is a necessity to keep the peace... I ...I promised. This could end badly. I don't know what the* H.E.C.C.*s will do if I don't deliver.* Peter stared directly at Kenneth and tapped his first two fingers on his left thigh, indicated their own unspoken code to play along. He would explain later. With one eyebrow raised, Peter explained Doug would join them shortly, but it remained imperative that Jayne steal away to Jonathon.

Dee insisted on pushing Jayne in the wheelchair. With one hand on his head, Jayne pointed the way with the other. His inside and outside worlds were colliding and creating new possibilities. The two men followed Dee and Jayne out and down the outstretched corridor. When they reached the door, they heard the horse play stop cold.

Strong pheromones and indistinguishable odors hit Jayne as well as the bright light from the sun. The heavy shade had been put away for the first time since Jayne worked there.

Heads bobbed under the water. One head came out and shoulders appeared at the edge. It was Jonathon. He saw Jayne and signaled with a slap of his hand against the surface of the water. Many heads appeared then.

"Jonathon!" The wheelchair almost tipped as Jayne put his feet down to stand up.

Kenneth and Peter caught Dee as she started to fall backward from the excitement. After she thanked the men, she insisted on going to oversee the food preparations. Jayne's focus was on his friend as he waveringly walked toward the water.

Kenneth caught up to Jayne and accompanied him to the edge. Peter helped Dee to the door.

Jayne ached to cannonball next to Jonathon, but decided against it with all the eyes upon him. He glanced at his swim trunks. After he eased into the water, he exchanged a mutually understood high-five greeting with his best friend.

{:-)-]~~{

Both agents climbed up the bleachers. Peter excused himself as Kenneth sat down. The stairs beckoned to him to burn off the heart breaking stress. Little crossed his mind as he ran up and down ten times. His meditative thoughts turned inward. Rejuvenated, Peter sat down next to his partner who handed him a bottle of water. Bogey had brought it to them as Peter was running.

A low rumbling in their stomachs reminded them that they were human and still had to care for themselves. The scene before them reeled in their attention. The rest of the H.E.C.C.'s gathered around Jonathon and Jayne as best they could.

Kenneth nodded at them with a slight angle and queried aloud, "So do we count Jayne as a catfish?"

"I don't know. Man, I don't even know what to make of all this. How are these people… these individuals… going to go back to their old lives? Take the gal that the nurses say that Jayne calls 'Hope'."

"Was she the one he kissed before he passed out?"

Peter nodded. "I think so." His hand flew to his chin. He scratched his neck under his jawbone. "Have you read her missing persons file?"

"Not yet."

"Her birth name is Marian Harrison. She hated the water. She was taken from her family years ago. Her parents are divorced. Her mother is remarried and her father has at least four girlfriends in three major casinos. What kind of a life will she have now?"

Shrugging his shoulders, Kenneth focused directly at his partner. He leaned in closer and whispered. "I heard the Heccs had difficulty in coaxing her *into* the water." He leaned back, searched the pool below, and slightly lifted his voice. "She looks like she is doing a little better now."

"That's good. Now, take Jayne's friend, Anth…"

Kenneth interrupted, "Jonathon?"

"Yeah, Jonathon. His real name is Anthony Rodriguez. He might adapt pretty well because he has always loved the water. However, he was a competitive swimmer…"

"Looks like he still is."

"Anyway…Officials are not going to let a H.E.C.C. compete in swimming competitions. It's not legal… or fair!"

"Hmmmm," was all Kenneth could reply. He leaned back and then Peter followed. Both men had never taken their eyes off of the watery arena.

Peter yawned without taking his eyes off the sparkling tails.

All sixty-one H.E.C.C.s were now involved in several activities. Kenneth was trying to figure out the sports and who was involved. "Look at the Heccs swim naked according to human civil laws, yet they have an instinctive form of modesty." He paused. "Speaking of which... Remind me to thank the doctor who brought the Heccwans swim suit tops.

"I take it. Heccwans are female H.E.C.C.s?"

"Yeah, and Heccans are males. Look at the silver tails when the sun hits them just right."

Peter stared hard. "They're almost iridescent."

Kenneth mused. "The glints from their rainbow colors make them look like exotic fish."

"Well, there's every skin color accounted for so no racial activist groups will have their panties in a wad. When I listened to them talking, I heard heavy accents in a few of the individuals, so there may be a bit of international involvement before long."

Peter had most of the stories memorized. "Yeah, they are naturalized citizens so we should be ok there. They had been in the US a while before they went missing. One man had crashed in a plane on a visit to his native land for a funeral of a relative. He and his pilot were presumed dead. Yet, here he is, alive and better than he had been when he left. His back trouble seems to be completely gone. Who knows where his pilot is." He shook his head in disgust.

The young Heccwans and Heccans were now playing tag and enjoying complete freedom from the fear of drowning, which was a new adventure in itself. The twins and triplets hung out together away from the crowd, soaking in the sun and conversation. One adolescent H.E.C.C. pair were engaged in conversation as they sat on the side, playing with their fins in the water. First their fins splashed separately and then together.

"I noticed the Heccs have different hair growth according to how long they have been catfish. They have a silver highlight shine mixed with their roots. Jayne hasn't been a fish as long as the others. His hair still has very little new growth in it." Kenneth commented as he stretched his back.

Peter openly shared his own thoughts. "It's hard to stare at them up close without them getting uncomfortable. The pictures that were taken by the three cameras made it easier to really look and get a better idea. There is a strip of silver on the back of their necks and it traces under their hair up to their ears. However, their faces look normal except for those ridges on their foreheads. And, well, the…"

Kenneth interrupted Peter, "Did you notice that the females have a small pattern on their forehead like a jeweled tattoo? I noticed it while they were being wheeled down the hallway. Each one has a mixture of different colors."

"Yes, I noticed that on the mug shots, but I never made the connection that it was only a feminine trait." Peter agreed. "I must have been too overwhelmed."

"Hey, I just remembered something that a doctor told me."

"What's that?"

"He told me upon his examination, he noticed that there is an extra function to their eyes than when they were human. He said they would need to be examined extra thoroughly to uncover their abilities. They can see under water better than humans."

"So they could be lip reading under water while they stare at us?" Peter shivered.

"Hey, isn't it our job to be the ones spying? Besides, the ripples in the pool should disrupt their line of sight like a mirage."

The two men warily leaned back, staring with disbelief at each other. They shrugged their shoulders and sheepishly smiled. After they relaxed their guard, they chuckled. An awkward nervousness set in so they shot each other a wounded glance before concentrating on the water scenery. After a few uncomfortable minutes, they whispered back and forth as they played the game of attempting to read the H.E.C.C.'s lips.

{:-)-]~~{

A group surrounded Jayne. When they wouldn't stop staring, he glanced around as if looking for answers.

The group continued focusing their direct attention on Jayne.

Jayne narrowed his eyes and ran his fingers through his hair. He lifted his voice. "What?"

Nathan Hawk boldly broke the silence. "We want you to be our ambassador. We are a new race and we will need to make some kind of agreement with the regular humans to protect us from any additional medical experimentation and to ensure our right to live freely in this country. We think you are the perfect candidate. Jonathon thinks highly of you as you have proven to be a good friend to him. You look as though you are part Hecc and part human and have superior physical abilities to move through their world. A biracial would be perfect to be our voice. How about it? Will you speak on behalf of all Heccs?"

Jayne's eyes widened as all hopeful eyes stared at him. "Hmmm." His right hand flew to his chin. He rubbed it from one side to the other. *I can still walk. I can go places they can't. Maybe humans will be more at ease with me being the ambassador. I could have the best of both worlds…what with the gills and all. I know what both the humans and the Heccs want.* Jayne stared at their faces and not their fish flesh. *They are people like me whose world has been yanked out from under them.* After clearing his throat, Jayne opened his mouth.

The H.E.C.C.s' heads craned for his decision.

"I think…yes, I can be your ambassador.

A loud cheer erupted. The dog pile was on as they entered his personal space and slapped him on the back. Jayne cringed and allowed himself to slowly sink underwater. After the joyous celebration calmed down, they dispersed. Jonathon reveled in his teaching role of the fine art of diving underwater before jumping in the air like dolphins. Most of them seemed to enjoy learning techniques from Jonathon, since he'd had the longest practice. Jonathon insisted Jayne join them, but was met with scowling resistance when it was suggested that they could give the tail-less one a boost.

Sadness crept over Jayne for he didn't like to feel inferior. He politely excused himself to talk to the others who had not approached him. When Jayne wasn't conversing, he liked watching the spinning tricks. For a while, he joined the circle of adults who were tossing and diving for rings. Jayne bounced from group to group to connect with each one.

{:-)-]~~{

"Well?" Peter raised his voice as he nudged Kenneth.

"Well, what?" Evidently Kenneth's friend had spoken to him without him even noticing.

"I said, what's going to happen? Where are they going to go from here?"

Kenneth blankly stared at Peter. He couldn't help himself and changed his Kansan accent to mimic his friend's Oklahoman drawl. "Well, they can't be turned into circus freaks." He paused and returned to his own accent. "Before long, there is going to be major media attention. I don't know how *we're* going to avoid it!"

"I don't know how *they're* going to avoid it from here on out!" Peter interrupted. He entertained the palms of his hands outstretched. "The media will fall all over themselves to get this scoop. They won't care whose lives they trample on. Missing people returned to their loved ones will be front page news! 'Missing persons who come back as *mermaids*' will be a bombshell!" Leaning forward, he let his arms rest on his thighs and his hands dangle in between his legs.

Kenneth nodded before he continued. "The first thing we do is fly them to their families before the media gets wind." He let out a small sigh of frustration. "How are we going to do that? I mean, Jayne needs water to survive, and the rest of them need it even more. They can't even walk! It hurts them. They're cripples in their old world, our world. They're free in their new world. How are we going to strip them of their freedom? We just handed them their freedom and we're going to take it away again? Come on!" It was his turn to pause. He dramatized the last sentence. "This also presents a citizenship and segregation problem. Boss said for us to let him know before we move so that the President can be privately informed."

"Without the media sniffing around." Peter sat back.

A movement in the doorway caused Kenneth to stare harder. Kenneth nudged Peter. Once they both stared in the general direction, Bogey signaled at the men to come to him. The two men came back over the walkway bridge to join Bogey. He led them to the conference room. Bogey explained the computers and Peter's mess had been taken to Jayne's apartment, the new official outpost. The tables had been redecorated like a medieval mansion's feast. Dee had brought in several large candlesticks from her vehicle. She had been meaning to take them to a second-hand store, but found a more fitting use for her toss-out-box, making an 'almost elegant' feast. There were mismatched sets of dishes from the apartments. Water filled each cup, goblet and coffee mug to the brim. Clean spoons, empty bowls, and sleeves of saltine crackers strategically dotted the table.

Jayne appeared in the doorway with a trail of water behind him. Although he told Kenneth and Peter that restroom breaks were a necessity, his distracted nose sniffed the air. The light meal of salmon and seaweed soup in stock pots on hot pads teased his senses. Saliva formed in his mouth. He licked his lips and swallowed.

Confusion once again lifted its ugly head and bit everyone with venom. Bogey located a workable amount of loading carts and wheelchairs to aid in the necessary, but difficult undertaking. Several agents pushed four to five Heccans per cart to various apartments. The Heccwans were assisted by the nurses using the wheelchairs to get them to the restroom.

All the H.E.C.C.s were pushed back down the hall where the agents parked the carts alongside the wall. Each one was helped to a chair in the conference room. Some had to share chairs. It was obvious to Kenneth and Peter that the happy reminiscing chatter of the pool area had ceased and sadness was developing because of their lack of mobility when away from water. The two lead agents helplessly watched with their own growing sadness and worries. Everyone else congregated outside in the hallway and lounge.

Peter and Kenneth weren't worried about the teams on outposts around the building since MREs had been delivered. Unenthusiastically, Peter and Kenneth ate their own MREs in the hallway. It was torture to smell the hot soup, but they were still on the job and Peter didn't want to take any chances of poison or tranquilizers being slipped into his team's food. The pet shop inhabitants were not suspects right now, but caution still had to be enforced. Kenneth was managing a handful of complaints about the MREs when the cell phone in Peter's shirt pocket started to ring. Peter sauntered down the hallway to answer it privately.

Jayne had already left the dining room several times to deal with his first Ambassadorial duties. Eating his soup on the run, Jayne seemed to be needed here or there constantly. He wasn't used to all this socializing, but he understood his important job as spokesman. The H.E.C.C.s were relying on him. During the meal, in an adjoining room, an agreement was discussed and presented to the United States Attorney General by video conference. Since the H.E.C.C.s already were established citizens before they were experimented on, the AG felt their transformation did not dissolve their rights as citizens or their human rights.

Now, Jayne was on a mission to speak with Kenneth. He strolled up to Kenneth and waited for him to him finish a phone conversation. Jayne took the precious minute to finish his cold soup.

Noticing him, Dee walked up to confiscate his empty bowl and give him a glass of water. A wheelchair stopped next to Jayne and Dee.

Kenneth's confronter had hung up in a huff. With a scowl, Kenneth turned around to face Jayne. His eyes calmed as he observed Jayne's interaction with Hope. Precious life flooded his sight, leaving a strong understanding smile.

Jayne looked over to see two enchanting eyes peering at him. She had awkwardly wheeled herself, using her hands. Embarrassed from being out of breath, Hope's eyes dropped to focus on her lap while she composed herself. Compassion moved Jayne when he carefully handed her the glass of water that Dee had just handed to him. "Here."

Hope looked up. Her eyelashes batted rapidly as she accepted his gift.

"Jayne, I am proud of you for taking care of everyone else, but you do need to take care of yourself, too." Dee scolded.

With a nod, Jayne answered Dee. His sunshiny expression missed the aim entirely. Instead of Dee, Jayne's pleasant look and adventurous eyes lingered on Hope's twinkling ones.

A bright winning smile lit up Hope's face as she stared up at him. Her eyes dilated. She hoped the glass covered her reddening cheeks while she sipped it down. When she finished the last drop, she didn't bother wiping it off her cheek. The drop of water fell down her cheek and throat, but disappeared in its journey. Hope handed the empty glass to Dee.

Dee ran off to get Jayne another glass of water.

"Did you need something?" Jayne asked tenderly.

"No, I just wanted to tag along and watch you work if that's okay."

Jayne nodded at her and the two turned, acknowledging Peter, who joined them.

Catching Kenneth's eye contact, Peter muttered with air quotes, "Well, they've started the 'gentle' process of locating and contacting families." He made an obnoxious face.

Hope's facial expression turned thoughts to reality. *How can I go back? No more jogging with mom on weekday mornings before she goes to work. How will I fulfill my dreams?* A rapid rhythm started as her heart picked up its song. She tensed up. *I wanted to be a computer tech or a librarian. I can't become either if I'm a mermaid!* Clamping her eyelids shut tight, she opened them several times, trying to change her reality by thinking it into existence. When she failed, her limbs trembled and a pain choked her throat and chest. *I want to be where the people are.* An emotional ladle stirred her thoughts over a heat that churned her stomach. *Up where they walk, not stuck in a pool of water.* Lost was her old world. *Up where they run.* The sudden nausea caused her head to reel. *Free to go as I please.* Hope was so lost in her own world that she didn't see Jayne's world collapsing.

Stabbing pains rippled through Jayne's back and limbs as gravity increased its tug. Butterflies crawled and bumped about, attempting to escape Jayne's stomach. Wrinkling his nose, Jayne's face soured with furrowed eyebrows framing his glazed eyes. His shoulders pulled into his chest as the emotions punched him repeatedly in the gut. The stinging words originated in Jayne's brain, but ignited a burning sensation on his tongue as it evaporated in the atmosphere. "Where will I go?"

His doleful question was nonverbally answered as Kenneth and Peter looked at each other, horrified. Peter and Kenneth had not thought of him. They did now. Both started to speak, but syllables failed them. Their lips moved like puppets, but no ventriloquist spoke for them.

To Jayne, Bogey materialized like a ghost, for he had not seen him walk up. The sudden appearance startled him. He jumped back a bit. However, Bogey's words were mush to Jayne. He could not hear the conversation at hand. Turning an about face, he lumbered in the direction of the stadium in a trance.

Alerted to Jayne's heavy steps, Hope woke up from her inward nightmare and wheeled in a fury after him.

Jayne slogged along, ignoring reality.

"Jayne! Jayne… Jayne," Hope frantically cried after him, but he was wrapped up in his personal thoughts and could not hear her. Frustration increased her body temperature. Tears formed in the corners of her eyes. "Please," she begged while she lost her breath. "Jayne, stop! I...I can not keep up!" Her chair stopped as her aching arms fell to her sides. She lacked the stamina to keep up. Straining the full length of her arm as she reached for him, Hope broke down in painful tears. The old Marian Harrison stepped out of her wheel chair, but fell face first. As her right cheek hit, her hands struck palm out, slapping the floor. With her breath taken away, a wailing moan escaped her lips.

The crash of the wheelchair broke him out of his trance. "Oh, Hope," Jayne chastised tenderly as he turned around and saw her rumpled body. He embraced her on the ground, picking her up. When he attempted to place her in the chair, she pushed the wheelchair away with a fin. It rolled back since the brakes had not been set.

Jayne sat down and let Hope snuggle. Her overwhelming hunger for comfort soothed Jayne's own hurting soul as he held her. She melted in his arms, but the choking tears continued to flow. She buried her face into his bare chest and clung onto his arms with tightened fists. Tears rolled down Jayne's nose and dripped onto her hair. He lowered his face and enjoyed the touch of her, rubbing his cheek against the back of her head. His pulse increased causing his back and neck to flush. The temperature in his thighs and hips increased. Agents escorting H.E.C.C.s passed by, but Jayne and Hope did not notice. Spectators avoided eye contact, too.

With a crack in his throat, Jayne whispered, "Life is sometimes unbearable; we don't know what will happen next! But I try to remember that our lives are like books, containing chapters that start and end with highs, lows and unexpected plot twists. Mixed emotions come when one chapter starts and another one ends. One must continue reading to enjoy the journey."

Hope sniffled. "I like books."

"I know," said Jayne. His soft words soothed even his own sadness and fears. Pouring out his heart to her, he told her his life story, giving her every detail concerning his affiliation to the pet shop. Without interruption, he explained how he'd met Doug and the complicated friendship they had developed. Fears for his own new chapter in life drove him to not miss a beat. When he finished, Hope lifted her head, gazed into his eyes and gave him a tight squeeze.

Lowering her head, Hope snuggled into Jayne. The increased beat of her heart spread a warm flush over her back and shoulders. The sound of Jayne's voice next to her ear heightened the awareness of a warm and swelling sensation inside her fish flesh. An aching in her right elbow from being squished suggested she move her hand. The pounding increased to where she shifted her hand. The warm sensation of his body heat radiating warmed her soul. The touch of his skin over the tight muscles in his chest radiated pleasure from the tips of her fingers to her brain. Allowing herself to feel anything psychologically and physically in that vulnerable minute of her existence shook her nerves. *I'm not supposed to be feeling these kinds of feelings right now*, she thought. *How can I think about liking a guy when I've just been turned into a fish?* Closing her eyes tight, Hope calmed her blood pressure and cooled the awaking desires of her flesh.

Sounds around the two faded. Insignificant shuffles of feet, squeaks of carts, and wheelchairs passed by. Uncomfortable agents cleared their throats as they passed, but disappeared into a vast of nothingness to Jayne and Hope. The connection they had to the floor under them faded. All the two could see, hear, smell, and touch was each other. They could taste the moisture in the air. Their sixth sense hovered on whether the other would break the spell cast on them. Broken tears dried up while hearts mended. Time exhaustingly ticked by. Jayne and Hope held each other.

A pair of feet abruptly stopped in front of Jayne. Jayne half-heartedly glanced at the white tennis shoes. A sweet smell beckoned to him, drawing his chin and cheek to settle back into her soft hair. The feet stayed there and didn't move. Jayne's eyes narrowed and sharpened. *Who could possibly need me now?* Hairy legs, shorts and shirt came before a goofy grin. Jayne's glare lightened to a crooked smile. It was Doug.

Embarrassed, Jayne cleared his voice. "Long time no see, stranger."

Doug knew better than to order Jayne around. "I'm forever done with my interviews and being grilled by the head honchos. I am going to go for a swim. Want to come? I bet I can dive deeper than you, oh Tailless One." He cocked his head side to side with a spirited attitude. "Hey there, Hope. Nice to see you finally out... and about. I've heard so much about you."

"Oh really?" Hope batted her eyelashes in confusion. She made a mental note to ask Jayne about that later. Right now, she had a more pressing matter on her mind. *Swim? Back in the water, again? Jonathon said...well...I guess my fear of drowning doesn't matter anymore.*

Jayne might not take that crap from the world, but he had come to enjoy the company of Doug. "You want to bet, oh gill-less one?" His eyes glimmered.

Giggling, Hope sat up. "I could use a game. Think you can take me on, oh tailless *and* gill-less ones? Don't make me beat you like a baby seal." She had heard the expression used by two sparing martial artists. Her eyes beamed as adventure lay around the bend. Her tear stained face did not steal the sight of her beauty.

"Ha! You're not playing, little fry! You're the prize!" With that comment, Doug hefted Hope up and threw her over his shoulder like a sack of potatoes. After he barged forward a few feet, Doug settled into a brisk stride.

Rattled, Jayne had to get over the shock of the snatching before he hopped up. His clumsy feet yearned to catch up to his body. His legs must have fallen asleep. Stiff, sore, and aching limbs protested. Loudly, Jayne yelled down the hall, "No way, Doug! She can't be a prize for an *ugly* 'ol polar bear!"

"What? No way! I want to be *in* the game, *not* a trophy for the winner!" Hope moved ever so slightly and realized her hips were slippery enough to cause Doug to drop her. Using his back as a prop for her hands, she hung rigid and tense. It was safer in his arms than falling on the hard floor from that height. "I can dive down to the bottom and be up in the air before *you* or Jayne *reach* the top!" Hope challenged him. She felt safe in his arms because Jayne had bled his heart out to her. She knew the whole story. She also understood Jayne's fondness for Doug, despite their rough start.

"I don't care if you can thrust both of your fins together. You're gonna lose!" He specified the number that she had to count to before she resurfaced. Doug tossed her to the other shoulder causing her arms to flail. It was a far-reaching walk to the show tank even with a fast pace. Doug's breathing increased. "More than a single helping of caviar is a waste, anyway!" He was losing his grip as her natural oils made her slippery. His lips curled up with extra ornery wrinkles before throwing his head back with a guffaw. Doug's loud laugh echoed throughout the whole hallway.

Jayne stumbled again, but he had been challenged. There was a fight to win. Getting up, he raced after the two giggling down the hallway.

Little did Jayne know, but a face was peaking at him from a doorway. Grinning like a Cheshire cat, Kenneth had put Doug up to the harassment.

"Doug likes his sardines with their heads on," Hope sang at the top of her lung capacity as Doug marched through the entrance.

"Yep! More fiber that way! Annd crunchy too!"

"EW!" Quivering with disgust, Hope slipped an inch or two in Doug's arms.

Doug walked to the water's edge. Heads had turned and now the staring began. Doug didn't care. He shrugged his shoulders. As far as he was concerned, it wasn't the H.E.C.C.s exclusive domain.

Several sunbathing Heccwans with full bellies were startled by the sudden and noisy entrance of Doug and Hope. Their conversation about what might have been ended abruptly. They pulled back from the water that had soothed their nerves as they dangled their hands and arms while laying on the edge of the pool. Once the Heccwans saw Jonathon signal the 'all's well', they returned to their lazy horseplay and gossip. Bruce and Roland were also startled by the incoming commotion. They briefly stopped their water sumo wrestling match. The surrounding spectators encircling them turned back to their cheering when the two Heccans continued their battle of strength and wits. Val sat alone, moping and ignoring the world around him. The remaining groups who noticed, turned back to their business when they saw Jayne grinning and running full speed. He was still threatening to win. He almost slipped on several patches of water, but it didn't stop him.

Hope felt the shift of weight, but realization came too late, "Noooooo!" She shrieked with a laconic, nervous scream. After her belly flop, Hope struggled as she turned around in the water. Her air had already exhaled before she immersed her head. Two kicks in the air allowed her to flat-out flee under the surface.

Unhesitatingly, Doug picked up a ring beside his foot and tossed it into the water and dove, hands first. He wasn't planning for Hope or Jayne to beat him. Jayne flew through the air and headed for the depths. The three dove as far as they could dive. Hope dove all the way to the bottom. She laid her face down and started counting to 50, as Doug had demanded when he challenged her. Meanwhile, Jayne was catching up to Doug. Doug and Jayne were side by side and tussled a bit underwater trying to get to the ring. Doug grabbed it and headed up. Jayne grabbed his foot to work his way up Doug's body, determined to steal the ring. They pushed each other away and Hope flew right between them, snatching the ring. Startled, they both hurried to the top. Hope reached maximum height in the air ending in a tail kick. Jayne came up last because he had given Doug a boost so that he could hurry and catch his breath.

As soon as Doug caught his breath and Hope returned to the surface, the water war began. Jayne splashed Doug before Hope splashed Jayne. The surrounding spectators whooped and hollered, but it did not bring peace. One by one, they joined the war until even Val was involved.

Water splashed and landed in the pool and on the concrete surroundings. Sounds of coughing from the constant transitions from air to water breathing and back again joined the song of the wind whistling around the giant arena.

Kenneth and Peter came in and raced like mad men to get to the top of the bleachers before someone splashed the laptops they had with them. As soon as they sat down, they noticed that there were no apparent teams, winners or losers.

In short order, Doug attempted to exit the chaos to stop from choking. Doug nodded his thanks when Nathan kindly boosted him out of the water. Kneeling down, Doug coughed and choked so hard it made his toes curl. Nathan and Bruce shielded Doug from the splashing to help him catch his breath.

Kenneth watched Doug as he staggered to a nearby towel and dried his face. Every couple of moments, Doug paused to spit out water and mucus. Bogey purposefully climbed the stairs, determined to address his superiors. Kenneth and Peter had seen him out of the corners of their eyes. They figured that nothing could be urgent, so they continued pulling up their satellite internet service.

Bogey preferred not to interrupt them. He pretended to be patiently waiting, standing at parade rest; however his skin was crawling with impatience.

Noticing Bogey's irritation, Kenneth sighed before taking a deep breath in, "Well?" Slightly annoyed, he cocked his head to Bogey's side.

Keeping his tone down, Bogey replied. "All the outside doctors and nurses that left, have checked in by phone after doing further research. They say exactly what the inside nurses hammered about. These victims of the vanished evil scientist will live out their lives as the new humanoid race: Human Electric Cave Catfish. There is no way to get them back to fully human form unless you want them as *dead* humans."

Peter and Kenneth shook their heads and rolled their eyes. "We already knew that," Peter huffed. Kenneth tried to wave him off, but he would not go.

"What now?" they answered simultaneously. Clearly, Kenneth and Peter could not hide their developing agitation. They had concerns blowing like Mount St. Helens, but they both had coveted a moment to de-stress.

"A lot *more* people know it too," Bogey answered, physically flinching. Taking a breath of profound courage, Bogey braced for the reaction before he dared to speak the next update. "There was a leak. Words out and there's reporters snooping around. But to make matters worse, the AG's office was alerted to email traffic from the associated press starting to investigate about the 'medical mutants'."

Peter Austin's face faded to ash white. He grabbed a water bottle and downed most of it to keep the contents of his stomach from escaping. He leaned back into the stands and threw the rest over his face and hair.

Kenneth Hershkin's face turned boiling red. If he were the fictitious Magneto, his super powers would have blown Bogey up from the inside out. "*What* do you *mean* we have a *leak*?" he roared. He already knew what it entailed, but he had hoped for a mere second that his openly expressed anger would change the fact at hand.

"I have our more experienced men outside forming a protective perimeter with their weapons ready. The rubber-neckers and lookie-loos have no clue why there is so much government activity, but with the leak, they will soon start putting two and two together. The rookies are helping with the loading of evidence." Bogey stopped there because Jayne's friend Dee showed up beside him.

"It's getting out of hand. The media and general gawkers are trying to push in!" Dee's limbs quivered like gelatin.

Bogey's jaw dropped.

Together, Kenneth and Peter slammed their laptops closed and sprang to their feet. It was then that Kenneth and Peter knew that H.E.C.C.s indeed had improved hearing. All eyes were glued on them except for Doug's. He hadn't heard a thing. In fact, he was still shaking water out of his ears. The H.E.C.C.s were hugging the wall closest to Kenneth and Peter and staring with greater fear in their eyes than when they found out that they were no longer human. A blue-green glowing light formed around each H.E.C.C. in the water. No human was close enough for damage. Kenneth and Peter had ducked down to the concrete ground. Noticing their reaction, Bogey's instinct forced him to gruffly reach out and bring Dee to her knees away from the metal rails for her protection.

Even though Doug was far enough away, he was still too close for comfort.

Kenneth watched as Doug considered his hands like there was a tingling sensation in them. Looking over at the H.E.C.C.s, Kenneth yelled, "Everything's going to be all right!" He toppled down a few steps with his right hand outstretched. "I won't let anyone in and no one will hurt you ever again. Please! Lower your charges! Calm yourselves!"

When the electricity didn't ease up, Kenneth and Peter started running up the stairs, avoiding metal. Bogey guarded Dee and shouted as loud as he could. "There is still too much current!"

Jayne jumped out of the pool, turned around to face his people, and yelled, "I'll take care of this. I'm your ambassador, remember?"

As their anxiety was reduced so was the voltage, but there was still an energized feeling in the air as if a thunderstorm could break out any minute. As soon as Peter gave Bogey the okay signal, Bogey led Dee out with a faster pace than she could naturally keep.

She yelled over her shoulder, "Jayne! You can stay with me."

Suddenly, Bogey released her arm. He snatched Doug and pushed them both out.

Bogey ordered Doug to run to the pet shop entrance and help the few agents there. The agent continued at a brisk pace. He spoke hastily. "I'm going to gather the nurses! We're leaving! Now!" Earlier, he had openly expressed his admiration for Jayne's role as an ambassador. He did not think less of Jayne for the hallway incident because he knew that even ambassadors needed quiet time to work things out for themselves. Bogey planned to work out his quiet time in the gym as soon as he could clock out. Right now, though, the H.E.C.C.s needed protection more than negotiations. And Bogey had an evacuation to execute.

With all hands on deck for the emergency exodus, the H.E.C.C.s would be loaded up for a brand new chapter in their lives. Kenneth arranged for the buses to come immediately, a day earlier than planned, while a hurried bathroom break was managed with caution. The nurses were encouraging them that everything would be okay and got the Heccwans to talk about rejoining their families. The agents tried helping the Heccans discover humanity and humility, which was challenging, as it was far too easy to lose those virtues in their line of work. They engaged the Heccans in talking about what they were eager to return to. Some even discussed what they retained from when they were taken hostage. Anything to distract them from the hurried exodus.

From the apartments, the next step was a pain for all involved. The freed individuals were to be loaded on buses that had been parked right outside the pet shop. The entrances to the buses were purposely parked toward the store front for privacy. The chaos was hidden from the view of the prying newscasters and locals who had heard the rumors starting to fly of a big scandal at the old oceanarium. Bogey had called the local police for backup. Their job was to keep the crowd at bay, beyond half a football field. Carts brought the H.E.C.C.s to the exit and then wheelchairs helped them to the buses. The agents lifted them up inside and when everyone was seated, Bogey went over orders with the head bus drivers. The agents still had their black uniforms on and stood around while giving emotionless looks which offered no clues to the nosy reporters. The agents could be seen by the public, but they kept Jayne out of sight. Jayne, wearing a black trench coat and black hat, stood with his back to the public overseeing the loading.

Peter was on the phone getting orders and relaying them to Kenneth. Peter hung up the phone and made another call, giving a fair number of orders himself. Hanging up again, he continued to make numerous calls.

Heavy in thought, Kenneth puffed on a cigar, dispensing directions and encouragement as needed. The sky was dotted with intriguing clouds that floated by. Kenneth mused over the past few days; there was still so much to do, he thought.

Peter decisively hung up the cell phone and turned to Kenneth. "Well, even if we shake the public here, there is a camera crew already sniffing around the first house we are due to arrive at tomorrow." They both knew they were not fully prepared for this first big step, but what else could they do? Hopefully they had made the right decision. Taking the H.E.C.C.s back to their original families now while they were still under Peter and Ken's authority was surely better than letting the Center for Disease Control or some other agency gather them up in a government lab or to just be made to 'disappear' for good!

"Well the fat lady has sung," Kenneth regretfully declared as he snuffed out his cigar. With that, the two men shouted orders to their men and groups of agents split up and piled in government vehicles. Off sped the convoy of buses and black vehicles.

$$\{:-)-]\sim\sim\{$$

Home Anemone Home

Safe for Whom?

Chapter 12

he schedule changes were interesting the first few weeks after August 7 when Tyler's entire extended family had invaded the vacation house. It was full and everyone was happy - once the adjustment process was over. Gabriella had a few instances where her nerves had been tested, but she conclusively relinquished household authority over to her mother-in-law. Secrets and sorrows, when it came to Gabriella's missing daughter, dispersed with complete truth. Emotional levels throughout the house cooled down. The newness of Mary having a missing sister wore off. In no time, she quit nagging everyone about Marian, especially since the old stories didn't change when retold.

Togetherness seemed to be functioning on a good note, daily, including Friday, September 3rd. Supper was over and most of the family had gathered in the 10ft ceilinged basement, dancing, playing games and visiting. Tyler's father, Jack, dropped out of the crowd to quietly read his book in the conservatory.

The noise downstairs overwhelmed Gabriella as she sat on a bench in front of one of the two marine tanks that topped out up in the conservatory. The two five sided tanks put together would form half of an octagon and were built into the front corners of the room. Concrete pillars formed the frame of three tall rectangular acrylic viewing windows almost from floor to ceiling. Heavy, knitted curtains tied back with hemp rope flanked her. Gabriella shuddered as she thought, *Ew. I haven't washed them in months. I haven't even been down here to care.* She slowly lifted and lowered her shoulders. *Spiders could be hiding in them, waiting to jump out on me.* Holding her breath, she peered up from her book and craned her head to see why unnerving shadows danced on the page in front of her. Staring through the window, she relaxed. Several Zebrafish and Bala sharks fluidly danced a beautiful ballet up, over, and around giant rocks and fake plants. One Plecostomus suckerfish fixated itself right above her. Gabriella smiled and returned to her book.

Peace and quiet had once lingered around the house, but now, in its place, constant noise and extra chores remained. Gabriella had certainly been too busy to mope. Wrinkling her nose, she stared over the top of her book, beyond the tables, at the circle of teenagers that mingled in the center of the room. Diverse perfumes from the teen girls lazily mixed in the air. Most congregated there and danced to the music. After Abney Park, Madison Rising loaded up on the six-tray CD player. When the last song played, various groups separated to find other things to do. Gabriella cringed as she heard a few distant loud rumbles from beyond the dance floor, indicating that the two lane bowling alley just found some bored occupants. Just as quick as the noise had started, it ceased. Gabriella sat taller and saw Marcy leaving the alley, having routed the bowlers. *They must have left to sulk by the fireplace, at least they aren't headed this way.*

Gabriella inhaled deeply. Without the blaring music or bowling alley, peace visited her. She was still holding her book like she was reading it; however, she was really enjoying people, watching at the card tables. She had left Mary hypnotized by the children's program on the TV opposite of the bowling alley. She knew Mary was safe with Mildred watching the kids in that area. A pleasant expression settled on her face. It was nice not to feel like the biggest liar in the world anymore. Her kryptonite had been banned behind bars of truth. Burning nerves tickled Gabriella's bottom, hips, and back. *I've sat long enough,* she thought as she gingerly placed her book next to her on the padded red corduroy covered bench. Her limited sly sleuthing skills failed her as she openly watched Tyler sitting at a card table next to the opposite wall from her. Calm serenity tugged at the corners of her lips. She smiled, buried in thought as her heartbeat increased slightly. Movement caught her eyes as the tweens meandered over to the card table on her side of the room. She didn't know what card game they started, but at least they had settled down. Leaving her book behind, Gabriella stood up and wandered over to their table.

"Omph," uttered Gabriella. She reached down to cover her stomach. Her fingers felt a head. When she looked down, she saw a head with a black buzz cut.

Small beady cornflower blue eyes peered up at her. "I'm sorry."

"Which one are you?" Gabriella straightened up. The pain had been brief.

"I'm Nick. We're playing cops and robbers."

A girl with black bangs and chin length hair collided with Nick causing him to strike Gabriella again.

"Nick?" Gabriella helped him catch his balance before she gently positioned him a foot away from her.

"Hart. I'm seven."

"Your mama's name is…"

Interrupting her, Nick eagerly spoke up. "Beverly."

"And the cop who is chasing you?" Gabriella sweetly grinned at the shy girl hiding behind Nick.

Nick side-stepped his cousin so she could be fully inspected. "This is Vanessa Burgess. She's eight."

"Of course," Gabriella leaned over. "Nice to meet you again, Vanessa. Last time I saw you was when you were just a toddler. I know your mama real well. Bonnie has been one of my closest and dearest friends." Gabriella reached out to shake her niece's hand. Vanessa giggled and ran off, pulling Nick behind her. Gabriella straightened up and approached the children's card table. Never before had she had the opportunity to get to know all her nephews and nieces.

When Gabriella approached the fraternal twins, Charlene and Charlie Hart, they acknowledged her with their heads since their hands were full of UNO cards. Charlene's black hair, chocolate brown eyes, and button nose was completely opposite of Charlie's strawberry blond hair, china blue eyes and blade-like nose. Other than being slim, they looked like they were from two different families, not the same parents.

Ten year old tomboy Blakie Clark waved her free hand.

Gabriella whispered, "She has her mother's smile. Marcy was truly blessed." She longingly sighed. "I want a baby." Her empty womb burned for the sensation of life dancing inside her once again. Clutching her tummy with both hands, Gabriella held her aching feeling like it would burst open her guts. Knowing that eyes watched her, she dropped her hands to her sides and put on a fake-it-till-you-make-it smile.

Blakie's other hand clutched two cards. "It's my turn!" Her brown hair styled with a pixie cut framing her doll face, complimented her blue eyes, even if she was irritated. Blakie blissfully challenged her peer, Tony Shaw, whose blue eyes sparkled. He and his identical twin brother, Mark, both sported chestnut brown blunt haircuts which proudly displayed their seashell ears. They even dressed alike.

Standing next to Tony, Mark objected, "Not yet, Blakie! That card is special!" He nudged his brother. "Check your hand, Tony! Look for all of the Potters!"

Gabriella chuckled with genuine delight and turned on her heel. The animated boys were at the age where their biggest fear was losing to a girl. Gabriella's eyes searched for all the adults. She approached the card table with Marcy, Clifford, Beverly, Marvin, Bonnie, and Kelly-She. They were playing the domino game, Eighty-Eight. Still standing by Beverly, Gabriella turned her body and focused her gaze on Tyler's card table. It filled up with adolescent nephews and nieces and two of her brothers-in-law.

Tyler observed his two brothers-in-law learning to play a new and different card game. The two had caught on fairly well after the second game. The three uncles had originally joined the young adults, unable to resist the table of laughter. After the rules were explained, they became full of youthful energy. They were now enjoying their third game. Eyeing each one around the table, Tyler practiced his own people watching skills. He was really concentrating on this game of Bullshit. He had played the part of ignorance by asking several questions during the explanation of rules and the first game. However, a keen understanding of the rules had been implanted in his brain way before this evening. Reading their faces intrigued him far more than watching the decks. Mysteriously, he watched them react even when it wasn't their turn, because he hid a secret in the depths of his bones. He would pull the sneaky, but perfectly legal, move again soon. This round had gone without any challenges so his next turn should be perfect timing. When his turn came, he piped up, "Three sixes." He managed to slip in a few more cards.

Gabe Clark didn't dare run his clean hands through his tousled light brown hair as he watched Tyler. The grease from his mousse clung to every strand. His athletic biceps rippled as he moved a hand from his peach-fuzz covered chin to his cards. Chords of Apocalyptica filled his ears from the headphones nestled around his neck. Confidently, he spoke loudly so all could hear. "Two sevens." Blue eyes twinkled.

The turn fell upon Billy Hart, who had mastered the art of constantly looking and sounding serious. His greenish-blue eyes focused on the task at hand. Strawberry-blond roots played peak-a-boo under his dark green dye-job. Wearing a dark green t-shirt and green camo pants, he articulated with a growly singsong. "It is one eight, I have." However, when he quickly placed the card down, it shifted the cards slightly, causing it to appear that he had played more than he acknowledged.

Staring straight at him, Jerome and Kelly-He yelled in unison, "Bullshit!" Sure enough they found the one eight as well as two sevens. They noticed the three sixes that Tyler put in and two cards that someone concealed underneath. They couldn't tell who had cheated. A big table-wide debate consumed them with much finger pointing. Tyler performed the difficult mission of trying to blame others, maintaining an innocent smile, all the while carefully restraining himself from a smug attitude.

At last, the arguments tapered off when Mildred arrived and insisted that it was her turn to join in. When she was met with debate, she raised her voice. "I don't care who did what. Start a new hand and deal me in!"

Two braided raven pony-tails framed Eva Clark's small ears and dropped over her shoulders. Her tails flicked about as she dealt. She sat in between the year older fraternal twins, William and Willetta Shaw. They both were slim and had brown eyes, but William's hair was a sandy brown compared to his sister's darker shade. Willetta adjusted her round false-lensed glasses before her fingers fidgeted with her purple feathered hat as she chose her play. After she finished, she smoothed the ruffles on her simple handmade Victorian dress before she glanced at her steampunk crafted watch.

The game continued with excitement and hearty genuine belly laughs - so hard that cheeks reddened and tears were spotted rolling down. Shrieks of hilarity and protests of innocence echoed in the large room. Gabriella realized that Bullshit was a very rowdy game!

When Jack briskly walked up, Willetta, nudged her cousin, Eva, who nudged William. Tyler's sly grin faded as Jack bent to whisper in his right ear. Horror-struck, his eyes and his lips tightened. The muscles in his throat twitched. His expression mimicked the gloom on Jack's face. Tyler's hands dropped to the table, his cards scattered. With a solemn face, he whispered questions. The answers caused his spine to slightly buckle. Without turning back around, he motioned for his brothers-in-law to follow as he abruptly left the table. Jerome and Kelly-He dropped their cards and bolted behind the two men.

Concerned, Zola took the elevator while Melista hesitantly climbed the stairs.

Gabriella had been watching Tyler and knew in her heart that unexpected trouble had reached a boiling point. She couldn't guess what it was as she attempted to fleetly follow. Gabriella spun around to see what or who had stopped her. It was her daughter, Mary.

Full of energy, Mary had grabbed her hand and was trying to pull her in the opposite direction. "Mama!" She was bubbling over from head to toe. "Mama! Come see! Come see!"

Although Gabriella was slowly being pulled over toward the television circle, her attention was with the men stomping up the stairs. But the grip on her jeans' belt loop wouldn't budge no matter how politely Gabriella tried to pry Mary's fingers loose. "Alright, Mary! I'm coming!" She faced her daughter and offered her hand in trade for the belt loop hold.

Jumping up and down, Mary grabbed her mom's hand and jerked. Gabriella pulled it away and massaged it.

"Look Mama! Look!" She pointed and bounced demandingly. As Gabriella approached, the rest of the family also gathered around the home theater. Breaking local news reports interrupted national newscasts on multiple channels. All were covering the same century changing topic. It was not a holiday parade on anyone's calendar, but crowds of people and news reporters bustled about on the screen in every scene. Smiling and laughing faces celebrated with waving hands. The guardian of the remote changed the channel to a local station, hoping to see how the weird news might affect them.

{:-)-]~~{

The three men reached the front door two steps behind Jack. Tyler opened it and bore down on a man who was poised defiantly, ready to withstand them all. Anger and protection filled Tyler's heart as he bellowed, "You are not welcome here! How did you find us?" Hardening muscles jumpstarted his heart to pumping as if one additional beat would send it flying out of his body. Choking pressure wrapped its ugly arms around Tyler's lungs. His jawbone danced around, introducing his teeth to a painful grinding sensation. Tyler growled, "Go back to the rock you slithered out from under!"

Then the man shook his head, before speaking loudly so all could hear. "I can't and I won't!" Brash, he planted his feet proving that he wouldn't leave.

"Don't you have a scam to pull somewhere? Or some table to bet at? Or some two-bit floozy to chase after?" Wrath boiled inside Tyler. He walked up and swung a fist at the man before a numb Kelly Shaw or Jerome could stop him. Tyler missed as his victim ducked.

"Hey! Whoa there, tiger," Shaw appealed as he leapt to stop his brother-in-law. As he attempted to stop Tyler, a flailing punch from the visitor landed squarely.

Shaw massaged his jaw. Tyler shrugged his shoulders.

Jerome knew who it was and he walked up, adding his own intimidation. The lone man was bobbing and weaving to avoid the punches that surrounded him. Shrugging, Shaw decided to join in.

"Boys! Control yourselves!" Zola cried out as she furiously waved her hands. "This is no way to treat a visitor."

Leaning against the wall, Melista was enjoying the action before her. She had never seen her brother or brothers-in-law in a fight before. She never dreamed that they could be quick on their feet. This new side of them was puzzling, but possibly admirable. Melista turned to Zola and quizzed her concerning the stranger's affiliation. She was answered with shrugged shoulders and horror filled eyes.

Confusion held Kelly-He at bay. He focused on Jerome and Tyler's body language. They were backing off, but kept their fists clenched and their eyes narrow.

The man nonchalantly felt his bloody nose before he popped his neck.

Kelly-He released his fists since he didn't know who the stranger was anyway. Confused, he looked at Tyler. "So... Tyler, are you going to introduce us?"

Jerome scoffed, "It's Gabby's ex."

Anger tightened Kelly-He's fists again.

"Marshall Harrison," ranted Tyler, huffing and puffing. "You got a lot of nerve showing up! What brings you here? Screw that! You're not welcome here! Don't plan to unhitch your trailer here. Get in your Cadillac and drive on!"

"But they found Marian!"

{:-)-]~~{

Chapter 13

Gabriella was starting to feel a bit claustrophobic as she was getting drawn through the growing crowd toward the television. Behind the newscaster, the newsroom displayed pictures and names of missing persons. She could not catch all the names, was Marian in the list somewhere? Pictures were also displayed of formerly missing persons, now confirmed deceased, some with funeral times and locations. More names would be released after their families were notified.

The bright overhead lights suddenly flooded the basement rec-room causing everyone to whine and shade their eyes while jostling each other for a sharpened view of the tv.

It was Melista who had turned the dazzling lights on. She walked over to the crowd and whistled with two fingers. Her family turned to look at her. When she had their full attention, she said, "Gabby, Tyler needs you to come upstairs." Melista raised her voice so all could hear. "Everyone else, stay put! You'll find out quickly enough! Mom, Marcy and Bonnie, you ought to come too." The Sharp women responded by hurrying to the elevator, the quickest route upstairs.

Beverly, Mrs. Shaw and Clifford immediately yelled for quiet and sent the young ones off to play, turning off the TV.

Keeping her head down, Melista refused to look at Gabriella. Harassing her all the way, Gabriella asked questions a mile a minute. Marcy and Bonnie fixated on each other. Melista shook her head from side to side, still not making eye contact. Gabriella rubbed her forearms with both hands, feeling goosebumps popping up everywhere. Giving up on questions, the women proceeded in silence. Reaching the front entry, Gabriella found Tyler, Kelly-He and Jerome blocking her view. When the sea of bodies parted slightly, there stood her ex-husband.

Gabriella's eyes widened, her cheeks reddened and burned. She unconsciously let her mouth drop before closing it again. She grasped at the air as if she were trying to break free from captors. In reality, the only captors she fought were the ghosts of past memories. They lingered in the air causing her face to pale. When she attempted to speak, there was only silence.

"Alright, she's here. Speak your piece and then, you can leave!" Tyler snapped.

But, there wasn't time for anyone to talk because the doorbell rang and a pounding interrupted the awkward silence. The captive audience turned to the door. That is, all except Jerome. He was glaring at Marshall as he stormed to the door. Tyler and Kelly-He stood like a wall between Marshall and Gabriella. There was very little room to squeeze through for a face-to-face conversation.

Opening the door, Jerome was rushed by three men shoving their way into the room. A tall nurse entered hurriedly followed by yet another short pudgy one. A wheelchair was pushed in by an attendant wearing a black trench coat. He reminded Gabriella of a 1930's gangster with his black trench coat, pants and large-brimmed hat. The upturned collar and big hat concealed his face, making him very anonymous. Gabriella lost her concentration on the mysterious man when another nurse entered. Turning back, Gabriella tried to focus on the person in the wheelchair, but she also was a mystery with her legs and feet covered with a bulky blanket and her face well hidden under a hat and veil. At least, Gabriella assumed it was a woman, based on the hat and veil. Her heart stood still with hope. Two extra men followed and shut the door promptly.

The deafening uproar was like a thunderstorm with high-pitched voices and the low angry tones directed at the intruders. Amidst the chaos, Gabriella noticed an even stranger commotion. Everyone within a three foot radius was being pushed away from the wheelchair by the man dressed in black. The other intruders seemed to take the hint and they started pushing people away too. An ear piercing noise came from the direction of the wheelchair, thus startling everyone into complete silence. It would have broken the skylights if they had been glass.

Silence weakened the hostility of the room except for two men who lingered in a tangled debate. Suddenly, Tyler and Marshall flew apart. A flash of light felt like a lightning strike. Static electricity caused the closer ones to wince. Gabriella noticed that only the man in black did not back away, nor did he flinch.

He removed his hat to reveal a blue bandana covering his forehead and ears. Next, he stooped over the wheel chair and removed the hat of the woman who also had a rag covering her forehead. Her first word made Gabriella Sharp crumble. Kelly-He had been close by and caught her. Although she straightened up, Gabriella still felt weak as she staggered toward the couple. The woman in the chair grasped the man's hand on her shoulder. Gabriella walked closer, with Kelly-He and now Tyler to help her.

"What did you say?" gasped Gabriella. Emotions strangled her throat. The muscles in her limbs weakened from shock and trembled.

"Mama," she cried again. "It's me, your lil lady bug." Marian's words broke into fearful tears. The H.E.C.C.s had split up and went home. Marian 'Hope' Harrison had helplessly watched as others before her were reunited with their families. Her fears stirred and bubbled overtime during the last few days, hearing about the reception other families had given their returning mutated loved ones. Because the catfish DNA in her didn't allow more than four hours of sleep a night, she was overtired and distressed in spite of knowing her mother truly loved her.

Gabriella gasped so loudly that the rest of the Sharps in the room followed suit. Although Gabriella had never told anyone she had called her daughter that, everyone knew immediately.

Marian's lips quivered as she queried, "Don't you remember me? Don't you want me back?"

"Baby, my baby! My sweet baby has returned," Gabriella shrieked as she sprinted to her daughter's side. However, when she neared Marian, she paused. Her trembling hands reached out and fingered tufts of her daughter's hair, which were spilling out under her head covering. Next she caressed her daughter's cheeks with both hands. Gabriella bent over and kissed Marian's cheek, fearing the moment would vanish. "Marian, my dear! Oh, how I longed to hold your face again. Your hair seems different and you've grown up, but you're still my girl." Gabriella ran her fingers through her daughter's hair that flowed out from under the blue and white handkerchief.

Marian responded by touching the back of her mother's head and holding her close. One corner of Marian's lips curled up happily and yet her doubtful eyes told a different tale. Her world had been turned upside down. Tyler deliberately paraded up behind Gabriella and placed his hands lovingly on her shoulders. Marian's eyes turned unwavering and cold as she stared at his hands. She had been told about her parents' divorce, but seeing it was strange. Her mother had another man's hands on her shoulders and it was not her father. "Um, Daddy?'

"Right here, Marian." Marshall stepped forward without laying a comforting hand on his daughter's shoulder.

Gabriella glanced to her left shoulder, tossing Marshall a dirty look.

Jayne felt Marian's grip tighten.

Gabriella turned to face Marian. "Come, let me get your wrap and… so you can be more comfortable." She met with resistance when she tried pulling Marian's gloves off.

Marian shook her head to display her discomfort, so Gabriella turned to pull off her daughter's blankets. Shaking her head, Marian tightly gripped the blanket.

The man with the broad-brimmed hat, Jayne, glided around and up to Gabriella. He declared with authority, "I will get Hope settled in. There are further needs to be met to put us all at ease."

Gabriella's hand shot toward Marian as if to protest.

"Darlin', is there a dinin' room or a conference room where we can go and converse?" One of the nurses approached and interrupted Gabriella before she could say anything. "Ever'than's olright. Can't ya see? Why, she's more nervous than a long tailed cat in a room full of rockin' chairs." Billi Joe Sparks tossed her head.

Bewildered, Gabriella stared at the tall nurse with confusion and disbelief. She didn't want to let her baby out of sight; she just got her back. Her husband kindly took her hand and guided her, turning briefly back to tell the nurse to follow them. She nodded and waved him on, hanging back. Agents Hershkin, Austin, Maxwell, and the others oozed toward the dining room.

Mildred stopped Marcy and quietly ordered her to stand guard over the two stairways leading downstairs so that she could keep the children from interfering. After nodding, Marcy stood away from the view of the leftover crowd in the conservatory.

Deeply inhaling, Marian and Jayne breathed a sigh of relief. They looked at Billi, who had stayed behind, with gratitude. She might have a standoffish attitude, but her strength was perception and she had straightaway solved Marian's problem. Billi politely smiled.

"I don't care what anybody else calls you. You will always be Hope to me." Jayne winked. "You were *my* hope. You kept me alive even though you were in coma."

Wrinkling her nose, Hope cocked her head to one side. After a pause, his movements and his soothing countenance worked. "I remember you in my dreams." She relaxed and returned a warm smile. "I'm not ready to expose myself, yet… but… I guess I have already lived long enough as a Hecc to understand that I got to do what I got to do."

Jayne set down the big black briefcase that he had been holding in his other hand. He slowly controlled the wheelchair down the ramp in the center to the main level. Billi marched down the two steps to the left of him.

First to come off of Marian were blankets and then her coat, gloves, and shirt. As soon as her covers were off, Marian enjoyed stretching her stiff muscles. Her hands gripped the sides of the chair, to secure her balance when she stretched her lower limbs.

Jayne took off his overcoat and pants. He kicked off his black crocks. It felt heavenly to get those heavy bulky garments off. He freely stretched every muscle he had, and glanced at Hope.

"Your towels were getting dry; you must have soaked up all your water. It's a good thing that we got here at a decent time."

"Yeah, Jayne," she answered absentmindedly while she eyed the big and little fish ponds in the room. She licked her drying lips.

"Let me check the water, first." Grinning, Jayne opened his case and pulled testing equipment out.

Staring at the ceiling, Billi broke her daze when she heard Jayne and snapped to an attentive stance. She took her heavy bag and set it down. Fishing out a bottle of water, she handed it to a grateful Marian.

The biggest aquariums were located in the corners to the left and right of the front door. Jayne stepped closer to the one on the right. "Wow. It's *way* deeper than it appears." He inspected the partial octagonal tank, leaning over the waist high wall to take samples.

"Looks like a hot tub without the harsh temperature," sang Marian.

Several diamond observation windows were embedded near the floor on the three exposed sides. He tested the water with his hand. "Hmm. The heater probably keeps the temperature in between 74 and 78 degrees for these tropical fish. Good. Hey, you've got to see these beautiful kissing gourami's." After he wheeled Marian over, he allowed her to marvel for a minute. "There are several different kinds of gourami's in here."

"Which ones are the kissing ones."

"See…" Jayne paused, made a kissy face, and turned to face her. The air in the inch between their faces warmed with their combined breath.

Blushing, Hope quickly turned back to spot the fish. "Oh, wait, is that one?"

Jayne nodded.

"Ready," Hope eagerly reached for the water. Her mind raced around an endless track, but she refrained from divulging her confusion aloud.

Grinning from ear to ear, Jayne picked her up and helped her in. Marian shivered a minute until her body accustomed itself, and then she lay down underwater staring at the mesmerizing bubbles fleeing the life-size fake treasure chest's lid. After Hope held still with her back up against the wall, the community fish scampered about, checking her out.

Watching the curious fish, Jayne licked his drying lips. Still wearing swim trunks, he pulled off his black shirt and eased in. Misjudging the depth, he slipped under the water with a splash.

Marsha had heard it, but thought better of leaving her post to ease her curiosity.

Billi busied about and picked up the articles of clothes and placed them neatly together on the wheelchair.

{:-)-]~~{

Chapter 14

In the spacious dining room, the family refused to seat themselves. They warily stood around four extensive homemade wooden tables. Backless benches lined each table and two arm chairs were scooted in on each end. One giant antler candle chandelier hung by a heavy rope pulley in the center of the ceiling. Two huge windows allowed light from the setting sun to dance in the room.

Confusion and shock filled the eyes that stared at the agents. Kelly-He and Jerome crossed their arms. With one hand, Tyler played with his favorite pen fastened to his shirt. His free arm protectively enveloped Gabriella. Jack stood behind Mildred and placed his hands on her shoulders. Leaning her weight next to Mildred, Zola stood with tears forming in her eyes.

"I am so sorry for this intrusion. We tried to call before we came, but the phone rang with no answer. I'm Kenneth Hershkin from the FBI," soothed Kenneth. "This is Peter Austin and Agent Maxwell." He pointed toward Peter and Bogey as they were named.

Tyler politely shook their hands, but kept his expression neutral. His brothers-in law followed Tyler's lead. Jack nodded his welcome.

As soon as Bogey shook the last willing man's hand, he backed up in the corner nearest the closest entrance. Standing at attention with hands clasped solidly behind his back, his alert eyes instinctively watched for trouble.

Speaking in a professional tone, Kenneth rapidly laid out their story using Hope's given name, Marian Harrison. Several times, he stumbled, but he caught himself before he said, 'Hope'. Peter knowingly smiled.

Marshall, who had already heard the story, stood by the huge window, occasionally looking out.

Shaking and still in profound confusion and distress, Gabriella at times missed words or sentences and begged the agent to repeat himself. Her very breath left her lungs. Tingles ran up and down her spine. Numb fingers shook as the blood fled from them. Many times, she had hoped that Marian would return. She had never wanted to accept the possibility of her death. Fear crossed with happiness wrote the wrinkles on her face. Details, bluntly spewed forth, about Marian's condition changed Gabriella's rejoicing to shock.

There was no tiptoeing around the subject. It had to be addressed before the family could mingle. Peter thought it was appropriate to show pictures of Gabriella's daughter so that the family could stare and have time to comprehend the changes. This was the time to openly express their horror, away from ears and hearts that it would hurt and possibly damage irreparably. In some of the first reunions, the mistake of letting the family mingle without preparing them had caused hard feelings all around.

Two profile shots of the head and neck showed the ridges on her forehead and her pointed ears. The pictures that Peter passed around next, showed the upper body profile. Gabriella swallowed hard when she saw her daughter in a bikini top. Her little girl had grown into a woman. However, it wasn't quite as disturbing as the fish features on her daughter's spine. The last couple of pictures showed her lower limbs and tails. The family present handled it well until that shocking sight. Kelly-He openly cried. Tyler gently guided his wife to sit down on a bench. She sat, fixated on the crowd in front of her.

Looking directly at Tyler and Gabriella, Kenneth explained twice that it was still a big shock to Marian herself. She didn't need increased stress about returning beyond what she already had. He begged the Sharp family to be extra supportive.

"How?" Jack needled with despair. "How did this happen?" He sat down.

Tyler shook his head. "Who gave that scientist the right to play God?"

"Who did the maniac think he was?" Jerome objected as he openly gestured with his hands. "Darwin? You haven't caught him, but when you do… can you force him to fix them?"

With dismay in the corner of his lips and a yearning in his eyes, Peter lamented, "Well, there is still a manhunt. We have several leads that we are checking into, but the doctor's office lacked any fingerprints. Some evidence was also misplaced during our analysis… His trash can was full of ashes from the surgical gloves he constantly wore. We don't have a description since he wore a disguise around all the nurses. He-"

"We have come to 'lovingly' call him, the 'I.V. Scissor King'," interrupted Kenneth, oozing with sarcasm. "That was Jayne's doing." When confused faces pondered in his direction, he noted, "The young Heccan out there who escorted your daughter in…"

Tyler abruptly stopped Kenneth. "But how can he walk and Marian cannot?" He scratched his head.

Kenneth stepped back. "Jayne is the only one who has gills, but no tails, we call him a biracial." He paused and stepped closer to his partner. Lowering his voice, Kenneth uttered, "We still need to find him a place…"

Waving his hands frantically, Peter loudly interrupted his co-worker. "Unofficially and you didn't hear it from us. We just don't have probable cause to get warrants on every doctor in the field of regenerative medicine. Everything was typed up and printed out so we have no handwriting to go on. The doctor was careful to take his laptop with him so we have no computer to search. The nurses did all of the filing in the cabinets we found." Peter shrugged and tossed his head back and forth. His shoulders drooped. "We have nothing to go on. Without someone coming forward, we're at a loss. The title and owner for the property of the oceanarium was managed by a man overseas who is untouchable. We're just sitting on our thumbs, trying to clean up the mess. The bottom line is that even if we catch him, there is very little chance that these people can be restored to a fully human form."

"How is humanity going to adjust?" Kelly-He, flabbergasted, raised his voice. "Humans have never had to deal with something like this!"

Tyler opened his mouth, but words failed him. Stiffened, he directed his ears to process the information, but his mind just could not come to terms with it all yet.

"She's pretty much an invalid in the human world, now," Peter stated sadly. He scratched the corner of his jaw.

"She can't walk?" Gabriella couldn't believe it. All her dreams for her daughter's return died. Even with Marian returning, the old normal routines with her daughter would never be the same. Jogging was what she had really missed about spending time with her daughter. On the other hand, their mother-daughter conversations did not have to end. Gabriella turned around and faced the table. Placing her hands on the table, she leaned to lay her head down. Marian's pictures were spread out on the table to Gabriella's right. She trembled as she scooted in front of them. Searching over the photos with her forefinger, she paused when she found the one that had been included in Marian's missing person's report. Picking it up, she closed her eyes, pulled it into her chest and hugged it. Opening her eyes, the recent 'mug shots' of her daughter stared back at her. Gabriella's frown straightened as she laid down the old one and picked up a recent picture. Staring at the figure in the picture, she suddenly grinned from ear to ear.

"Gabby? Honey?" Tyler broke the silence. All eyes, dry and tear-stained, were upon him. "What do you see?"

Everyone turned to stare at Gabriella.

"She's not dead! Tyler, she's alive. My daughter! She's back." Shaking her head, she said, "Having her as a... uh... uh..." She lost her confidence as she peered up at Kenneth. "What did you call them? A Hecc?" Facing Tyler, she grabbed his hand and stood up. "That's better than her being dead or locked up in someone's

195

basement. She's home! Just because she's not completely part of the human race now, doesn't mean I can't love her like I always have! We can make the necessary adjustments even if we have to move. She's home. My baby is home! No more missing puzzle pieces. She *is* found! Marian's *here!*" Gabriella's words choked her.

Kenneth and Peter were immediately bombarded with questions from every person in the room. "How do we take care of her? What doctor will we take her to? How do we know if there is a problem? How much of a normal life can she have? Will she have a shortened lifespan?" Peter and Kenneth lost track of who asked what and gave them answers which sounded like TV channels being rapidly flipped through.

The questions to the two strangers stopped. All attention diverted to Gabriella as she blatantly put the screws to Marshall, "Now, Mr. Harrison, how do you fit into all this?" It was her ex-husband's turn to be stared at.

Kenneth gasped as he inhaled. It was the first time he realized that trouble was brewing and that this wasn't the happy extended family that Marshall Harrison had made it out to be. Kenneth expected Harrison to respond vocally instead of shifting his weight back and forth.

"Mr. Harrison was actually the easier parent to contact in this case. He had put up the reward and been involved in the recent missing persons show so his contact info was readily available." Facing his partner, Kenneth then urged louder than necessary, "You know, Peter, the boss gave us some leave to finish up on paperwork and to rest. And I don't *have* to be anywhere soon. We didn't really help the other Heccs ease into their new lives. Maybe we could hang around a bit?" He turned toward Tyler. "If that would be okay... can you give us directions to the local hotel?"

Tyler nodded with approval, but then shook his head. "The local hotel is too far a drive. We can find you comfortable sleeping bags or cots."

Jack chuckled. "This is a vacation house. There's *plenty* of room."

Kelly-He snorted. "Yea, I'm sure there's spare bedding somewhere."
The group de-stressed with a hearty laugh. The agents chuckled.

As soon as the last person quieted, Tyler stood taller, smiled, and lifted a hand palm upright toward the door. "Well, gentlemen, if we are done here, do you think we could get back to my stepdaughter and get her settled in?"

With a faraway look, Peter shook his head and browsed through the file in front of him. "Not yet, there's another issue that… needs to be discussed."

Gabriella startled everyone as she bolted for the door. She couldn't wait any longer.

Everyone else politely looked at Peter to see if he was going to officially stop her.

A knowing countenance eased onto Peter's face as he shrugged. Two by two, the room cleared out as though in a race. Next, he gathered the pictures up and tossed them in his briefcase. The file with pictures of suspects in his hand that he was planning to show them would have to wait. He placed it back in his case. With a flick of his wrist, he snapped it shut.

With peace filling his heart, Kenneth sighed. Things had gone very smoothly, considering the situation. He had spent the most time with Hope and Jayne. Peter, Kenneth, and Bogey had developed a fondness toward both of them.

Marshall waited in the dining room, staring out the window. Kenneth and Peter found themselves in a jammed dimly lit hallway. Someone had stopped. The domino effect happened even though there was enough room to get by on either side.

Gabriella swayed as she stood in the hallway. No one passed her. She turned around to whisper in Tyler's ear. "What do we…when do we… how do we… introduce Mary? How will our family change? What if Marian decides to go with Marshall?"

Tyler gave her a half-squeeze and a gentle push toward her firstborn daughter. "It will all be okay. I will go talk to Mary and bring her here. You just go on to Marian. Okay, honey?"

Forcing a smile, Gabriella sighed. Continuing on her journey, she eagerly walked into the conservatory only to suddenly stop again. The lonely front door stood wide open. "Marian!" Gabriella yelled as she broke into a run toward the door.

The nurse charged through the open door in a panic and peered around.

A splash of water resounded, a cough, and then a soft voice. "I'm over here, mama!" Marian had sympathetically hollered as best as she could as she continued to clear her throat. A splash sounded and another splash followed.

The crowd hurried in the direction of the voice.

Still a little panicked, Gabriella ran toward the tank and slipped on a wet spot on the white large tiled floor. Reaching out, she grabbed the thick edge to stop herself from falling in face first. Gabriella backed up as Marian appeared right in front of her. Jayne popped up on Marian's right startling Gabriella into jerking even further back.

Jayne coughed.

Marian and the stranger had both taken off their handkerchiefs. Gabriella's startled expression morphed into love and acceptance. No one spoke. Mother and daughter made eye contact until their giggles turned to laughter. Marian coughed and her eyes sheepishly darted away. Gabriella's incredulous stare was distracted and briefly searched the room before her roaming eyes again fixed on her daughter.

Suddenly without warning, Marian wildly threw her arms around Gabriella. "Thanks, mom."

Gabriella's soaked white blouse and blue jeans absorbed another dousing. "For what, baby doll?" She gently pulled her shirt away from her skin.

"For not ever giving up on me and still loving me."

Mildred walked over and whispered to Marsha. Mildred stood in the middle of the two stairways while Marsha disappeared up the stairs. She returned and handed a towel bundle to her confused sister-in-law, Gabriella, who was soaked to the flesh.

Looking down, Gabriella noticed how unsuitable her white shirt was in a room full of family and strangers. She made a mad dash to the closest bathroom. Out of the corner of her eye, she saw Tyler enter with a bouncing Mary.

Within five minutes, Gabriella returned wearing a floral one-piece swimsuit and blue see-through beach dress. She stood out of sight and watched. A loving expression spread over her whole face, making her glow as if she were a new mother. A movement caught her eye. Marshall sauntered out the front door, left it ajar and paced in and out of sight, talking on his cell phone.

Standing tall, Gabriella walked up to Mary, Marian, and Tyler. "Where did everyone go?" Gabriella whispered to Tyler.

"Honey, everyone up here said hello and then went down to talk with the others. The two lead agents went with them. The other is right behind you." He pointed at Bogey, who beamed.

Jayne surfaced with a splash.

Mary giggled. Completely satisfied with having a sister, she didn't realize someone else was hidden under the water.

Marian winked at her mom while she told Mary, "This here is my friend, Jayne."

"But, *Jane* is a *girl's* name," Mary whined.

A poker face grin crossed Jayne's lips before he let a brittle chuckle escape. Winking in Mary's direction, he teased. "Not always, little lady. Mine is not spelled J-a-n-e; it's spelled J-a-*y*-n-e." Turning to Marian, he excused himself. "Hey, Hope, I'm going to go take a walk, okay?" She nodded her approval. As Jayne hopped out, Tyler handed him a towel.

"He called you 'Hope', big *sister*," protested Mary. "Why?" She was genuinely concerned. "Doesn't he know your name?"

A light clicked on in Gabriella's mind. She jerked her head to watch Jayne. That wasn't the first time she heard him call her 'Hope'. It was, however, the first time that she made the connection.

Coming across as oblivious, Jayne used the towel to dry his feet and legs. The rest of his skin enjoyed the water dripping and running toward gravity's pull. It had a pleasant cooling sensation considering the late summer heat. Stepping outside, he yearned to talk with Marshall and have a look outside. Jayne nodded at Marshall, stopped and stared. Beyond the prairie grass stood a tall black iron fence built into two columnar brick fence posts. Black iron arched over the driveway with the family name 'Sharp' forged with sharp edges. Under the archway, busy-body reporters, FBI, and the closest local police danced in conversation while pacing the property line.

Hysterically laughing, Gabriella tottered into the pond. In between breaths and keeping her head above water, she said, "I never imagined… I would be swimming… in our fish tank! I never… realized how deep this is. I knew it went into the basement, but…" Gabriella's head searched to look at her husband. "Tyler! This must be why you said that you didn't want to change the occupants unless you had to. You couldn't catch them even if you wanted to!"

"The tanks depth from here…" Tyler's right hand hovered over the edge. "…is exactly 14 feet down to the bottom." He placed his hand palm down over the edge of a side. "Its wall is only three feet above this floor," explained Tyler. "From the corner of the house, they have an eight foot radius. Access to the pumps, filters, heaters and other maintenance equipment is located in the side walls of the walk-in game closet which is in between the two tanks in the basement." For emphasis, he pointed to the coat closet behind the tank before returning his hand to his side. "We were originally going to put sharks in there, but evidently they need a round tank instead. I forgot to consult with a tank expert about it before we built it. Dad was mad. He won't let me help with planning architectural structures anymore. Don't you remember?"

Gabriella focused inward. The ghost of days past visited her and her mind flashed through years of walking in a daze. Never fully recovering from her grief, life had always been held at bay. Even the positive days were shadowed with sadness. Her daughter returned alive, gave Gabriella a miraculous second chance. *What would have happened if she was never found? Would I have ever found my way back to happiness?*

Noticing his wife's faraway look, Tyler knowingly smiled. "Come on, Mary, let's go play downstairs." He stood up. It was a wonder that Mary politely agreed. They went downstairs hand in hand and ran into the cousins pouring upstairs.

"Line up, children. Form a line. Please," Marsha shouted above the slight roar. "Just a quick 'hello-glad-your-back or nice-to-meet-you' then off you go!"

The children complied and arranged themselves in a line with stragglers standing in small packs.

Jayne walked back inside the house. Hope motioned for him to approach her.

"There's so many of them," Hope whispered to him. Her eyes pleaded with him to save her.

Leaning forward, Jayne lowered his voice. "Didn't you tell me back at the shop that you *wanted* a big family?" He reached into the water and splashed his face because he could, not that it was exactly necessary at the moment.

"I met some of them before..." Hope's low voice wavered. "They were just mom's friend's kids... back then."

"Now they are family."

"Step."

"Step is family. At least they want to be family," hissed Jayne. He lifted his voice with tenderness. "Welcome them as such." Hope nodded as Jayne turned on his heel and picked his way to find a semi-remote location.

Standing by the masculine fountain, Jayne's lusterless eyes soaked in the never-ending line of cousins. The fact that he had never been in the same room with so many people tainted his view. First, it was just him and his mom, and then at the pet shop the most he was with at one time was, maybe, twelve people. Immediately, Jayne knew what the animals felt like when affected by zoochosis, but with all the stares aimed at him. He might not have been a complete

H.E.C.C., but he had features that were just as noticeable. Feeling self-conscious, he snatched up his bandana and punctually tied it back on. This was the only home where he had stayed to help a H.E.C.C. adjust. Duty called upon his strength again, so Jayne faked a pleasant demeanor. Sitting down on the circular bench surrounding a tree and flowers, he focused his eyes on Hope. Darkened thoughts wrote a stale glaze over his eyes and furrowed his eyebrows. Here, spread before him was a huge loving family while Jayne had no known family to escape to. *If only Dee's living arrangement included a bedroom. Where am I to go? I'm too old for an orphanage, or adoption.* A quick sideways glance over his shoulder told him that no eyes were directly on him, so he let his shoulders droop. His body slumped as his eyes darted about. They fixated on the nearby old-fashioned claw-footed porcelain tub. Three large goldfish scouted to and fro over the bottom. Glancing back up at the crowd, Jayne sadly sighed.

One pair of eyes noticed the faraway, miserable exhale and the dark cloudy expression on Jayne's face. Gabriella attempted to make eye contact with Marian, but failed. When Marian wasn't politely answering questions or asking how each cousin was related, she dove under to catch a breath of peace and a gill-full of water. Gabriella crept out of the water and grabbed her beach towel. She hurriedly patted her face and covered her body with it before she marched up to Jayne. It took a bit of maneuvering through the cousins and the men, but she managed.

Jayne startled. Correcting his posture, his eyebrows danced trying to straighten into a happy wrinkle. His lips managed to straighten out, but failed to lift his cheeks.

"Young man, perhaps you will join me for a cup of tea in the kitchen?"

Speculating and trying to read her, Jayne deliberated before answering. "Yes, ma'am."

Gabriella spun on her heel and walked away. "Follow me, please."

Jumping on his toes, he sprinted to catch up with her. They excused themselves through the lengthy line to squeeze into the hallway. Once they reached the kitchen, they were told to stay put. Marsha insisted on them not entering too deeply into the kitchen because Zola, Mildred, Marsha, Bonnie, and Beverly were busy making a late snack. Marsha found a teapot in the cupboard. On the double, she hurried to the open fireplace. To the right of it, she grabbed a hot pad off a hook and used it to pour water from the hot kettle into the pot. Bonnie briskly met her with a teacart, stopping to give her a chance to set the teapot down before she pushed the cart to Gabriella.

Taking over the cart, Gabriella pushed it toward the tea-room. Jayne followed.

Peter and Kenneth greeted Gabriella and Jayne in the hall.

"Would you gentlemen like to join us?" When they politely smiled and nodded, Gabriella backed up. She pushed the cart into the wooden room. The four then sat down for a cup of tea.

Gabriella played hostess and 'Guardian of the Tea Pot' as she poured the water in their cups with one hand. In the other, she held an ornate wooden box that contained a variety of tea to choose from. Once she sat down with her own cup, she broke the silence, "It is… Jayne." She blew on the surface of her tea and sipped it. "Right?"

Jayne nodded with a half-smile and leaned forward.

Opening her mouth several times, Gabriella remained speechless. She gave up and closed her lips tightly without uttering a word. Sitting back, she sipped her tea.

Jayne's voice quavered. "Do you have questions about your daughter?"

"No," Gabriella hesitated. "Jayne, I brought you in here to talk about you." Setting her cup down, she said, "Would you care to share your story? I haven't heard it yet."

"My story…ummm…. What? My story…. Hmm…what now?" He stumbled through his words because he had already concluded from his visit with Marshall that Gabriella's only concern was her missing daughter. "Where do you want me to start?"

"Why don't you start by telling me about where you were before the pet shop? Do you have family to go back to? Where's your mother? Just talk and tell us your story before you met Hope."

When Gabriella referred to her daughter as 'Hope', that got his attention making him straighten up. He felt noticed.

"Why do you call her 'Hope'?" Gabriella admired his renewed strength. "Did you name her that?"

Jayne answered her previous questions and then went on to new ones. He greedily ate up her attention, eager to have a new acquaintance. Jayne expressed all that he could recall with many details. He talked a lot about Jonathon and Doug. He told the stories of their difficult friendship. He dove into the good moments and the hard times with great enthusiasm. To the surprise of the two men, Jayne ended in tears.

Peter and Kenneth were farther away from the other two and gave each other a look. No considerable thought had been given to the vast length of time during which Jayne acted strong for the rest of the H.E.C.C.s while he himself struggled. The fact that he strutted around on two feet seemed so normal that they had forgotten that he too was one of the victims. They gave each other a knowing glance and hid behind a sip of tea. Neither drank hot tea often, but they were sure there would be bountiful supplies of it in this house. At least it was pleasing, even if it tasted like a poor coffee substitute. Kenneth and Peter looked around uncomfortably, but soon, the masculine scenery put them at ease.

Despite how painful it was, Jayne discovered how healing it was to let it all out. Gabriella comforted him from a distance. She had tried to not lose eye contact even when she got up to get him a tissue, but he shook it off before she could grab it. It pleased Jayne the delicate way the tears soothed and wet the skin on his arms even if they hurt his eyes when they welled up.

Gabriella herself was rushing through a healing process. She was getting over the shock of her reunion with Marian and having been given a second chance. Gabriella refused to pass up this chance of living again. She decided at that moment that if she lost another loved one or Marian again, she would continue living life to the fullest. Gabriella visited with Jayne about life at the Sharp family vacation home, hoping to ease him into the comfort of their home.

Jayne skipped the part where he had kissed Hope and when they held each other. He concluded with their departure from the pet shop.

Silence once again fell over them, causing time to tick by with everyone finishing their last drop of tea.

Without warning, Jerome popped in to call them to snacks. The agents followed him while Gabriella rounded up the teatime mess. Jayne took off toward Hope, only to find that she wasn't in the aquarium. Deciding that he could not do without a refreshing dip, he stepped in for a short but sweet soak. After Jayne coughed and clambered back out, he toweled off completely.

Bitter and sweet smells taunted him from the hallway. Each nostril tickled with delight as he followed them to an open doorway crowded with a few stragglers. Marsha, Mildred, and Bonnie rolled in after Jayne. A loud shrill whistle parted the air signaling everyone to sit down. Finger-food, bowls of cheese, crackers, jerky, and fresh vegetables dotted the tables. Apple jelly, dried apples, apple butter and apple wine were passed around to those who had the acquired taste. Jayne was overwhelmed. Other than the 'feast' at the aquarium, he had never eaten with more than three people before, but he took it all in. Gabriella's comforting words, *Our home is your home*, reassured him that it was safe to eat and enjoy the company. Billy, William, Willetta and Gabe included Jayne in their pleasant conversation and humor.

Snacks were politely passed, but greedily gulped down. The newness had worn off and the huge family and strangers became one. Conversation was in an uproar. Dessert was served. The late hour brought on a sneak attack of yawning all around. Peter and Kenneth asked to sleep in the wooden room and, to their satisfaction, Jack granted their wish. It wasn't hard for most to yield to the sandman; they were tired from the long, stressful day. Bogey, the rookie agent, and the nurses left. The nurses wanted to get back to their own lives.

The reporters were promised interviews if they left the property and followed Bogey to a removed, but disclosed location.

Marshall went out to his car where a pop-up camper trailer was hitched. He had set it up while the cousins met Marian. He ate snacks with the family, said goodnight to Marian and then rushed out to the camper.

After changing into her purple silk shirt, silk pants, and a pink cotton robe, Gabriella hurried about on the second floor. Her arms pumped as she raced from one room to the next and back again. Tyler gently stopped her in the hallway, but he spoke up as she attempted to sidestep him.

Confused, Tyler tugged her up against him in his white t-shirt and jogging pants. "What are you doing, honey?"

"I am finding beds for Marian and Jayne." Her intense eyes looked down her nose at him.

Slowly shaking his head, Tyler still didn't understand. His hands lifted and rested on her shoulders. "Honey, they're staying in the conservatory."

"Do you think I'm going to let my grown up daughter sleep by someone of the opposite sex?"

"I think that it is the farthest thing from their minds right now."

Shrugging her shoulders, Gabriella left Tyler in a huff. After she had moved a few nephews and nieces around, she walked down the stairs to the conservatory. Marian was floating patiently in the water. A repetitive whooshing sound reached her ears. One crumbled up mess of blue plastic lay next to Jayne's foot. The purple one filled with life as Jayne pumped up the floating bed with a foot pump. Once it had reached its max, he closed the tube shut and handed it to the awaiting Hope. She had no trouble placing it in the water behind her and took a dive while she waited for Jayne's bed.

"Uh…" Not knowing what to say, Gabriella played with the surface of the water. Hope surfaced, coughed, and crisscrossed her arms on the edge to hold her head out.

Gabriella started speaking in a whisper, but ended her suggestion with a normal tone. "There's a bed in the toddler room for you. It's right by me and it's in the same room as Mary. You could sleep in my private bathtub."

"Um… No thanks, mom." Marian continued eyeing Jayne's every movement as he pumped up the bed. "This will be more comfortable."

"There's a bed for Jayne in the boy's bunk room, too."

Overhearing the conversation, Jayne politely butted in. "Until we know more about how long we can stay *out* of the water, I think it would be best to sleep *in* the water."

"Oh" was all the concerned mother could say.

After Jayne finished, he handed his floatation device to Hope and placed the pump back in his huge black military duffle bag. Locating a dry spot on the floor, Jayne used it to hop onto the edge of the tank. Spinning carelessly around, he fell into the water. "Whee-heee." *Splash*

"Hey!" Gabriella protested as she was splashed. Her silk pajamas clung to her skin.

The two arranged the beds as best they could in the small space they had to work with. Gabriella stifled giggles. The two crawled precariously into their beds and slipped underwater several times.

Mildred entered the room. Her bright eyes and pleasant nature warmed the atmosphere. "Now, Marian, Grandpa Jack and I are in the bedroom right there." The name grandma had spoken, rolled off her tongue just like it had when she visited Marian when the girl was ten. "If you need us, just holler. Okay?" After Marian nodded an okay, Mildred left. She knew that Gabriella wished to be the last one to leave her daughter's side.

"Do you want me to find a cot and sleep by you?" Gabriella didn't dare leave Marian's side for fear that she would close her eyes and the healing dream would end.

"No, Mama." Marian read her mother's worried face. "I'll be okay. We'll be okay. Don't worry. I'll be here in the morning. Get a good night's rest in your bed. Hecc's like the moonlight so we probably won't go to sleep right away."

"Oh… Okay… Good night, Marian."

"Sleep tight."

Gabriella hesitated, "Don't let the bed bugs bite." Their old routine seemed silly now.

"If they do," asked Marian without skipping a beat.

"Take a shoe… and stomp that little critter right in two."

Marian giggled, her warm smile showing her pearly whites.

Blowing her a kiss, Gabriella reluctantly shuffled back. Marian playfully caught it and put it on her cheek. Smiling, Gabriella then walked upstairs with a faraway gaze. She bumped into Tyler on the stairway and he escorted her in his arms up to their room.

The house quieted down. The wind whistled against the windows. Crickets loudly schemed with each other to irritate the occupants.

In the front room, Jayne and Hope could not sleep. They could see each other by the sparkling moonlight that shone from the tall rectangular sky-lights. They whispered, sighed, and giggled. Quietly they splashed each other. Their social bonding tightened. There wasn't really enough room for a whole lot of fish-play and diving with the 'beds' in there. They also had to watch out for the other occupants. Besides, it was supposed to be bedtime. The H.E.C.C.s didn't need the long human sleep cycles and they especially didn't want it during the night, when the moon called to them. The peaceful darkness seemed to bring out stored-up energy. Three hours before daylight, the silence of the house finally caressed the two into a deep sleep.

{:-)-]~~{

Birth of an Octopus

Good News for Whom?

Chapter 15

ayne and Marian were included in the new schedule at the Sharp's. Jack, Mildred, and Melista rented out their house and moved in to help Tyler. Tyler's sisters and their families returned to their homes for three weeks before returning as well. A steady stream of guests flowed through the house. This cool and cloudy first Wednesday of November was no different.

Jayne sat with his back against the large white planter in the conservatory. Delicate leaves of a mimosa hovered above his head. Both arms crossed tightly against his chest. His rigid muscles rippled with tremors. The tension sent burning chills throughout his body. Knots tied his uneasy stomach to his throat. His green swim trunks were completely dry. Cold eyes bore holes into Hope's aquarium, shifting to the closed front door and back to the basin again.

Diiiiiiiinnnnnnnggggggg. Dooooonnnnnnng.

Hopping up, Jayne bolted for the door. Politeness toned his sharp wrinkles into a composed smile. Opening the door, he greeted the visitor. "Oh, so glad you could make it! How was your flight?"

"It was delayed a bit, but I am here. Finally." The Native American with athletic build firmly shook Jayne's hand with his right hand. In his left hand, he clutched the handle of a briefcase and a black leather bag that could pass as a small gym bag. His fingers awkwardly gripped a folder. He set his load down. "With all the flying I do now, I ended up selling my place." His right hand caressed the blood back into his left hand.

"Where's your stuff?"

"At my mother's cabin in Colorado." Dressed in a black suit, tie and white shirt, his shoulders dropped as he sighed. The man straightened his shoulders and stood taller. Hazel squinty-eyes over a slight hawk nose searched the room. "Where is she?"

"Over here," Jayne nodded in Hope's direction and closed the front door. "She's hiding."

"Probably thinks I'm here to discuss politics with you." The Indian winked at Jayne as the two descended two steps and proceeded to casually walk over to the tank. He hesitated. "Did you tell her to expect me?"

"Nope." Shaking his head, Jayne reached his hand over the edge of the water and swirled it. "Hope, he is here to see you. Not me."

The visitor leaned over the edge and stared at the surface of the water.

Near the back wall, the surface of the water broke with her hands. Hope's face appeared. She coughed and hugged the wall with her back.

"It's true, Hope," soothed Jayne. "He's not here to talk to me or to talk about politics."

"No dark horror stories of Hecc families selling their kin to settle the debt of looking for them?" Hope tossed her head with sarcasm. When she stopped talking, she swam slowly toward Jayne's open arms.

"Martin said those claims were unsupported." The visitor raised his eyebrows. "Allegations were made, but since there was nothing for the police to go on, the matter was dropped."

Jayne reassured Hope that she was safe from any circus side shows.

When Hope reached the edge, she hoisted herself up on it. The splash forced the stranger to back up to remain dry.

"Who's Martin?" quizzed Hope in her blue bikini top. Flicking her hair, water was flung against the back wall. She lifted her lower limbs over the edge one at a time with her thighs tucked tightly together.

Kneeling over, Jayne cocked an intense stare at Hope as he set the brakes on the wheelchair.

Oblivious to Jayne's annoyance, Hope seductively smiled and batted her eyelashes at their stunning visitor. His shoulder length black hair sparked her attention. Every time he shifted his head, a tiny braid with a feather flashed into her view. His thin side burns moved a little as his strong jaw shifted into a courteous expression.

With Hope and her admirer making eye contact, neither noticed Jayne speaking through gritted teeth. "You would have known if you would meet people with me when I ask you to."

The man said with a syrupy voice, "He's the Hecc's official lawyer, Martin Tucker."

Hope reached with open arms hinting to the stranger that she solicited his help. She shrieked when Jayne roughly grabbed her and plopped her in her wheelchair.

"Jayne," objected the visitor with a snarl. "That was uncalled for!"

Thump thump thump could be heard coming from the stairwell, followed by heavy panting. With all eyes watching the stairs, Jayne released the wheelchair breaks without anyone noticing.

Gabriella appeared completely out of breath. Instead of her usual comfortable clothes, she wore a nicely tailored fitted shirt with blue jeans. She held her stomach in agony as she could not find the balance for her lungs.

"Aha," exclaimed Tyler with a sing song. "Your way is faster, Gabby." He winked at her as he confidently strode over to where she stood, tenderly pulling her up to a standing position. Love wrinkled his face with genuine concern and a joyous air about him. "Gabby, honey, breathe in and out." Wrapping his arms around her waist, he pulled hers into his. Gabriella stared deeply into his eyes and caught her breath. They turned around and faced their guest.

"You must be Dr. Derrick Jensen." Tyler lurched closer with his arm dragging his wife along. Reaching his hand toward Derrick, Tyler noted, "Glad you could make it."

The wheelchair groaned as Marian reached with both hands, trying to scramble back to the safety of the tank.

Suddenly and without warning, Jayne whisked Hope away. "Ah, ah, ah!"

Derrick firmly shook Tyler's hand. "Yes. You must be Tyler and Gabriella. I've heard more about you than any of the other Hecc families." He grinned.

Marian crossed her arms and slumped into the chair.

Jayne stepped closer to Tyler and Dr. Jensen. "Out of all the osteopath candidates, the Heccs chose Dr. Jensen as their official doctor for his compassion, raw talent, and humor. Hope was the only one not to vote."

"Ah, honey," fretted Gabriella. Narrowing her eyes, she tilted her head and looked at Marian. Her disgruntled daughter did not return her gaze.

Dr. Jensen hurried to the door and scooped up his briefcase.

Jayne stared hard at the folder in Jensen's hand.

"Yes, Jayne, this is yours." Dr. Jensen handed Jayne the folder.

After skipping away from the commotion, Jayne found a place on the floor and tore into the folder.

"What's that?" inquired Gabriella. She rested her hands on the back of Marian's chair. Marian twiddled her thumbs.

"The FBI finally released complete copies of the files left at the pet shop by the 'I.V. Scissor King' to me," Dr. Jensen opened and reached into his briefcase. Pulling out a file, Jensen said, "Here, this contains 'Hope' Marian Jennifer Harrison's. There are also papers from the Centers for Disease Control and Prevention. By order of the Director of the US Dept. of Health and Human Services, all H.E.C.C.s will be giving bi-monthly samples of blood, skin and excretions. The CDC will receive copies of all lab work and physical exams that I perform. They have also issued a ban against all the Heccs from dating or sexual relations."

Hope rolled her eyes.

Jayne snorted.

"Wait," Tyler scoffed. "How are they going to prevent the ones that are already married?"

"They made me issue birth control to them. Actually I have to give it to all of the Heccs."

"Wow... wait," interrupted Tyler. "Wouldn't the rules of sterilization from crossbreeding apply here." Tyler's face wrinkled as his lips soured puckered with distaste.

Inhaling deep, Dr. Jensen faced Tyler with his body. Compassion kept his voice steady and strong. "The CDC is really much more concerned about the effects of a second generation than dating. However, since what we knew as concrete "separation of races" has been interfered with...well...I can understand why they do not wish to take any chances." Entering into Tyler's personal space, Dr. Jensen lowered his voice as his body quivered with justifiable fear. "What if the birth control doesn't work? That...is the main reason for them to discourage dating. They cannot overstep their... They cannot legally forbid married couples."

Tightening his chin, Tyler nodded. He did not continue the difficult subject.

Dr. Jensen cleared his throat. "Mrs. Sharp," His lips curled with a courteous smile in her general direction. "I did not get many files from the doctors you gave me."

"No?" Gabriella hobbled toward the doctor.

"Marian was getting close to the age where she would have been legally declared dead."

Gabriella's knees knocked. Tyler shifted over to stand beside her. He wrapped his arm around her waist to comfort and steady her.

"I also included a small portion of research to aide in meeting Hope's... I mean, Marian's dietary needs."

Tyler and Gabriella's eyes met and their shoulders shrugged.

Dr. Jensen continued. "She will need to increase the portions of fish in her diet and seaweeds like hijiki, miyeok, and carola..."

Tyler interrupted. "We knew about the fish." He laughed. "It's all we can do to keep the freezers stocked. We had to purchase an extra freezer."

"Yeah," Gabriella chuckled. "We have had to increase the portions of fish in our own diet. Did you include any recipes? I could use something new." she said with a wry grin.

"Come to think about it…" Dr. Jensen placed a finger to his chin in deep concentration. "I did find a recipe for miyeok guk."

Gabriella and Tyler simultaneously blurted, "What's that?"

Dr. Jensen politely smiled. "It's a Korean soup that is traditionally eaten on birthdays."

"Hmmm." Tyler lifted his chin momentarily to look at the ceiling. "Does it have fish in it?"

"Not traditionally, but I'm sure your daughter would like it, if you added it." Dr. Jensen sighed.

Gabriella regarded her stomach. "We have definitely accustomed our taste buds to sushi. Marian loves salmon, rice, cream cheese, and vegetables wrapped with seaweed."

Tyler swallowed as he licked his lips.

"Hmm." Eyeing the door, Dr. Jensen tapped his foot. "As soon as the nurse gets here, we'll get started."

"Nurse?" Gabriella left Tyler's side to stand next to Marian.

"Yes." Dr. Jensen's pleasant expression turned upside down. "I have had the darndest trouble with hospitals not cooperating with me for simple things like lab work. The Heccs lead such a bubble-like lifestyle that all I really need is the use of their facilities for check-ups. I would like to use the original H.E.C.C. nurses, but we are waiting on the courts to get through with them first. With Martin's help, I have privileges to use hospitals in emergencies and I have full cooperation with the lab…"

"But?" Tyler raised his right hand with the palm up before placing it back at his side.

"But," Dr. Jensen hesitated. "All routine visits will be performed in the homes. Home Health Aids from the community hospital are supposed to come and assist me as needed."

Bang bang bang echoed the front door.

Jayne didn't look up. The papers spread out before him took precedence.

"Speaking of the leech," sang Dr. Jensen.

Tyler and Gabriella both giggled. Tyler answered the door and welcomed the stocky black nurse.

Filters on the tanks echoed their disdain toward peace and quiet. Jayne continued reading the copies in his medical folder. All voices became indistinguishable and unrecognizable and sounded similar to Charlie Brown's teacher; "Wah waw waw." Jayne silently read and reread the 'I.V. Scissor King's words that jumped off the page cradled in his hands. '*Suffocation caused by submersion in water...* The giant room visually buckled and swayed for him. *...subject recovered with shock therapy, but nonresponsive...* The bright lights in the room increased and burned Jayne's cheeks. *... subject in vegetative state with oxygen mask...* He dropped the record as the words before him turned into chaos and scribbles. Lifting a hand in front of his face, Jayne stared intently as the fingers visually outnumbered his hand. Closing his eyes, Jayne breathed deeply in and out. A deathly silence filled the blackness in the focus of his tightened eyes and cheeks. His protesting teeth angrily ground against each other.

A presence blocked the light and towered over Jayne. He ignored the nurse as she drew his blood.

Jayne refused to look up or open his eyes as another person entered Jayne's personal space. When the second person wouldn't budge, Jayne wrinkled his nose and momentarily opened one eye. His eyelash did not allow for Jayne to distinguish the person. He opened the one eye again and then opened both eyes. Tilting his head up, he saw Dr. Jensen's kind face calmly eyeballing him. Jayne relaxed and returned the genuine smile.

"See," said the nurse with a strong rich voice. "That wasn't so bad." Holding the large needle with one hand, she pulled out a tube and placed it in a special courier box designed for the transport of blood. Reaching with her free hand, she grabbed another empty tube and drew another sample. She released him and finished loading the courier box.

With a deep inhale and exhale, Jayne squatted in front of his mess. Right away, he gathered the strewn papers and slipped them into his folder.

Dr. Jensen turned on his heel. Absentmindedly, he gathered his paperwork and his bag.

Standing up, Jayne strolled his way over to the bench and set his folder on it. Then, he turned and edged over to Hope.

The nurse swiftly and quietly gathered up her things. With a nonchalant air, she excused herself saying she had to make haste to deal with the blood samples. She fumbled out the door and closed it behind her.

Tyler and Gabriella held each other as they faced one another. They positively conversed about possible recipe alterations, substitutions, and new ideas. They rejoiced over Dr. Jensen's findings that Marian's muscle tone and stamina had greatly improved. Dr. Jensen assured them that he would consult with some dietitians for ideas for recipes.

Placing his right hand behind Hope's back, Jayne soothed. "Yeah, Hope, that wasn't so bad." Making full eye contact, Jayne placed his left hand under her. Hope's fingers traced his forearms and ran them over his biceps up to rest around his neck with a vice-like grip. Without complaint, Jayne cradled her. The corner of his mouth twitched as he stole a sideways glance at her.

Hope's dilated pupils never left his, but Jayne's eyes shifted to search out the whereabouts of the tank. Placing one foot in front of the other became difficult for Jayne. His eyebrows raised as his closed mouth settled into a firm smile. Blood doubled through his veins as Hope's closeness affected his rising temperature.

The fingers on her left hand traced the Heccan bumps on the back of his neck. When he didn't look at her, Hope liberated her right hand. She caressed the bare warm skin on his chest which reacted by firming his fit and athletic pecks. He was bouncing her to where she had to clasp her hands around his neck. Placing her head on his shoulder, Hope's eyelashes fluttered as she inched her lips up to blow on his ear. Reaching the tank, Jayne grinned wide and set her on the three inch edge. Both startled as Dr. Jensen's voice boomed.

"There will be none of that." With sorrow in his eyes, Dr. Jensen coaxed. "Jayne, you are their ambassador. They look up to you. It is the utmost necessity that you set the best and most compliant example. You knew about the ban before it even became enforceable."

Hope disappeared under the water with a splash.

With a plastic grin, Jayne nodded and plodded down the hall toward the wooden room to light a wine tasting Hookah, a sad substitute for Hope's sweet lips.

{:-)-]~~{

Chapter 16

Constant visitors and phone calls gobbled up more of Jayne's free time. His ambassadorial duties were demanding all his energy and he was hiding in his busyness. Several weeks passed with Jayne carefully avoiding Hope. Being close, but not allowed to care, to love, was too much for either of them. *Better to suffer separately,* he thought.

Alone and in the dark, Jayne sat on the couch in the den at eleven o'clock on a Saturday night. Sharp stabbing pains crawled over him. He licked his dry lips. Crushing pounds pressed on his lungs. The lights and shadows flickering from the television cast an eerie phantom that mixed with the words booming from the religious program, throwing emotional, ghastly grenades at Jayne. The television preacher ranted angrily and openly that the sins of the hags' forefathers had caused this disease and that it served them right. Grabbing the remote off the coffee table, Jayne flipped the channel.

Another program and yet one more intolerant charlatan who did not know or want to know Jayne Flynn. Tears fell from the reddened cheeks of the famous TV preacher as his hands danced about to the audience behind the lens. With great emotion, he emphasized every word. "The Apocalypse is here. The time is now. Repent. Dark times are here. Repent. The first of the four horsemen has arrived. They are conquering us by infiltrating the pure bloodline of humanity. These Human Electric Cave Catfish will be the death of us all. Their souls are possessed with the spirit of Dagon!" He cringed. "Pray. Pray! Pray for your souls! Your families' souls! Your neighbors! ...And if you call and make a tax deductible donation, I will personally pray for the safety of *your* soul. We need to pray for the protection of all the God fearing individuals from the plague of these... these 'Fish People'! The sins of this nation will cause God's wrath to be poured upon us. The end draws near. Listen, brothers and sisters, humanity has been tampered with..."

After Jayne muted it, he flipped on the quick menu. The TV flashed as it changed to a news channel. As the mute came off, the funny cheesy chip commercial soothed Jayne's soul. Then, anger hardened his heart and tightened his jaw. Leaning forward, Jayne slammed the remote on the coffee table in front on him.

"Easy there, tiger."

Jayne jumped up and faced the intruder with both fists armed and dangerous. His unique eye trait sparkled brilliantly in the low light of the room.

Dressed in black sweat pants and a white t-shirt, Tyler wore a cautious mug. He bounced his hands in the air in Jayne's direction. "Easy, Jayne. It's me... Tyler." When Tyler saw Jayne disarm by dropping his hands to his sides, Tyler approached him. "Hey, you need a tag team?" Placing one hand on Jayne's shoulder, Tyler gently guided Jayne to the couch to sit down. Tyler sat on the edge ready to jump at a moment's notice.

"Tag team?" asked Jayne as he sat down. He quickly placed both hands on his head, resting his elbows on his knees.

"You know, someone to take over when you crave a quiet minute to yourself."

Commercials on the television ended. A repeat of the evening news began. After an introduction from the anchor, a scientist dressed in a blue lab coat pushed his explanation for the 'uncommon virus'. "A new incurable strain of Ichthyosis must be affecting the public. We must quarantine those contaminated so we can get answers on how to stop it! We need to get samples of their blood and create a vaccine so that we can keep this disease from spreading!"

Standing up, Jayne turned his back on the TV. With both hands on his head, he paced the den never looking at the TV, but not turning it off.

Tyler's mouth dropped.

Humanistic racists hijacked the evening news with their hate. "If we let them live, scientists will be experimenting on everything. What's next? Bovine/humans? Centaurs? Werewolves? Next thing you know, we'll have sparkling vampires! Where would the moral issues end? Would the bovine/humans be considered meat or men? Would it be considered bestiality for them to be wed with a human?" Others held tight to their conspiracy theories. "The government defends their existence! It was all a governmental experiment! Who will they experiment on next? Political opposition?"

Promoters of evolution commented next on the H.E.C.C.s. A sample of their DNA would prove that they were right all along. Once they had that proof, they declared that Darwinism needed to be forcefully pushed into private schools.

The news anchor objectively announced, "Ever since the Heccs were rescued, petitioners have hounded the victims' families and stirred public opinion. These individuals want to keep those that perished during the experiments from being buried and the evidence destroyed. Several of the bereaved families actually backed the petition saying 'Our loved ones died so that others could live!' During the heated debates, memorial services had been conducted for the victims, but included empty caskets. Comparisons were drawn to the Nazi doctor, Josef Mengele, resulting in the I.V. Scissor King's nickname being regarded with the same dread fascination. The Supreme Court announced today that the need for preserving these unique remains outweigh the privacy concerns of the families. Therefore the remains shall be remanded to the control of the National Science Foundation for determination as to which researchers may access them."

Tyler's cheeks drained and his jaw dropped. "Why don't we change the channel?" He objected as he reached for the remote. "I'm sure there is something else on."

"No!" Jayne whirled around. His incredulous eyes made direct eye contact with Tyler's fearful eyes. "I have to hear these things. I'm their ambassador."

Without looking down, the pretty anchor lady declared, "Video coverage of an anti-H.E.C.C. rally went viral on the Internet today. After we show you the clip, we will interview the motivators of the rally." Coverage showed The East Burro Church holding signs on sidewalks near the homes of famous H.E.C.C.s including the lead actor in the *Try Hard* trilogy, Roland McGregor. "Fish R ICHy!" "God hates GENE Splicers!" "God hates HAGS!" "God hates HECCS!" "Ichthyosis Quarantine!" "Save the human race!" "Stop the Ich from spreading!" "Flush the Fish People!"

"That's enough of that! Jayne." Tyler turned the TV off and switched on the flashlight in his hand. For extra visual effect, he cast the beam in his face. Lowering his voice, he said, "You are staying in my house and you are under my rules. No TV in the den after eleven o'clock!"

"Seriously?"

"No, but you are dehydrated and you will go to bed." Tyler scooted closer to Jayne and placed a reassuring hand on his shoulder. "This ban won't be forever. They can't ban you for..."

Jayne interrupted with a high-pitched whine, "But what if they do?"

"Then... Gabby and I will move... where they can't ban it. You can join us." Tyler stood up and faced Jayne. "Now it's time for you to get a good REM sleep and let your lungs have a break. You need to rest. You need to unplug. You're getting a bit testy. You haven't been in a tank for a week. Sneaking water in the bathroom doesn't count."

"I don't get human REM sleep anymore."

"I don't care what quality the Hecc sleep cycle allows. You need to get some acceptable sleep for you." Tyler reached down and grabbed Jayne's hand. "Let's go. I'll even read you a bedtime story."

Jayne snorted. "Okay. Can you read the one about the ugly duckling? He and I might have something in common."

"Yes," said Tyler. "Your both quackers. Quack Quack."

"Ha Ha, Very funny."

Waving the beam in the direction they needed to exit the den, Tyler ordered, "Come on."

"What about Robin Hood?"

"No. I'd be asleep before I finished it and you would sneak back in here to watch the latest scandals. Oh, I know. Mary has a book. How about the fish that swam across the ocean to save his son? That has a happy ending."

Jayne skipped in front of Tyler. The beam of light showed Jayne's sly grin while he walked backwards down the hall. "No. That has a scary creature with shiny metal teeth in it that shakes fish until they're dead." He paused. "It might give me nightmares." Faking a sniffle, Jayne wiped his nose with his knuckle.

"Alright. We don't need you crying like a little *girl.*"

With a hop, Jayne faced forward. The moon lit up the conservatory. "Ty, where's the wheelchair? Where's Hope?" Jayne's eyes narrowed and his eyebrow's knitted as he measured Tyler.

"I thought you didn't care about her."

"You know I do."

"She's upstairs. Mary was somehow convinced that Marian had promised her a slumber party in our bathroom."

Slowly closing and opening his eyes, Jayne stared at the aquarium. The water beckoned to him. Tight lips relaxed and danced into a wry grin. Focusing on Tyler's beaming eyes, his lips parted. A shrill voice escaped his lips with one word repeating like a broken record, "Mine, mine, mine."

Flaring his nostrils and lifting his cheeks into a wide sly grin, Tyler nodded.

Pumping his arms at his sides, Jayne raced to the second tank. As if he regularly practiced track and field, he hurdled over the edge. *Sploooosh.*

"Nighty-night Knightly-Knight." Tyler disappeared in a sprint up the stairs. His lilting voice echoed in the conservatory. "Just keep swimming." He hummed all the way upstairs.

The water swayed to and fro until it settled down, rocking Jayne into a deep sleep.

{:-)-]~~{

Chapter 17

On a cloudy May 2nd, the creaking front door woke Jayne. Breaking the surface, he coughed as he gimlet-eyed the giant wall clock above the hallway door. Six o'clock. He thought, *Hmmm. Less than two hours of sleep.* The unique smell of a new day wafted in through the door flooding Jayne's nose with life. Irritation curled one corner of his mouth as he stared at Hope's empty basin. With a deep sigh, Jayne's curious eyes watched as Tyler stood, holding the door open.

A big box and a medium one appeared through the door, then the man who was carrying them. He wore ratty jeans, a blue football jersey and a blue baseball cap. The two men whispered their greetings.

Jayne hopped onto the edge. "Tyler. What's going on? Who is the visitor? Why this early?"

The visitor pulled off his sunglasses, then a curly black wig with attached cap, and straightened his own hair. Under the disguise, Tyler's brother-in-law Jerome stood grinning like he had won a world cup. "Hey, Jayne. I just got back from doing a simple undercover job."

"It's okay, Jayne. I had Jerome pick up a present for Gabby."

"Oh, yeah. It's her birthday." Jayne ran his fingers through his hair. Water squeezed out and sprinkled in the pond. "What else you got?"

"Why?" Tyler leaned his head back slightly and slowly batted his eyelashes.

The left side of Jayne's mouth lifted into a crooked tired grin. He sniffed. "You and Jerome have guilty expressions on your faces and Jerome has a disguise on."

"Um," Tyler faltered. "I guess we got caught. I know you went to bed late." Tyler swallowed and set his jaw. "You can look at it later," Tyler soothed as he closed the door. "It's just a bunch of tabloids."

"East or west coast?"

"Both," noted Jerome. He struggled with his burden and rearranged his shoulders.

"And British ones that I had mailed in." Tyler lifted up a giant white envelope on top of the box, holding it for Jayne's determined eyes to see. "Why don't you dry off and meet us in the wooden room?"

"Jerome," asked Jayne. He rubbed his arms and looked around. "Did your disguise help you ditch the paparazzi?"

"Wasn't too hard," sang Jerome.

Jayne's stomach rumbled. "I'm going to grab something to eat first." Water splashed on the floor as Jayne hopped out. He slipped, but caught himself as he wearily stepped over to the portable metal towel rack. "Hey, Tyler, we really need to get some non-slip mats for around the tanks."

Jerome and Tyler nodded before they scurried off to the oversized den.

Once Jayne toweled off, he strode down the hall. In the kitchen, he found Mildred scurrying about. The warm kitchen was filled with the bittersweet smell of chocolate. Colorful bowls of homemade icing rested strategically on the counter.

"What are you doing up so early?" Jayne smiled with a wink.

"Nothing, Jayne." Mildred shook her head. Her innocence faded as mischievous corners painted a different portrait. "Absolutely nothing out of the ordinary." She walked into the walk-in fridge and returned to him with a jar of lox, a package of cream cheese, and a bag of dried crushed wakame seaweed. Jayne graciously accepted his peace offering. She scuttled off to busy herself about again.

"What?" Jayne looked at his arm-load. "No bagel?"

"Sorry, Jayne. I got a lot on my mind."

"I'll get it."

"No, I'll get it. You sit."

With awkward coordination, Jayne carried his breakfast over to a dark table, settling onto a matching wooden breakfast stool. A cupboard attached above the table supplied Jayne with the necessary utensils to eat his meal. Mildred handed Jayne a pitcher of water and a bagel before she hurried off again.

After Jayne gulped down his meal, he speedily placed his dishes in the sink and stretched his dragging muscles as he meandered toward the men's hangout.

Opening the door, Jayne found Tyler and Jerome kneeling. Closing the door behind him, Jayne never let his eyes wander from the magazines spread out on the floor. Numb from head to toe, Jayne sat with his legs crossed. British and American tabloids featured tales of the H.E.C.C.s with each one being more sensational that the one before. All to sell more copies and whip the supermarket crowds into an all-out panic with articles about the 'fish people'. The lurid stories even topped the latest sighting of Elvis. One story discussed the possibility of the fish DNA technology raising Elvis from the dead. Some of the readers now lined their underwear with foil to protect their genitals from being shot with supposed governmental mutation ray guns producing catfish offspring. Jayne snorted when he read the last headline.

"What?" quizzed Tyler.

"This." Jayne burst with laughter. He handed Tyler the magazine and pointed to the article with a picture of foil-lined underwear. Jerome crawled over to where Tyler knelt and hovered, reading over his shoulder. "Hmmm. Are those TSA approved? I need one of those."

After Jerome guffawed, Jayne and Tyler joined him with a hearty laugh. Jayne abruptly paused. His nose and mouth twitched. A crestfallen look painted the corners of Jayne's lips.

A knock on the door forced them all into silence. Mildred pleasantly smiled as she held a phone out. "Jayne, it's Martin."

After Jayne accepted the phone, he placed the receiver to his ear. "Hello?"

"Ambassador Flynn? This is Martin Tucker, the official H.E.C.C. lawyer."

"Yeah, I know. What's going on?"

"I'm losing the case in Hollywood."

Stunned, Jayne shook his head and shifted it back. "I don't remember. You'll have to refresh my memory. You have been busy with so many cases lately."

"Hollywood produced the horror movie, 'The Spawning; Beaches Forsaken'. We have been able to hold it from being released so far. However, the defense claims that the ocean people don't look anything like Heccs, but instead creatures out of the most recent pirate film. The mere idea is enough to incite trouble. They're releasing it. I lost. We lost."

Jayne sighed deeply. He shook his head and placed his heavy head in his hands. "This is not encouraging news." He paused. The line remained silent on both sides for a minute. "Anything more I ought to know concerning the movie?"

"They are taking it further. They're making it a trilogy. 'The Spawning; Rivers Quarantined' and 'The Spawning; Aquifers Abandoned' have been announced today as already in production."

"When will this end?" Jayne raised his voice as he repeated the names of the films. He turned where he could see Tyler's reaction. Tyler and Jerome sat back completely, their rears flat on the floor. Tyler lifted a magazine with the titles in it. Jerome's hands were placed on the back of his head, staring at Jayne. With hands trembling, Jayne's voice tarried before he continued. "Do you have anything else for me?" He turned on speaker phone and motioned for the others to join him.

Papers rustled on the other end of the line before Martin answered. "A few of the Heccs that returned to their jobs found them impossible to keep. We filed lawsuits under the ADA against the ones that we found to be obviously discriminatory. We have won those and placed a portion of the money in the giant fund for Heccs. Those bosses that were careful to meet the letter of the law, haven't had cases filed against them."

"So are they finding other work?"

"Yes and no. Hey, with all the venom being spat at the Heccs, your friend Dee Graham has started up a Pro-Hecc charity."

"She did?"

"Yeah, it's called H.O.H.—Hooked On HECCs. She's rallied a few religious organizations and some support groups whose missing children were not regenerated into catfish. She has come up with counter press ideas like: 'HECCs Happen', 'Let HECCs Live,' 'God Loves HECCs', 'HECCs have souls', 'HECCs are Mammals too', 'HECCs are People too', 'HECCs were born Humans', 'Blame not the victims'. Which one is your favorite?"

Jayne asked him to repeat the various catch phrases. Martin complied and Jayne picked 'HECCs Happen'. Tyler and Jerome nodded their approval.

"And that reminds me," Martin paused. He cleared his throat away from the phone before returning. "...There is another case you should be aware of. I am still representing the Heccan, Dinison Shane Wyllis in his legal battle to return to the Navy Seals. It hasn't been released to the public."

"So, when will it?" Jayne bit his lip.

"The judge ruled today. Dinison returns to his job tomorrow!"

Whooping aloud, Jayne jumped up and out of his chair. "Hec'yeah! All right!" He almost knocked the others over as they quietly shook their fists with excitement.

"Speaking of jobs. A few Heccs have found work as divers for off shore drilling, gold dredging in the Bering Sea, and salvaging for archeologists."

"That's good. That actually is really good news. I hope for their sake... they have understanding bosses."

"They do. I hear the boss in the Bering Sea is a real nice one who invented a new type of dredge. He called it 'the Dragon'." Martin sighed, but he slowly continued, "I have other news."

Jayne's shoulders dropped. His brows knitted and his expression flattened. With a low frustrated voice, Jayne said, "Ok." He walked into the middle of the room away from the others and paced.

"Washington is going to announce tomorrow that an official H.E.C.C. embassy will open in Washington, D.C. That means that you, as the official Hecc Ambassador to the USA will have an office inside the Beltway."

Tyler's handmade chair caught Jayne as his knees buckled.

"Until you are ready, of course, your calls will be routed from the switchboard to the cell phone that I will be delivering to you in person later this week. Oh and not everyone will have access to the number. I have several papers for you to sign. My office will be moved there and so will Dr. Jensen's. Anything relating to the well-being of Heccs will be moved there including Dee's official HECC charity."

"Okay. I don't think I'm ready to move quite yet." Jayne ran his fingers through his hair and rolled his neck. Staring at the ceiling, he quizzed, "Anything else?'

"I'm sorry to be the one to inform you, but the chemotherapist-"

Jayne abruptly interrupted, "Let me *guess*. Mom's doctor passed away before he could help the FBI with the identity of the 'I.V. Scissor King'!"

"Yeah."

"How'd he die?"

"Heart attack."

"Is there an investigation?" Jayne cowered.

"Since the coroner didn't find any foul play, there will be no official investigation. The paper trail for your mom's bills lead nowhere. It's a dead end." Martin's voice turned upbeat. "Well, I am out of news. Is there anything on your end that I should know about?"

"The Hecc's that call me, continue to grow increasingly uneasy with their human environments. All sixty complain about being confined to mobility chairs, bathtubs for beds, or even one room apartments. The adults do not enjoy going to the store or swimming facilities because of all the stares or harassment that they receive. What can we do to make their lives easier?"

"I don't know, but we need to find something."

"Thanks for keeping me updated."

The two ended the phone call with well wishes.

"You okay, Jayne?" Tyler stood up from his chair with knitted brows and the corners of his lips turned down.

Jerome stood up from his chair and crossed his arms.

Numb as a brick, Jayne stood frozen to his spot.

"Jayne." Tyler immediately started pacing the room in a circle. "Outcry from both sides is touted on talk shows, defending with compassion or speaking against all the catfish humanoids with fear and hatred." Raising and lowering his hands, Tyler spoke with emphasis. "Even the Pro-Life and Pro-Choice groups are divided on the subject of H.E.C.C.s. This nation is suffering as families divide over the hatred and fear, or desire for tolerance and peace." Tyler bumped into Jerome causing both of them to catch their balance.

Hanging his head, Jayne sighed. "Each group claims that civil war lurks around the corner unless the other side backs down." Jayne's voice grew louder as he lifted his chin. "Everyone seems to have an opinion...all across this planet... especially any who have access to TV or the internet!" Standing tall, Jayne shook a fist at the heavens. "It's time the world knew what *our* opinion is! It's time we, Heccs, stand up for our individual rights of life, liberty and the pursuit of happiness. Come on, are we thinking, intelligent souls or just fish?"

"Watch out, world! Ambassador Jayne Flynn is ready to fight," declared Tyler.

"I don't have gills," said Jerome as he uncrossed his arms. "But, my good man, you have inspired me. I'm in!" Jerome walked up to Jayne and slapped him on the back. "Let's do this!"

Staring wide-eyed, Jayne grinned from ear to ear.

"So... what's our first step?" Tyler sauntered into Jayne's view.

Jayne shrugged his shoulders.

"How bout you start by letting Jerome and I be your tag team and screen some of the news for you and tell you if it's important enough to worry about."

"Okay."

Chiming in, Jerome beamed with a big smile. "I also think you need to take care of yourself by having some fun."

"Fun?"

"Yeah, Jayne," said Tyler. "Your life can't just revolve around news and the needs of your race. You need to take care of *your* needs..."

Jayne interrupted, "I do."

Without rhythm, Jerome and Tyler both shook their heads.

"Jayne, Jayne, Jayne," Tyler scolded. "You don't sleep. You don't unwind. It's leaving you nothing, but a ball of raw nerves. How can you get humans to fight for you or love your fellow survivors if you walk around with a short fuse that could blow a bomb any minute? Eating, drinking, sleeping, and swimming are not your only needs. You need to do some adjustment by watching some movies, bowl, play some board games. Too much of something is a bad thing and you have had too much seriousness in your life. Play pool. Take walks around the property. Enjoy life!"

Brief encounters danced in Jayne's mind. Many times he had told Hope's cousins that he didn't have time to play games. It had been several months since anyone asked him. Jayne swallowed hard. His stress levels had increased in part because of his lack of socializing.

Gabe appeared in the doorway. A wry, ornery expression spread across his face. "Everybody's ready, Uncle Tyler."

"Already?" Tyler checked his watch. "Time for Gabby's surprise party. Hmmm. Speaking of having fun..." He nudged Jayne.

"What?" Jayne stared at Tyler. "Uh...Oh!" Jayne pulled on his chin with his right hand. "Gabe?"

"Yeah?"

"I owe you a game of pool." Jayne exhaled and held his breath.

"Okaay..." Looking for guidance from his uncles behind Jayne's back, Gabe's eyebrows raised. They were softly bouncing their hands with encouragement. Staring at Jayne's uncertain face, Gabe confidently answered. "Actually, you owe me a game of pool..." He glanced at the ceiling as if in recollection. "...a game of Bullshit,

Monopoly, Risk," Sending a caring scowl in Jayne's direction, he ended with, "… the list goes on."

Jayne's mouth dropped.

"Yeah, dude, I kept track of all the times that you rejected a friendly game. In fact, you were supposed to be my teammate so I could finally beat the undefeated bowling 'team Will'!"

Sighing, Jayne smiled. "So, what game do you want to start with?"

Lost in conversation, Jayne and Gabe left the room debating on the details.

Not wanting to leave the magazines sprawled out, Jerome and Tyler quickly gathered them into a pile and set them back into the box.

Traipsing into the crowded dining room, Gabe and Jayne abruptly ended their conversation. Noise flooded Jayne's senses and a headache tickled his nerves. A waving hand let Jayne know that Hope still acknowledged his presence. Jayne politely smiled. He searched the room. "Where's Gabby and her mom?" He whirled about to find Tyler. He repeated his original question.

Without making eye contact with Jayne, Tyler guessed, "Upstairs."

"Oh."

Kelly-He broke the chaos of the huge extended family with a shrill whistle.

Mildred stood up with a big grin. Placing both hands on her cheeks, she said loud enough for the present company to hear. "Okay… Let's see. Everyone is here. The children want to yell 'Surprise'. Plates, napkins, silverware, and cups have been passed out. The carts are here with the cake and punch." With the closest hand, she pointed at the extravagant three-tiered snowy mountain of sugar and flour. Green leaves, laced around pink and purple flowers, complemented the cream cheese icing with pink and purple framework. Next to the scrumptious mass, sat two large glass punchbowls filled almost to the brim with pink and purple punch. Two ladles lay within a hands reach.

Letting her hands drop to her side, Mildred hesitated. "I'm lost... What are we missing?"

Billy stood up with lively confidence. "Aunt Gabriella is the reason that, all gathered, are we. She is not, hmm? If she partakes in her journey not, then gathered for no reason. All is lost. Yes, hrmmm." His low squeaky growl ended in a choke.

The table full of preteens opposite of Billy snickered before they erupted into laughter.

"True. Billy. Too true." Melista's eyes sparkled as she answered her nephew.

The dining room door opened cautiously. Grandma Cook entered, holding the door.

Gabriella marched in. Her eyebrows raised high and her lips questioned with a smile.

"Surprise!" The children stood up and yelled without coordination.

"Oh." Gabriella reeled back. "Oh," she said, stepping forward again. She couldn't think of the last time she had a birthday party. One table in the corner was stacked with neat, but less than perfect, colorfully wrapped packages. Her animated, but fearful eyes appraised the room.

Tyler snuck up behind Gabriella and snatched his arms around her.

Gabriella shrieked. Her arms flailed outward. When she craned her head, she saw Tyler lean in to look at her. Gabriella's muscles relaxed into the warmth of her husband's masterful arms.

The room quieted down.

"May you be blessed with peace, wisdom, health and strength. May your mother be blessed for giving you to us. May you enjoy cake, laughter and good company. Have a happy birthday. I love you! " Tyler grinned from ear to ear and then brushed his lips across his wife's smooth cheek.

Dolores placed her loving hands on Tyler's shoulder as she excused herself past him. "You're a good man, Tyler Sharp."

With a sigh, Gabriella beamed at her mother and her husband. Dolores left her daughter's side to join Mary and Marian. They had a lot to catch up on.

The festivities took off with an instantaneous bang and trekked its way down a mountain.

With a happy distracted heart, Gabriella glowed as she swallowed her first bite without even chewing. She feared she would blink and miss out on all the planned activities. The animated party continued with engaging conversations between gulped down sweet disorder.

Gabriella set her plate on the bench next to her and started opening her cluster of gifts. Various family members chipped in together including the adults. First, her nephews and nieces handed her their homemade crafts, pictures, and baked goodies.

After the last niece approached her, sister-in-law Marcy tapped a beaming Gabriella on the shoulder. A pink and purple striped box rested in her hands. Marian sat in her wheelchair with Willetta behind her. Both girls stared with eager eyes and smiles.

"What's this?" Gabriella raised her eyebrows and held her hands out with surprised confusion. She stared at the giant purple curly ribbon bow as if it had the spines of a prickly pear. After gently poking at the bouncing three inch round bow with both hands, she stroked the two inch wide ribbon tails down the sides of the box.

"Well, don't just gawk at it." Marcy squealed, "Open it, silly." Her hands pushed at the air in between the two.

"Yeah, open it, mom," sang Marian.

Startled, Gabriella's lips parted from her closed smile into a wide toothy grin. Her hands pulled the ribbon apart and opened the lid of the white box.

"Oh," gasped Gabriella. Her right hand pulled out a glass milk bottle filled with layers of pink and purple bath salts.

"I got to help make it." Marian beamed.

Blinking the joyous tears forming, Gabriella stared at her faithful friend. She expressed her thanks to Marian and Marcy. Opening the lid, she deeply inhaled the sweet bitter red rose scent. "Hmmmm," her slow exhale released what was left of the euphoric smell that her lungs processed. A peaceful countenance relaxed her stiff shoulders.

Gabriella shifted to place the bottle in the box and then on the floor next to her.

Willetta and Marian left Gabriella's side to go mingle.

Marcy's face and shoulders dropped. "Don't stop. There's more!"

Gabriella sat up and handed the bottle to Bonnie, who stood on her other side. Sticking both hands in the box again, she pulled out several pretty homemade soap bars zipped up in small plastic baggies. "Did you make these?" She glowed as she scrutinized the pumpkin spiced oval bar inlaid with a profile of a woman in white. A hazelnut coffee scented sea star soap bar and a chocolate coffee sea shell bar filled her nostrils and tickled her taste buds. The rectangular one in her left hand begged for deeper concentration. Puzzled, Gabriella looked up. "I thought you only made natural products like bath salts and oils? These have coffee and I don't know what these are made with."

"Aw, you know, got to follow the market. Some naturalists say that glycerin soap, coffee, and man-made dyes aren't natural enough, but I have been playing around with the novelty market to add some extra income." Marcy shrugged. "I picked up a few new interesting molds to test out. I couldn't find any mermaid molds, but the ocean themed ones seemed right, aannd it was kinda last minute. There really isn't a mold that is quite right for Hecc's. Sorry, sis. Ssooo.... what do you think?"

"I like them. They are cute," said Gabriella, smiling. She lifted her left hand. "What's this one? It looks like a little pistol and a little hand...What's it made out of?"

"It's a pun. See...hand...gun." Marcy pointed the two shapes out and laughed. "It's a hand gun soap. For the freedom-lovers in your life. (*Giggle*) The clear glycerin soap encases the molded dyed goats milk."

Jerome snatched the gun soap and interrupted. "Hey, can you make me an army camo-colored gun?" He held his hand open as Gabriella placed the bar in his hand.

Marcy's face concentrated hard. "Yeah, it could be done. It's just going to be a little more time consuming."

"Cool." Jerome bounced his head in affirmation and handed the gift back to his sister-in-law. He sauntered off to rejoin the festivities.

"Thank you, Marc."

"Don't thank me, yet." Marcy mysteriously beamed. "You're my guinea pig. I need someone to try it out first."

"Have you come up with a name for your business?" Gabriella sniffed the soap through the plastic baggie.

"Yeah. I think I have." Marcy stooped in front of Gabriella and gently took Gabriella's presents from her and placed them in the box at her feet. "I'm going to call it: 'Author's Soap'. You know, 'words creatively painted into pictures'… even if they are punny."

"I like it. Thanks."

"Now, that's all the presents." Marcy stood up. Her mothering voice conquered her best friend voice. "Time for you to finish your cake." She handed the unfinished delectable to a teary-eyed, Gabriella.

"Yesss ma'am."

Gabriella scarfed down her cake, nuts, candy and punch. The food helped her retain control of her overwhelming emotions. The noise toned down just when she finished her last bite. Tyler stood directly in front of her with his feet set wide apart. Both hands were firmly held behind his back with his torso regarded high. He lifted his eyebrows when Gabriella acknowledged his presence. Warmth spread over her from head to toe. She unconsciously raised her eyebrows in return and fastened eye contact with him. Tucking her chin into her right shoulder, she blushed.

"Hey," said Tyler as he tilted his head in her direction. After his shoulder rolled back, his posture straightened. His left hand plunged to his side. Flaring his nostrils, his wide mischievous grin softened into a peaceful open expression.

"Thanks, Ty. It's been a great birthday."

With his eyes twinkling, a headstrong Tyler flirted with his sensual expression. His daring left hand slowly swept to rest on his six-shooter, cylinder rotating, revolver belt buckle. He gave it a few quick twirls causing Gabriella's eyes to fixate on his buckle and his jeans below his belt. Cricking his neck, Tyler's hand shot up to smooth out the ruffles in his hair. Her dreamy naked neck called to his hungry lips. Rubbing his chin, he licked his lips. "Um, Gabby."

"Yeah," breathed Gabriella. Saliva increased in her mouth. Blushing cheeks framed her lips as they parted and developed into a small smile. The nagging desire to erase the distance between them flowed through her veins. A shiver ran up and down her spine, which brought pleasure to her body, spirit and soul. Gabriella set her empty plate back down. Shifting in her seat, she focused her dilating pupils back on her husband's eyes. Her hand delicately rose, stroking her throat.

Tyler offered his hand palm-up to her.

Gabriella responded by placing her hand in his and standing up with feminine grace. With an open stance, her body melted into his. A hum escaped her slightly open mouth before she concluded her exhale with a groan. She wrapped her delicate arms around his chest and followed both his delicious biceps down to his hands tucked neatly behind his back. A semi-smooth but rough stiff texture caught her off guard. "What's this?" Gabriella's reluctant smile faded as confusion painted her from forehead to toes. Bringing her hands in front of her, her hand held a mysterious package tied with hemp twine. "I thought that Marcy said that I opened all the presents."

"Honey, you know husbands keep the best for last." He shook his head with a mischievous grin.

Gabriella covertly blew him a tender kiss and lightly sat down in her chair. She focused whole-heartedly on the white paper wrapping, which she greedily tore open to find a family picture blown up to a horizontal 8x10. Imitation gold and stones framed the portrait of the four of them as they sat on the circular bench in front of the huge tree in the conservatory. Tyler wore light blue jeans and a dark blue shirt. With a forced straight face, Tyler sat as conservatively as he could next to Gabriella. Her wide eyes and red cheeks complimented her open mouth with curled up laughing lips. Gabriella sported a purple shirt and dark blue jeans. In front of Tyler's feet sat Mary cross-legged in a purple t-shirt and blue jeans. Marian 'Hope' Harrison, in a purple bikini top, sat with her fishy thighs and fins together, stretched out in front of Mary's knees. Marian's hands rested in her lap with her head tipped slightly up, while her mouth stood ajar. Gabriella brought to mind that moment frozen in time. Willetta, William and Billy had stood behind the camera goading Marian beyond a timid grin while Clifford stood ready to capture the moment at the tripod holding his digital camera.

Tenderly, Gabriella hugged the memory and whispered her thanks. Tyler nodded and leaned forward. His right hand softly held her shoulder as he bent over and brushed a kiss on her forehead. With a quick turn on his heel, Tyler hurried about, helping Mildred pick up the mess.

Tyler's thoughtful gift distracted Gabriella to a faraway heaven-like fantasy world. Her polite, but excited smile accompanied a nod as she thanked individuals passing by her with well wishes. The 'holiday' continued as the crowd streamed down into the basement, dancing to loud bumping music. The bowling alley opened with teams and the general din escalated, but Gabriella didn't mind or feel claustrophobic for once. It had indeed been a happy day.

{:-)-]~~{

Chapter 18

Summer arrived with few changes in Jayne's life. Tension continued to hold Hope at a distance. Jayne and Hope sometimes spent a few awkward moments alone together. Jayne visited and played games with Hope's cousins and uncles when they were around. His personal cell phone rang off the hook from the lawyer, doctor, and other H.E.C.C.s. After months of begging, Hope convinced Jayne to turn off his phone in the evenings and take her for daily walks in the gardens.

On a Sunday night, Jayne had dropped Hope off at her tank and found Mildred waiting for him in the hallway. Smiling, she handed him the cordless phone. "It's Jon."

Jayne snatched the phone out of her hand and ran down the hall. Laughing, Mildred turned on her heel.

Quickly, Jayne shut the door to the wooden room. He plopped in the chair that he made with the Sharp's help. It looked like a wooden canoe that had been cut in half with one end nailed upright for the back rest. Two lobsters which had been taken through a taxidermy process were mounted on both sides. Seashells and other ocean decorations covered the outside. Jayne's favorite decorator touch was the fluffy 'faux hide' of a polar bear that covered the cushion on which he sat. Arranging his body into the lotus and his butt to comfortably sink in deeper, Jayne placed the receiver on his ear. "Jon! Jonathon! Bro, I haven't heard from you in *two* months!"

"Sorry, man. I've been busy fighting the system. It's totally choof."

"Yeah, what happened? The last news report showed you protesting to regain your right to return to the competitions."

"It's over, brohein." Jonathon's voice cracked with despair. "I tried real hard to follow human breathing cycles at the swim meets, but I was too fast for them. No matter how hard I tried to separate my kicking, adrenaline or instinct kept forcing my fins to work together. They passed a rule forbidding Heccs, including tailless ones, from competing with humans."

"The Olympics too?' Jayne lifted his hand and placed it atop his head bringing his elbow down to rest on his knee.

"Yeah, duuuude. It's totally choof."

"I'm sorry, Jon. Really."

"Hey, we've all had dreams stolen and sold to the highest bidder. Anyway, me and some other Heccans are going solo. We're going to throw our own competition where we compete for a prize donated by the spectators. I hear some crippler Heccwans are going to work it at some oceanariums."

"Jon, you're an intelligent being." Jayne raised his voice. "You're not an animal to be gawked at! You're not a circus side show! You're a person!"

"Jayne," Jonathon returned his friend's fury. "I have to make a living. I need to be somebody besides a victim."

"I know." Jayne lowered his voice into just above a whisper. "I know."

Charm trimmed Jonathon's distaste with a mischievous tickle in his throat. "Besides," Jonathon chuckled. "The sardine tips are to jump for."

Jayne's lack of response left the line to fill with awkward silence.

"Dude." Jonathon snorted. His voice lowered with each consecutive word. "I'm tired of being only a catfish. It's totally choof, brohein." As he changed subjects, his voice softened. "I found a barber. He's dope. Did you see my 5 o'clock shadow and my short bowl cut?"

"Yeah. Okay."

"Shyau. The old one just couldn't cut it."

"Hey!"

Jonathon chuckled.

Jayne traced his forehead with the fingers on his free hand. "Have you heard the news?" Resting his forehead in the palm of his hand, he sighed.

"You mean," Jonathon swallowed. "About the increase in drowning among human children? Sure, brohein."

"There are a lot of parents blaming the Heccs." Jayne adopted a professional tone. "The families described exaggerated symptoms of the 'fish disease'. Sadly, fears were expressed by 30% of the United States population about a possible outbreak. A whopping twenty five percent of the world's population remains fearful that the United States will spread their 'Fish' disease." Unsure of the outcome, Jayne hesitated. "They claim their children are going off and drowning 'to become a freak'."

Jonathon interrupted. "Ahh Son of a Fish!" Raising his voice, he lamented. "Freak? Freak? Do they think we chose this life? Do they think we were born like this? Those stupid stinkin' walkin' landlubbers don't know anything about anything!"

Sitting up, Jayne bit his lip. He slowly inhaled and exhaled. Taking a deep breath, he soothed his distraught friend. "Hope's family is really nice. They aren't so bad. Don't forget..." Jayne paused. "I still walk."

"You don't stink."

"Says you," snorted Jayne. "To the humans, I smell like I danced the tango in an omega 3 packaging plant!" He shifted his weight.

"Speaking of fish, Tuna Boy," taunted Jonathon. "I took my wheelchair for a spin around the block." Mirthful silly laughter choked his words. When he could untie his tongue, he explained, "All the neighbor cats were following me, dude!"

A huff of air escaped Jayne's nose before he cackled.

Jonathon joined Jayne in a superb hearty laugh.

"Whad'ya do?" Jayne rocked back and forward holding his sides. "Did you tell them the fast food was down the street? Wait. Wait. I got it. Did you stop and let them give you a bath?"

"Nah fish," Jonathon guffawed. "I beat it around the block. I was up to my nar-nars in cats! They didn't want to just lick my fins! Mi madre was right!"

"How so?"

"She taught me from when I could hang five: Fire – hot; Water – wet; Kitty – *sharp*!"

The two laughed hysterically. After their jokes slowed down to a trickle, they promised to get in to contact more often. The call ended with a click. Bringing the phone down in front of his face, Jayne stared at the receiver.

{:-)-]~~{

Chapter 19

On the last Sunday in July, clouds were nowhere to be found. The moon shone bright while the cool mountain air played with the trees. Clothed in a blue cloth vest and black basketball pants, Jayne shivered to adjust his body temperature as the atmosphere dropped a few degrees. His navy blue Crocs slightly squeaked as he dawdled along, pushing Hope in her wheelchair. The semi-smooth brick path through the Sharp's flower garden provided an easy route without extra planning.

Individual scents from hollyhocks, cosmos and blanket flowers tickled their nostrils. Jayne bent over, picked a colorful hollyhock and handed it to a grateful Hope.

Lifting the sweet flower to her nose, Hope enjoyed two deep inhales. She brought it down in front of the football jersey that Jayne had given her. Resting her hands on the black blanket across her lap, Hope merrily sighed. Life pumped through the flower's tiny green veins sucking it from the snapped stem. The soft petals felt nice and smooth to the tips of her fingers. Her vibrantly colored fingernails sparkled in the moonlight. Hope petted the individual petals as her wheelchair moved on toward the herb garden.

Every muscle in Jayne's body twitched. The sparkle in his eye shined with an intensity likened to high tide. No matter how many times he swallowed the lump in his throat, it wouldn't budge. Shifting his head, his sharp eyes darted about. The wind blew a cool breeze on his bare forearms.

Lavender, rosemary and sage flicked their scents in the slight breeze. Pausing, Jayne knelt before the lavender. Reaching with both hands, he gathered a handful of leaves. With a sense of duty, he approached Hope in her wheelchair and hovered.

With a dreamy expression, Hope dropped the flower in her lap. Greed drove her open palms to reach for Jayne's gift. Instead of dropping it carelessly, he placed his hands in her cupped hands and withdrew them leaving the leaves behind.

Hope rubbed her arms and neck with the powerfully scented leaves. Every damaged leaf gave off enchanted sweet perfume on her skin and in the air. With a pleased heart and mind, she sighed.

Still facing Hope, Jayne's disarming smile turned plastic. "Hope." His cold eyes burned and withered with direct contact. "We need to talk."

Hope's lips curled down and deep wrinkles formed like an old redwood tree. She closed her once tender eyes. "Must we? Can't we just enjoy the night?" She turned her head away from him.

"Hope." Jayne reached a hand out and placed it on her shoulder. She flinched and jerked her shoulder away from his tender hand.

Jayne pivoted and stared at the magnificent horizon, his eyes focused into a fuzzy haze. Without raising his voice, Jayne remained cool and collected. "You think this has been easy for me? Heccs everywhere are giving into the public craze, and they are letting themselves be interviewed. People are beginning to wonder why I won't. My people deserve better from me."

With a skip start, Jayne paced in front of her wheelchair. His head jerked several times, avoiding her wayward eyes. Crossing his arms, he paced in deep thought. He tried to form sentences in his mind so he wouldn't come across as a dope or a jerk. "Half of them call me constantly." With a sigh, he paused. "I don't get a minute's rest. It's time I accept my duties fully. To be a fitting ambassador, I must go. I have to join the fight for our very survival, for justice and equity for our race. I need to take the interviews as part of a stronger campaign to convince the public that we are not monsters, not a disease, not idiots."

Opening her eyes, Hope begged. "Please. Please don't go." She reached her hands to him, but even her leaning did not allow for her to snag him. "You... you can't go... not yet."

Standing in front of Hope, his cold eyes changed to sorrow. "Don't make this more difficult than it already is. Hope, I can't be your ambassador if I'm here all the time. I can't fight for your freedom, or any Heccs' freedom if I'm not out there making our case to the public." Kneeling down to her level and taking her hands in his, Jayne pleaded with his eyes and his heart. "They won't let us have love if they don't start loving us and treating us like the victims and not the perpetrators. We didn't ask to be turned into a different humanoid race. Right now, we need to fight for the right to exist. We're not circus freaks. We're intelligent beings that hunger for a chance to prove that we can live and care for ourselves. Don't you want true freedom?"

Hope rested her chin against her chest.

"If I stay here and fight from the sidelines, then I'm not going to accomplish anything, really. I need to lead the charge for civil rights on the frontlines, not from the sidelines."

"I know."

"I understand that you don't want to be interviewed, but I really don't have a choice. I not only have to let them interview me, I have to take it to them. I cannot hide behind 'adjustment' any longer." Jayne stood up. His uneasy hands cracked his knuckles. "Do I have your blessing?"

Hope did not answer. She raised her chin and stared with vacant eyes at the middle of his figure. Both of her hands fidgeted, stroking her blanket toward her fins. As she gazed at the house in the distance, her eyes turned sad.

Jayne cleared his throat. "They are good people. You're in good hands. Your mother loves you. She always has."

Hope's despondent eyes grieved as she looked up. "Yeah," she confided with a crack.

"You have a sister who adores you."

"I don't think she knows that I longed for a sister too."

With duty in his steps, Jayne positioned his feet directly behind her chair and pushed her on the path. "At least Tyler got her to quit tapping on the windows on the tank." His face brightened and then saddened. He would be leaving the most welcoming home that he had ever known.

"Yeah," Hope eagerly said as she sat taller.

Jayne marched on in funeral silence. His steps became slower and less determined for his goal.

In the front of the house, Tyler's car faced the exit, ready to depart. Tyler sat lightly on the hood with his arms crossed. When he saw Jayne and Hope, he hopped up.

Gabriella padded from the porch to greet them.

"What? You're leaving *now*?" Hope squirmed in her chair. With sharpened eyes, she glared at her mother. "You knew?"

Tyler opened the passenger door.

"Honey," Gabriella hesitated. "His flight leaves in a few hours. He needs to go."

"Oh," Hope cried. "Go. Just go!" She crossed her arms and tucked her chin.

Gabriella lovingly pushed Jayne toward the car and stood behind Hope, ready to wheel her inside.

Jayne tiptoed around to face Marian. Jayne's arms ached to hold her against his chest as he leaned over. Gently biting his lower lip, his tongue barely peeked out in between his lips as he wet them. *How I remember the touch of your full lips pressed up against mine.* He raised his eyebrows as his ears honed in on the beat of her heart. Although she refused to look at him, he stared deeply at her as he longed to hold her gaze with his eyes. His cheeks burned with passion as he recalled the memory of her soft hair warming them.

Marian's head shifted as she glanced at him. Once she briskly turned away, her left hand flew up to her head where her fingers found several strands of hair to twist.

"Hope," breathed Jayne. In short order he leaned over again, but Marian refused to look up. Jayne growled as he turned away from her and stared angrily into the heavens.

"Jayne," hesitated Tyler. He placed a reassuring hand on his shoulder. "It's alright. It will be our secret. Kiss her goodbye." Tyler and Gabriella exchanged nervous merry glances before they turned away from the two young lovers to give them a brief minute of privacy. Their lack of view gave them alibis in case anyone interrogated them.

Jayne nodded. His face relaxed into a glowing wide grin. He bowed down and carefully grabbed Marian's feisty head with both of his masterful hands. Lifting her limber chin up, Jayne moved closer to her. His lips parted before they brushed lightly on the crown of her head. Warmth and electricity ignited slightly from Marian as Jayne's lips pressed firmly against her fishy jewel causing Jayne's own organ to increase its intensity ever so slightly. As quick as the energy started, it ended.

Marian tucked her chin again and crossed her arms.

Gloom clung to Jayne's eyes and muscles. He shrugged his shoulders and turned on his heel.

Tyler heard Jayne trudge to the vehicle. With a skip and a hop, Tyler sat behind the wheel and started it. With a weary heart and mind, Jayne sat in the open passenger's seat. After he closed the door, he rolled the window down. Leaning his head out the window, he raised his gentle voice. "Hope? Please don't be mad."

Worry creased Gabriella's eyebrows as she stared at the back of her daughter's head.

The vehicle shifted into low gear and slowly crawled away.

Gabriella's hands grabbed the handles with a start as Hope spiritedly shifted forward in her chair.

Hope yelled, "Jayne! Call me?"

Leaning his head out the window, Jayne placed his hand to his ear.

Hope cupped her hands to her mouth. Effort forced air from her lungs to her mouth. "Call me!"

With a delighted expression, Jayne returned his answer. "I will. I will!" He wildly waved his hand at Hope and Gabriella.

Mother and daughter watched in sorrow as the car exited the driveway and started its lengthy journey down the road.

"Come on, honey." Gabriella pushed the wheelchair around to the front door. "Let's get you in bed."

In a dream-like state, Marian 'Hope' Harrison watched the world become a fuzzy place. The bright lights in the conservatory did not aide her sight. Her eyes could not focus as Kelly-He with alert eyes stood waiting in the conservatory. All life froze in Marian's veins. Her sluggish limbs willingly allowed herself to be helped into her tank. The cool water warmed her soul as Marian's gills took over.

Gabriella's hand stirred the surface of the water. Her normal voice clouded through air and water. "Honey, it will be okay. We'll do just fine. Goodnight, Marian."

Marian closed her burning eyes. She rolled over. With her eyelids closed, she saw the lights turn off. Footsteps faded. The atmosphere crushed Marian's very existence. The sandman forgot to visit the conservatory. Minutes turned to hours as Marian tossed and turned. Even the tiny heartbeats of the fish pounded in her head like a busy construction site.

The huge wall clock ticked, but never tocked. The filter's soothing voice lost its note in the middle of its endless song and sang off key for the rest of the night. Marian opened her eyes and then tightened them shut hard. Sleep knocked on her mind, but she jumped with a start when her bottom bumped the wall. Turning round, she stared angrily at it and made a face. Using her hands to cover her face, Marian closed her eyes again. At 5:45 in the morning, sleep finally paralyzed Marian's limbs. Her arms drifted away from her face as she floated near the surface.

A watery mumble alerted Marian to an awakened state of mind. Her mother called to her. Water rustled on the surface. A loud splashing brought Marian up to the surface. She coughed, flabbergasted "What? What?" Looking around the tank, she noticed all the fish were dead. She must have accidentally ignited her electric organ during the night Not one beating heart besides her own. Marian swallowed the lump in her throat, but it did not remove the pains stabbing her heart. She sank to the bottom.

"Wake up," repeated Gabriella louder. "The phone is for you. It's Jayne."

This time, Marian appeared above the surface. Her mother cradled a cordless receiver and towel away from the tank.

Eagerly, Marian sloshed out of the water and sat on the edge. Using both hands, she flattened and combed her hair away from her ears. Grasping at air, she greedily accepted first the towel. After Marian blotted her face and ear, Gabriella handed her daughter the phone.

"Hello? Jayne?" blurted Hope. "Did you already get where you're going?" She grasped the phone with both hands.

"I'll be over by the hall." Gabriella whispered. "Just holler."

As Marian nodded, Gabriella padded out of the conservatory and stationed herself just inside the hallway. "Jayne?" When extended silence ensued, Marian's voice trembled. "Are you still there?"

"Yes," said Jayne in a rush. "Sorry. I had to talk to someone."

Marian merrily sighed. "Did you get to where you were supposed to go?" She gazed at the wall clock and adjusted her focus. The clock read a quarter past nine. She must have slept through the morning rush.

"They are getting ready for a special interview. It will be on tomorrow...if you wanna watch." Jayne paused for her to answer. When she didn't, he continued. "I really need your support. I really need you to watch it. I will do better if I know you are watching it."

Timidly, Hope replied softly. "Okay."

"I don't have much time. I just wanted to let you know that I'm safe and I'll call as often as I can." Jayne sounded like he was speed reading.

"Oh, okay."

"I've gotta go. Bye."

The click echoed in the receiver like a gong on a bell tower. Marian stared dumbfounded at the phone. Lifting her voice, she cried, "Mom!"

Gabriella raced into the room and halted as she reached Marian's side. "Here I am. Honey, What's wrong?"

"Here," quipped Marian. Devastation haunted her eyes as she tossed the phone to her mother. "Why was it so short? I didn't get

to talk to him. I mean he just up and left. I didn't have any warning.
I miss him." Her voice trailed off.

"He hasn't been gone very long and he called you to let you know
he was safe."

"He doesn't like me." She stared at her mother with her aching
soul on her shoulders.

"You know that isn't true. It's time for him to come into his own.
He has *vacationed* and *lingered* here long enough. This is not a hiding
place. It's time he actually earned his title as ambassador. He can't
work if he is on the phone with you all the time." Gabriella placed a
loving hand on her daughter's shoulder.

Marian relaxed her tense shoulders.

"Oh, Marian. At least he called. That shows he cares."

A pleasant visage lifted Marian's chin. "Yeah….at least he called."

"You can always catch a glimpse of him on the news. He said he
was going to be doing a lot of interviews."

"Is there a TV that you can bring in here?" Placing her hands to
rest in her lap, she waited for an answer.

"Hmmm." Gabriella lowered her head to stare at the floor.
Popping her head up, she raised her free forefinger. "Tyler's not
back yet. He had extra shopping to do. Maybe he can find one, if I
catch him."

Marian's chin lifted up. Her smile increased with a touch of
genuine happiness.

Immediately, Gabriella lifted the phone to her ear and dialed
Tyler's cell. Walking two feet at a time, she disappeared down the
hall toward the tea room where the base unit rested.

Mildred appeared with a trash bag. One at a time, Marian
handed her adopted grandmother the deceased remains of her once
lively companions. Marian blankly stared at Grandma Sharp as she
left the room.

Loneliness and water beckoned to Marian. Without aiming, she
fell backward lifting her hands to the ceiling. Splooosh. The water
swirled over and around her. The side of the tank grabbed at Marian's

fishy flesh as she raked against it. The rug burn shot through her nerves and hit her brain. Her lungs heaved several times forcing water out of her gills as she lifted a cry of pain. Both hands grabbed at her bruised flesh. For several minutes, she clung to her injury making sour faces. Although there was not even enough blood to tint the water, Marian could taste it. *Yuck.*

Gabriella's voice rang out above the tank, "Okay, Marian. Tyler is going to grab a TV for you. He said he would find one with a remote. Hopefully, we can put it in a Ziploc bag and you will be able to use it."

{:-)-]~~{

Hours passed for Marian with little to do in the empty tank. She lay on her stomach on the bottom, stacking pebbles until they fell. Giggles in the conservatory broke her boredom. Marian swam to the surface to where she could spy out the diamond window to see who passed through. Her sister, Mary, and her cousins conspired almost below a whisper. Lisa cradled a pretty plastic doll and stroked its black braided hair. Nina held one with red fuzzy hair and a red dress. There were two dolls in Mary's hands. One sported a fluffy birthday dress while the other wore a flowing purple dress. A brush lay tangled in its hair. Mary let out a sharp gasp. A doll and a forefinger pointed at Marian. The girls disappeared down the stairs.

Marian rolled over and hid behind the concrete foundation inside her aquarium away from the windows. No footsteps sounded louder than the rhythm of Marian's heart. When she felt the coast was clear, she carefully peeked out the diamond window. No one. Marian backed up to where she floated in the middle of the tank. The curtains on the basement windows were no longer drawn for her privacy, but had been opened up. Lisa and Nina's faces were planted on the window with their mouths open and their noses squished against the glass at weird angles.

Waving and flicking her hands, Marian desperately tried to shoo them away. Instead, they made faces with their mouths and eyes. Dropping their dolls, they used both hands to emphasize their weirdness. All four hands took turns on their own or each other's heads with their thumbs. Once they finished that routine, they pulled on the corners of their mouths and eyes.

Marian rolled her eyes. Wrinkling the corner of her mouth, she stuck out her tongue. The girls giggled, grabbed their dolls and ran off past the card tables.

A shrill roar echoed above the surface of the water. Marian's spooked stomach churned. Annoyance radiated from her eyes as she glared at Mary sitting on the edge. With a start, Marian closed her eyes and used both hands to cover her head as something slipped out of Mary's hands into the tank. Once it bounced off of Marian's head and hands, it settled to the floor.

Mary let out a squeal and jumped down. She loudly raced down the hall.

Marian rigidly outstretched her hand. Her body instinctively guided her to the floor where she swooped up the intruder. Two flings of her fins forced her skyward reaching her hand above the surface. Marian prepared to launch it.

A glimmer of green caught Marian's eye as silver confetti paint dripped down her hand. Pulling the doll back under the surface, Marian held it at arm's length to study it. With both hands, she precisely peeled off the purple dress to reveal a mermaid doll with a painted bikini top from the manufacturer. The silver confetti paint could very well have been painted on by Mary, whose attempt to color the doll exactly like her sister intrigued Marian. Silver streaks in the dolls hair resembled Marian's own hair. The doll's nails were not perfectly painted with the sparkly glitter for the entire hands were covered with it. An amused smile crept onto Marian's lips.

No one watched as Marian lost time as she made the doll swim all over with a variety of hand and tail positions. Over the rocks and fake coins, around the treasure chest, and through the fake grass, they went. She heard the loud rumbles and cheers coming from the bowling alley.

Clumping in the conservatory caused Marian to hide the doll behind her back. She heard Tyler groan as he knelt to the floor with his load.

Leaving the doll to dive to the bottom, Marian swam to the surface. She coughed as she watched Tyler open the box with the giant flat screen TV. Eagerness drained from her bones when she heard Tyler announce that the satellite installer wouldn't arrive until the next day.

Playing with the doll during the night with the moon shining in, consumed Marian. Sleep entangled her in its tentacles just before sunrise.

At eleven in the morning, the blasting TV mounted on the wall to her right startled Marian awake. After her eyes popped open, she sat up straight. A brand new suckerfish scampered away. Pebbles shifted as Marian shot away from the floor. Without a glance at the closed curtains, she raced to the oxygen-rich atmosphere. Breaking the surface, she choked on her cough causing it to escalate with violence. Pain stabbed at her throat and chest. The culprit of her distress in clearing her lungs sat blaring at her; where was the remote? A harmless tray of food on the other side of her tank filled her senses with pleasure, but where could the remote be? She watched Gabriella disappear down the hall. Marian inhaled deep, allowing her lungs to fill with air. After a few routine coughs, Marian devoured the pickled fish, roasted Korean seaweed snacks, and sweet rice balls. She opened the pink thermos and guzzled the water.

Several commercials later, a special news program flashed on. The older Caucasian man rattled on in a deep serious tone. "It's been almost a full year since 61 imprisoned individuals were *all* found under one roof..."

As the newscaster explained the name and nature of the H.E.C.C.s and compared their mutated abilities to humans, Marian's facial expressions turned cold.

The TV continued, "...They are the first documented living humanoid race found in the Milkyway. They weren't openly welcomed at first, but thanks to increasingly available information and understanding in the US, the outcry against them lessens. They were born human before they were stripped of that title by a maniacal doctor. The kidnapped, mutated individuals have tried to re-enter society like nothing traumatic happened. All they want is to live in peace, in a semblance of their previously normal lives. With the recent close calls that Heccan Dinison Shane Wyllis has had in the depths of the ocean, a number of anti-HECC groups beg for a permanent solution of all H.E.C.C.s being dumped in the sea to live, or die, among 'their kind'..."

Marian closed her eyes and shivered.

"It is a very unkind solution," the anchor soured. "Sharks usually mistake humans as seals or other marine buffet items, but they are far more enthusiastic predators toward the H.E.C.C.s. Since Pro-H.E.C.C.s have accused the government of dangling Heccs in front of predators as some sick scientific experiment, the Navy Seals are not taking any additional chances with their Heccan crewmate or with the heated media debate."

A lump developed inside Marian's throat. She cringed as she thought, *There's no freedom on land and there's no freedom without an extreme price in the oceans.* Swallowing hard, she listened intently as her eyes soaked up the madness. Groaning, Marian turned around and disappeared under water.

"Here with us today to talk about the latest happenings with H.E.C.C. politics is Hecc Ambassador, Jayne Flynn."

Perking her ears up, Marian jumped to the surface and sprawled her arms over the edge. The sight of Jayne on the television thanking the viewers for allowing him to be on the show struck pride in Marian's heart. Her soul leapt sky high at the sight of him. Instead of cowering behind a bandana, he proudly wore a sparkling green vest showing off his muscular arms, a silver tie against his oiled bare skin and dress black slacks. His sandaled feet revealed silver toenails glinting when the light caressed them. Fear did not emanate from his eyes or his straight posture, causing strangers to assume he was entirely at ease. Although his hands rested in his lap, Marian could tell his arms flexed with tension.

"Hello. Thank you. Good news first, Roland McGregor of the Try Hard movies will be returning to his career as an actor." He paused before he continued with a straight face.

Marian rolled her eyes when the studio lost power briefly. She knew in her heart that it had been on purpose so the shadow on Jayne's face accustomed the viewers to seeing Jayne's glowing eyes as he turned to a more serious topic. He didn't skip a beat as he continued. "I am sad to report that the Navy will be giving Heccan Dinison an honorable discharge on August 1, complete with a public ceremony. Before his unfortunate kidnapping, he had earned medals for courageously completing several difficult missions. The Navy lost a great asset when he went missing in action. However, when he returned, he found that his co-workers fought against him being reinstated. They wanted to deny his chance to obtain what was rightfully his: freedom to earn a living and achieve the American Dream. H.E.C.C.s everywhere should be able to live, work and own their own material things. They should not have to rely on the charity of others to prosper." Jayne never lost eye contact with the camera. He spoke as though he wouldn't back down from any pending battle.

Jayne's voice faded in Marian's mind as her heart fluttered. The water deceptively crushed her chest. Visions of her former life overwhelmed her with an itch to take a step with her lower limbs. Straightening her limbs, she sank to the bottom of the tank on one end of the small pebbled wavy path dividing the tank in half. Staring at the curtain covered window, she straightened her knees. One by one, she inched forward, but her knees jerked up with every point of pressure. The joints that used to be ankles could not fully bend to ninety degrees.

Exasperated, Marian opened her mouth wide. A scream resonated underwater. She tried again and again to walk under the water. Without being aware, she generated an electrical charge which built from her ankles to her hands. When she released it, she whirled about. Right behind her, the new suckerfish did not twitch. His lifeless remains haunted Marian. Shaking fists replaced delicate hands.

Marian wailed. In short order, she repeated her angry cry. Bursting through the surface, Marian threw her arms onto the edge. After she coughed, horror stiffened her limbs and dilated her pupils as she stared at eyes looking directly through her soul.

Billy, in his signature green pants and shirt, stood with his back leaning against the wall. His spiked green hair jumped off his scalp. His warm eyes did not shrink back from Marian's fear.

Marian stared back at him with irritation and frustration. "When I went to sleep, the fish were fine. I woke up… and…and… they were all dead! I killed them! Every last one of them. I even killed the new suckerfish Tyler just bought!"

"Nightmare, you had, hmm? Worry about bad dreams, do not. Heccs and humans alike experiences bad dreams. Yes, hmmm. In fact, nightmare last night, I had. Your instincts just kicked into gear. You used the force and…" Billy nodded his head. "An accident, it was. Yeesssssss…"

Sniffles attempted to escape Marian's taut lips. Clouds rolled in over Marian's eyes. Her face puckered with sadness, anger and fear.

Billy's concerned eyes did not glance away. He lifted his forced, cute growl. "Died as a human, you did. Rejoice to be transformed, you should. Mourn the past do not. Miss it, do not. A beautiful young Heccwan, you are. Embrace her future, a Hecc should. Should she not, hrmm?"

Silent cold moments passed before a disarming smile eased onto the corners of Marian's lips. With a deep inhale, she sighed. "I should, shouldn't I… oh, wise Billy-Wan Kenobi?"

Taken aback by the warm zing, Billy jumped away from the wall. Instead of being offended, Billy swallowed the lump in his throat. With affection, he answered with a mischievous grin. "Come on, now. Mock me, do not. Kill you to listen to me, I think not. I really am wise. Hmmmm… Understand I see things. Try not. Do. Or do not. There is no try." He zigzagged toward the aquarium. "Leave behind the dark side. Embrace your future, you should. Hurt you to find your talents, I think not. Embrace your destiny, you should."

Marian's jaw dropped. She gasped. "But… how? Why?" Lifting her voice, she shrieked, "I was afraid of water and here… here… I *am*, stuck in it. My worst nightmare came true! How? How, you goofball!?" Pausing, Marian tucked her chin to her chest and shook it back and forth. "How can I embrace the life of a cripple? I'm all alone."

Leaning forward, Billy waved under her chin with his right hand.

Lifting her chin up, Marian stared with hardened eyes.

Compassion radiated from Billy's eyes, tenderizing the broken life before him. "Alone, hrmm? Alone? You are not! A total of sixty-one H.E.C.Cs., there are! Much family here, you have, hmm? Yes, hrmmm." Once Billy finished, he sat down on the floor with his back leaning on the wall next to a window. Pulling out a popular science fiction book, Billy flipped the pages until he found his place.

Marian stared dumbfounded at the top of Billy's head. Warmth filled her heart.

{:-)-]~~{

Over the next few weeks, company comforted Marian by resting near her as she watched special news reports and interviews with H.E.C.C.s.

Public protests died off, except for a few remaining supremacists including the East Burro Church. Overall, public opinion now pushed for mankind to protect the new-found race. Every H.E.C.C. along with Marian/Hope developed confidence and optimism as the media no longer searched for stories of 'freaks', but of the tales showing strong individuals who had escaped a maniac. Human interest stories of how loved ones were reunited headlined talk shows. Most TV programmers gobbled up the increase in ratings.

Excitement filled Marian's fins as she watched several Heccwans in the broadcasted shows working at oceanariums. Envy stirred the blood in Marian's veins and her eyes glazed over when shows contained H.E.C.C.s in swimming pools displaying their talents. Positive media attention stirred admiration for the new race. As the novelty wore off, understanding broadened and wisdom was encouraged in dealings with the H.E.C.C.s. Jayne's media campaign was working and the Hecc's were becoming more accepted. However, what they truly desired was to be on their own and keep the money they made. Not letting the humans they worked for take advantage of them. They really didn't want managers or agents; they just wanted a life on their own of freedom without fame and fortune.

Disheartened and lonely, Marian ignored the TV as the interviews slowed down. The front door never opened with Jayne back from his tour. Marian gave up looking for a phone call from him. Gabriella saddened as she realized the huge Sharp family wasn't feeding the full need for companionship that her daughter longed for. Radically embracing the life of a hermit, Marian refused to talk to Marshall on three phone calls. She hid from family and sulked underwater for hours on end. She avoided anyone who splashed the water to get her attention. Diving toys lost their appeal. Marian dreamed about her life when she was human. Running, freedom to roam about, and ordinary electronics were things of the past. There just wasn't a lot to look forward to in a future stuck in a tub. Phone calls were rejected with frequent excuses. Her deep persistent funk worried those around her more than she would have believed.

Just Keep Swimming

To Tread or Not To Tread?

Chapter 20

n a beautiful day in early September, Jayne sat comfortably on the brown vinyl couch in the large cyber tea-shop. Its main room comprised of a counter and shelves upon shelves of all sorts of things to buy. Books, fancy boxes of tea and coffee were on the lower shelves whereas the breakables were placed higher. Teapots, press pots, tea sets and all sorts of utensils were encased in glass-fronted, vertical oak cases that lined the walls. Another room accommodated a coffee/tea bar, complete with several tables full of college students working on socializing or homework on their laptops. Reference, fiction and best sellers covered one wall from top to bottom. Board games and tables filled the lounge room. Sweet flowers and potpourri seasoned the air.

Looking around the room, Jayne glanced at his watch, *he's late.* With a navy pseudo turban wrapped around his head, Jayne sported a full length navy blue overcoat, the collar of which partially covered the back of his neck. He wore a black vest, white loose-sleeved shirt and baggy black trousers. The tension of being in the human world, kept his posture straight, tall, and stiff.

The shoulder-length blonde-haired employee seductively smiled at Jayne as she arrived with a tray. Sporting a black knee-length skirt and a form-fitting white shirt, her ravishing good looks failed to help her zealous flirtations.

Jayne returned a half-smile. His mind was focused inward and elsewhere.

Bending over to where the top two unbuttoned buttons revealed a rose tattoo, the sassy young lady lifted his cup up off the round tray she carried. She set the large blue teacup steaming with hot chicory coffee on the table in front of him on a coaster with the cafe's logo. Next, she placed a glass of ice water on another coaster.

Without even an upwards glance, Jayne put two fingers in his water. After he fished out four chunks of ice, he dropped them in his coffee.

"Sorry," said Jayne as the waitress took a napkin out of her short black apron and wiped up the small spill.

"It's all right. No harm, no foul. My name's Summer, like the hot season." Summer's extended eyelashes batted. The rose blush on her cheeks slightly moved with her sensual expression. She stood momentarily, straightening her curtailed skirt with her free hand.

Millions of light years away, Jayne's mind seemed trapped in a wormhole. Oblivious to picking up and sipping, he set the cup down again. All plans and emotions flew back to one continuous thought, *Will this work?* The scratched record played over and over again with a heavy, worried heart.

A movement caught Summer's eye. Doug, wearing a navy blue suit, grinned like a Cheshire cat as he silently crept up on Jayne. His right hand signaled for her to keep his secret. Summer shrugged and quietly removed herself from the situation to find a chore to accomplish.

Each foot picked up and tiptoed down slower than a box turtle crossing a highway. Inch after inch, Doug situated himself behind Jayne. He waited until Jayne set his cup down again before he roughly placed his hands on Jayne's shoulders.

Jayne didn't move or jump.

"You're no fun," whimpered Doug as he slogged around to plop beside him.

"I might be deep in thought, but I can still hear and smell better than *you* or any dog. You can change your clothes, but you will always smell the same to me. In fact, I'm going to buy you a new aftershave when I get my next paycheck from the Embassy." Turning his head toward Doug, he made direct eye contact. The corner of Jayne's smile twisted his lips into a mischievous grin.

Leaning back, Doug's lips tightened into a straight disapproving line. "Better not be salmon oil!" Doug's visage went from grimace to somber. "Anyway, sorry that I missed the last few meetings." Shrugging his shoulders, he lifted his ankle up to rest on his other knee. He placed one hand on the back on the couch and the other in his lap.

"I see you're missing a GPS tracking device on your ankle."

"Yup."

Jayne lifted his cup to his lips and sipped it. Looking up at the ceiling, his nostrils flared ever so slightly as he smelled the air. When he placed his cup down, he lowered his voice, "How's community service going? I just wish you didn't have so many hours."

"Ah, you know, full of work." Doug's sarcastic statement ended with a very forced smile. "It really ain't that bad. I could have been given serious time, but the prosecutor and the judge agreed if I did community service to work off my debt to society; the charges would be reduced." Doug's lips twitched from a frown into a weak smile. "He made it lighter 'cause the Heccs begged him. Instead of being a jailer to the Human Electric Cave Catfish, I have now become a servant to them. Jon's testimony of me sneaking him food against the doc's orders made the difference between prison and community service. A few nurses accidently testified to it too when they found me skipping meals."

"I didn't know you snuck him *your* food."

Doug ignored Jayne by looking around the room. His hand caressed a sliver of a scar on his throat. Fear sparked an intense fire in his eyes.

Jayne stared at Doug and quickly changed subjects. "I still don't know what's going to happen to the nurses yet. Dr. Jensen is still advocating for them. He insists that he needs their expertise." Jayne moved closer to the edge of the couch and gingerly placed his hand on his chin.

"Anyway, thanks for moving the meetings here." Doug hesitantly announced, "I have some news."

"Oh, yeah?"

"Yeah… I went to court today."

"You didn't tell me you had court! I thought you were just trying to make a new fashion statement. Martin never told me."

Doug pulled at his collar and chuckled. He put his foot on the floor and sat up. "Yeah, I told him not to. It was supposed to be a sur…"

Jayne interrupted. "So tell me!"

"Martin represented me and got the Judge to give me a different kind of community service."

"Quit dragging it out and tell me!"

"I'm stuck being a gofer." His shoulders drooped for emphasis. "I gotta work for a snobby ambassador… go for this, go for that. You know… a *gofer*!" Doug stared at Jayne waiting for a reaction.

Jayne's face wrinkled up trying to figure things out. His perplexed face was suddenly crossed with a growing ornery grin. "Which ambassador?"

"One who has bad taste in dress and cologne."

"No, really? I know a few like that. Which one?"

"Spain!" Doug jeered. "Bubble brain, the Hecc Ambassador!"

Mischievous peace pulled at the corners of Jayne's mouth. "Inconceivable!"

Full of joy, the two merrily repeated the word innumerable times as they laughed. Jumping off the couch, Jayne and Doug high-fived each other and whooped their enthusiasm. They concluded with a bear hug. Both quickly ended it. Out of the corners of their eyes, they noticed Summer's silhouette. With feline grace, she strode up while humming a song about being a hot woman. They backed away from each other. Any sailor would let his dry tongue hang out when he calculated the measure of her ravishing waist where more than a handful was a waste to greedy, calloused hands. A flash of gold over her bellybutton could be seen peeking through the thin material.

Doug's heart skipped a beat. Both his starving eyes scoped out her shapely legs dancing under her curvy hips. As if under the spell of her mysterious sweet spicy perfume, he turned his superb torso to her and aligned his feet with his square shoulders. Lifting his powerful chest higher, his husky biceps rippled as he placed his strong hands on his hips above his warming thighs. Doug's chest firmed as he raised his eyebrows. His eyes twinkled with increasing infatuation from the surreal thoughts in his passionate mind.

"The rest of your party is here, Ambassador Flynn," announced Summer, pleasant in her attitude and sultry countenance. Touching her luscious lipstick on her lips with her smooth forefinger, she curtsied with reddening fair cheeks. Her flirtatious finger moved precisely and elegantly, enticing them to follow without question.

Jayne scooped his backpack up off the floor from under the table and skipped two feet to catch Doug and the server.

The young woman's hour-glass figure moved to the rhythm of the music in the spellbound background. Her curvy legs crisscrossed a path toward the conference room. *Boom boom boom* went the beat of her desirable hip drum. *Click click click* tapped the confident thin three inch heels.

Doug didn't mind admiring the prize. His eyebrows rose as he slightly tilted his mesmerized head to exercise his eyes and thirsty neck. Jayne absent-mindedly reached over and snapped Doug's slacked jaw. They were here for business; not for luscious distractions.

"Refreshments will be here shortly. Restrooms are located on the east wall." Summer spoke with a slight lacy sing-song. After she opened the door, she retained it as Doug walked through. Flitting eyelashes stopped so a flirtatious wink could be directed at Jayne. "Is there anything else I can do for you, Mr. Flynn?"

Jayne inched to the opposite side of the doorway. Reaching his hands behind him, he hugged it with his back. "No… No, thank you."

Summer pranced toward Jayne, but he managed to slip in unmolested.

"Ambassador!"

Summer shied away as she reluctantly closed the thick door.

Even though Derrick was born and raised in the US, his parents' Irish accent popped up frequently. Jayne knowingly smiled.

"Jayne, my good man." Derrick vigorously shook Jayne's hand while placing his free hand on Jayne's shoulder. "So good you could arrange this!"

Jayne sang, "Mr. McKinney!"

"I cannot wait for this idea to be revealed to the world!" Derrick, with short-clipped red hair, stepped back. He was a pleasant, courteous man whose height and build matched Jayne's. Business was his life, but he refrained from being a workaholic. His broad genuine expression and dancing blue eyes could part murky business dealings easily.

Stepping five feet into the room, Jayne surveyed it. Bright blue carpet framed the large glass covered oak table. Black leather chairs skirted it. Three smooth white walls framed up-to-date abstract colorful art. Efficient, comfortable and private, a good place to bring together all of the diverse group of people he had been planning and negotiating with these past few months.

Joseph Vang, a short Asian man, demanded attention and respect from everyone, taller or shorter than he. His blunt-cut black hair didn't quite cover eyes that bored into one's soul. Without allowing distraction, he hurried about opening his briefcase and putting papers on the table in front of his chair. Briefly looking up at Jayne, he briskly nodded before returning to his important task.

Jayne nodded at Sonny Leddon, whose idea of dressing up included a blue silk shirt with a black stringed bolo tie, nice blue jeans and brown cowboy boots. In his right hand, he carried his tan rodeo hat which, before entering, had covered his thin-on-top jet black hair. A home-stitched brown leather portfolio stamped with the initials of his huge family farm dangled in his left hand. Sonny's handlebar mustache moved side-to-side and up before straightening out as his nose twitched.

"Where's your brother?" asked Jayne.

"Al couldn't break away from the farm. He's tryin' ta save money. He discharged his help. He an' his dogs are workin' the critters. His wife and daughters are milkin' while his sons are harvestin'."

"We could use more men like Albert." Jayne nodded and scooted past Leddon.

Lee Biggs, Eric Fox, and Buddy Graham turned around in their chairs to acknowledge Jayne. They were elegantly dressed in matching black suits, white shirts, gold watches, and formal ties.

"Don't get up. Mr. Biggs, Mr. Fox, Mr. Graham." Jayne nodded at each individual as they sank back into their chairs. One eyebrow lifted. "Lee, Buddy, I didn't think you could make it."

"My employer, the cruise line, was sniffing around, monitoring *my leave*, which hastened my decision to *leave*." Buddy's smile inverted as his lantern-jaw tightened. An angry flush brightened his tan skin. "I am ready for dry land. I've been away at sea all my life."

Lee cleared his throat before answering in his natural bass tone. "My company made a counter offer to retain me, but I'm ready to co-run our amusement park. We moved our families to Eric's Missouri rental properties."

Inhaling deeply, Jayne exhaled a deliberative sigh. "Thank you, Mr. Fox. Do you still have a job?" He continued to pick his way toward the head of the table. Alert, Jayne never lost eye contact.

"They are letting me stay on… for now."

Hunching down, Jayne carefully dropped his backpack in the seat.

Click. Squeak. The door opened. Summer appeared briefly, flicking her hair. Jayne drooped to the left and ran his fingers over his face allowing his head to dip down.

The bright-eyed server strutted aside revealing a sweaty Stanley Jordan. Scuttling in, his stubby legs knocked against his beer belly causing it to rhythmically bounce. His reddish five-o'clock shadow slightly hid his freckled face. The windy day had ruffled his unkempt hair, causing him to appear as though he had arrived straight from his bed. Words barely wheezed out of him. "Ssssorry. Hyme late."

"Ah. Hakuna Matata, Stan. We're right on time I say," a deep voice echoed from outside the door.

A sudden small light danced about. Jayne closed his eyes and slowly shook his head.

A large man's right hand suddenly appeared, grabbing the doorframe. On the man's ring finger, a garish amount of diamonds glimmered on a golden NBA championship ring, reflecting the lights. In ducked a head of close-thatched raven hair covering coal black skin. Intense green eyes twinkled while a grin spread that could melt a hardened woman's heart. The neatly rounded goatee and pencil mustache complimented his square jaw and high cheek bones.

Cautiously, Jayne re-opened his eyes. Maybe the lights should be dimmed with all the bling that just came in.

"Jambo," said Edward Spleers, as the rest of his long-limbed, 6'8" body jerked ungracefully through the open door. His smoking guns danced, drawing attention away from his broad shoulders. Toned, firm pectoral muscles rippled under his blue silk shirt as he balanced his weight.

Startled, Stanley gasped, "Hey." Towering black slacks was all that Stanley, a slouching 4'5, could see momentarily. In short order, he waddled away with his wide eyes focused on the predator behind him.

"Hello," enunciated Edward as he nodded toward the grinning Jayne. Pulling a signed red jersey out of his black duffle bag, he tossed it at Jayne.

"Thanks." Jayne waved the jersey in Edward's direction, folded it and tucked it in his own bag.

Edward darted three steps at a time, rapidly making his way around the room. While he made eye contact with everyone, he told them "Jambo" or "Hello". Constantly, he focused on the adventure of the here and now. "Oh, Jayne!" Tossing Jayne a look of concern, the edges of his smile curled down. Edward stated, "My business partner, Gerald Murphey, will not be here."

"Everything all right," asked Fox.

"Yes. He took his pregnant wife to the hospital. Again. Maybe this time they will keep her." Edward's face persisted as bright and cheery. "She was due last week!" He scratched the spot where his shoulders met the back of his neck. Laughter erupted out of his mouth as he pulled his hand down.

Doug positioned himself to the left of Jayne and crossed his arms. Jayne introduced him in a flash.

The bright lighting encouraged the men to settle in the windowless room, wanting to get down to business. Some unfolded their laptops and/or briefcases on the table. Each one set about finding files, papers, or notebooks before the meeting officially started.

Jayne slipped into the bathroom. Feeling at ease, he unwrapped his head and took off his outer clothes leaving on his blue-striped black swim trunks. Dropping his clothes onto his backpack on the black leather sofa, Jayne greedily ran to the sink and turned on the life-giving water. Sticking his face under the cool water, he lost track of time.

Doug entered. "You coming?"

Bumping his head on the faucet, Jayne shook his head, nodded and coughed. Fumbling about, he clumsily turned the cold handle which brought the water to a screeching halt. When he walked into the room, no one looked up. They were deep in conversation. Water dripped down his back and trickled all the way to the floor. Instead of sitting down, Jayne remained standing. Looking around the room, Jayne flashed a greeting at Marshall who had arrived while he had been in the restroom.

{:-)-]~~{

It had been almost a month since Marian had talked with anyone. Gabriella knew she was still alive, since she could see her daughter swimming about under water. There was also the healthy sign of missing food from the tray. On September 2, Gabriella broke down and called Marshall on his cell phone. She was in her room and away from Marian, so she was able to talk freely about her frustrations. Tears poured down as she anxiously vocalized her fears without letting Marshall get in any word that would derail her.

"Marshall, she is absolutely depressed, refusing any life outside of that *tank*! It's become a pain to try to get her to even eat. It's gotten to the point of leaving a cooler next to *the tank* with food and water in it because she will leave a plate there for hours. We *even* put a portable camping toilet close by *the tank*. She refuses to clean the algae. Nobody wants to go in there to clean it for her and she has killed every sucker fish we put in there! I don't know if I should believe her that their deaths are accidents or if she is charging the tank on purpose. Jack has had to replace the maintenance equipment way too many times lately...Our savings to buy a house are evaporating! I haven't talked to her for *two weeks* now. No *one* has!" Gabriella cried while Marshall just listened. "Billy, William, and Willetta can't even coax her out!

The next thing she knew, Marshall whispered. "Listen, Gabby, I'm working on a solution right now, okay? Now I've got to go." As quick as he had said it, Marshall hung up.

{:-)-]~~{

"Listen," Derrick growled. "Mr. Harrison, we were polite and quiet while you were on the phone with your social call, but we are conducting a meeting here. Is there anything that you need to tell us concerning our business arrangement?" Sarcasm oozed in his voice, "Or can we get on with the meeting?"

"Who says it's social? It is about the root problem that has brought us together; the welfare of my daughter and every other Hecc in this crazy nightmare!" huffed Marshall.

Seated next to Marshall, Jayne stared wide-eyed at him. His heart pounded painful drums in his chest and ears. His breath failed as Gabriella's words preyed upon him. Jayne's nostrils flared.

Desperation and frustration required all his attention to be whipped back under control. He inhaled and sighed, keeping his thoughts to himself. *This project needs to continue moving forward. Maybe it would move faster if it was made public.* Jayne sat back and stared at the ceiling. *Sneaking around and avoiding the Sharp's must end. Responsibility for the Heccs includes responsibility for Hope too.*

The thought of Hope's smiling lips warmed Jayne's soul and his body. *I am closer to her than the others, even Jonathon.* Momentarily, he permitted his mind to be captured by memories of his recent sojourn with the Sharp's. Many times, the two would wake up from nightmares about the pet shop or kidnappers. Several times, they lit their environment with electricity from their disturbed dreams. The two would secretly hold each other, shivering with anxiety. The terrible flashback of the day the Doctor forbade him to leave the pet shop stole the very air from his lungs. It was the day after his mom's funeral. He thought to himself, *I can talk to her and share my deep thoughts. The others are my racial responsibility…and they look up to me. They need me…but…*

The daydream of Jayne 'bringing home the bacon' warmed his mind and heart. *But, from the day I saw her, I promised myself I would save Hope and give her a life, a home…no matter what…* His cheeks reddened. He missed the way her gorgeous eyes batted at him, as the sound of her feminine voice intrigued him. *I promised her my heart. I've become her main source of comfort in this new world.* Recollections of being mesmerized by the jewel on her forehead, of being drawn in like a treasure hunter to the compelling sparkle of precious metal, pleased him.

Jayne's beaming eyes shifted to his hands, unconsciously massaging his starving thighs. The glint in his eye molded into self-hatred. Every muscle in his body froze for his heart no longer pumped desire through veins, it flooded his cells with ill feelings. *But no! Here I am deserting her! When she needs me the most… I left her hanging out to dry like raw meat! I haven't been calling her because I promised…* Jayne's eyes darted a stiff glance at Marshall.

A sweet smelling, triangular butterscotch scone sat untouched in front of Marshall. He pushed it and the cold cappuccino toward the middle of the table as he leaned forward to listen. Having a tender stomach allowed him to take only a few sips. An irregular rhythm pumped the blood through his veins. A trickle of warm sweat rolled down the back of his frigid neck. Marshall used his left hand to swab it into his shirt collar. His knee bounced with a nervous twitch while each investor discussed their ideas. Derrick carefully noted down each possibility.

Marshall, Jayne spat in his head. *I know she can pry things out of me… But! I'm the reason she is moping. Not being allowed to call her is affecting us both! Gabby said I could call until midnight.* Jayne's conflicting thoughts were interrupted by the irritating sound of Marshall's intestine serenading anyone close by. Jayne stared at Marshall's plate and then at him. *But, that will still delay their bedtime. Ah, but if I don't do anything… Gabriella sounded like Hope needs a cure and maybe a phone call from me would help soothe things. Surely Hope will talk to me.*

The discussion morphed into the possibility of having a casino worked into the plans. Each individual eagerly vocalized their ideas, but Derrick whined with pessimism, "The Kansas government has a monopoly on casinos. Private individuals or groups cannot compete."

"Indians have casinos." Vang responded without looking up from the papers spread out in front of him in neat piles. "They are their own nation."

Nodding, Jayne raised his forefinger. "I bet since the Heccs are now considered their own nationality, the Kansas government can't squawk about it. I can get Martin to push for it."

Marshall stood up. "It will have a unique location, we can definitely compete with anything in the area; if we build a high quality casino, we should be able to draw from around the country." Like wildfire, it raised his interest. "I will invest in it. I've got some additional money besides what I originally put in."

Derrick stood up. "You got additional money besides what you raised for the reward?"

Marshall nodded. "Yes, it's pretty substantial.

"You gonna run it?"

"No. I just want to invest in it."

"How much?"

"I've got somewhere in the ball park of just above 6 zeros."

Derrick sat down before the numbness hit his kneecaps. "I thought you had a few major gambling debts to pay off."

"Gentlemen, living off of gambling has its ups and downs, like any other job. I found an up I haven't shared. I just recently ran into a few guys who decided to pay off a debt they owe me. I persuaded them to pay up early."

"How'd you do that," questioned Jayne.

"I simply increased their interest rate and they came up with the cash."

"You got it here?"

"No, but I should have it in ten days."

Everyone around the table nodded their guarded approval.

Derrick rubbed his hands together as if they needed to be warmed up. "I guess we could have a casino." He paused as his eyes gleamed. "It would enhance the business income brought in by the tourists."

Jayne started to open his mouth to counter Marshall's tale of good luck, but perhaps Marshall didn't tell him everything. Movement caught Jayne's attention so he closed his mouth. Doug's waving left hand fell to his side. With his right hand, he motioned, in no formal sign language, that he was leaving early, his lips forming the words without a sound. Jayne nodded and indicated sotto-voce he would catch back up with him at the hotel.

{:-)-]~~{

Chapter 21

Listening to the click of the receiver as Marshall abruptly ended the call, Gabriella sat dumbstruck as to what solution might be available in this human dominated society. The H.E.C.C.s were the smallest minority that she knew of. She didn't know what to make of it. Turning around, Gabriella found herself sitting right next to Mildred's belly. Placing the phone back on its cradle on her dark wooden vanity, she turned around and stood up from her round wicker stool. When Gabriella faced her mother-in-law directly, she found Mildred's eyes begging her for an explanation of the conversation. Gabriella sighed. Her cheeks stung from her hot tears. She fixed her hair and kneaded her face.

"Dear, what did he say?" Mildred yearned to help any way she could. Her mothering desire illuminated her compassionate soul. "What was he talking about?"

"I don't know," Gabriella lamented as she touched her head. Her tightened facial muscles hinted a stress headache would emerge if she didn't focus on the positive atoms in life. Thinking about possible solutions presented a path down the road to madness. She carefully shook her head and shrugged concern off of her shoulders. There was nothing she could do about it today.

"Marian is five years older than Melista, Isn't she?"

"Yes." Gabriella smiled at the fond memory of being a mother around Mildred's surprise miraculous pregnancy. A wicked grin brightened her cheeks. "You and I are 20 years apart."

"Don't remind me. Jack was 17 and I was 16 when I had Marcy. Jack's folks gave us a shotgun wedding." Mildred turned away, lost in time. She straightened her shoulders and focused on Gabriella. "Don't change the subject. I'm not falling for it anymore."

The wicked grin wiped off of Gabriella's face leaving a dark loneliness in its place.

"Melista and Marian were sorta close right before Marian went missing. I wonder why they aren't close now?"

Shrugging, Gabriella sighed.

"What about her IQ?"

"Mood has nothing to do with IQ. The doctor said that when Marian was kidnapped and held in a comatose state, she missed out on years of physiological and educational experiences. She didn't drop in IQ; she just acts like a teenager because she missed out on eight years of growing up. Doctor said it's normal for being so traumatized."

"She's definitely a handful right now."

Gabriella moaned, lifted her face to the ceiling and growled.

Mildred placed a reassuring hand on Gabriella's right shoulder. "Marian has gotten close to Billy, William and Willetta. What do they say?"

"Marian has hid from them too." Gabriella yanked her shoulder away and started off in a huff. "Well, if you'll excuse me, I'm going to go find Mary. At least I still have one daughter who will talk to me." As soon as she finished speaking such ungraceful words, she briskly walked down the second floor's hallway toward the elevator and stairs.

"It doesn't do any good to avoid her," Mildred hollered wryly after her. She quickened her steps to follow Gabriella into the hallway.

Gabriella had heard Mildred, paused in her tracks, and grimaced. She started on a determined path again, but rolled her eyes and stopped. Sadness crept over her frozen stance as she thought to herself. *She's right, but how can I relate with her if she makes sour faces and dives under water to avoid me? Doesn't Marian know how that feels?* Gabriella trudged to the elevator and rode it to the first floor. The door opened with noisy gears. She inhaled and let out a deep sigh as she shifted her weight. Changing her mind, she pushed the button to the basement.

Gabriella searched all over the basement, interrupting merriment and conversations. She could not find Mary. She went up the stairs that ascended into the conservatory. She was not thrilled about searching in this direction, but perhaps Mary was harassing Marian again.

As Gabriella reached the main floor, she heard Melista and Mary giggling. Instead of frankly announcing her presence, Gabriella covertly peeked around to see what was so funny. They were seated next to Marian's aquarium, reading a book. Mary, curled up in Melista's lap, pointed at the page.

"No, see, that's why..." Mary couldn't finish her sentence as she rocked back and forth and squirmed. Her thin little arms flailed and clung to her sides.

Melista tickled and argued with fake displeasure.

Gabriella smiled with pleasure, enjoying the scene. She casually folded her arms to keep herself from openly breaking the spell. Movement caught her eye. Quietly, Marian popped her head out of the water to covertly watch the giggle fest. Mary and Melista could not see the warm delightful expression on Marian's face, but Gabriella could. Slowly, a sinister smile played with the corners of her mouth, a wonderfully devious idea had popped into Gabriella's head.

Two nieces surprisingly ran into the room from the opposite stairway, breaking the serene spell. They shouted, "Mary! Mary, come quick!"

A startled Marian disappeared underwater, leaving a whirlpool behind.

Mary's face changed from bright laughter to wrinkled begging. "Um... Aunt Melista?"

"We can finish the book later," Melista smiled pleasantly and helped her niece jump up. Melista watched the noisy commotion as her three nieces ran down the stairs.

Gabriella tiptoed into the room, making her presence known to Melista. Placing one finger on her lips, Gabriella's free hand motioned in a coming manner for Melista to join her. Shrugging her shoulders, Melista wrinkled her nose. She gathered a small stack of books next to her, hopped up, and then softly crept to her sister-in-law. The two conniving women disappeared downstairs out of ear shot of Marian before Gabriella disclosed her plan.

{:-)-]~~{

Chapter 22

Intense discussions challenged Jayne's patience. The meeting would not end. He imagined his hair increasing its length. Jayne had said what he'd planned to say. Now, his knees bounced nervously, while Marshall had calmed down, lost in planning a new casino. All his thoughts surrounded Hope. He sighed. Looking at Derrick, he excused himself with a whisper.

The tiny sink reminded Jayne of a prison. He shook his head and turned the water on. The water that dripped down his back drained off a commendable amount of stress hormones. He cupped water in his hands, while he exhaled the air in his lungs. Lowering his head with forbidden glee, he bumped his cheek as he situated his nose and mouth in the running water. His engaging gills commandeered his lungs while Jayne instinctively 'breathed in' the water for more than a few minutes.

Coughing, Jayne required his lungs to transition as he supported his balance with his hands placed on the edges of the sink. Turning off the water with a flick of his wrist, he encouraged his weary eyes to close. Free as a disembodied soul, water dripped off his face and hair into the sink. When he tried to flush his mind from stress, he recalled the time he sat with Jonathon and plotted escape plans. After the FBI rescued them, the idea to stay in caves had now slowly evolved into creating a city that looked like it was built in a sea-side cavern. Making that a reality was proving to be more than challenging to all involved. Distracted, Jayne did not pay attention to the countless minutes which passed by. Just as an idea struck him, he was startled back into reality by the sudden and unexpected creak of the door echoing in the room, followed by a bang against the wall.

"You alright?" Passion fueled the spring in Marshall's step and his furrowed eyebrows.

Petrified, Jayne dared to collect his thoughts and forced his muscles to move. He realized he held his palms out toward Marshall with a defensive posture. Dropping them sheepishly to his sides, Jayne forced a happy poker face.

"You coming soon?"

"Yeah."

Marshall took back his presence from Jayne's view as he roughly shut the door behind him.

Jayne's left hand raised and flattened his hair to his head. He placed his hands back on the sink and stared at his reflection in the mirror. "Maybe life will be different." Conflicts about the meeting ran through his brain. The future of day-to-day mundane jobs looked brighter. However, he was getting tired of living like this, having to stay wet and hydrated by constantly using a sink faucet on long days when no pool was available. It was a pain to live in the human world as he had once done. Joy turned to sorrow as he thought of the impossibilities of the discussions in the other room. Arguments had to stop and agreements needed to be made for the utopian city to ever be built.

Jayne whispered, "Mirror, mirror on the wall, should we just live on the coasts?" As he rolled his eyes and heaved a sigh, he turned away from the metallic painted glass. "I guess," Jayne pondered in a normal voice. "The city... it would be nice to live without being on the bottom of the food chain." Worry seeped in, wrinkling his brows, as he faced the mirror again. "Will this ever become reality?" Without another question or answer to himself, he straightened up, dried off leftover drips and bolted for the other room.

Jayne started to enter and found several pairs of eyes watching him. Pausing just outside the door, Jayne hesitated. He looked down. His eyes widened as he discovered he had forgotten to put his disguise back on. His feet prepared an about face.

"Hey Jayne," Marshall gave him a nod. "You look like you have something on your mind."

Jayne backed up against the bathroom door and rested his hand behind him. "I... uh," he stuttered momentarily. Standing tall, Jayne stepped away from his escape route. "I had an idea come to me. Why not call our indoor city, 'Centerearth Caverns'? I mean, we already decided to *make it look* like a cavern."

After exchanging glances, Lee, Stanley, and Sonny nodded. They beamed as they focused on Jayne.

Sonny piped up, "That's a great name. I like it!"

The words "Centerearth Caverns" were muttered several times by all to see how it rolled off their own tongue.

"Centerearth Caverns... it is!" Derrick announced. Vang nodded while everyone else applauded.

Creak. The outer door surprisingly opened and stood ajar. In waddled a pudgy Irishman and three trim Caucasians. Jayne's eyes fearfully widened.

Jumping up, Derrick dashed to Jayne's side. He thundered, "Who are you?"

The newcomers froze in their tracks as the rest of the investors stood, wary and enigmatic.

The crowd of newcomers was suddenly parted, being weed-whacked by elbows. A confident 5'2" breasty wasp-waisted doll faced individual declared, "Excuse me, gentlemen." Her annoyed sing-song voice rang out like a loud bubbly gospel singer. Her thick brunette French braid bounced as she walked. "Derrick! We have spoken over the phone. I am Jacqueline Hodge and I will be the owner of The Cafe in the town that we are building." Pointing at the men, she introduced them. "Tommy O'Hayer will have the grocery store. Carl Stevenson has an idea about a casino. Frank Greenwood has a bar and grill idea he'd like to bounce off you. Percy Gillis, here, is interested in building a dance hall for the human inhabitants."

"And Jayne of course, I hear he can still dance." Derrick shook their hands. "Good. I bet we can modify it to include the full-blooded ones too. Yes. Good to have you aboard. We just discussed having a casino. The more the merrier, but this here is the man, you need to go through." He pulled Jayne by the arm and thrust him into their reach.

"Remember the ambassador, I told you about?" questioned Jacqueline as she nodded her approval to her companions.

Disarmed, Jayne reached out to shake their hands. Smiling, they cordially greeted him.

After Jayne shook the second man's hand, a shrill scream stabbed the peaceful atmosphere. Jayne cringed, tucked his head inside his shoulders. With one hand he covered his cranial ridges, while the other covered his ear.

All the men fixated on Jacqueline, the only invited woman. The focus then turned to the person behind her. All eyes shot daggers at the once languorous blond server, Summer, who stood with both hands entangled in her crumbled hair. Her jaw dropped even further. She pulled a hand out as she vacuumed the air around her. Finding her voice, she screamed again. With a shaking finger, she pointed at Jayne as he turned away from her. The Heccan spinal trait strutting before her, blinded her to all else.

Jacqueline started to inch toward Jayne before whirling about to take a giant step in Summer's direction. Her bright eyes dimmed as her incredible smile faded. Concern wrinkled her button nose. She threw her hands in the air and then tried to escort the defiant and hesitant Summer out. Derrick and Spleers helped quicken Summer's decision to leave by physically pushing her out. Jacqueline reached back and closed the door behind her.

Derrick called the room to order while Jayne slipped into the restroom. Talking about new and old business broke the awkward moment. Jacqueline returned and nodded as she found an empty seat.

Jayne returned, fully dressed in his disguise and carrying his backpack. A forced smile planted its roots on his lips. Muscles in his throat tightened against reflux as his stomach twisted with stress. Reaching into the side pocket of his pack, he pulled out his flip phone and turned it on. As soon as the phone powered up, it vibrated with message alerts. Pressing the speed dial, he called his voice mail to see what was in store for him. The texts would have to wait. Jayne listened to the voice mail. Pale death painted his cheeks. Blood started to drain from every cell in his body and his lungs no longer thirsted to process oxygen. The air itself rattled like rocks inside his lungs and gravity increased around his body. Three times, he replayed the messages to get every detail.

Derrick stared at Jayne. He signaled everyone to fall silent. A few partners who were not paying attention had to be nudged.

Closing the phone, Jayne stopped himself before he lashed out with his electric organ. Placing his hands on the table, he stayed upright and supported. Sorrow, anger and fear caressed his mind. After Jayne dismissed his electricity, he felt a hand on his shoulder. Expecting to turn and find Marshall, he hesitantly glanced up. His eyebrows lifted in surprise and he straightened up. It was not Marshall, but an unexpected response from Derrick.

"What is it, Jayne? What's happened," Derrick inquired gruffly. His eyebrows furrowed and his nose flared.

Looking around the room, Jayne no longer felt like a pawn, but someone that they truly cared about. "There were at least five voicemail messages. The first one wasn't really anything, but the second one..." Jayne slammed his hands down on the table. "In the middle of the night ... Phil Colin Reva, he was only 17... a 17 year old Heccan, passed away along with his mother..." He gulped hard. "... father, and sister, Salina. She worked at the embassy." He sniffed as he paused. "The entire family was found after a family disturbance complaint was called into the local police station." Pausing, he inched to the edge of his chair. "The police took over three hours to respond. By then, the family was *dead*."

Making eye contact with each individual, Jayne continued. "It's no longer considered an accident and further investigation is being taken up by several law enforcement agencies, including the FBI. The third call was to tell me that several major media outlets are spreading the rumor that the young Heccan killed himself and his folks with his electric organ... out of hate for his condition and all humans. The fourth message was the local CSI team's final analysis of the crime scene. There had been an intruder. The parents' wrists had been bound along with their son's and daughter's. Their waste basket contained sixteen Irukandji jellyfish and a sticky note with the number 61 on it." Jayne sat back in his chair. "The sadistic murderers..." Jayne choked on his words.

Derrick and Edward exchanged fearful glances. Vang's mouth twitched. Jacqueline chocked on her tears.

"They...they...." Jayne wrinkled his nose as painful tears streamed down his cheeks. "They must have stayed and watched the family die of unspeakable horrors." Fidgeting, he cleared his throat. "They didn't even stand a chance." Jayne gasped. "Salina died of asphyxiation on her vomit from her mouth being covered by duct tape." His restlessness did not stop. "Jellyfish! Ha! Jellyfish as a weapon!"

Jacqueline shuddered and covered her face with both her hands.

Jayne rubbed his hands on his thighs back and forth to keep from exploding from the inside out and hurting the H.E.C.C.'s cause. Focusing his energy and emotions inwardly took its toll on his eyes. He shut them and tightly winced. All eyes focused on Jayne.

Rubbing his hands on his face and head, Jayne tried desperately to maintain self-control. He clamped them tight over his ears as he trembled. "The last phone call was a government representative saying that protests outside the Hecc Embassy had escalated. My mother's friend... my friend, Dee..." Anger stopped Jayne's tears. His body shook and jerked. Jayne tightened his jaw and gritted his teeth.

Those near him trembled and slowly inched away.

Suddenly, Jayne slammed his fists on the table. He left them there while his pupils focused on his fists.

No one spoke. They remained frozen in their seats, canyon-like wrinkles forming on their faces. Jacqueline trembled. Sweat formed on everyone in the room except Jayne.

"The anti-HECC protesters broke their way inside and in the chaos… Dee was trampled. Her lung was pierced by several broken ribs. By the time…" Jayne stood up full tilt and faced the wall. Mustering his emotional strength, he placed his hands on the wall. "…rescuers found her…" Turning around, he sank to his knees. "She had bled out internally. She didn't make it."

Jacqueline rushed to Jayne's side. Briefly, she felt the air around him before she placed her hands on his shoulders.

Oblivious, Jayne didn't look up. His hands fell to the floor and he stayed on his knees. Several awkward minutes passed. Jacqueline left Jayne's side and sat down in her chair.

Jayne stood up and stared at the ceiling. Raising his voice, Jayne lifted a fist in the air. "Until further notice, every Hecc is on lockdown. For the 'safety' of Heccs and humans." Jayne's words drifted off. Moving his fist slowly to his mouth, he bit his knuckle. Turning on his heel, he ran to the restroom.

Buddy's phone rang with the lonely song of whales. He politely answered and explained to the caller that he was waiting on a call. The gentle sound of a kitten mewing from Percy's ringtone caused everyone to give him a puzzled look. He shrugged everyone off and he verbally excused himself to his caller. Eric's phone buzzed with dancehall glee. After Eric turned down his own call, funeral stillness took over.

The Beach Boys 'I Get Around' sang loudly from Jayne's phone as it vibrated on the table. No one budged as they stared at it. Derrick and Marshall focused on the men's room. Jayne did not appear. The phone played a number of times before it finally ceased. The atmosphere took on an edge. It was sullen and everyone remained unapproachable.

A shrill ringtone sounded as another cell phone rang. When Vang answered, he excitedly motioned at the rest of the room to look at his phone. "Yes… No… We good? Yes. He's here. Call him again."

The restroom door opened. Out walked Jayne in his swim trunks, his disguise left behind. His eyes transfixed on Vang with uncertainty. Water dripped from his hair and followed every curve until the droplets were able to fall on to the expensive carpet. A longing vague look of hope emanated from his face as he waited for Vang's phone call to end. The investor kindly looked at Jayne, smiled, and nodded.

Jayne's phone rang. He answered it. "Yes... Uh-huh.... Uh-huh... okay... Uh-huh...yeah...thanks...okay...bye." Looking at each pair of eyes, he managed a deep breath before exhaling the joyous words. "Fight's over...We've won! Every last plot of land is ours! We can build the wonderful city of our dreams according to the plans we have created in these last few months! Washington intervened by giving us a grant and declared eminent domain to get the rest of the land we needed! H.E.C.C.s finally won't have to hide; a place where we can live safe and comfortable lives! Construction will start next week. Let's hope we can survive until it's finished!" His voice lowered before drifting off.

Shouts of excitement filled the room and echoed. As congratulations died down, Jayne made a hasty phone call to Martin. Not many words were said on his part, but he got what he wanted and hung up. "We're not going to be locked up; however, we do need to take extra precautions against public hostility." The room filled with a hurricane of relieved sighs.

{:-)-]~~{

Chapter 23

Gabriella made a bee line for the giant walk-in game closet while Melista rounded up several adults. William and Willetta helped Gabriella lift a folding table out. When they were filled in on the plan, Willetta grabbed several card decks and four board games. They precariously walked upstairs with their loads. Gabriella inelegantly carried the checkerboard box and a second folding table.

Bonnie, Jerome, the two Kellys, Tyler and Melista met up with Gabriella and her crew in the conservatory. They all helped arrange the folding tables. When it was almost done, a few men excused themselves to grab folding chairs from the closet downstairs. Gabriella slyly noticed a curious Marian looking at them through one of the windows before slipping away.

When Tyler, Jerome, William and Kelly-He returned, the mirthful conservatory group was loudly chatting amongst themselves deciding on what game to play first. Billy, Eva, and Gabe followed the men upstairs with a number of chairs.

They were soon set up, thanks to teamwork from the whole group. They continued playfully arguing on which game to play first.

"I could whoop you up, little girl!" William joined in the playful debate.

"Oh no, you couldn't, heel-grabber." Willetta spouted. "You might have the looks, but I got the brains." She pretended to lick her forefinger before placing it on her hip while making a sizzling sound.

"I think we should play Monopoly! We've got Spiderman Monopoly!" Bonnie challenged Jerome. "You owe me a game and this time, I'm winning!"

The game "Lord of the Rings Monopoly" was chosen unanimously by the young adults, outvoting the adults. The scheming began. Bonnie and Willetta teamed up while Jerome and William huddled. Tyler and Kelly-He partnered while Melista and Gabriella schemed. Kelly-She and Eva challenged Billy and Gabe, the last team. The quick method was chosen, since it was close to suppertime. The "ring" began to advance as the die was cast. The conservatory was filled with joyful hollering and round after round of fun. Most were enjoying themselves and forgot why they started playing in the first place. Gabriella couldn't forget. She had situated herself where she could see her daughter.

Underwater, Marian noticed that she could hear with a higher quality than on the surface. It became a game to pop up and down under the water. A pleasant visage formed over her lips. Out of old human habit, she refused to laugh or giggle underwater. Knowledge from past experiments dictated that she could open her mouth and make funny faces. After trying different ones, she made a fish face like she and Jayne used to do together for amusement.

On the Monopoly board, the 'ring' rounded its last corner. Very few sat in their chairs. They were either standing or at the edge of their seats hopping up and down in anticipation. Soon, the end space was past with inches to spare. Willetta raised the roof and slowly twirled around. After Bonnie whooped, she burst into laughter as she watched Willetta. With renewed youthful energy, Bonnie bunglingly attempted an imitation of Willetta. Smiling, but annoyed, the defeated Jerome and William put away the game since that was the pregame deal. The competitors all shared a laugh and exchanged the greeting, "good game" all around.

"It was definitely fun. Let's play a card game now," said Tyler.

Zola heard the celebratory commotion from the group and popped in.

Games were debated on again and William mentioned the game "Bullshit".

Zola scolded him. "That's an English cuss word that you should not be saying."

"It's okay, Aunt Zola, it's just a game" said Gabriella. She kindly placed a reassuring hand on her shoulder.

When the others agreed and convinced her it was a real game, Zola softened. She expressed that although she had never heard of it, she would like to learn. Bonnie protested, but then gave in and sat down for a game.

"I certainly would like to play again since we were interrupted the last time I played," quipped Tyler.

The rules were explained to Zola as the cards were dealt.

Marian yearned to sigh, for, to her, the confining surface game had lost its appeal. She stopped bobbing her head up and down. Her smile drowned to sadness as she let herself sink to the floor. She turned over and laid facing down with her nose and face plastered on the floor. Morbid thoughts caressed her senses. *I couldn't even willingly drown myself if I wanted to.* Tossing over, she stared at the ceiling. *Even if I could crawl to find a hair dryer, there's not enough electricity in the house wiring to do the job.* Life without Jayne crossed the wires in her brain. She pondered being awakened from her induced coma by his kiss. Her face relaxed as the corners of her mouth pulled at her lips. A look of pure contentment etched across her face. *Jayne.* Closing her eyes, she touched her lips with her first two fingers. *He was my constant companion here,* she thought to herself. Her left hand slowly crept to her head where her slender fingers found safety in twirling her waist length hair. *He was the first one who welcomed me to this alternate universe. Before the coma, I hated water. Even though I still hate it, Jayne gave me a reason to like it. We sure had fun splashing each other. After a few weeks, mom put her foot down after how many times she mopped the floor.* Marian's pupils dilated. *Mom and Tyler like him. He kissed me.* She lightly bit the nail on her forefinger. Suddenly both hands shot straight to her sides and tightened into rock hard fists. Flexing her muscles in her hands, she tightened her fists before she released her imaginary grip on life. *I was so mad... I can't believe I ignored him...*

How stupid I must have looked. He left. He just left. How could he just leave like that? Why couldn't he have stayed? The water swirled when she shook her fist. The movement of the water tickled her senses. Angry as she was, something instinctive about making the water develop into currents around and over her soothed her from zapping the world with her electric organ. Marian twirled and spun in circles as best she could without hitting against a wall.

Meanwhile, after two rounds of working with Zola, the real game began. In the middle of the game, Marcy and Beverly served finger foods for supper, complete with napkins. Zola had been told about the plan for spending time in the room ignoring Marian, but letting her see the action. Although she still didn't fully understand the game, Zola bravely continued to play along for Marian's sake.

Jack and Mildred came in, holding their plates and cups. They waited a minute while Clifford opened the two folding chairs that he had brought in for them. They carefully placed their plates and cups on the TV trays that Mark and Tony brought in.

Gabriella never bragged that she was superior at any card game. People were constantly calling her bluff. She stopped trying to pull the wool over her husband's eyes. He seemed to know her so very well. Every change or lack of movement in his facial features reminded Gabriella that she had missed out on a lot of things outside of her self-centered, grief filled life. Her shoulders dropped and her face flushed. A remorseful look haunted her eyes. With writhing lips, she thought, *I've been so selfish.*

Straightening her posture, Gabriella focused on the others around her.

Caught in her lie, Zola botched her attempt at innocence with her incomplete sentences mixed with English and Swahili.

With a jerk, Gabriella tucked her chest closer to her knees. Laughter without sound caused her body to convulse. Her lips formed the letters, a, h, and o without uttering a sound.

Bemused, Zola looked at Gabriella while continuing to stutter excuses of ignorance.

Zola's pretended innocence increased Gabriella's level to hysterical. Tears rolled down her cheeks and she choked on fits of laughter.

Marian abruptly came to a halt in the middle of a spin. When she surfaced, she coughed. Worry written all over her face, Marian propped her hands on the edge. From Gabriella's open mouth escaped a few awkward giddy laughs. Measuring one happy face to the next, Marian settled her arms on the side and propped her chin on her hands to watch the scene. Her lips twitched, contorting her face before settling into a delightful countenance. Laughter fit her mother like a comfortable glove. Lately, her mother had irritated her as she busied about, trying to find ways to cheer up Marian, but it was pleasing to see her truly laugh with joy.

Spotting her daughter above the surface, Gabriella attempted a wink in her direction. Her subtleness failed her for her whole head bobbed. After taking two deep inhales, Gabriella announced, "I have to be excused to use the ladies' room." She lifted a hand to cover her mouth. With a few jerks, her hand fell off and she burst out again with full-fledged laughter.

Everyone placed their cards face down on the table and made themselves comfortable while they waited.

"I bet she was laughing so hard, she had to pee," Melista piped up.

Faces around the table changed from ornery smirks to hysterical tearful laughter. Zola excused herself, followed by Mildred. Bonnie's giggling morphed into hardcore laughter, holding her sides.

Marian continued to politely smile, but took no part in the laughing. Peace perched on her shoulders. Life filled her lungs and soul.

Collected and calm, Gabriella briskly walked back into the room. Merrily, she sat down with a sheepish grin. She snickered. Those who surrounded the table were attempting controlled breathing techniques to compose themselves.

Mildred and Zola returned. Soon everyone settled into their chairs and picked up where they had left off in the game.

Still propped up, Marian stared directly at her mother. Gabriella returned her daughter's pleasant expression. A movement out of the corner of her eye caught Gabriella's attention. Her head turned, cocked to one side, and her eyebrows wrinkled.

Marian's chin lay on her wrists while her elbows sustained her weight. Marian's right hand was making a hand motion. Gabriella's eyes widened.

"Bu..." Gabriella started, but didn't finish the words, *But what*?

When everyone looked at Gabriella and then looked around, they did not see Marian as she had silently slipped underwater.

"What is it honey?" Tyler quizzed.

Willetta placed her cards down and proclaimed the numbers. Her shoulders dropped while she waited for her brother to play.

"Bull..." Gabriella hesitantly recovered. Then with confidence, she spilled, "Bull! I said, 'Bull'. I call you, little frog!"

William checked the pile. He guffawed.

"Ah, man!" Willetta carped as she drew cards.

Vengeful and grateful chuckles filled the air.

"Nice one, Gabby," acknowledged Tyler with gentle admiration.

As soon as eyes were diverted away from Gabriella, she covertly looked for the spot where Marian had been. Sure enough, Marian popped up and signaled the American Sign Language sign for 'no' again. Confidence lit up Gabriella's eyes and her posture. She called out Willetta's fraternal twin brother, William. Play after play, Marian's help raised Gabriella to the podium of Bullshit champion.

After supper, a few additional challengers, including Clifford, wandered in. To accommodate them, Gabe and William fetched another card table and additional chairs. Even though the original play had begun as therapy for Marian, they ended up forgetting why they started the game in the first place. The room was filled with thunderous noises from laughing and moaning when they had to pick up extra cards. No one noticed why Gabriella excelled at discerning the truthfulness of the people around the table.

The young Heccwan was thoroughly enjoying herself. At first, Marian only helped her mother on her side of the table. However the real fun began when Marian noticed she could see the reflections of the other players' cards off of the mirrors around the rooms. They were small mirrors for decoration, but effective. Marian's new eyesight suited her just fine. She couldn't think of a more fitting asset. This new discovery renewed her taste for life. She found if she focused her eyes underwater at the mirrors for an adequate amount of time, she could see the cards around the table. Then having the images stored in her mind like she never had before, she was able to help her mother. A few times she had to look at several different mirrors to catch a complete view.

Since Jack and Mildred Sharp were only spectators, they became aware of what was going on between Marian and Gabriella. They whispered to each other and exchanged impish mugs.

Momentarily, Bonnie glanced at her parents. A second look turned into a stare. "Um… mom… what's… going on? What are you two whispering about?" She scrutinized them both to see if she could figure it out.

Rubbing his protruding Adam's apple, Jack said, "Just talking about grown up stuff, Bonn."

"Ew," emphasized Bonnie and she went back to her cards.

Willetta rolled her eyes. She carried a heavy burden that never seemed to stop growing. Her tangled thoughts persisted as a jumble in the game. *What luck, what's with all these unmanageable cards?* In her moment of huff, she dropped several cards on the floor. Bending to pick them up, she saw Marian's hand sign 'no'. Willetta's eyes widened. Leaving her cards lay, Willetta sat up and searched each face.

"Bull, Bonnie," exclaimed the eager Gabriella.

Tyler also noticed Marian signaling. Knowledge struck Tyler like a bow and arrow.

With reddening cheeks, Willetta defiantly shook her head. "Oh!" She laid the rest of her cards down and raised her hands in the air. "No! No way. Now that's some stinky bullshit!"

Everyone else stared at Willetta in complete confusion.

Tyler stood up and pointed at his wife. "So that's how little *Miss Innocent* got so good at playing Bullshit!" He pointed at the cowering Marian. "She had help! Bullshit! Uh-uh. That's bullshit!"

Jack and Mildred Sharp were laughing so hard that they almost fell off their chairs.

Marian popped up, locking her elbows. Her head darted about absorbed in the action. If pillows were available, Marian figured there would have been several aimed at her.

Everyone looked toward Marian and saw her guilty concerned face. Laughter filled the room. Bonnie and Tyler tag-teamed a squirming Gabriella, using both hands to tickle her.

"You little turd!" Bonnie chuckled.

"Do you know how many cards I had because of you?" Willetta stuck her two cents in.

"No fair," hollered Melista. "No fair!'

Billy placed a caring hand on Willetta and said, "The game is called Bullshit. Is it not, hmm? If look like a pile and smell like a pile, then it, what is, hmm? Pudu! You can expect more, I think not. It can not be turned into diamonds. Can it, hmm? Hmmmmmm."

Scrutinizing the room, Jerome noticed the mirrors. "Hey, I know how the little fry did it too! Look!" He pointed the mirrors out to Billy and the two Kellys.

Kelly-He shook his head. "Ah, man. No wonder I had no luck." He snorted ever so slightly and folded his arms. "I'm usually pretty good. Hey, even Tyler was losing."

"Your luck? You and I had a friendly side bet going and I think that makes me the winner," Kelly-She bragged before bursting out in a devilish laugh.

"I was winning before Aunt Gabby started cheating!" Eva yelled into thin air because no one seemed to listen to her. "Arrrrg!" Her tightened fists hung sharply at her sides. "She… hah… sure… hah… had us all!"

Billy tried to talk while he was laughing but couldn't. He doubled over and slapped his thighs.

"Next time I play, I'll know to pick a room full of mirrors, and maybe a helper." William greedily rubbed his hands together. He knew a few close friends to try it on even if it wasn't exactly legal. It was 'Bullshit' after all.

Zola was the only one at the table who didn't stand up, but she laughed all the same. "I *require* a rematch, *dear* Gabby!"

"You had an accomplice," yelled Jerome. His elbows shoved Tyler and Bonnie aside and hoisted a laughing Gabriella like a sack of potatoes. "Slimy fish of a school should all swim together!"

Backing up, Marian watched with captivated curiosity.

Without hesitation, Jerome tossed a shrieking Gabriella into Marian's aquarium.

Gabriella had only shallowly inhaled before she went under. Her lungs begged for air.

Quick reflexes helped; Marian cradled Gabriella before she hit the bottom and rushed her to the surface. When they reached the surface, they separated. Hands of the scam victims splashed the water, effectively spraying both offenders. Melista and Billy scrambled to move the games and tables away from the excitement. Marian floated on her back and used her tail fins to lightly splash her aggressors. Gabriella shielded her face and made it to the safety of the back corner before climbing out of the tank.

She and Marian were both laughing as was everyone else. Although it was a dirty trick, it had been a fun one all around.

Bonnie, Jerome, and Kelly-She picked up the cards and put them in their appropriate boxes. Billy and Eva skipped downstairs, laughing out loud the whole way.

Willetta and William chatted with Marian.

Tyler mischievously grinned. Gabriella had achieved her goal. It had been a far-reaching journey, but it was satisfying. He watched as she headed for dry clothes.

Mildred interrupted William and Marian. "Hey, hon... how about joining us for a sleepover party?"

"Sounds good, Grandma," said Marian, smiling.

Mildred caught herself from losing her balance. It was the first time that Marian called her that since her return. "Hope, is it? How 'bout we have a naming party tonight?"

Marian 'Hope' Harrison's eyes sparkled.

"Can we break out the *keki*?" Zola asked Mildred as she gently touched her shoulder from behind.

Mildred nodded her head with approval. "Time for cake!"

The conservatory was cleaned up and word spread. Sleeping bags and children poured in like two rivers colliding.

William helped Marian into her wheelchair for the first time in a month. She let him push her around while she clung onto Willetta's hand. Marian started dictating where everyone's bags would be placed. No one argued since she seemed to know them well. Bean bags and blankets were brought in and spread out in the middle of the room for the grand social gathering. Marian couldn't keep track of the comings and goings of her extended family. Everyone busied about to get situated before the last minute festivities. Every member had their own task to accomplish to make it enjoyable for all.

{:-)-]~~{

Chapter 24

Back at the hotel, Doug waited for Jayne in the lobby with his overnight bag. When he saw Jayne, he stood up.

"Hey," said Jayne as he bounced a quick head nod. "I don't feel like talking."

"Ok."

"I *want* to hit the pool, *now*. You got my back?"

Concerned, Doug nodded. Jayne hadn't waited for Doug to respond, but took off at a fast pace. Startled, Doug fumbled with his bag. After slinging the strap of the blue sports bag on his shoulder, he bolted to catch Jayne.

After Jayne unlocked the door, he pointed and ordered, "You get the bed. I get the tub."

Doug closed the door and plopped his bag on the bed. The side zipper easily opened. Blue swim trunks tumbled out. In a flash, he dropped his jeans and pulled on his trunks.

After noting that Doug felt at home, Jayne disrobed near the closet and hung up his disguise. Kneeling over his suitcase, he found a blue shirt and pulled it over his head. Standing up, Jayne carried a ball cap with a comical paper bag character on it. He stood in front of the mirror. *I'm tired of being bullied*, he thought. Summer's scream echoed in his head from memory. A tear crept to the edge of his eye, but did not dare finish its path. Slowly his fingers traced his cranial ridges as he plodded closer to the counter. He paused as his completely silver covered fingernails glistened in the light. His nails did not give him away in public because the beneficent nation naturally handed out forgiveness for bold statements such as 'painted fingernails'. Head ridges, after thousands of years of culture and well-defined body identity, invoked fear and riots!

"Come on, dude. Rise up," comforted Doug. He slowly reached in front of Jayne, holding a large towel. Acknowledging Doug, Jayne accepted and threw it around his neck. He hastily pulled the ball cap on over his ridges and bandana. It didn't allow much extra room to watch where he was going. Jayne nodded at Doug and flew out the door. They barreled through the hotel until they found the pool. Relief soothed Jayne's aching limbs. It was deserted.

He tossed his towel at Doug. Positioning himself with his back against the side of the wall of the pool, he eased into the water, clothes, hat and all. A smile crept over his lips. Relaxing with his arms on the edge, he bolstered his chest and head out of the water. Jayne looked up at the ceiling. He softly growled. *What's taking him so long?* He turned around to see if Doug tagged behind him. Instead his friend lay stretched out on a chaise lounge. Jayne snorted. They were indoors and there was no sun. A soft peaceful expression grew wide on Doug's face as his muscles relaxed.

Inhaling deeply, the brilliant intertwining smells of the indoor pool and the surrounding plant life flooded Jayne's enhanced senses. The moonlight sparkled through the four skylights and danced on the water.

A deep snore rose from Doug. Jayne's glowing eyes darted back. He shook his head and cringed. The hotel towel tucked under Doug like a pillow restricted his airway, not opened it. The room tickled Jayne's fantasies of what a future home could feel like. Even though Jayne was at ease, he still kept his forehead and ears covered with his bandana. Quietly, he pulled his wet shirt off with his cap and flung it on Doug.

Doug snorted and woke up, giving Jayne a dirty look. Shrugging his shoulders, Doug stood up and sat on a chair that allowed him to have a full view of his environment.

Drawn by the moonlight, Jayne stared at it. He whispered the words. "That's it. The land is ours. It's a go." It played over and over in Jayne's mind like a broken record. Jayne smiled and sighed. For once, it wasn't bad thoughts that cycled. He ducked under the water and aimlessly drifted. Brief flashbacks of the confined pet shop only touched the tip of his mood. He thought to himself. *We did escape... all together. We're safe. Most of the humans... accept... us.* A frown crept on his face, but a happy expression returned swiftly. *We get to live in a giant cave! Hope's free and she likes me. Thank God, it's not just one-sided. The land is ours! The land is ours!* Celebration lit his soul on fire. Elated, he swam to the closest wall and caught himself with his hands. Bouncing off, he did the same to each wall before he stopped in the middle of the pool. A dog-like instinct took over causing him to chase his feet until he had enough exercise.

Exhausted from burning off energy, Jayne settled to the bottom. Through the water, Jayne stared at the moonlight with his arms crisscrossed under his head. His mind played tricks on him. Guilt tugged at his heart. Dee had helped rescue him and now she was dead because she worked at the H.E.C.C. Embassy for him and his new race. *But at what cost?* Joy and sadness struggled over Jayne's soul. Sleep tiptoed in and defeated the two foes.

Jayne's cavern fantasy manifested itself into a real in-depth dream. *Dashing headstrong Jayne and eager Hope plunged in the vast warm bouncy ocean as they held silken hands under the starry night. Everything that the humans enjoyed above the surface, the Heccs did too. After the intimate beautiful wedding, the trustful two swam to a vacant steamy cave where they were greeted by pet dolphins and tropical fish. He carried Hope up the shiny stone steps to find a glorious candlelight dinner for two.*

{:-)-]~~{

Chapter 25

The Sharp's conservatory thundered with conversations flashing a mile a minute. Tyler closed his eyes and smiled at the hustle and bustle of a real home. A gentle touch on his shoulder startled him. He jumped from his metal folding chair and whirled around. The dim lights danced from several lanterns placed about the room. Oil lamps cradled in wooden frames on the walls shone bright. The already adventure-filled night illuminated when Gabriella pranced into Tyler's view. With her eyebrows raised, she smiled at him. Tyler watched her hand rise from her side and her fingers parted to twirl her hair. He became increasingly aware of the rhythm of his heart. From head to toe, his body longed for Gabriella's touch. Reaching his hands out, Tyler leaned toward her.

Giggling, Gabriella turned around and sprinted through and around the cousins.

Pumping his arms, Tyler chased her. "You better get back here, young lady."

Gabriella's reckless path would soon intersect with a kneeling disgruntled Beverly whose fiery eyes stared at Gabriella's projected path. With motherly instinct, Beverly reached out toward her freckled four-year-old daughter and snatched her out of danger. Tannen's curly strawberry blonde hair bounced. Dumbfounded, her cornflower blue eyes were puzzled as she stared at the two sprinting adults.

"Gabby," Beverly's anger ended with hesitation as she summed up Tyler's mischievous grin and heard Gabriella's laughter.

One obstacle at a time, Gabriella gained distance on Tyler. They ran all around the conservatory, dodging the potted plants.

Billy, holding two gallon jars of orange spice pickled eggs, blocked Gabriella's road, so she used a giant potted tree as a shield from Tyler.

"Children, take it outside," fretted Mildred. White buckets of dried apples burdened her arms.

Tyler swayed back and forth, calculating his advantages. Taking a chance, Gabriella ran toward Bonnie whose identical twins clung out of fear to their mother's legs. Gabriella's focus went from Bonnie's eyes to her knees as Tyler grabbed her around her waist from behind.

Emma's button nose scrunched before she hid her emerald eyes in her mother's pant leg.

After Gabriella gasped, she laughed hysterically.

Hannah shook her head with bouncy raven hair at her aunt and uncle. "You're silly!"

Since Tyler was out of practice, he gracelessly lifted Gabriella to an erect position. She faced him with bright eyes and tears pouring down her reddened cheeks. Tyler's laughter slowed to a halt as he pulled his wife's waist to his own. They wrapped their arms around each other and closed their eyes. Their souls drew to each other as they slowly locked lips.

Ashley Shaw's eyelashes squinted over her greenish eyes. "Ew!" Her long chestnut brown hair flipped about as she turned on her heel. In her arms, she carried a humongous cookie sheet full of lavender sugar cookies.

"Ah, fourteen year olds," zinged Tyler as he waved a hand in a downward swoop in her direction.

"Yea!" Eva carried one big metal tin in each of her arms. "Get a room!"

Heat crept over Gabriella's cheeks as her blush deepened.

Tyler peered inside Eva's scenic decorated metal tins. Scents of salt and fresh warm butter wafted up from the hot popcorn. "Om-nom-nom-nom!" He reached his free hand toward the popcorn.

"Not yet, Uncle Tyler!" Eva continued her path to place them on a coffee table that had been brought in for the occasion.

"Let's find you a seat," noted Tyler with a reassuring face aimed at Gabriella. One step at a time, he lovingly guided her with her hand in his. When he found a green cot for her to sit on, he left her to stand near the front entrance. Its stage-like platform would do for the evenings events.

The deafening roar of happy chatter died when Kelly-He loudly whistled for attention.

Eyes focused on Tyler, who hot-footed onto the stage. He waved his right hand. Once he found all eyes and ears on him, he passed the attention to Aunt Zola. Dressed in fitted black pants and a stage shirt with black beads framing it at the knees, she walked up the stairs with bare feet. Her small braids bounced free from her usual pony tail. She gracefully placed herself in the center of the stage and turned her back to the room. Tyler left the front to sit next to Gabriella.

Taking his cue, Billy ducked into the closet. After fiddling with the CD player tucked in the closet, the in-wall speakers breathed life into the room. After four beats of drums, Zola whirled about and danced beautifully to the fun rhythm with a Soukous dance. The fingerwork on the acoustic guitar plucked the audience into clapping along. She then danced to another piece.

Billy appeared out of the closet and quietly shut the door. Zola strolled center stage and stretched out her hands. A lonely sounding song in Swahili filled the room. Zola's hands floated rhythmically with the notes, drawing all eyes to her.

Mouths opened as food went in. They chewed like cows careful not to make disturbing crunches. For one heavenly moment in time, the children guarded every limb still and zipped their lips as the foreign words enchanted the atmosphere.

Marian sat with her legs straight out in front of her on the floor. On Marian's right, Willetta, sat with her knees up. Melista sat crisscrossed on Marian's left. William sat on a cot behind Marian. The wheelchair had been placed away from the group. Feeling a part of humanity for a few minutes, Marian smiled from ear to ear.

Sitting like the rest of them, she didn't feel inferior. Her lips parted and moved with the music coming from Zola's heart.

The performance Zola gave was so awesome that tears welled in most of the mothers' eyes. No one knew what Zola sang, but it was an emotionally moving song. As Zola ended her song, the crowd erupted with a huge cheer.

Marian had been moved and didn't want to open her eyes to her surroundings. Her hands lay peacefully in her lap.

Getting ready to sing another song, Zola parted her lips. Instead of her voice, another song lifted high in the air. Eyes darted around to find the source of the solo. Marian's voice echoed like she was in an opera house. With a shiny expression on her face, Zola gracefully padded back from center stage.

As suddenly as Marian started, she stopped for she had startled herself.

Setting her hot cup of blueberry tea down, Gabriella leaned forward and soothed. "Keep going, dear, it's lovely!"

Others hollered for an encore, but Marian didn't smile until Zola begged. Then the unique music flowed smoothly once again.

Gabriella whispered to Tyler, "She never learned opera when I had her. Did she learn it during the time she was away?"

Without looking away from Marian, Tyler softly recalled, "Peter said she was unconscious the whole time. I think she's discovering new abilities."

The song crawled under Marian's skin and released on the tip of her tongue. Her very soul seemed to spew out into the open air. She ended in a choke and wildly waved in a welcoming manner toward William.

William intuitively nodded and skipped to her wheelchair. He pushed it lickety-split near Marian. Bringing it to a stop, he set the brake. Melista aided Marian who refused to look at anyone. William unlocked the chair and pushed her back to her pond. Before he set the brake again, Marian tumbled out onto the floor, grabbing the raised edge of the pool. She hung there by her arms.

Jaw tightened, William placed his hands under Marian's arm pits.

Marian thrashed behind her, pushing a scowling William away. William, stricken, backed up. When a warm body obstructed his getaway, he turned around to find it was his sister.

With a determined visage, Willetta placed a hand on her brother's shoulder to stop his flight. She then grabbed Marian by the head with both hands, forcing Marian to make eye contact. "You don't have to do this alone!"

Marian's shoulders drooped. "Oh, okay." She let Willetta and William give her a boost. Marian slipped over the edge and disappeared under the surface. She reached her hand out and grabbed Willetta's wrist. She popped her head up, coughed and hoarsely whispered, "You will stay, please?"

Willetta said in a normal tone, "Sure, Will, come here." She cleared her throat.

The room filled with awkward silence while several faces bore deep frowns. Gabriella stood up. Her strong voice rang out as she walked onto the stage. "I think you all know who I am. I don't need an introduction."

Gabriella's loved ones soaked up her every word, admiring her newly found courage. It was unlike her to be so assertive anytime in the last decade.

"If you don't, then you are an intruder and need to be kicked out." She paused dramatically to allow for someone to get up and leave, causing genuine laughter to fill the room. "Alright, since you all know me, let's continue." Gabriella's face radiated courage, humor and love as she smiled. "We have come together tonight willingly, as a family."

A grin crept across Tyler's face.

"Perhaps," Gabriella used her hands to convey her heart. "Today is not only a day of birth for Marian, but a day of rebirth for our whole family."

Tyler noticed how his wife had changed a great deal within the last week. It was very apparent today. Leaning in to catch every word, he fell more in love with her. She allured him with mystery again.

Tyler's eyes sparkled and the corner of his mouth twitched into a slight grin.

Listening to her mother, Marian glowed. She had family, she really did! Whether or not they were H.E.C.C.s, she had a home filled with love. She swirled around underwater with delight. William caught the bubbles with his hand that had been resting on the surface. He motioned to his sister. Willetta nodded and smiled.

Gabriella gave it her all. "Family. What does family mean to us as individuals? What does family mean as a whole? I will tell you what I think it means. I think it means diversity with loving unity. I think a family is like a car. When the pieces are apart, they might not move or turn this way or that way, but they are individual parts of a whole. They don't look the same and they have different functions, jobs or talents that drive them to a mutual purpose. There might be a few parts that get replaced along the way, but the greater good is bigger than all of us individual parts." She glided from one side to the other to make eye contact. "We must keep driving and working to get over the endless hill called life. I am proud of everyone here today. Many in my life have put up with my grief over a child missing. This family has accepted her with open arms upon her return. I thank you all for uplifting Marian in her difficult task of accepting herself. I think she has finally come to the top of the hill with open arms. She is ready to be given a new birth. Let the festivities continue and we will name her at midnight!" Starting from her hip, Gabriella punched at the ceiling.

Everyone cheered and craned their necks or bodies to catch a glimpse of Marian who was propped up on the edge, smiling. She sheepishly tucked her chin into her shoulder. Applause filled the room. Raising her head, Marian used one arm to anchor herself and used her free hand to blow a few kisses.

"Now," Gabriella motioned at Melista who was standing next to the stage. "Let's continue with a poem." Gabriella confidently walked off stage. On the way back to her cot, she shook a few hands and patted nieces' or nephews' heads. Sitting down, she cuddled into Tyler's open arm. Laying her head on his shoulder, she shivered. It was nice to get back into shy oblivion.

Agreeing to the request, Melista took center stage without a paper. When all quieted, she began.

"'This Little Fishy' by Jae Byrd Wells

The Maker plans each catch with infinite detail.
Multiplication stays hidden in the depths below.
Calm waters hasten the preparations to sail.
Outside still remains a stable place for you to grow.
Fast and obnoxious winds say that two is too much.
'They will break the line and the rod that holds them up.
Others say that when it comes to your heart, more will touch.
Oh, how I never expected the feelings to overflow my cup.
Your eyes enchant me and draw me in with a reel.
I am a sucker fish for you.
Your strength glows brightly and dangerously like an eel.
I am a cuttlefish for you.
You will see as I tell you in the light of the moon,
This little fishy went to school.
This little fishy stayed home.
This little fishy ate plankton.
This little fishy had none.
This little fishy…
This little fishy…
This little fishy…
This little fishy went bloop bloop bloop, all the way home."

With the last stanza, the children erupted with goofy laughter. They did not catch the meaning of the first few. However, it did not matter that it went over their heads. They enjoyed the 'fishy game' played on their toes instead of 'little piggy'. The adults understood the meanings according to their own hearts and experiences with the precious little lives that they were blessed with.

"Please excuse us for intermission." Melista flitted down the stairs. "Kids that are supposed to go with Bonnie may be excused." The children obeyed and ran to Bonnie's open arms. Loud conversation ensued as the audience stood up. They mingled, grabbed some snacks, or found a different place to rest their hind ends.

"What's next? Who's next?" Marian eagerly nudged Willetta. When Willetta pretended to zip up her lips, Marian bugged William.

The noise abruptly ended after a shrill whistle. Marian's bright eyes focused around the room intently on everyone's face. Giggles and snickering sounded as the little ones marched in costume up to the stage. Melista had helped them arrange in the order that they practiced. Willetta pointed at the children and whispered commentary. Marian giggled as they watched the cute chaos unfold. With a contented sigh, Marian rested her back against the far wall as she soaked in the entire room and its inhabitants.

Conversations quickly hushed when the children sang a cappella. Their sea creature costumes sparkled when the light touched them as they sang a song that encouraged swimming upstream despite the difficulties.

Marian's eyes closed as she soaked in every word. She thought, I *am like a fish now.* I *belong in the sea.* The next song startled her. It was as if they could hear her thoughts and broadcast them for all to hear. Marian shook her head. Her cheeks squished her eyelids as she smiled the biggest grin she ever had, since returning to her mother. No one would ever know how encouraging their voices were tonight. She openly laughed as her cousin in the lobster outfit spun around at the end.

$$\{:-)-]\sim\sim\{$$

Inside the Mouths of Oysters

Does Beauty Always Require Pain?

Chapter 26

n hour passed. Several loud splashes alerted Jayne to open his eyes. Horror-struck, Jayne's dulled senses built to a climax. He had been in a deep sleep and did not even hear visitors entering. Normally, Jayne hopped out of the water before other guests arrived. Underwater, he snarled at Doug. He saw Doug's toes test the water with an 'x', signaling his location. Jayne swam up to the surface next to Doug. Instead of popping up, he eased his way up, finding his ball cap which Doug dropped in the water. It was then that he saw the two boys with super hero swim trunks playing with rubber ducks on the shallow steps in the water. A trim brown haired woman sat reading a book. As soon as Jayne's head was all the way out of water, Doug apologized softly. "Sorry, man. I went to the restroom."

Jayne froze with his back to the wall. Doug crept to the lawn chair and picked up their towels. Upon returning, he dropped one onto Jayne's neck. Still facing the visitors, Jayne pulled himself out of the pool with his arms and sat on the edge. Doug joined him. They both dangled their feet in the water.

"Let's see how long they'll stay," whispered Jayne.

"Well, let's look less suspicious by talking." Doug snickered.

"What do we talk about?"

"How about what happened after I left?"

Jayne and Doug became engrossed in catching up. Forgetting the visitors, Jayne tossed the towel off and faced Doug in the water. He repeated the voicemails to Doug leaving him speechless. Giving Doug a minute to digest, Jayne drifted to the bottom. A thought lit his feet and he raced to the top. The water fueled his adrenaline as it rushed over his back and neck. He knocked his ball cap and bandana off when he broke the surface. He couldn't wait to finish coughing. He sputtered, "Will you (*cough cough*) come (*cough cough cough*) with us? Will you (*cough*) work," he swallowed, "...with us? With me?" His eagerness mounted as his eyes danced. Things had pretty much completely healed between them. Doug spent time with him without reporting to anyone including the 'I.V. Scissor King'. Doug remained a friend that Jayne had met in an unlucky situation.

Two pudgy senior citizens, a couple, entered through the door along with the boys' three girl cousins. The woman dropped her jaw, screamed, and pointed at Jayne's mutated neck and spine. Wide-eyed, Jayne faced them. The three girls joined in the screaming fest. Like greased lightning, Jayne ducked underwater. Swimming to the deep end, he found and hugged the floor. Voices plainly rang in his ears below the surface as if he were still above water. With clear vision, Jayne did not miss a movement.

The aunt stood up with her book from her chair and bawled at the boys to get out.

"No! I don't want to." Both boys grudgingly got out of the water and argued with their aunt in unison. The eldest boy wailed, "Mom said we could swim. We've *wanted* to ever since we *heard* about the stupid wedding." The younger one agreed.

Doug watched with horror and anger. It was obvious that Jayne, who wasn't even considered a full blooded H.E.C.C. was still harassed just as much as the others. Doug felt very protective about Jayne, no one knew him like he did. Standing up, he folded his arms.

The aunt grabbed the older boy and yanked him toward the exit. The older one fought his aunt, while the younger stood and wailed. The older boy's arm flailed and accidentally knocked the younger one into the deep end of the pool.

Doug knelt at the edge of the pool. Flicking the water three times, he waited momentarily before he mouthed the words, "Come on, Jayne, let's go."

The child cried at the top of his lungs as he hit the water. Panicking, he clumsily tried to get out of the water, only to fall back under again. His delicate hands and knobby elbows thrashed at the surface. Coughing, crying, and inhaling mixed as well as oil and water, Water clogged his throat. He could only inhale water and he started to drown.

The grandmother noticed that the youngest was not with them. She looked around for her grandson. The girl cousin pointed him out as she screamed his name. They all turned and started to scream.

"Oh no!"

"Help!"

"Do something!"

"I (*gag*) I ca (*gag*) nn't (*gulp*) swi...." His voice disappeared under the water.

Making a face, Jayne swam full force. He grabbed the boy, forced his head out of the water, and pushed him toward the pool's edge. Jayne lingered under the surface. The boy violently coughed.

The commotion and cries for help had hurried the whole family into the pool room.

When Jayne reached the edge, he lifted the boy up and placed him on the concrete. As Jayne's hands receded underwater, a man grabbed his wrist and clutched it tight. Fighting, Jayne pushed his feet against the wall.

Doug stood on the sidelines, hard-eyed with twitching muscles. When he saw Jayne's hand, a prisoner, he rushed to the other side. Having to dodge puddles slowed him down and he still slipped.

A woman told the captor to "set him free", but he refused.

"No, I will not!"

Another man stepped up and gave him an anchor. Several additional men arrived and kept Doug from aiding Jayne. Clearly in charge, Jayne's captors managed to pull him to the surface. Jayne coughed and lost the tug-of-war. His butt landed hard on the concrete. Jayne flinched.

The boy's mother came, knelt, and cradled her shivering son who had just escaped death's jaws. She had been the one to order

Jayne's freedom. The boy's uncle helped deliver the prisoner to the air breathing world.

Looking around, Jayne sulked as all the beautiful humans stood gazing and staring at him. Maybe a few were ugly, but to him, they were all beautiful and powerful in this man's world. Although Jayne boasted little self-esteem while he worked at the pet shop, he lost all of it the day he woke as a biracial Heccan. Lonely, he didn't fit in with the humans and neither did he fit in with the H.E.C.C.s. Jayne looked up at the man who now only held his hand, having loosened his tight grip. His blue eyes were tender and caring, not hateful and despising. Jayne twitched a hesitant grin. The stranger carefully helped Jayne to his feet and shook his hand. The mother cried and thanked Jayne for saving her son's life.

Jayne adjusted his shoulders with more confidence. The hold on Doug was released. The crowd parted so that Doug could stand beside Jayne. Three additional eager men zealously shook Jayne's hand. A round of cheering overwhelmed him. The aunt and grandmother who had screamed and started the madness shyly approached him. They thanked him too.

"Alright, alright. Give the hero some room," said the athletic six foot man who had grabbed Jayne's wrist. His deep New Yorker accent and the twinkle in his greenish eyes could make any woman need to find a fainting couch. That cherubic face with his thick nut-brown mutton chop whiskers could con a cub away from its mother. Gently, he nudged the crowd aside. "Hi, I'm Paul Walkere. We're here for a wedding tomorrow. I'm the best man. The boy you rescued here is Daniel Holland." He pointed at the boy whose mother embosomed him in a death grip with one hand and patted his head with the other.

Daniel responded by breaking loose to stand in front of Paul. "Thank you mister." He looked at Jayne without fear. Curious and awed, he stared at Jayne's forehead.

"Yes," Paul exclaimed. "Thank you! You must accept a gift of appreciation. I'm a stockbroker and fairly well off. I can afford to thank you properly."

"No." Jayne emphasized with a quick shake of his head. "Any child's life is worth it.

Doug quickly jabbed Jayne in the rib and piped up. "Jayne, what about a donation to the cause?"

Paul peered cautiously at Doug. "Cause?" His shapely ears perked up.

Rubbing his ribs, Jayne again denied the gift and then thought harder on the subject. "We could …we could use more… investors… or gifts…" Pausing to ponder, he nodded. "Yeah, I guess we don't really have the luxury of turning down any help with as big of a project as we are building."

Curiosity filled Paul's veins. He was always interested in investing money into something new and different.

"Let's go somewhere else." Placing his arm around Jayne, Paul guided him out the door.

Doug grabbed Jayne's shirt, cap, and bandana before he caught up behind them. Paul teased, "Is that your bodyguard?" He chuckled. "We weren't properly introduced."

Jayne answered without a touch of sarcasm. "Yeah, I guess you can say that." He enjoyed Doug being overprotective. "Doug's just a good friend." Turning his head at a backwards angle, Jayne winked at Doug.

Paul swallowed, but felt as though, somehow, he had put his foot in his mouth. His broad grin slowly faded.

Heavy footsteps behind them alerted Jayne. He saw a beefy black man two inches shorter than Paul, kept pace two steps behind Doug. His steely blue eyes never left the back of Jayne's neck. Short curly raven hair covered his head while the only trace of hair on his face was an imperial beard. Flaunting the air with an upper class stature, he carried his chin high.

Doug and Jayne were led into the conference room that was apparently, from the number of decorations placed around and on the tables, holding the wedding reception. Jaw dropping as it was for any woman who dreamed of a big wedding, it was all just hyped up frill to most men.

The four sat down at an undecorated and empty table. Jayne dove into explaining the H.E.C.C.s plight, his concerns, and his involvement in creating a safe haven for them. Doug continued his silence throughout the meeting, encouraging Jayne with his solid presence. The men were briefly interrupted as they were introduced to the bride and groom. Gratitude was poured on Jayne and Doug before they were invited to the wedding and reception. Jayne and Doug kindly and politely accepted.

The meeting went late into the night with Paul's companion listening intently, but remaining silent. Jayne focused on Paul's face, the stranger's face, and then back again, expecting an introduction. Instead Paul controlled the conversation by continually grilling them with many questions, including Jayne and Doug's history of how they met. As though rehearsed, Jayne and Doug kept their answers brief and positive. Jayne concluded by writing down contact phone numbers for Paul to reach both the H.E.C.C. attorney and himself. All departed company.

Jayne and Doug wearily sauntered onward. Deep in thought, Jayne stared ahead.

Doug waited until Paul disappeared around the corner. "Wonder if that was Paul's body guard?"

Jayne sniggered at the irony. "No really. I wonder how come we weren't properly introduced."

"Maybe we will find out at the wedding."

In the hall nearing their room, Doug and Jayne were stopped by the passing night manager. He said, "Hey, there were several guests that heard what you did. Your room has been paid for through your two week stay."

Jayne and Doug exchanged glances and shrugged their shoulders.

"Also…" The night manager paused. "…the day manager will be by in the morning to give you the receipt and his personal thanks." Then he quickly excused himself and hurried about his business.

After Doug pulled the key out of his pocket, he handed it to Jayne. Jayne knowingly smiled and opened the door. After

Jayne sprightly entered, he bee lined for the bathroom. Turning the shower on, he let it run while he tested it for the perfect temperature. Doug announced that he was going out to find food and left. Jayne nodded and closed the bathroom door. He proceeded to take off his swim shorts and rinse off the strong chlorine of the pool. After four minutes, he plugged the tub and found a clean pair of green swim shorts. Stepping into the tub, his body drifted to the bottom where he soaked with his head underwater. The cool water not only refreshed his gills, but it soothed his soul. Being a Heccan, steamy hot showers and baths were a thing of the past. The cool, soothing and euphoric effect cleared his mind of problems.

Whistling as he walked through the door of the hotel room, Doug awkwardly carried his bounty. He paused and carelessly tossed two tuxes swathed in plastic wrapping on the bed. "Jayne. I'm back!" When Doug didn't receive a response, he banged on the door to the restroom with his free hand. Like any human new to this whole water breathing concept, there was still a hint of worry of accidental drowning. "Jayne? Jayne, you okay in there?"

This time, Jayne popped out of the water, coughed and responded. "Yeah, be out in a minute." He drained the water.

Doug cringed every time he heard Jayne cough, even if it was considered normal for H.E.C.C.s, "Hurry up before you wrinkle," teased Doug as he cackled. He knew Jayne's skin didn't wrinkle. He set the food on the table.

Rolling his eyes, Jayne snorted at his humorous friend. Opening the door, he came out tired, but smiling.

Trying to look serious as Jayne entered, Doug crossed his arms.

Jayne pulled out a pair of sport pants to cover the swimsuit. They would get wet, but hold the moisture on his legs a while longer. He dried his face, arms, and hair with a towel because he hungered to eat his meal dry. After pulling the towel away from his face, he eyed the two tuxes on the bed. Curious, he asked Doug about them. "Where'd those come from?"

317

Doug shrugged his shoulders and explained, "They were at the front desk when I came back in. The night manager said they were from your 6 foot tall investor friend."

Shaking his head, Jayne spoke up. "I guess we really have to attend the wedding, now, huh?" He was a little concerned with having to be around innumerable strangers. Still, he felt at peace since the evening had turned out the way it did. It could have had a totally different ending. There was still plenty of bad publicity for the H.E.C.C.s.

"Yeah, I guess so," said Doug. "I wouldn't worry about any problems. The family is grateful you saved the little one."

Jayne wasn't entirely convinced. He snorted. "I wonder if the tux covers up my fish flesh." Taking his hand, he waved it around his forehead and around the back of his neck without touching his skin. He danced both set of fingers in front of his face so the silver fingernails sparkled when they hit the light from the ceiling.

"Come on, Jayne." Doug's nose twitched and the corner of his mouth twitched. "Let's eat." Doug opened the bags on the table. "We've got to get this night over with so we can get up and go to a wedding. I'm exhausted."

Doug flipped the TV on before he sat at the table to scarf down his burger and fries. Jayne sat cross-legged on the bed with his water, fish and fries and thought about what a day it had been. The land was theirs and the construction started next week. But Dee was dead and so were a Heccan and his family. He had rescued a small boy and found a new potential investor of Centerearth Caverns. And tomorrow he had to wear a tuxedo to a wedding, certainly something he had never done before! Too bad it wasn't his own wedding with Hope; someday, he promised himself, that would happen too.

{:-)-]~~{

Chapter 27

The littlest entertainers enticed everyone to never give up with one last ocean inspired song. After they finished, they stiffly bowed in their bulky costumes. Happy noise followed them as they dispersed. Tannen, the last girl to leave the stage, wore the oyster costume. She tripped and landed on her pearl made out of a craft ball. She stood up and was in the process of dusting her knees off when her pearl fell to the floor. Tannen wailed. Her mother, Beverly, ran to her rescue and took her off to another room to care for her.

Marcy stood up and patiently waited. Once the room quieted, she announced, "We are ready for our next act. Kids, come on down. While they are getting ready, we have a special commercial break brought to you by our very own director... Billy-Wan Kenobi!"

Billy ran from behind the stairwell to the closet to change music.

Marian grinned from ear to ear. She exchanged smiles with William who stood next to her. *So this is the surprise they were talking about.* Turning her focus back to the stage, Marian attempted to clap louder than the rest of the family. The cheering died down as a full orchestra and choir from a sci-fi/fantasy movie series echoed in the room from the surrounding speakers.

The fateful symphonic music was joined by Eva and Melista who winked at a smiling Marian as they passed her aquarium. The two barefoot young ladies were clothed in tannish-brown knee-length robes and entered from stage left. Eva wore brown pants while Melista strutted in with black pants.

A black hooded barefoot figure entered from the opposite side of the stage. The person's slow march was fluid, without jerking movements or flaws. After pausing, Willetta slightly kneeled as her shoulders rotated with her arms rippling. Dropping her robe, she <u>revealed</u> a red and black ski mask, black knee-length robe and black pants. Slowly standing up with several hip bumps, she dramatically lifted a wooden cane, her right hand supporting the black painted center. The florescent blood red painted tips spun menacingly as she precisely belly-danced with lethal confidence around the stage. Eva and Melista daintily reached behind their backs with hip figure 8's and pulled out black handled, painted straight canes of their own. Melista performed a vertical ribcage circle with undulation before her florescent green tip carefully collided with one end of Willetta's. Eva skillfully whirled her florescent blue tip about before landing it on the other end of Willetta's. The three shifted with glorious horizontal, diagonal and vertical core moves all over the platform twisting their hips and ribcages. Occasionally, they coordinated their standstills with their heads rhythmically sliding back and forth.

The audience cringed and gasped as the villain's sword broke in two. One half carelessly dropped on the floor with a clunk. With near perfect dance isolation techniques, the villain mounted a strategic pose in front the tall young lady whose upright arms towered above her, forming a pyramid. The masked figure viciously poked the red end into the heroine's undulating abdomen. After Melista arched her back, she crumpled to the ground, holding her stomach.

Engrossed in the powerful interpretive dance, Marian placed her chin on her wrists in sympathy. What 'could have been' haunted the depths of her eyes. I *will never be able to dance like that… I could have died in those experiments*, she thought to herself. Fear and worry pulled on her cheeks and shoulders, but she tried to shrug it off. The dramatic dance drew her back.

Eva 'killed' the villain and bowed with outstretched arms to the audience. She knelt to cradle her teacher's head in her lap. After a brief pause, she bowed her head. The audience cheered with exuberant delight as the music ended. Marian gleefully applauded as the three dancers hopped up and sprinted to the back of the room.

She grinned from ear to ear. Out of all the cousins, Marian had spent abundant time with them so she knew how much effort they put into their performance. Pride, contentment, and love filled her heart.

Tonight was a perfect time for a home school play. Preparations for a Shakespeare play had been gone over in class a week ago. They hadn't originally planned for this evening, but performed by memory. There were a few minor mistakes, triggering laughter, but nothing critical enough to spoil it. The shadows from the lack of lights, plastered an eerie effect on the story. Many times, the low lighting haunted the audience in serious moments. Tears were silently shed. The adults had to be coached a bit, needing prompting to bring lines back into memory several times by Ashley. Engrossed in the book with a flashlight, Ashley occasionally rocked in her comfortable lotus. The younger actors presented their lines with souped-up accuracy.

Since Gabe and Melista were the oldest students, they had the most familiarity with the story and played Romeo and Juliet beautifully. The two Kellys played the Montague's while Bonnie and Jerome appeared as the Capulet's.

Adam and Billy executed the two Friars with vigor. The whole family eagerly took in Billy's role. Although he wore his normal olive green B.D.U. pants and green shirt, it was one of the few times that he didn't use his Yoda accent.

Eva loved to overdramatize the role of Juliet's nurse. She frequently received an enthusiastic roar of laughter.

A bit bored, Marian looked around. She was alone. William and Willetta had left Marian's side to be involved with the play. She sighed as she thought to herself, *I saw Romeo just over a year ago. Oh, wait… I was unconscious for several years.* Marian swallowed. *Part of my life is missing. All those years, those days are lost.* Flashes came to her of her recent nightmares. *I don't know if I'm just having nightmares or if they're memories of me waking up during transitions.* Trying to push the dreams deeper, she blankly stared at every movement in the scene before her. She shook her head at the abridged scenes, used for a shorter presentation. *Throughout all Shakespeare, Macbeth is still my favorite.* The actors shot Marian winning smiles. Marian sat up. *They're doing this for me.* Gabriella's word, 'family' boomed in Marian's head. Out loud and to no one, Marian said, "Family." On her fingers, Marian counted her family when she had been kidnapped. Bringing her fingers closer to her eyes, she counted again. *"Mom, dad, me, Grandma and Grandpa Cook.* Five fingers staring back at her. Her fisted hand clenched tighter. *My father's family exists, but…* Marian's eyebrows danced up and down under the ridges on her forehead, they never froze high in contempt. *They didn't want me… Mom's an only child. I never had cousins.* When she tried to conjure up a picture of her father, Tyler's eager expression flashed in her mind. *Tyler's made an excellent stepdad. He's been a good husband to my mother. They don't even fight like mom and dad used to. I never saw Dad hit Mom, but I wondered sometimes.* Marian stared at her mother. Gabriella leaned into Tyler while he lightly touched her bicep with his arm around her. His free hand gently stroked her knee. When Marian's eyes darted to the stage, she saw her stepfather's family genuinely smile as they stole moments to peek at her. Billy snuck a hand wave by his waist. A disarming expression creased Marian's lips. *His family makes my life feel complete. I have cousins, aunts, and uncles now.* Her internal focus went back to the scene at hand. As the scene before her played out, what felt like spiders crawling on her now burned like wasp stings.

Touching her lips with her two fingers, Marian's heart crumbled. Although her head disappeared under the surface of the water, Shakespeare's Romeo and Juliet, Act 5, Scene 2 continued. Inch by inch, Marian 'Hope' Harrison sank to the floor. A crushing sensation clutched her chest and tightened at her throat. The last lock of Marian's hair pulled underwater. Shaking her head, she could not escape the sounds outside the fish tank. She clutched her throat with both hands before they flew to her ears. She pushed hard against them, but her hearing maintained a higher quality. "Stupid Hecc," she silently enunciated underwater. Through clenched teeth, she uttered, "Stupid… stupid… stupid Hecc vibration gland. I can hear everything. It's like the opposite of being deaf. It's like hearing whispers in the dark. I hate being a freak. I hate being," with enunciation, she spat the words, "a Human Electric Cave Catfish!" Hooking left and right, she punched the water. With her jaw set and her teeth clenched, she boxed the undistinguished mounting feelings. In her thoughts, she screamed as loud as she could, I…*uhg*…I wish I were human! Shaking her head back and forth, she recollected life as a human. Old fears of avoiding water boiled. She spat, *Water. Water.* Cutting the water with her hands doing karate chops, she said, "And *now* I have to *live* in it!" Marian growled.

With a loud voice, Gabe dramatized, "Arms, take your last embrace! And, lips, O you. The doors of breath seal with a righteous kiss."

The younger children giggled and whispered amongst themselves. They watched Gabe kiss Melista's forehead instead of her lips like he was supposed to if he were a 'real' actor. They were not a kissing family.

Ignoring the heckling giggles, Gabe continued. "A dateless bargain to engrossing death! Come, bitter conduct, come unsavory guide! Thou desperate pilot, now at once run on. The dashing rocks thy seasick weary bark! Here's to my love!" Cracking open a wax candy drink, he toasted. With a loud glugging sound, he chugged the small 'vial' to please the children. "O true apothecary!" His voice cracked. "Thy drugs are quick. Thus with a kiss I die."

The children attempted to hide their hysterical giggling and snickering. A few quieted down in short order when they saw disapproving glares from their mothers.

Still underwater, Marian whispered, "Jayne." She closed her eyes and covered her face with her hands.

Tears were silently dripping from already tear stained cheeks as the drama played out its conclusion. Some spectators even had new tears over freshly dried cheeks.

The heart that was breaking in the tank in the conservatory thirsted to cry openly. Noises spewed out that Marian didn't know existed. Pulling her hands away from her face, she opened her eyes. Sounds roared from her mouth and bounced off the walls in the tank.

Leaning in, Gabriella desperately tried to concentrate on the drama's conclusion, but found she could not hear it above the odd noises. Like a bird, she looked around for the source. Gabriella whispered to herself, "Is something left on? Has a machine gone bad?" A few others searched around including the actors. Hand gestures were made trying to figure out the direction.

Willetta caught Gabriella's attention with a frantic two hand wave as she jumped up and down. With a repeated punching motion, her forefinger pointed toward Marian.

Jumping up, the worried mother stripped off her shirt.

A few adult and teenager's faces paled, including Tyler's. His cheeks flushed at the sudden display of her skin until he realized that his brilliant wife had determinately caught on to the new drama. His jaw dropped. Gabriella wore a blue and white floral bikini swimsuit under her clothes. He had never seen her wear a two piece before and his mind forgot about the noises. Gabriella's legs pumped as she sprinted to her eldest. A mischievous grin formed as Tyler closed his mouth. This new, confident woman piqued his curiosity and interest.

Although in a hurry, Gabriella did not wish to startle Marian. She tapped the surface of the water. *Ripple-ripple-splish-splish-splish-splish-splish. Splash Splash.*

Marian heard her mother's unique tap and stopped in her tracks. Hesitantly, she zigzagged to the surface. They looked at each other in the darkness. Marian's eyes flashed with their unique H.E.C.C. glow. Gabriella refused to break eye contact. Shadows danced across their faces until a moving lantern flooded the area. The light illuminated the bearer's face. Concern etched the corners of Willetta's face and lips. Soon Zola appeared. Marian made direct eye contact with her. Motherly love kindly removed Marian's scowl. Zola saw Marian's grief-touched face and put out a kind hand to embrace the lonely cheeks.

Gazing upon her daughter, Gabriella recognized that particular look. Briefly turning to glance at Zola, Gabriella focused back on Marian. She thought, *Misery and longing means one thing. Marian is in* love. *My baby girl is in love. But, but she's not old enough.... oh wait... she is. I'm just not ready for her to be.* Gabriella also reached a comforting hand out to hold her daughter's cheek. Zola placed her hand on the other one. Marian's face was sheltered by the two women.

Willetta searched the three women's faces trying to figure it out. Zola removed her hand slowly.

"It's okay, honey. He'll call soon. He's just been a little busy," soothed Gabriella. She knew that Jayne still cared for Marian.

A train ran over Willetta's mind. She smacked her forehead with her right hand.

William smacked her from behind her head. "Just stay clueless, sis. You're better off!" Maniacal laughter burst forth from his mouth. The contagion hit those around him causing them to giggle, laugh or chuckle while Willetta scowled.

Marian semi-smiled before her lips returned to a slight frown.

The silence around the aquarium disappeared, for it became surrounded by children of all ages. "What was that noise?" was multiplied by additional people besides Lisa, Charlie and Tannen.

"How did you do that?" Charlene excitedly piped up.

"Sounded like a whale to me." Vanessa mused.

Rolling his eyes, Nick responded, "Nuh-uh. It was more like a dolphin!"

"Are you hiding any whales or dolphins?" Charlie eagerly asked, having misunderstood the conversation in all the commotion.

"Dolphin? If she gets a dolphin, can I have a koala?" Mary fussed. She thirsted to have everything big sister had. It was a bit hard for her to give up her rank since she was no longer the only child.

Surprisingly, Marian didn't hide from the crowd gathering around her personal space. Gabriella gazed fondly at her eldest. She became a proud, outspoken mother. "My daughter is grown up now."

Marian turned from the noisy children to look at her mom with curious eyes. She cocked her head to the right.

Zola answered with her own statement. "She is indeed ready to be named."

Gabriella responded. "I think she needs a godmother too. Are you up for the job, dear Aunt Zola?"

Grinning from ear to ear like a possum, Marian was ready to proceed.

The children cheered. "Yay! It's almost time for cake!" Nina Shaw skipped around the room followed by Hannah and Emma. They squealed and giggled with girly delight. Nina and Hannah tripped on a few blankets, but no tears were shed. Cake was around the corner! "Cake! Yay! Cake!"

The lights came on and Marian was helped into the middle of the room, water dripping everywhere. She felt like a lone Heccwan as she sat in her wheelchair in the middle of the sea of human Sharps. Her fears departed when her mother put her loving hands on her shoulders.

Zola placed a wreath made out of flowers on top of Marian's head. She raised her voice and said, "Attention Sharp family! Attention, please!" The crowd settled in and around Marian. They quieted down.

Gabriella spoke as loudly as she could so all could hear her. "Years ago, I gave birth to a wonderful daughter, Marian Jennifer Harrison. She is no longer the young woman she was years ago. Marian reached a crossroad in life and walked into a new world, a new life. Jayne, who was a stranger at the time, was also at a crossroad in his life. He looked down the road for answers and saw Marian. He didn't know her name, but the name Hope illuminated the atmosphere around her. She was the reason he wished for a new life with great expectation. She was his symbol for a new life. She gave him strength to keep swimming in the wide ocean of life despite the wailing winds pushing him down." Gabriella ignored the giggles concerning her well placed pun and continued. "From this day forward, Marian will be called Hope for she is my wish, my dream, come true! She has given me new life, new love. She is my hope. Marian, as your birthmother, I name you this September 2nd, the date of your new birth." Gabriella turned to the rest of the room.

"I introduce to you, my eldest daughter, Hope!" Two or three cameras alternately flashed their approval.

The glowing smile of approval on Hope's face welcomed the onlooker's delightful gaze. Tyler signaled the cheers. "Three cheers for Hope!"

"Hope!" everyone yelled.

"Hope!" The whoop was louder.

"Hope!" The name was hollered even louder than the first two times.

"Congratulations on your naming ceremony!" was repeated to Hope a few times before it vanished behind the sounds of the noisemakers around the room. The deafening sounds were slowly silenced by Beverly.

Beverly stood up to signal to the audience to quiet down before she made the announcement. "Gabriella," said Beverly. "The children have an additional presentation." Gabriella nodded her loving approval.

Hope was taken aback. She had thought that the small ceremony had ended. She hadn't expected anything other than cake. Soon, all the Sharp children came up by threes and fours to present Hope with gifts. They pulled towels and blankets off of their art projects. Seashells, pretty rocks and fake jewels were decorated in many different ways. There were trophies, necklaces, bracelets, rings and sculptures of things one might find in the sea. Hope treasured the unique sculpture in the shape of a seahorse that Willetta gave her. William had also given her a gift, a wooden trophy with the burned inscription: 'Hope, an Inspiration to Many'. Hope embraced that one tight to her chest while a few additional gifts were presented. Attention went from Hope to the commotion coming from the hallway. Hope didn't mind, but when she saw the cause of the commotion, she too had to vocalize her awe. The cameras took turns to flash their admiration of the spectacular cake which had been tucked away in the walk-in freezer. Prepared to celebrate Marian's one year reunion, the party had been postponed due to her depression.

Bonnie, Beverly and Zola had wheeled in a giant three-tiered white cake, decorated with blue and green icing-shaped sea plants. Clams made out of chocolate were placed strategically to give it a unique effect. Blue and green candy sprinkled all over magnified the sweet moment in time, increasing its desirable color. Three plastic mermaid dolls were placed back to back on the top as a centerpiece. Green and blue ribbons spiraled in between the plastic flowers to connect the cake layers. The awestruck cake admirers turned to protest at the sight of a threatening knife poised by Jack Sharp. A mixture of booing and cheering echoed in the room.

Jack dramatically backed away from the cake and stepped aside. The crowd changed their vocalized votes. A rectangular cake beautifully displayed on another wheeled metal cart entered with the help of Dolores and Jeremiah. Hope and Gabriella clapped their hands enthusiastically at the site of their loved ones. The Cooks had gone home, but had surprisingly returned for the occasion. Everyone else just welcomed them with hugs and gentle pats on their backs.

Mildred and Melista started to pass out the cake that was being cut by Jack. Eager hands reached out for it.

"Don't we get to eat that pretty cake?" Mary popped the question. She tugged on her mom's shirt.

"Not tonight dear," Gabriella answered. She was a bit distracted with the huge commotion. "We will have it for lunch tomorrow! Does that sound like a plan?"

"Oh, yes, mother! Yes, that sounds like a good plan." Mary ran away happily and enjoyed the cake that had been handed to her.

Not all mouths chewed their food properly. The tasty morsels disappeared in happy gulps. Cleanup took place quickly because nerves were frazzled. It was so late. Everyone scattered to brush their teeth in different bathrooms.

They reappeared in the room to settle into their blankets and sleeping bags. Silence was not demanded, but it took place anyway. Eyes and heads were foggy. Limbs sluggishly moved. Sleep rolled in as soon as children crawled into bed. Some didn't have a chance to bundle up before the sands fell upon them. They sprawled partially on their bedding and slightly off. While the adults were settling into their cots, the phone rang. A few sleeping children stirred but did not wake up. They were dreaming of a Mount Cake-more to be conquered after the following lunch.

Zola wondered aloud. "Who could be calling at one thirty in the morning?"

"I'll get it," Melista insisted for she was closest. "Hello?" She fell silent a few minutes, and then she responded into the phone. "It is okay, Jayne. We've been expecting your call. No need to apologize. We were up. No. Everything's all right. Yeah. She's on her way." She gently put down the phone.

Tyler and Gabriella heard the name Jayne and hurried to get Hope to the phone. Hope greedily reached for it. She fumbled with the phone a minute before she could answer. "Hello, Jayne? Hi!" She didn't know where to start.

"Hope. Hi." Jayne warmly answered. "I'm sorry my phone calls have been so spread out."

Hope answered shyly. "I've been waiting for you to call. What have you been up to?" Her timid voice then morphed into a more bold and challenging tone. "Where have you been? Who have you been with?" She looked around and brought her voice down to a whisper. "Seriously, what's up?"

Taken aback, Jayne replied, "I've... I've been busy. I'm sorry. I should have never been too busy for you. I was afraid of waking up your family, though. I really didn't know if they had adopted a new schedule or not." His excuses ran out and he realized how much he missed her. "Oh, Hope, I am truly sorry. I should have taken extra time out for you. I have been working on something that will make it so that we never have to be apart again. It's something that will improve all the Heccs' lives."

"Really?" Hope changed subjects. She knew better than to badger him. "What else have you been up to? What happened to your interviews?"

"Well. I've had so many TV interviews that I lost count! Various politicians, and lobbyists for political action groups have tried to end my speaking career. They seasoned and grilled me like a hot potato in front of the Senate and Congress…well… along with a few 'expert' biologists and geneticists." After pausing, he lifted his voice with a sour sing-song. "Yeah, that was fun."

"You make any new friends?"

"Not really."

"You have someone nice to talk to?"

"Doug's here. He's nice enough."

"They let him off for good behavior?"

"Since he did what he could for me and Jon at the pet shop, they gave him community service. He joined up with me and he has been watching my back in this human world."

Hope snickered. "Really, how is he? What mischief has he gotten you into?"

Jayne let a drawn-out, "Well." He exaggerated. "He didn't warn me when I was in a swimming pool before I got outnumbered."

"Oh, no!" Hope sat up. "What happened?"

Jayne rushed through the story about the boy almost drowning. He left out the details concerning the contempt for the H.E.C.C.s. Then he reassured her. "It really turned out okay. The boy's relatives invited us to the wedding tomorrow and one of them is going to invest in our future."

"Wait," Hope protested. "What future?"

"I can't tell you right now. You're going have to trust me to tell you the details later. I gave my word." Jayne hoped she wouldn't pester anymore. He yearned to leave the conversation on a positive note. If she kept prying to find out his secret, their conversation could abruptly end from heated debate.

"Hmm." Hope could hear his tone changing. She tried to lighten the mood. "You're climbing a slippery slope there, buddy!"

Jayne gulped down his guilt. "Well, anyway, anything new at the summer house?"

She excitedly told him about the naming ceremony and the presents she received. She concluded with sorrow, "I really don't know where I am going to display or put them all. I really don't have a bedroom."

"I know that one," Jayne felt depleted of material possessions himself. "I travel from hotel to hotel. When I get a place, I guess I will have to come up with a different hobby. As a boy, I always wanted to get involved in miniature trains. I wonder what other hobby I could have."

"Well, you do seem to enjoy marine life, even if you were thrust into it." Hope was cautious as she carefully trampled on a possible testy subject. She didn't want the call to end yet.

"Yeah, but I need a hobby besides work."

"True," said Hope. She hesitated. "True. Very true. What about collecting fish?"

"That still seems like working. I've always liked Legos and Castles. I wonder how Legos would build underwater." He gave a sad chuckle with a twitch of his mouth.

Hope clamped her hand over her mouth at the thought of Legos scattered around floating in her basin. Her cheeks briefly puffed up with air before it escaped into a snort and a gaspy chuckle. "How would you get them to stay on the bottom?"

"I guess when I build a bigger and more efficient tank; I will have to put some panel foundations into the floor. Or... I could design them out of a heavier material." He snickered at the thought of the challenging idea.

Sleeping family members stirred. Imagining similar thoughts, Hope bit her lower lip to stop her laughter. "I really can't talk a whole lot right now. Everyone is ending the party with a sleepover."

"A sleepover?" Jayne paused for a minute thinking about that statement. Unconsciously, he lowered his voice. "Is *everyone* in the conservatory?"

Looking around with fearful eyes, she softly answered him. "Yeah. Zola is still here. She delayed her flight again. Grandma and Grandpa are in cots and they look so cute holding hands above their heads. Mom and Tyler have fallen asleep here beside me. They're sitting here by me waiting to help me back into the tank."

Sadness crept over Jayne. "Ahhh, I miss it there. I didn't realize how much until imagining everyone crowded into that room. It felt like my first home since before mom died. Are the Cooks still there?"

"They went home, but surprised mom and me tonight. They arrived late." Hope explained.

"That's neat. Anyway, I just wanted to check in with you." He paused for a minute. "I really do miss *you* most of all."

"You do? Well I miss you, too." Hope longed for his reassuring hand on her shoulder. She placed her free hand on her shoulder and hugged it with the nape of her neck. "I am starting to settle in a bit. If I didn't feel welcome before, I should feel it now. I just wish I could feel freedom again. I wish I could go out into the world again. I feel so confined in the wheelchair. I miss jogging and feeling the wind in my hair." Hope momentarily drifted off into her own world.

"I'm working on something that will give us all freedom. Well, I'm just helping. There are other people making it happen." Pride flipped to being humble.

Jayne's statement brought Hope back to the present. "I wish you could tell me additional details about what it is. The more you hint at it, the more curiosity pains my soul." Pausing, she merrily sighed. "I had so much fun tonight."

"Well that's good. How's William?"

"He's good. Willetta tells me he misses you, but he won't tell anyone but her."

"I miss hanging out with him too. He was the first friend that was of my choosing." Jayne's thoughts diverted. "I mean... oooof."

"You okay?" Hope asked sympathetically.

"Doug hit me," Jayne griped. He was still being distracted. "Ow! That hurt, you overgrown ape!" He fought off the playful battering.

With her lips spread apart, Hope laughed hysterically.

Tyler stretched his legs. Gabriella rolled her shoulders and opened her eyes.

As quick as Hope started, she ceased her hysteria. "Jayne," she cleared her throat. "Jayne, will you call me again soon?"

Gabriella and Tyler both sat up at the sound of the conversation ending.

"Yes, I promise. I won't make it so far in between. I guess I had better let you go." Jayne hated to say goodbye. It felt like a very brief conversation.

"Yeah. I guess," Hope sadly answered. She changed her voice to teasing. "Well, goodbye, Jayne, my dear friend."

"Goodbye, Hope." Thinking about her full lips spread in delightful character, Jayne hung up with a roguish smile himself.

At the sound of his click, Hope hung up also.

{:-)-]~~{

Jayne and Doug were exhausted. They simultaneously yawned.

"Goodnight, dude." Doug searched through his suitcase and found a pair of boxers shorts.

"Yeah, 'nite, Doug."

Doug picked the tuxes up off the bed and hung them in the closet. He sat down on the bed and took his shoes off. While Doug took his shoes off, Jayne headed toward the bathroom. Doug changed into his boxers. With attitude, Doug proceeded to plop on top of the covers, all sprawled out. They left the trash on the table.

Jayne left the door open and took his sports pants off. He filled the tub with cool water. Stepping in, he yawned again. It had been an emotional roller coaster ride all day. After lying down in the tub, the water reached his desired level. He naturally exhaled before plunging his face underwater. His gills took over and he immediately fell into a deep sleep. Dreams about the future filled his mind with hope. He softly smiled.

{:-)-]~~{

333

Wearily, Tyler and Gabriella helped Hope into her aquarium. Then they went to their cots and fell asleep as soon as their heads touched their pillows. Hope exhaled and dipped underwater. She became aware of how tired she was. Her gills welcomed their job with open hunger. The water filtered smoothly and Hope fell into a deep happy sleep. She had heard Jayne's voice. She couldn't control the dream where she walked hand in hand on a beach with Jayne in the sunset.

Chapter 28

The bright morning sun on September 3rd crept in between the window and the curtain at the hotel. Doug turned his head over and planted the other cheek on the hard pillow. "Errg." He tossed over again. He rolled his eyes. The noise continued that had been in his dream. Only this time, it wasn't his dream. Clearly, a knock pounded on the door. Hopping out of bed, he mumbled his way over to the door. Peering through the spy hole, Doug straightened up and swung open the door. "Oh, I'm so sorry, sir. Did we oversleep? Is there a problem?"

The hotel's day manager walked into the room, followed by Paul Walkere, Paul's friend from the previous night, and a stranger. Paul shook his head. "No, no problem. We might be earlier than you set your alarm." He beamed. "Sorry. Hope you had enough rest."

Doug read the manager's name tag.

Manager Vince McGilly spoke louder, "Where is he? I want to meet him. Where is this young hero, Jayne?" A bit off-key, he sang "The Hero of Canton" from the 'Firefly' TV series, but he switched words to make it fit his hotel and the incident.

A young and pretty Latino hotel staff member wheeled in a cart filled with breakfast. Looking around, Doug's whole body blushed as he noticed the maid blankly staring at his bare chest and heart boxers. If Hope had been there, she would have harassed him about his rapidly reddening cheeks.

A loud splashing came from the bathroom and everyone looked toward the door. Jayne heard the voices. With fluttering eyelashes, he grabbed a towel. Sleep still clung to his eyes. Stumbling, he fell in the doorway. Paul reached out to catch Jayne, but thought better of it and pulled back. Doug helped steady the half-awake Heccan. Then he grabbed his jeans and shirt out of his duffle bag, went into the bathroom and shut the door.

The sight of Jayne dripping water all over the floor startled the men. They guffawed and slapped their thighs. However, the young lady gave him a small scolding for dripping water all over her floor. Jayne started to turn back toward the bathroom, but found the door shut.

The short woman turned to the manager and sniveled about the water damage. The manager's laugh faded as he shooed her out the door. With both hands, he closed the door before turning to his guests. "Here, Jayne, have a seat and wake up a minute." He guided Jayne to the table.

The bathroom door hastily opened. Doug raced in, apologizing as he cleaned off the table. The manager grabbed a dishrag from under the cart and washed off the table.

Paul waited until the table was clean and then sat down in the opposite chair. Doug sat on the bed and rubbed his eyes. He looked at the clock. It was definitely earlier than he had wanted to wake up on a Saturday morning. He turned toward the others and watched with glazed eyes.

Vince McGilly handed Jayne a cappuccino and started to set the table with food. The stranger walked over to the cart and grabbed a black coffee and a donut. Bananas and oranges were also on the grab and growl menu for Paul, his friends, and Doug.

Looking over his choices, Jayne grimaced and lifted a glass of water and gulped it down. The manager handed Jayne a container and lifted the lid. Jayne's grin completely engulfed his face. The room filled with friendly smiles and friendly banter. Excited, Jayne grabbed a fork. The bagel with salmon, cream cheese and pickled capers disappeared quickly as Jayne gobbled it down.

Beaming, Vince admitted that he had his sources. Then he changed subjects. "I want to deeply thank you for your act of kindness. You are welcome to stay here whenever you are in town. I will make sure that you get no harassment here ever again. I am sorry that you had to save a life to be recognized and respected as a person." Pausing, he shifted his weight. "Would you like for me to arrange for the swimming area be open to you and your friend after closing time? We can loan you a key so you can lock the public out. Once the wedding is over, there is no guarantee of the outcome with any new guests."

That statement startled Paul. He had never thought about how often Jayne received harassment because of his differences. Originally, he hadn't planned on giving over a few thousand dollars. The manager's statement made him think again.

"The chlorine in the water makes it difficult for me to sleep in there longer than an hour," said Jayne, "but we will appreciate being in there until midnight or two, if you can arrange it." Only after he finished the fish spread and bagel, did he reach for the cappuccino and donut.

"Yes, sir, Jayne, I will arrange it. Now if you will excuse me, I will leave you to your guests." They nodded goodbyes before Vince eased himself out of the room.

"Jayne." At first Paul Walkere sounded as though he hesitated, but continued with confidence. "I brought Tony because last night before bed, he mentioned that he wanted to match my investment. You remember Tony Smith from last night? However, before he and I could talk this morning, I decided to make a significantly larger investment; possibly of hundreds of thousands." He slightly waved at Tony.

Tony glanced quizzically at his friend. He had talked to him this morning and there was no mention about making any higher investment. They had even made a few phone calls to check on the legitimacy of the project. He wondered when his friend had decided on investing extra money.

He turned toward the stranger and introduced him, "This is Malcolm Leeds, another family friend." With only an inch of height difference between the two tall men, he was more solidly built. Close set beady brown eyes intently peered behind small glasses. Malcolm had been with them during their discussions this morning and had become curious about the project.

Without missing a beat, Paul continued. "I thought about it last night and I think it is definitely worthy of greater financing. Malcolm here, wanted to hear from the horse's mouth before he invested any money."

Although they understood Jayne's plan to be legit, they let him explain in endless detail. Jayne rattled off a couple names of some of the other investors. The potential new investors examined him with many question. When there was nothing left to talk about, Paul asked Doug what he thought about it.

Doug politely smiled. "Well, I know the Heccs personally, so I am biased. All I know is that the Heccs need a home. I don't believe that we humans have the right to kick them out of the states, or dump them in the ocean, and split them up from their families. They weren't born H.E.C.C.s, they were kidnapped and mutated into them. They used to have human lives that they still crave. I think this idea will give them the best of both worlds." He paused. "That's my opinion." He crossed his powerful arms.

The three men looked at Doug and looked at each other.

Tracing his pencil mustache, Malcolm blurted, "Jayne?"

Jayne looked at him. "Yeah?"

"What do you think about arranging a meeting with your group to which we three can accompany you?" Mr. Leeds pointed to the three of them.

Running through everyone's schedules in his brain, Jayne concluded aloud. "I'll make some calls. After the wedding, I'll let you know what arrangements I have been able to set up."

"Alrighty then. Keep us informed." Malcolm turned to his two friends. "We will rendezvous after the wedding festivities?" They nodded in return.

Malcolm and Tony left, but Paul stayed behind to help Doug and Jayne into their tuxes. Jayne snuck off to freshen up with a shower first. Although Doug had worn one once, it had been many years ago. Jayne was the one that required the most help. The three of them went downstairs and rode in Paul's limo. They went to the church wedding and then returned for the reception at the hotel. Jayne had wanted to sneak out to find some water during the ceremony, feeling dry and jittery, but managed to refrain for fear of disturbing the joyful occasion. He was starting to feel land-locked and welcomed the sight of the hotel on their return. Once he walked through the door, he raced upstairs for another shower, all he had time for before the reception.

Doug ended up trailing after Paul as he introduced him to people as one of the two who saved the young ring bearer. It was one enlarged loop of conversation that he was glad to share with Jayne when he finally appeared.

Once the reception wrapped up and people were mingling, Doug and Jayne excused themselves from the strange family that they had been thrust into. They fled to their room, and shed their tuxes. Anxious, Jayne was ready to go, while Doug dragged his feet about going for a swim. Jayne droned on about how slow Doug's feet 'slogged, like a snail'. Doug told him to 'quit nagging and call Hope'. Jayne pouted, then made the phone call, telling Hope about the wedding and the discomfort of wearing a tux, secretly wishing it had been them up there and wondering if she felt the same way. By the time Jayne hung up, Doug was ready.

The two headed for the swimming pool and found it filled with people waiting to swim with a real live H.E.C.C. The young boy Daniel refused to ever swim again unless Jayne held his hand as he entered the shallow end. The shy Jayne didn't like the attention, but politely managed it for the child's sake. Doug went for a dip and then stood around watching, just in case a supremacist slipped in unnoticed. He spotted the new visitors before Jayne did.

Hope's father, Marshall Harrison had brought a few men with him. Doug was a bit shocked since Jayne's morning conversation with

Marshall had set up a meeting for the next day to let the potential new investors meet with the planners. Paul also walked into the pool area. Doug was not going to be the one to introduce them. He whistled sharply.

Jayne caught the signal and excused himself from the confining crowd. When he walked up to Doug, it took him a minute to see Marshall hidden behind the backs of Sonny and Albert Leddon. Jayne anxiously welcomed them all.

The pool area was too loud for Jayne and it was starting to drain him, so they headed for his room. On the way out, Paul's associates joined them. They all followed Jayne to his room and found amassed owners and investors waiting for them.

There were too many people for a meeting in his room, so Jayne excused himself to contact the manager about a possible solution. He reappeared in the hallway and asked the group to follow him. Manager McGilly joined them and directed the group to a conference room.

{:-)-]~~{

The Sting of an Eel

Shocking Ain't It?

Chapter 29

aturday morning marked a week since Hope's naming party. She emotionally floated on a cloud the entire time. Jayne called every night at nine. On several occasions, he ended the phone call by calling her, 'Sweeting', which he had picked up from watching too many episodes of his second favorite sci-fi show. No one had to stay up past their bedtime to help her back into the tank.

Although Hope longed for enhanced freedom other than a wheelchair, she welcomed the idea of getting out of the house. For two days, she had worked to convince her family that she was ready for a road trip. Most H.E.C.C.s had already gone out into the public, but Hope Harrison had not been thrust into the city or public dealings. She led a very sheltered existence after her return to her mother. Today was the day she was aspiring to escape her cabin fever. Bubbling with excitement, Hope's eyes danced on the unusually warm Saturday morning. She constantly talked about the list of places that she wanted to tour. Everyone in arm's reach got an earful of the things she missed about each place. The old Marian showed through because libraries and museums were at the top of the list. The oddest place she desired to visit included a grocery store. Willetta helped Hope dress in a floral beach dress and a large beach hat.

Tyler and William helped her into the wheelchair and pushed her to the car parked outside the front door. Gabriella and Willetta walked alongside with a number of loaded bags. The two women placed their bags at the back of the vehicle and walked over to help Hope get in. Tyler dashed back into the house while William tucked the bags away.

Gabriella, the victim of a long-winded one way conversation, finally managed to get a word in edgewise. "Honey, we will be able to stop by and grab fuel for our trip to the zoo. But, dear, it's a long drive so we don't have time for the library or a museum, today."

Giving a fake forced pout, Hope showed her discontent. It did not last a lengthy amount of time for she was very excited. "I want to see the penguins, the jungle, gorillas, lions, tigers…"

"And bears! Oh, my!" Willetta teasingly interrupted. The two looked at each other and knowingly laughed.

"Hey, hon, Mary is riding with the Kellys," Tyler told Gabriella as he arrived.

Smiling, Gabriella nodded her assent without making eye-contact. She straightened her knee length floral dress with her hands.

Before Hope's door was closed, she hollered at her mom, "Hey, Momma? What's today's date?"

Closing her eyes, Gabriella had to calculate in her head before responding. "It's September 10th, honey. It's been a full year since you came back to us." She winked at her daughter and quietly thanked the Creator for bringing her daughter home again. Gabriella helped her shut her door and settled herself in her own seat.

The drivers of the caravan signaled each other. Everyone was accounted for and ready to travel. The whole household was taking the trip, including Zola. Off they went, one following another, with Tyler in the lead. The Cooks drove their own vehicle because they were heading home after the field trip. Melista and Gabe took her Harley, but she trusted Gabe to be in the driver's seat. He had a license, but not a motorcycle. They were planning on visiting a friend of Gabe's before reuniting at the zoo with the family. The Kelly's drove their 10 passenger van while the Hart's took theirs. An old school bus brought up the rear of the strange caravan with the rest of the family, kids and all. A parade on the way to the zoo!

It took over half an hour to get to the closest town. Hope acted like a little girl. She couldn't take in enough scenery. She played a car color game with Willetta and William. She rolled down the closest window and took in the smells. It soon turned into a game with William as he challenged her to describe each different scent. No human had the keen sense of smell like the H.E.C.C.s did. William enjoyed asking Hope about her heightened senses. Tyler pulled up into the parking lot and parked the vehicle. They got out and helped Hope out. The first place the ladies went was the bathroom to help Hope get quenched and drenched. The guys joined Kelly-She and Jerome as they sought out a few last minute essentials for the trip. They met up with Gabriella and Willetta pushing the wheelchair. Hope didn't feel any different than any human there as she received pleasant looks from the other customers and the store employees.

Soon it was time to head to the zoo. The caravan mounted up and moved on. It took two and a half hours to get to the big city. They stopped at a gas station and let the kids overrun it for bathroom breaks. As they loaded back into their designated vehicle, they received a sack lunch. Each had brought their own thermos and those in the bus could make a break for the cooler to fill them up again. As soon as all were accounted for and ready, they drove the remaining thirty minutes to get to the zoo. Hope still could not get enough of the scenery. Everything was beautiful to her; the tall buildings, the cramped rows of houses and even the stores. Time had definitely moved on without her. There were old and new vehicles to be in awe over. Although she did not remember time passing, it had. Hope again expressed her abundant desire to own a computer and to spend countless hours in a public library. She hadn't seen a library since she had been kidnapped.

Ready for a stretch of legs, the drivers eagerly parked in the zoo's parking lot. Melista and Gabe hadn't arrived yet and called Tyler on his cell phone to let him know their estimated time of arrival. Everyone clambered off of the buses and waited for Tyler and Gabriella to unload Hope, and the Shaw twins. The Sharps,

Cooks, Clarks, Harts, Shaws and the Burgesses all meandered to the entrance with Jack and Mildred in the lead. Mildred gave the piece of paper with the written number of visitors to the clerk. The visitors had been categorized by ages to make it easy for the lady to tally the total. Jack paid with a credit card and would be paid back by the individual families later. Gabe and Melista were going to be on their own.

They entered the zoo and split up into groups. The grandparents and Zola went off on a slow walk while the younger ones ran on ahead.

Kelly-He yelled at William as his group took off. "William, you're in charge! Keep them from joining the monkeys while they're here!"

William Shaw hollered back, "Sure thing, Pops!" Then William turned to Billy and the two mischievously whispered. Ashley and Eva huddled to get details on where they planned to head first.

Mary begged to tag along with Lisa and Nina so she gave her mom and dad a kiss before heading off with her group.

Last of all, Tyler and Gabriella followed Willetta as she pushed Hope in her wheelchair. Hope kept a bottle of water with her and doused herself a few times. The air hit her with new and exciting smells. At first, it was a bit overwhelming, but Hope learned how to tune out the strongest ones.

Tyler and Gabriella sported a bit by playfully shoving each other. Their rekindled love for each other showed as they enfolded their hands and intensely looked into each other's dreamy eyes. They slow danced by the panda bear exhibit. Snickering, Hope and Willetta pointed at the two intoxicated lovebirds. Tyler masterfully chased Gabriella in and out of trees, while Hope gazed at the elephants and zebras. Hope tried to holler at her mom a few times, but Gabriella could only answer briefly and out of breath. Soon, the Sharps couldn't sport anymore: it seemed like the zoo became crowded. There were people meandering around them so the two just passionately held hands as they jubilantly walked from exhibit to exhibit. They intently conversed, scrutinized each other from head to toe, and modestly leaned on each other.

"Hey, Mom," Hope uttered.

"Yes, sweety," her mom answered while not taking her eyes off of Tyler's lips.

Willetta and Hope giggled.

Gabriella looked over at her daughter. "What's up, Hope?"

"Can I have a slushy?" Hope's eyes danced.

Tyler glanced at Gabriella before looking at Hope. "How many do you want?"

"Really?"

"Of course, silly."

"Can Willetta have one too?" Then she turned toward her cousin and inquired, "You did want one, right?"

"Sure I do." Willetta grinned.

Tyler kissed Gabriella and started to walk off. Hope protested, "Tyler! Wait! Mom, you can go too. We don't need to be babysat. We can handle ourselves."

Gabriella snuck a quizzical look at Willetta.

"Yeah, we don't need any watching," Willetta teasingly quipped before sweetly telling them, "Go on, you two! Go have a mini-date."

Smiling like a school girl, Gabriella took off with Tyler. The two flirted with each other as they headed for the closest snack shop.

{:-)-]~~{

Gabe and Melista sailed into the large zoo parking lot picking a, brightly painted parking space close to the old school bus. This time, Melista was controlling the reins and enjoyed pulling a few zigzags. Once parked with the engine turned off, they took off their helmets and padlocked them to the bike. The two didn't have a whole lot to say because they had chatted with their helmet mics off and on the whole journey. Gabe had met his friend at the mall while Melista went shopping for new nose rings.

Gabe paid his own way and so did Melista. Gabe grabbed a map and opened it briefly. Melista peered over his shoulder.

"Let's head there," Melista said as she pointed to the African Plains. She pined to see the big cats. Gabe nodded and started walking toward their destination.

"Too bad our free time is over," Gabe pondered.

"What do you mean?"

"I like my cousins for the most part, but a couple of them get on my nerves."

"Like who?"

"Billy, for example. He's such a geek. I don't know how his parents put up with him talking *Yodish* aalll the time."

Melista laughed with her signature higher to lower note. "Yeah. I agree. I can only take it so long before I excuse myself. I do try and accep-" She was cut off by a passing conversation.

"Come on children. Hurry," the frantic woman in a business suit whimpered. She and her family scuttled by Gabe Clark and Melista Sharp.

"But," blonde-haired girl bellyached, "I don't want to leave yet! I haven't seen the gorillas!"

"We have to leave before we catch that contagion." The strange woman rolled her eyes as well as her head.

The boy paused. "What's a contagion?"

"It's a disease, I don't care what they say. Now, shut up! Move it," the father commanded as he roughly grabbed his two whiny children.

Wide-eyed, Gabe spoke softly, "Did you hear what they said as we passed them?"

"Yeah, I did," Melista replied. She swallowed the lump building in her throat. "I wonder if someone threw up." They shrugged their shoulders and continued. Gabe and Melista shook it off. When another group passed in a hurried gait, Melista and Gabe looked at each other as they eavesdropped.

"I saw it. It was one of those freaks shown on the news," a man told his girlfriend.

"No way! It was here? Was it in an aquarium?"

"Gosh, I can't believe they let those things out in public."

"Let alone live."

"Yeah."

Fear drained Melista's face of any natural flush. She shook her head slowly. Gabe started to get a little concerned. They picked up their pace. Melista's face was turning green. She didn't struggle when Gabe grabbed her arm and pulled her along to look for their family. Additional rude and mean comments passed by them. They were getting a tolerable idea what was taking place. Yanking her arm out of Gabe's grip, Melista ran to the side of the path. Her upper body jerked while her feet remained planted. Vomit shot out of her mouth and nose, landing in the grass. She cleared her throat and spit a few times. She knew she would never hear the end of it, but she could not help spewing her emotions.

An employee driving a cart rolled up the path as Melista had upchucked. Pausing, he investigated and evaluated the situation. From a distance, he vocally assessed if she was okay and if she needed him to contact medical aid for her. Gabe and Melista both shook their heads no.

Gabe reassured him and then said, "Thank you."

The employee left and Gabe grabbed Melista's cell phone out of her back pocket and her water bottle off her belt loop. He headed over to the closest fountain. Gabe filled up Melista's bottle before trying to call Tyler on his way back to her. When he arrived back at her side, there were two teenagers talking to her. He noticed Melista looked a little sharper as he walked up to her. Then she turned pale and started dry heaving. He heard the two young ladies talking as he walked up. Gabe flipped the phone shut.

"Oh, my God! Oh, my gawd!" She then emphasized every word, "I bet she's got the fish disease."

"Let's go, Helena, before we catch it. My father said I already had all the plastic surgery that he would pay for."

"Oh, my god, the Ich is spreading! You know my dad. He will sue if I catch that awful disease. Ugh, and I wouldn't be head cheerleader anymore!"

"Cover your mouth! You might breathe it in!"

"Maybe it's not a disease at all. Maybe we should stop by the office and tell them that one of their exhibits got loose." The two girls laughed with their high pitched voices.

Gabe's feet wouldn't listen to his brain. It was like he had tromped into wet cement. No matter how hard he tried, he could not put one foot in front of the other. When the conversation faded behind him, he became sickened and bolted for Melista. He stuck the phone in his pocket. He told Melista, "I'm sorry, but you're going to have to grow some balls." When she wouldn't budge, he picked her up and carried her like a sack of potatoes. Gabe started searching for friendly faces. His breathing was becoming labored, but he had so much adrenaline coursing through his body that he walked like a lone soldier in a war zone. As though enemies could jack-in-the-box any second, he skirted around the trees. He hurdled over uneven spots in the path as though they were landmines.

It was eight minutes before Gabe heard the sound of a familiar voice. William Shaw screamed on the other side of a spread out row of tall hedges. Gabe couldn't make heads or tails of the loud conversation so he shouted, "Will! Will! Is that you?" He perceived a voice behind him in the maze of tall grasses and hedges before he could reach Will. "The kidnapper was seen heading this way!"

Another voice answered. "Come on men, pick up your pace and keep your eyes open. Our daughter's lives are at stake! They're grabbing pretty women for their new experiments!"

William, Billy, Adam, Ashley and Eva, Willetta, and Hope all came around the corner to Gabe's surprise. They almost crashed into each other. The group breathed a sigh of relief when they saw

Gabe, however when they saw Melista, the females grew concerned and reached for her. Gabe gladly passed Melista into Hope's open arms. Fearful of his cousin's tear stained faces, Gabe grilled, "What's going on with you guys?"

"Other than we're being followed," Adam snarled, "everything's great. Just great."

Billy rolled his eyes.

"Come on guys," Gabe said. "Let's go find our parents." He didn't know if he could protect all his cousins by himself. He turned around to see several men glaring at him. Gabe swallowed hard.

Alarmed, Billy yelled, "Look! Hey, look you!" He pointed at the men. "Possessed by demons, are they."

Adam and Billy took over for Willetta and started to turn the wheelchair around, but, it was too late. They were surrounded. Melista gathered her weary strength and hopped off to lighten the load. She knew that Hope was safe for right now, maybe she could help keep it that way.

Gabe looked around and ordered to the group, "Follow me!" Then he looked at Melista. "Have you got my back, now?"

Melista assured him with a firm nod. Steam built up in her engine as she lifted her fists. The teenagers that had followed Eva and her group no longer threw rocks at them, but ducked to escape Gabe and Melista as they plowed their way through. Gabe and his cousins picked up the pace and started to run for open ground. When they were in a clearing, they stopped and turned around. They were being pursued by one posse with their fists waving menacingly and a lynch mob shouting insults. Gabe passed the phone to Willetta and told her, "Here! Call! Now!" Willetta almost dropped the phone when it was thrust into her hand.

The boys made a ring around the girls, with Hope in the middle.

Fists closed and a fight was pending with the arrival of fear-spreading insanity.

{:-)-]~~{

Tyler and Gabriella walked around glancing casually at each exhibit and reading the labels.

"Where do you think they went?" Gabriella nonchalantly picked her husband's brain. "You don't think they went back to the vehicle, do you? Maybe they're looking for us?"

"I don't know. I was under the impression that they were staying close by where we left them." Tyler was starting to get concerned. Using his free hand, he called the adults and teens in the other groups to see if they had seen Hope and Willetta. The paper cones sloshed in his left hand. He briefly found out that the group with the small kids had gone out to the bus and the reason would be explained later. He called the next group. He was on the phone with the group of men, when he heard a commotion.

Gabriella heard it too. "I wonder what's going on. Maybe an animal is loose."

Tyler waved her to be quiet before answering. "No, Jerome, we can't find them anywhere." He listened to the other end while in deep thought.

As they got closer to the commotion, Gabriella grabbed his arm. "Tyler! Tyler!"

He tried to ignore her, but as they got closer, he said, "Wait, a sec. Hold on." Tyler looked harder. "Uh, Jerome? I think you better meet me next to the building with the jungle." He hesitated momentarily, but then he saw three men roughly pulling Hope out of her wheelchair. Gabriella pointed a shaking finger at the group as her jaw dropped. The snow cones in Tyler and Gabriella's hands fell to the ground and exploded under their feet. Tyler cried into the phone. "Hurry! There's trouble!" He forcefully punched his hand with his phone behind him toward Gabriella. Heat filled his bones as his tight fist shook the phone back and forth. Gabriella understood and grabbed it.

He and Gabriella simultaneously started yelling out names since they didn't know who was or wasn't there. They sprinted toward the madness.

Pumping his fists, Billy frightfully struggled to escape the man's grabby hands. After he lost his grip on Billy's shoulders, his nails clung onto his shirt. Billy cried out in pain. Lastly, the man's hands imprisoned Billy by holding onto his stuffed green alien backpack. Billy howled as he released his treasure one arm at a time. The man threw down the teen's backpack and chased him again.

Tyler saw William flat on the ground, being imprisoned by the knees of an aggressive strange man. His fists were protecting his bloodied face while the man freely punched him. "Get off of him, now!" When the man wouldn't budge, Tyler bulldozed him. "William, it's me, Tyler! I'm here! Get up!"

Shaking, Gabriella fumbled with the phone as she saw Melista on the ground unconscious. She clumsily went through the phone numbers and found the one that she was searching for. She pressed the button to call.

Tyler punched the man holding William down. He helped William up and they circled the brawl. "Hey! That's *my* daughter! Leave her *alone*." Hope clawed at three male aggressors with her semi-long fingernails while they carried her off. Her fins alternately kicked as she kept her thighs tucked tight together. Natural oils made her a difficult and slippery capture.

One man shouted, "Cleanse our bloodline!"

Another screamed, "Get rid of the Ich before it spreads in our town!"

The heavy stranger bulldozed Tyler, knocking him to the ground.

"Oh my god!" Gabriella shrieked. "Oh my god!" She forgot about the phone, holding it away from her ear. She yelled to whoever in the zoo would hear her. "Help! Help! Help! Help!" The phone rang three times. Gabriella could not hear Jayne answer above the commotion. She screamed and held the phone at an arm's length as two men ran toward her. One of them coiled his fist at his waist ready to strike. Running away but staring at her aggressors, she pleaded, "Help me! Someone, help me! Murderers! Help! Hope! Help! Someone help us!"

{:-)-]~~{

Chapter 30

Sitting in his hotel room on the bed, Jayne froze as he turned on the speaker phone. His heart threw multiple left hooks, jabbing his ribs like a punching bag. The horrifying background noises rang out from his cell phone. What Jayne heard, made him ill and shake from head to toe.

A knock at the door snatched Doug away to unwillingly answer it.

Vince McGilly, Malcolm Leeds, Tony Smith, Marshall Harrison and Paul Walkere barged in. Their joyful smiles turned to fearful frowns.

Doug snatched up the hotel phone and dug in his wallet to find a phone number.

The guests heard screaming and pleading coming from Jayne's phone.

"What is going on? Where are they? What have they done to my daughter?" Marshall turned to Jayne, yanked him up off the edge of the bed, and angrily cried into his face, "Why is Gabby screaming?" Realizing his aggression was misdirected, he consequently left Jayne to fall to his knees.

"Hello? Hello?" Doug had dialed the one eight hundred number in his wallet and got a quick response. "It's me, Doug. There's…" Jayne looked up as he noticed Doug was interrupted by the other caller. Confounded, Doug hung up and turned to Jayne.

"What?" Jayne eyed Doug. "Well?"

"That was Special Agent Hershkin. He was yelling orders and they were on their way. With the recent attacks on the H.E.C.C.s, the FBI have been keeping up with their whereabouts. Hope is at a zoo near the Sharp's vacation home."

"Oh, Hope! My Hope! Is this happening all over or only to the ones I am close to?" Jayne cried in agony.

Paul observed the increasing load of anguish, which fell on Jayne, and he was greatly concerned. Clearing his throat, he spoke up. "Tony. Malcolm. I'm going to have to excuse myself. I believe I have the means to take these three where they need to go." He paused, deep in thought.

"Gentlemen," said Malcolm with confidence. "I've still got the jet plane I rented at the airport."

"That's quicker than what I had in mind," Paul mused.

Tony concluded, "Let's go."

"Gather your stuff and meet in the lobby," Paul Walkere ordered.

Horrified at the mess around him and choosing to help, Vince McGilly searched his mind for possibilities. He quietly recommended, "I bet I can get you guys to the airport with a police escort."

"Good," the others replied in unison.

{:-)-]~~{

Chaos spread throughout the zoo. Word rapidly traveled from human to human. Guests were being escorted out and directed to leave. Zoo security hurried to assume control of the brawl. They called the local police and the county sheriff's department. Animals near the biggest commotion cried out their alarm and concern. Other startled animals became uncontrollable and jumpy. Volunteers comforted and soothed the bigger, friendlier animals before they could cause themselves harm or injure zoo keepers.

Gabriella's foot returned from finishing a kick to a man's groin. Leaving him crumpled, she escaped that particular menace as she raced in the direction of Hope and her captors. Abruptly, she stopped in her tracks as someone yanked her hair from behind. Gabriella almost lost her balance with the whiplash. Regaining her footing, she whirled around only to be roughly punched by a red-headed teen attacker. Blood flowed from her lip and ran down her chin. Another punch struck her straight in the eye.

Arriving nearly out of breath, Jerome and his group raced up. They bulldozed a path to the young girls and formed a circle around them to prevent them from further harm. Clifford ordered the younger boys to stay off the path near the trees. One by one, the girls were being pulled to the side and out of the action.

Zipping down the path, zoo security drove precariously in a golf cart. They screeched to a halt and piled out like clowns from a Volkswagen.

Gabriella, knocked to the ground by a punch in the face, repeatedly attempted to stand up. Her adrenaline-filled aggressor attacked her time and time again. Jerome pulled the man away by the back of his shirt. Gabe walked up and swung as hard as he could, landing his fist on the man's jaw.

Zoo security didn't know who were the aggressors and who were the innocent, but noticed one group trying to get the women out of harm's way. Billy managed to get the empty wheelchair over to their temporary base. One security guard took up the precarious occupation of protecting the unconscious Melista from being trampled. Another guard received a broken nose. His two co-workers immediately dog piled the aggressor.

The local police soon arrived on the scene in numerous golf carts with zoo security. While they were breaking up the last fight which included Gabe and his aggressor, the young men and women voiced their concern over the missing ones. Too busy trying to find out who started what, security would not listen to the fearful questions from the Sharps.

"Where's Tyler?" Kelly-He surveyed the injured.

Teeter-tottering, Gabriella wearily stood up only to fall to the concrete on her already bloody knees. Gabe broke away from the security guard three times before he reached Gabriella's side. He picked her up and placed her arm around his neck, walking to the nearest bench.

"Ty... Ty!" Gabriella weakly pleaded. "Hope! Please, help Hope!" She waved her arms to stop the fainting fairies from buzzing around her. Gingerly, she placed her hands on her temples to stop her head from falling off.

Frustrated, Kelly-He bent to her eye level. He growled, "Which way?"

Gabriella's trembling forefinger pointed in the direction of a nearby building.

Jerome and Kelly-He both heard what Gabriella yelped, looked at each other and began to run.

When the security men saw two sprinters, they pursued. "Stop! Stop! I said, stop! Get back here!" A few policemen joined in the chase.

The sign above the building towered over Jerome and Kelly-He, causing them to briefly pause and swallow. It read *Reptiles, Amphibians & Crawlers, Oh My*!

After stepping through both sets of double doors, Kelly-He and Jerome paused. Their eyes slowly adjusted to the darker lighting. Humidity, dirt and the smell of tropical plants tickled their noses.

"Where do you think the kidnappers and Tyler went?" Kelly rubbed his bruised jaw, trying to foresee possible outcomes.

Worry tripled Jerome's fears. "Let's split up?"

"I'll go this way," they both said, pointing in separate directions.

In tumbled four local police, knocking both Kelly-He and Jerome down.

"Let go of me! My brother and his daughter are still in danger!" Kelly-He defiantly threw off their grabby hands.

Two security men holding inner and outer doors yelled one after the other for their boss to hurry. The head of security entered and, after listening to the advice of his men, asked the police to let their prisoners search on. He and the zoo crew tagged behind.

Racing down the hallway, Kelly-He paused to glimpse around every corner. As if being chased by fire, he darted past the small aquariums that lined the wall. The frogs, toads, snakes, and small turtles were oblivious to the trouble brewing. The huge turtles were outside on display, but underneath their circular fenced table, a young black couple fearfully huddled.

"Where," heaved Kelly-He. "Which way?"

The man pointed down the hall. On down the hall, Kelly-He ran across one man sprawled on the ground. When he saw that it wasn't Tyler, he shouted to Jerome, "This way! This way!"

The security boss stopped and placed a reassuring hand on the moaning man. "He's alive."

Before Jerome and the others could join him, Kelly-He cautiously peered around the next corner. Four feet ahead, Hope's floral dress lay bloodied and crumpled on the floor. Following walls and corners splattered with blood, he expected to see death's cold grip at the end of the tunnel. A crushing sensation gripped his jittery stomach and chest. His tear ducts pained him.

Thunder rumbled through the halls as Jerome and his team joined them.

Placing a hand on Kelly's shoulder, Jerome cried, "Tyler! Hope! Tyler! Hope!"

Screeching to a halt, the rescuers turned the corner into the spacious alligator and crocodile observation room. A large Komodo dragon in a glass and metal cage hissed when the group startled him. His menacing eyes pierced with a foraging hunger.

A security guard stopped to bend over a fallen employee sprawled on the floor. With two fingers, he checked the pulse on the employee's wrist. "He's alive, just unconscious." Moving the man's hand ever so slightly, he exclaimed, "Ugh! His middle fingers are broken."

A nip on Kelly-He's ankle alerted him to the floor. He screeched like a little girl. "Wow! Hey!" The coiled up rumpled ball that he was stepping on made him jump back a foot. "There's a snake! It bit me! *Why* is there a snake loose?"

Jerome scanned his environment for answers.

"Is it venomous? Do I need to *panic*?"

"No….no. It's just a flesh wound. I can clean it up for you later."

"Well, what is it?"

"It's about a 4 foot Ball Python. The sign says: *Snake petting at 11:45, 1:45 and 3:45.* You'll be fine." Jerome's eyes darted to make direct eye contact as he said, "Right now, we got to find Ty. I fear he is in *far* worse of a situation than we are." Flashing the non-lethal, slightly agitated snake a dirty look, he nudged it to the side with his foot. He searched the room again. "Where is he?" His voice boomed, "Ty, answer me!"

"Where could they have gone?" Kelly-He yelled at the top of his lungs. "Hope, talk to me! If you can hear me, just holler!" Tears poured down his cheeks, blurring his vision. Spots of blood splattered the floor.

"Hope!" Jerome froze. His limbs struggled to collapse, but his knees locked. Still as death, Hope lay inside a huge rectangular aquarium on a raised shelf. Trickles of blood from her wet arms painted the dry rocks ending in the water. Her wet hair clung to her head and shoulders.

A ten-foot female saltwater crocodile lay in the water on the floor next to the observation window with death written all over its face.

"Wait! WAIT!" A plump security guard danced around like a madman. "Where's the second one? Where's the second croc?" he screamed.

The local police officers and county sheriff's deputies startled, wide-eyed. Backing up, they pulled their weapons in a ready position and scanned for threats. This situation, completely out of their area of expertise, shook their once steady hands.

To the left of the aquarium, a groan and a moan echoed from an open metal door. A bloody handprint on the frame cast a dark spell on the searchers. The zoo guards sprinted toward the doorway and down the corridor. Passing one hallway, they continued down the hall which echoed with another groan. They shuffled gently when they reached the holding room. Puddles of bloody water trailed to the right of the holding room down the hall from the huge aquarium.

Three beat up men were sprawled out inside the holding room. Two were regaining consciousness, the other man, who turned out to be Tyler, was still out of it.

"Hey, help over here," one guard hollered back to the police.

A tall skinny policeman answered, "Coming!" He roughly grabbed Kelly-He harder than he intended. "Let's go!"

Jerome pounded on the glass. "Come on! Wake up, Hope!"

After Kelly-He disappeared down the corridor, he yelped. "Come quick, Jerome. It's Tyler!"

Jerome came on the run and checked Tyler's pulse while the officers helped the others to their feet.

Entering the room, the missing and bad tempered nine foot crocodile sniffed the air.

With wide eyes, Jerome un-tucked the back of his black t-shirt from his blue jeans and drew a Glock from his holster. He aimed it at the crocodile.

The police officer fumbled for his weapon. Taking aim at Jerome, he threatened, "Drop it! Drop it!"

Aghast, Jerome yelled, "There's your threat!" He waved the gun in the general direction of the croc. Looking back at the policeman, he volunteered, "I have a firearm permit."

Ancient blood flowed through the croc's veins as she growled and hissed. The verbal warning let all know that she was still on top of the food chain. Baring her teeth and snapping menacingly in their direction while tasting fear in the air, she stood taller with her head inside the holding room, trapping all inside.

"Right… right," said the policeman who immediately focused his weapon on the hissing beast. When his gun discharged, the bullet wedged itself into the doorway.

Screams and shouts echoed throughout the corridor.

The others cringed while Jerome never wavered. He aimed, then lowered his finger onto the trigger.

"Don't shoot her!" The zoo security guard shook his head. "We'll get some help!"

"Back! Get Back!" The policeman waved his free hand.

No one needed persuasion. All but Tyler scrambled back.

"Come on," Kelly-He pleaded. "...help me get Tyler!"

Still pointing the gun, Jerome warned, "Tyler, Tyler, get up. Move!"

A security guard grabbed a broomstick and poked it in the croc's direction. The movement of the broom caught the crocodile's eyes resulting in a deeper hiss. Kelly-He grabbed the soaking wet Tyler under his armpits and pulled him to safety. Blood mixed with water left a crimson trail behind from his jeans, revealing a bloody wound on his thigh.

The crocodile snapped the wooden broom in half, startling the guard, causing him to shriek and jump to safety on top of the metal table. The policeman took aim, but hesitated.

Jerome slowly lowered his Glock. A semi-smile formed. "Don't shoot! It's Hope."

Hope was scrambling up behind the reptile, using her arms to pull herself onto the back of the reptile. Her nostrils flared with fear and anger as she struggled to secure her hold on the croc.

Kelly-He looked around. He wildly flailed his arms about and blurted, "Get away from metal! Get away from the metal!"

Without questions, the men obeyed. One of the instigators jumped down from the metal table.

Jerome and the armed policeman quickly unloaded and placed their weapons and mags on the metal examining table and jumped away from it.

One guard was on the radio for backup, "Croc loose! Man bitten! Need..."

Jerome interrupted. "He said metal! Drop the radio!"

Hope used the majority of her weight to pin the crocodile down. Shifting her hands, Hope placed them on both sides of the crocodile's mid-section.

"Hiss!"

Bash went the radio against the wall next to the crocodile.

Snap went the reptile. She failed in her attempt to turn her massive head and back up with Hope weighing her down. Hope closed her eyes and ignited her electric organ, zapping the crocodile.

Even avoiding the metal, the whole group swallowed a tickle of electricity and sat down in a daze. Their nerves tingled with a dash of pain. The crocodile lay unconscious with its foot twitching.

{:-)-]~~{

In the Belly of a Whale

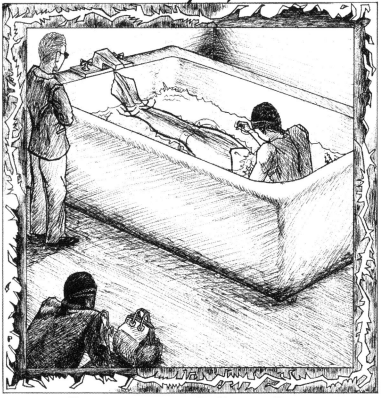

Sitting It Out

Chapter 31

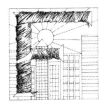ive hours after the incident at the zoo, a nurse walked in the room that was assigned to Tyler. "Mr. Sharp!" Then she yelled to the nurse at the desk. "Not again! That does it! Find him! Get him back into this room, now!" Another nurse convinced her to grab the bed and follow along.

Down the hall in another room, Tyler sat with his hands on his face. He heard the nurse calling for him. He moaned softly. Closing his eyes, he fell asleep in the chair. His hands and head were bandaged.

Leaving the emergency room, Gabriella entered the hallway where the receptionist told her she would find her family. As she was walking, she fell off balance as someone bumped her from behind. "Ooff," she huffed.

"Oh..oh... Mrs. Sharp," Agent Ned 'Bogey' Maxwell apologized as he caught her before she hit the floor. "I'm sorry. I didn't mean to." He stepped back to look at her from head to toe. "I'm amazed you're released from E.R. Look at you! Your arm is in a sling! Are those bandages from your fingers clear up over your elbow?"

"Oh, Ouch." Gabriella moaned. She gently shook her head in misery. "It's alright, Bogey... I mean, *Special Agent* Maxwell." Gabriella changed names as a nurse hurried by. She made eye contact again. "The resident said I have bumps, bruises, and scrapes, but I'm not critical." Her nasty black eye didn't compliment her, nor did the stitches on her chin. She cringed as a ringing in her head kept her movements slow and concise. With her free hand, she gently tapped the back of her bandaged head. "Did you arrest the jerk who pulled out a chunk of my hair?" The corner of her mouth twitched.

"We can talk about that later. They are at another hospital under guard. Your injured family members were all brought to this hospital by helicopter and ambulance. The rest of your family drove back to the house."

Switching her balance from one foot to the other, Gabriella sighed. "Where is Tyler?"

The two turned and walked toward the commotion in the hallway. Two nurses had wrestled Tyler into a bed and started to push it back to his assigned room. A doctor intervened and waved them all back into the room they had found Tyler in.

"Speaking of Ty," Gabriella stood taller to focus on the distant scene. "Looks like they're moving him to another room."

"Yeah," Bogey said as he grinned from ear to ear. "I bet they are moving him to Hope's room." His deep smile turned upside down. "Despite what he's been through, he's been giving the staff up here extra things to do by sneaking away to Hope's room whenever they aren't looking."

Case Agent Peter Austin and a policeman approached them.

"This way, Mrs. Sharp." Peter reported, "He's the second biggest casualty in the family after Hope. We thought he was going to need a blood transfusion, but he's made it without one."

When they entered, Gabriella stared at her husband. His broken nose worried her. Bloodied white gauze covered his bleeding and bruised knuckles on his right hand. Bandages on his left arm covered a couple of stabs from a key. His puffy and blackened eyes did not compare to the horrible contusion on his chin. Bloody bandages covered the shredded flesh on his right thigh. Gabriella cringed and rested a reassuring hand on his shoulder. Tyler lifted a corner of his mouth and closed his eyes.

Peter hung behind Gabriella and handed a couple of papers to a nurse at the nurses' station. He quietly conversed with the policeman in charge. The policeman ordered all the men in the hallway to rally to him. They gathered around the agent as he addressed them. Several nurses darted their eyes from the paperwork to the crowd gathered in front of their desk.

After Gabriella stared sadly at the nosy nurses, she left Tyler's side and went to gaze at Hope. She kissed her daughter's bandaged forehead and then meandered into Melista and Billy's room. Her nephew, Gabe sat in a chair with Grandma Mildred's hand resting on his shoulder. Besides his cuts and bruises, a cast covered his hand.

Gabriella sighed and thought, *Things could have been worse. Much much worse... and he even knew how to defend himself.* Gabriella turned around to face a sleeping Billy. His peaceful expression reassured her despite his scratches and bruises from head to toe. The shuffling of Jack's feet irritated Gabriella's pounding head. Gabriella approached him. Instead of trying to gain his attention, Gabriella followed his gaze to his quiet baby girl, who seemed to have a few minor cuts and bruises. As Jack continued his irritating noise, she halted him with her hand outstretched. Only then, did he make eye contact and stop in his tracks. Gabriella whispered a question to him about Melista's neck brace. Jack's response, garbled with tears, explained the support that the neck brace provided. The doctor had ordered her to be under tight surveillance because of complications caused by a severe case of whiplash.

"Melista," whispered Gabriella. The flashback became unbearable. *She was just there. Not moving when Ty and I found her.* A tear ran down her cheek as she swallowed what could have been. Surprised at a rustle in the doorway, Gabriella jumped around.

"Gabriella," Peter spoke softly. "You need to rest. Ty's asked for you. You can rest in their room."

Yawning, Gabriella followed him into Hope's room. She stood next to Tyler's bed, too tired to think anymore. Seeing he was asleep, she carefully tucked the sheet next to her husband and lay down. He stirred briefly to place a reassuring arm around her. Peace cuddled her. It was splendid to know that the love of her life was still alive. Her eyelashes fluttered before she slumbered.

Peter cautiously smiled at the sleeping couple before he posted guard by the door. The local police hung around, but there were FBI men in charge now. Friendship was not an adequate reason to claim FBI jurisdiction, but the murder of one Heccan and the attack on Hope were in two different states. It gave the FBI a legal motive to take over protection and investigation. Peter stood taller, proud of his involvement. He and the original rescuers had been given permission to stay on the job. Peter knew the H.E.C.C.s wouldn't like strangers hanging around. They were more comfortable with the men and women who had originally rescued them.

The nurses' station staff was startled when the doors on their floor flew open. An angry young biracial Heccan burst through with a mouth full of obscene words and threats. The commotion had also alerted the policemen and the FBI. The Federal Agents recognized Jayne and Doug and signaled the all clear, so everyone relaxed their guard. Bogey marched in front of Jayne. "Jayne... cool it now, before anyone else gets hurt!"

Jayne had planned to keep walking, but when he saw Bogey, he swayed to a stop.

"Doug!" Bogey scrutinized Jayne. "He really looks like he needs to hit the shower. Doesn't he?"

"I'm fine," huffed Jayne.

The muscles in Doug's neck tightened before he nodded his head. He folded his arms gruffly.

Bogey knew that Jayne could be stubborn. Aware of his duties, he tilted his head slightly toward the strangers. "These men with you?"

Doug nodded a secure yes and unfolded his arms.

Bogey jerked his head, passing a signal to Doug. He and Doug roughly pounced on Jayne and pulled him into the closest unoccupied hospital room. Jayne fought them. He didn't care about his own health because he was worried about Hope. A nurse tried to stop them from entering the sanitized room, but Bogey pulled Jayne on. She started to protest, but Peter motioned her away.

Feeling the hair on the nape of his neck tingle, Doug grew uncomfortable. He half teased, "Don't taze me, bro!" When the tingling sensation didn't stop immediately, Doug started to panic. "Jayne, if you shock me, I will walk out on our friendship!"

"Good." Bogey felt the tingling back off. "That's a good decision. You should know that we're not going to stand by if we need to take care of you."

They pushed him to the bathroom and threw him in the shower stall, clothes and all.

Jayne threw his hands up. "Okay. Okay!"

Bogey yanked Jayne's shirt off. Jayne cooperated and pulled off his sports pants leaving his swim trunks.

A screech and a squeak and Doug had turned on the cold water. Jayne stuck his head under and even placed his face directly in the path of the water. He braced it there for a few minutes. Doug shivered and turned to Bogey. "I hate it when he does that. So, how've you been?" The two walked out to greet a shocked group of men. Paul, Tony and Malcolm all had wrinkled brows, but when they saw Doug grinning, the wrinkles disappeared.

"You're a good friend, Doug," said Bogey.

Doug nodded and placed a hand on his head as he stretched his neck.

Bogey followed by stretching his own muscles to relieve some tension. It was still weird to deal with the H.E.C.C.s. He liked them and had no problem with them, but walking, talking, shocking intelligent humanoids roaming on Earth still crossed the line of brand new ideas. He liked Jayne as a person and had bonded with him the most. When Jayne threatened Bogey with electricity, his body coursed with adrenaline. "So, how's it feel to tangle with a Hecc all the time?"

"Kinda like peeing on an electric fence...you only got to do it once." Memories from the pet shop caused a crushing sensation to wrap around Doug's colon. The time when he and several others were zapped by Jonathon sent chills up his spine. He clutched his chest as he remembered being hit with the tingling and pain, while the dying nurse suffered from seizures, change in skin color, nasty blisters, coma and respiratory arrest. Shaking off the fear that constricted his guts, Doug loudly greeted Agent Austin from thirty feet down the hall. He barked. "Hey, Peter! Where is she?"

Sharp and unwavering, Peter peered inside the open doorway. He frantically waved Doug over with one hand while shushing him with the other. Doug leapt the first foot and then shuffled toward the door with his hands at his sides, pumping to and fro.

Paul, Tony and Malcolm were in a new situation, amazed at all the law enforcement personnel in one hospital, so they felt lost. Doug knew the federal agents and they didn't. The three men followed Doug anyway. Marshall dragged his feet. Peter switched from the far side of the doorway to the near one.

Doug squeezed past Peter, knocking him slightly off balance, and hurried into the room. Surveying the room, he stood in the middle of both beds and placed both hands behind his head. A growl escaped through his nose when he realized that he did not dare disturb them for answers.

Marshall scuttled in, continuing his slow journey until he paused two feet away from Hope's bedside. Marshall didn't touch his daughter's head; he just stood there staring at her.

Pale and still, Hope lay covered with a white sheet tucked around her up to under her shoulders. Some damp towels were placed over her, but the exposed skin was cracked. Bandages covered her forehead and a shower cap covered her hair. The spirit of death caressed her still slender arms covered with bandages. Band-Aids covered each fingernail.

With a slightly dropped jaw, Doug tiptoed near Hope's pillow. He gently laid his hand on the hospital gown that covered her shoulder.

Jayne and Doug's companions didn't introduce themselves to Peter as they entered, but kept their distance. Peter waved them in.

They entered politely, but Tony and Malcolm hugged the wall. Paul walked over to Doug. Marshall staggered away from Hope, opened the shades, and stared out the window at the parking lot.

The rattling from the shades alerted Gabriella to the crowd's presence. Tyler stirred. They startled when they saw the strange men.

Gabriella screamed, "Get your hands off her!"

The man touching her daughter whirled around and soothed her. "It's me, Doug. You know, Jayne's friend. I meant no harm!"

"Oh, Doug!" Gabriella lamented. "It's you." She forgot her injuries and ran into his chest. Tears flowed, draining her body of the last bit of strength that she had harbored for herself.

Taken aback, Doug lifted his arms. He held his arms at a distance away from her and patted her with one hand. "Hey, hey now, Gabby." Doug placed his hands on her shoulders and manipulated her to stand away from him, still using his words to comfort her. "Jayne is down the hall. He will be here in a minute."

Tyler recognized Doug. Sinking into the bed, he groaned and moaned.

A shrill voice forced shoulders to cringe. The nurse that popped her head in carped. "What's going on in here? He shouldn't be racing his heart!" The short plump Latina nurse crossed her arms. She made individual eye contact with each, giving a glare that could incinerate a baby-less mother rhino. Wagging her forefinger in Peter's direction, she objected, "There shouldn't be all these people in here! It's too crowded!"

Placing his hand on the harried nurse's back, Peter escorted her back out. "Everything's okay and the guests *are* completely necessary." She acknowledged his authority by disappearing from the room, grumbling all the way down the hall. He knew Doug and Jayne were, but he shot a questioning look toward the newcomers.

A dry dirge sang forth from all the nurses as they raised a chorus of complaints.

Doug and Peter understood why, once they saw Jayne appear. Water dripped from his Heccan flesh and swim trunks onto the floor. He briefly looked around at the occupants of the room before rushing to Hope's side. Tracing her cranium ridges through the bandages with his fingers, he stared longingly at her. He kissed her forehead. The occupants in the room exchanged glances.

Observing this, Paul stepped over and nudged Tony, whispering, "So she is the breath in his gills? I didn't know he had that kind of a *girl* friend." He winked.

Without looking up, Jayne scowled.

"Jayne," Gabriella sniffled. "I'm so glad you're here." Leaving Doug's side, Gabriella scanned the room for a tissue. "She's fading. I don't know what to do." Her head slightly rolled. Closing her eyes, she placed her hand on the back of her head.

"She doesn't smell right," said Jayne as he sniffed the air. "I bet they've never treated a Human Electric Cave Catfish before," fumed Jayne, his voice carrying outside the room. "Idiots! Morons!" Whirling about, he bellowed at Peter, "Get her out of here! She needs to get out of here!"

Peter started to shake his head in protest. Looking beyond Jayne at Doug, he stuttered, "Hey… uh… wow… uh…"

One by one, Jayne pulled the Band-Aids off Hope's unscathed silver fingernails. Without remorse, he flung the sheet to the foot of the bed. After he was careful to lift her head, Jayne pulled off Hope's cap and uncovered her forehead. His head shook, tilted, and jerked as if looking for answers. Then, he shot a Doug an icy stare. Nudging Doug with his head and eyes, Jayne lifted Hope's hand.

Doug leaned in closer and stared dumbfounded. He exchanged a look with Jayne before shrugging his shoulders.

"Rrrrrr," Jayne spoke in a low and slow growl as he clenched and unclenched his fists. He pointed at Hope while giving Peter a malicious stare. "There are no injuries on her ridges or her fingers. They just wanted to hide her Heccwan features!" Inhaling and exhaling, Jayne paused to stare. Suddenly, Jayne rushed to Peter and shook him. "They're drying her out! She will heal. I promise. Just get her to water!"

Peter's shoulders drooped. He huffed.

Another man barreled in. It was the H.E.C.C.s' official doctor Derrick Jensen. "He's right, Agent Austin. She needs to be immersed, not dampened!"

At that statement, Jayne turned to Hope and ripped the bloodied bandages off her fishy thighs. The snaps of her hospital gown protested as he broke them apart. Jayne muttered and growled as he pulled the bandages off her fishy ankles and fins. Although clearly angry, he carefully pulled out her I.V. and took off her heart monitor.

Protesting nurses tried to break through the barrier of men with their hands and elbows.

"Ace," Peter commanded. "Move the nurses back. We're coming through!"

Doug saw Tyler struggling to lift himself off the bed. "No, sir, you may not!" he ordered and then reassured Gabriella. "I'll help you keep him here."

Gabriella gasped and then sunk into the chair as Paul and Doug settled Tyler into bed.

"Tony! Malcolm! Come with me! Peter, we need to get her to water, now!" Even though Jayne had been in authoritative roles, he had never issued orders like this before. As he picked her up, her bloody wounds stained his chest.

A few agents were ordered to follow them. There had been no open protest of Hope being in the hospital, but the FBI had brought in extra agents, prepared for war to keep the peace. The aggressors at the zoo had been taken to a different hospital, but their families knew where Hope was being treated. Additional physical trouble could be brewing, so the agents were on their toes with their senses and body alert.

Gabriella waited until the room cleared before she kicked Hope's bloody bandages under the bed. Slowly, she sat down and stared after the commotion, straining her ears. Doug managed to guide the groggy Tyler back into bed once again and get him quieted down. Not long after his head hit the bed, Tyler fell asleep. When Doug saw Gabriella move to sit alertly by Tyler, he walked over and gently pushed her shoulder back against the bed. Staring up at him, she closed her eyes. The protests of the nurses echoed throughout the hallway.

A resident attempted to stop them with his hands and loud deep voice. Dr. Jensen pushed a piece of paper in his face giving him all medical authority where the patient, Marian 'Hope' Harrison was concerned. He then demanded the resident show them to the nearest bathing room.

The resident quickly led them down the hallway and around a corner. Directly to the right, he opened a wooden door that led into a room lined with closets and an opening to a wheelchair accessible shower. Jayne followed, but plowed his way past to the room beyond. He scrutinized the giant whirlpool tub built against the back wall. Without hesitation, Jayne stepped in one foot at a time.

Arriving behind Jayne, Bogey immediately turned the water on.

Jayne carefully set down Hope's legs and butt before laying her shoulders and head to rest on the bottom. Staring at her still closed eyes, Jayne sat next to her. Although his nerves were dancing around like heated molecules, Jayne sat rigid with a deep frown. Water droplets splattered from the strength behind the inlet pressure.

"Here are the controls for the whirlpool," the resident doctor pointed out the panel on the wall before turning on his heel.

Peter nodded. Without looking up, he waved the doctor on. The resident disappeared out the door.

Millimeter by millimeter, centimeter by centimeter, the tub filled. When the water touched Hope, it mixed with her blood. Jayne hastily collapsed beside her where he could focus his eyes on her chest, willing her to breathe, to live. Reaching his hand out, he firmly grasped her wrist. After several minutes of touch and sound, Jayne shook his head. Placing his ear on her chest, he closed his eyes.

The squeak of the water turning off disrupted Jayne's perception. Darting his eyes toward the surface, Jayne threw Bogey a dirty look. Bogey shrugged.

A tall thin nurse discreetly slipped past Tony and Malcolm, who were confused as to the best course of action. The nurse bumped Peter.

Agent Peter Austin pointed a shaking finger at her. With a growl, he ordered, "Bogey! Get her out, now!"

Bogey pulled the protesting woman out by her upper arm while Tony and Malcolm apologized to the agents.

"Bogey! Arrange better security for this area," Peter shouted. "You two," he said to Tony and Malcolm. "Against the wall!" They obeyed with displeased and apprehensive looks pasted on their faces.

Doctor Jensen elbowed his way through the agents and sat with open legs on the floor. Racing death, he opened his med kit. He was a human and could not feel her wrists or hear her heartbeat in her chest as she lay underwater. Jayne could feel and hear both because of his heightened senses. The doctor passed something from his kit to Peter who nudged Jayne's shoulder. When Jayne felt a tap, he reached out to grab the end of the special stethoscope that was handed to him.

Listening on his end of the specially modified stethoscope, Dr. Jensen let a low grumble accompany his sigh. The commotion behind him increased with loudly protesting voices. Looking up, Jensen motioned with a wave of his hand for Peter to deal with it. The agent nodded and closed the door with Bogey outside. Bogey glowered at Peter as the windowless door closed. The five nurses argued at the door threatening him with loud clucking and hen pecking.

A broad grin crossed Bogey's lips when the hospital doctor parted the nurses with his hands.

The resident doctor's voice boomed with absolute authority. "The papers from Agent Peter Austin, Dr. Jensen and Martin Tucker have been checked and confirmed. They are fully authorized to take over the responsibility for the care of this patient. Go tend your human patients! The girl, Marian Harrison, was born human, but she is no longer and does not need your medical expertise. She is a Human Electric Cave Catfish and will have to be looked after by their doctor. She is in his care now. We are supposed to loan him our facility and any aid he needs. Now, get back to your rounds." He confidently ordered the staff's dispersal with a flick of his wrist.

Peace and quiet tickled Dr. Jensen's strained ears. Now, he could listen to his over-sized and super stringy stethoscope better. A small monitor attached to the interesting stethoscope, showed the slow dancing steps of Hope's heartbeat.

Sucking in his breath, Peter exhaled, "It's abnormally low... even for a H.E.C.C." Looking up, he frowned at Tony and Malcolm. The glint of hope in his eyes vanished.

Flabbergasted, Tony lurched toward Peter and whispered, "You mean the doctors *here* were letting her *die?*"

Peter sadly nodded. "Yes, they didn't know how to treat her." His eyes shimmered with tears. Under his breath, he mumbled, "... or they didn't want to." Standing a little taller, Peter shortened and expanded his neck as he swallowed.

Jensen looked back and forth between the tub and his battery-powered equipment. "Mr... uh... er... uh?" He alternately snapped his fingers and pointed at Malcolm.

Malcolm leaned toward the doctor and quietly answered, "Leeds."

"Mr. Leeds, can you look at Jayne for me and see his responses when I ask him questions?" Doctor Jensen had a look of concern on his face.

Malcolm answered by obediently moving where he could see Jayne's face.

"How were her gills when they took over," queried Dr. Jensen as he repositioned his legs wider.

"Jayne, how were..." Malcolm said as he turned away from the doctor, but stopped midsentence. Seconds after he focused on the surface, Jayne's hand popped above. "Um. uh... wait... Jayne is signaling two fingers."

"Okay." Dr. Jensen rapidly continued, "How was her heartbeat when her gills took over?"

"Jayne's signaling two fingers again." Mr. Leeds responded.

"Okay. How are her gills now?" Dr. Jensen sat up. He was feeling unsettled. Hope had always been his favorite patient.

"He's signaling one finger now."

"Okay. How's the heart now?"

"One finger now."

The doctor shook his head.

Malcolm whispered, "Wait, what does that mean?" His stomach was turning and he was feeling anxious.

"It's a scale from one to five. Two means that they weren't doing well. And one indicates that they are decreasing."

Malcolm looked back into the water at Jayne. "Um, sir, he's signaling by curling and uncurling his middle three fingers."

The doctor blasphemed under his breath and then said, "All right, Jayne, do it." He yanked the end that Jayne had and pulled it out of the water. "Malcolm, step back! But keep your eye on him." The doctor was still seated in a lotus on the floor with his gadgets and notes spread out on and around him. There was no way he could stand up fast enough to see over the edge.

Malcolm did as he was told.

"Okay, Jayne, we're safe." Dr. Jensen winced.

"He put her head on his lap and he's putting both hands on her chest." Malcolm started giving a play by play. "Wow! Sir! The water is blue around them."

"One thousand one… one thousand two… one thousand three." The doctor paused his counting.

"The water's not blue anymore." Malcolm Leeds kept his eyes fixed in morbid curiosity.

"You know, Jayne, this is experimental right?" The doctor raised his voice.

"There's that blue glow, again!"

Dr. Jensen immediately counted, "One thousand one…one thousand two…one thousand three."

"The glowing stopped." Malcolm's anticipation grew. The glowing didn't appear again and the doctor didn't count anymore. He expectantly looked at the doctor.

The doctor answered with a sharp shake of his head and he motioned for Malcolm to stay put.

Malcolm relayed the details as he watched Jayne put his head back on her chest and his hands back on her wrist.

"Okay," noted Dr. Jensen. "Now we wait."

Seven intensely quiet minutes passed. Malcolm excitedly raised his voice, "Doc! Doc! He's got three fingers up!"

The deep inhale of the doctor took the whole room's breath away.

"He's got four..." Malcolm started, but was interrupted. A splash with a hand appeared above water. "...fingers up now!" Malcolm didn't have to finish his sentence, but he wanted to anyway. Jayne's four fingers excitedly waved.

Dr. Jensen breathed a sigh of relief. "Jayne you take a breather. Relax a bit. Let her sleep." He gathered his medical equipment. Once he finished packing everything, he said, "Peter, tell Bogey to go update everyone. I'll stay here. What were your names again?"

"Malcolm," confessed Malcolm as he shook the doctor's hand with both hands.

"Tony," was the answer with another handshake.

"Thank you for helping, Malcolm. You guys can go about your business now." The doctor stretched his stiff muscles.

Tony announced, "I think I'll go stretch my legs and check up on Paul."

Malcolm nodded. "I'll stay here if you don't mind."

"It's going to get boring." Dr. Jensen hesitated. "They're both going to take a nap."

"I'll stay a few and then stretch my legs." Malcolm responded and positioned himself on the driest edge of the tub.

Dr. Jensen threw his voice toward the tub. "Jayne, in a few minutes, I'm going to freshen the water and turn on the jets."

Jayne held up a fist and nodded it.

Peter and Tony crept out the door, closing it behind them. Peter dismissed Bogey and took over his post. Bogey followed Tony. They peered in on the sleeping Billy and Melista. Tony dared not interrupt while Bogey whispered the news to Jack Sharp so as to not disturb a sleeping Gabe in the recliner. Next, they went into the room where William and Willetta were being cared for. Bogey told Jerome, Clifford and Beverly the news. They walked out of the room and quietly shut the door.

As they meandered toward the room with Tyler and Gabriella, Tony whispered to Bogey. "They're family, right?"

"Yeah," explained Bogey. "They're cousins on Hope's stepfather's side. Even though, they're not blood, they sure spilled their own to save her."

"That's for sure." Tony mused as he pointed at their intended door. When they quietly walked in, Marshall was nowhere to be seen. Doug and Paul welcomed the news about Hope.

"Let Gabriella sleep. Don't wake her up for good news," said Doug.

Tony and Paul agreed. "Paul?" Tony didn't know how to start.

"Yeah?" Paul answered.

Tony looked at Bogey and played with his goatee. He ended up speaking his mind. "I'm going to go ahead and sell all out. I'm going to invest in the condo option. Jayne and Hope need the help. I also want to help save the rest of the Hecc race. They shouldn't have to live in hiding. Humanity should embrace this new race and protect them," he drifted off and swallowed, "not exterminate them."

Doug nodded his head in approval, smiled, and slapped him on the shoulder.

The slap startled the sleeping Tyler and Gabriella, but only momentarily. The men held their breath as they waited for the two to settle back into their dreams.

"We can discuss it later at the meetings that will be arranged." Paul whispered. "I'm planning on doing the same. I'm not married yet, so I only need the condo with an office and spare rooms for entertaining."

"Maybe we can finally be neighbors in the same city. Hey, maybe we can be in the same building!" Tony's enthusiasm surrounded the fact that he would enjoy living near his old schoolmate again. The two men quietly slapped each other's backs and whispered plans for get-togethers.

"Psst," Bogey interrupted. "Hey, promise not to tell anyone, yet?"

The two men looked quizzically at him. That was a dangerous question coming from someone that they didn't know well and who was also an FBI agent.

Bogey paused as he briefly checked on Gabriella and Tyler to see if they were asleep. Paul and Tony followed his gaze. When the coast was assumed clear, Bogey continued. "A couple of us in the unit that rescued the Heccs are going to surprise them by retiring from the FBI to become head security at the complex." Bogey received thumbs up from Paul and Tony. "I'm going to move in with my fiancé. We're going to settle down and have the family she has bugged me about. We're finally going to get married."

Paul and Tony congratulated him and teased him that he should wait to have the wedding on opening night. The three men casually planned what things they desired to take with them to make it a new home.

Simultaneous yawns interrupted their plans.

"I think we'd better crash for now." Doug claimed the chair in the room and fell fast asleep in it.

Tony and Paul left to find Malcolm and retire in the waiting room. The night pushed 4 am.

{:-)-]~~{

Chapter 32

At 7:13 in the morning, Hope slowly stretched her limbs. Startled, Jayne opened his eyes only to close them again. Noises around him filled his ears. A shrill squeak sounded as the door opened. Dr. Jensen's normal sounding voice assured the nurses that they could peek in on the two. He ordered them not to disturb Hope and Jayne as he went to find a cup of coffee and breakfast.

Two to three at a time, nurses semi-quietly entered the room and stared at the occupants in the tub. They whispered back and forth about the old and new business of the shift changes. The nurses thought that they weren't heard, but being a Heccan, Jayne heard everything they said including the friendly and unfriendly gossip about H.E.C.C.s. One subject included Hope's mending wounds. A group of three nurses started to leave the room. One nurse who was still staring at the tub loudly pointed out that Hope's ankles were slightly moving. A crowd of nurses all came running in. Those who arrived for the new shift were briefed about the interesting patients and told that a few would be assigned to Dr. Jensen and his unique patient.

An hour later emptiness filled the room with peace and quiet. The surface of the water in the tub broke as Jayne stood up. Sleeping in a small Jacuzzi style tub was difficult for one, let alone for two. Jayne's attempt to move as little as possible so as to not disturb Hope made for light sleeping. After rolling his head, Jayne arched his back to stretch his sore, cramped muscles.

Glancing down at Hope, Jayne sat on the edge of the tub. He was in no mood to be awake yet, but was actually considering a large coffee. The agents' conversation abruptly stopped when they noticed him through the open door. They quickly strode into the room. 'Ace' excused himself and Peter waved hello. "Hey, how's your love?"

"Hmmm…" Jayne thought hard. "You know, Peter, I guess you're right. There are a lot of Heccwans to choose from, but I'd do anything for Hope. I want to be near her for the rest of my days, even if she doesn't feel the same way."

Peter smiled a toothy grin. "You look like you could use a walkabout."

"Indeed, I could. I might even be considering a cappuccino." Jayne stretched again before stepping out of the tub onto the towel on the floor. "Besides, I wanna check on Hope's family." Peter reached in the cupboard near his head and handed Jayne a towel. Graciously accepting it, Jayne dried his face, hair, back and his chest.

The water swirled causing Jayne and Peter to jump. Peter's cup of hospital coffee drenched his shirt. They turned around to face the noise. A bikini-less Hope propped herself on the edge with her arms. She stared bleary-eyed first at Peter, scrambling to cool his burn, then at Jayne.

Jayne's stared back, frozen to his spot.

Smiling, Peter turned on his heal. "I'll go get Doc Jensen." He dropped his cup in the trash can and disappeared around the corner holding his shirt away from his skin.

Jayne and Hope's fixated eyes lingered on each other. Their mouths twitched, but didn't quite curl into pleasant expressions. Awkward silence scared away any pins that would dare to drop on the white tiled floor.

Shaking off his nerves, Jayne gingerly walked up to her. When he gently placed his hand on her cheek, she nodded her head feeling the love radiating from his hand. She looked down at the water, closed her eyes and slipped under the surface.

Panic overwhelmed Jayne. He jumped in after her. Water sprayed and swayed in the tub. Startled, she sat up fearfully, then focused on him and smiled faintly. When she lay down, he saw that she had drifted back to sleep. Holding her wrist, he counted her pulse. Sighing, his shoulders relaxed. Hope would not be leaving him alone in the land of the living. Slowly, Jayne sat back on the edge of the tub as she fell deeper and deeper into REM. Drained from her experience, she obtained an unusually deep rate for a H.E.C.C. Placing his head in his hands, emotions tumbled around in Jayne's brain. His hands rubbed their way back from the bumpy ridges on his forehead to the back of his head. Footsteps padded loudly through the door.

Peter and Doctor Jensen stared at Jayne and shrugged their hands and shoulders. A store bag rattled as Jensen relaxed.

"She went back to sleep. She didn't say anything." Jayne whispered and shook his head.

"That's okay, Jayne," the doctor answered. "Why don't you take a walk while I sit awhile?" When he sat down, he opened his bag. Pulling a floral bikini out, he promptly used his pocket-knife to cut off the tags.

Peter reached out for Jayne's hand. When it was accepted, he helped him down. Jayne stretched his upper body and limbs. As their end goal was breakfast, Jayne repeated the process of drying and threw on his pants and shirt. The two left for their walk, Jayne closing the door behind him.

{:-)-]~~{

The dreary room jolted alive with the annoying sound of a beep that wouldn't cease.

Gabriella mumbled. "Oh, turn it off. Please." When the sound continued, she stuck her head under the pillow without looking around. "Come on, Ty, turn your alarm off." She huffed and sat up. When she opened her eyes, an unfamiliar ceiling stared maliciously back at her. She jumped to an alert position. Her eyes searched for greater details as to her whereabouts. Instead of the safety of the vacation house, she was sitting in one of two hospital beds. She lay on a blanket, which to her horror covered up a bloodied sheet, bandages and a hospital gown. There was an I.V. monitor that was beeping beside the other bed. Gabriella gasped when she saw the end of the I.V. nestled in a small pool of blood on the sheets.

A nurse appeared at the doorway thinking she had the easy task of shutting off the beeping and putting a new bag in. When she saw the situation, she walked over to the woman in the room that was staring at the I.V. monitor. The nurse forcibly grabbed the woman's wrists and found that she was not a willing patient.

"Excuse me! Let go of me!" Gabriella tried to pull her wrists away when the nurse examined them.

Nope, the nurse thought to herself and started to walk over to the other bed to find the clipboard with the patient's name.

Before the nurse could reach the clipboard, Gabriella remembered everything. *Oh my gosh*! *Tyler*! The nurse and Gabriella stared at each other briefly before Gabriella said, "Marian! Oh, honey. Hope! Oh!" Gabriella popped right up out of the bed and raced out the door with the nurse on her heels. Flailing her arms, Gabriella paused while trying to regain her balance and her bearings. The nurse got caught behind Gabriella and tried to push her way out on Gabriella's left side. Gabriella immediately ran that way first. The two were neck and neck in the race down the blue carpeted hallway. No matter how fast the nursed walked, Gabriella increased her stride to stay ahead. Adrenaline caused Gabriella to be first to the open door next to Bogey. The nurse had been trying to get in front of her to stop her. Gabriella barely stopped herself from bulldozing into the room. She protectively kept her free arm out to hold onto the door and keep the nurse out.

The commotion at the door startled several of the occupants.

Gabriella looked around the room, searching the faces. Jayne was not there. Doug was not there staring at her. The only two people she recognized were Tyler and Hope.

The strangers stepped menacingly to the door.

A man soothed the nurse fighting to enter behind Gabriella. "Marie. It's all right."

When both newcomers heard that statement, they eased off from their struggling to oppose each other. Gabriella dropped her hands and the nurse pushed past her.

"Explain. How?" Marie sneered at the doctor.

"I was making my rounds this morning when the Hecc doctor came in, insisting that I bring in Tyler Sharp. The gentleman was due to have his I.V. removed this morning, so the doc and I both thought it wouldn't hurt to go ahead and take it out so we could get him on in here."

"Why? What's a Hecc doctor and where is he?" Marie looked around.

The head resident doctor ignored the nurse and kindly explained to Jayne's associates, "This is Gabriella Sharp, Hope's mother." After he finished, he focused on Gabriella with kind, sympathetic eyes. "Doctor Jensen went down to look for Jayne, Doug, and Peter."

When Gabriella scrutinized Paul with fearful distaste, he spoke up. "Mrs. Sharp. I am Paul Walkere. This is Tony Smith and Malcolm Leeds. We brought Doug, Jayne, and Marshall."

Gabriella didn't care about Marshall's whereabouts. She eased her shoulders and turned to assess the health and welfare of her loved ones. Tyler was holding Hope as one would hold an overgrown child. Wearing a bikini top, Hope's wounds on her skin and fish flesh were noticeable, but mending. At *least they have stopped bleeding*, she thought. The two were positioned outside the bathtub on a couple of towels. Hope curled up beside him with her head resting peacefully on his bare and mostly hairless chest. Bruises dotted his skin. Hospital shorts hardly covered his bandaged thigh. Hope's arms were tucked under her chin, resting comfortably.

Tyler, awake, stared at the top of Hope's head. Bright-eyed, he lovingly glanced up at Gabriella. She noticed his bewildered visage. Tyler explained in a whisper. "She asked for her dad. Not Marshall, but me."

Weakened, Gabriella would have broken her fall with her already damaged knees, except that Paul and Malcolm caught her. She looked up at each of their faces including Tony who was in front of her. "She has never called him that..." She paused before she finished her thought, "...before..."

The doctor and nurse displayed their discomfort with the moment of family bonding by heading for the door. The resident doctor said loud enough for the room to hear, "Get the paperwork started, Marie. Let's get them packed up to go home." When the two reached the hallway, they briefly conversed before splitting ways.

Paul and Malcolm, dressed in clean suits, helped Gabriella sit on the floor beside her husband. Gabriella cautiously placed her head on his shoulder. He slowly moved and put his free arm around her. Tony handed her two folded towels to increase her level of comfort.

When all were settled, Tony, Paul, and Malcolm hugged the wall. One by one, they sat down and soaked up the pleasant view.

Noises thundered from a distance, but quieted down as it reached the room. A huffing and puffing Jayne appeared in the doorway. Holding the door frame, Jayne used it for balance as he caught his breath for he had broken into a run as soon as the grinning HECC doctor said 'Hope'. Running was not his thing anymore. Jayne's worried expression morphed into a brave smile. Tyler look pleased from ear to ear. "She's fine, Jayne. She's even been talking a little bit."

A nurse peeked around Jayne, holding a glass of water and a small cup of pills, saying "Tyler Sharp, it's time for your medicine. Here, take these, please."

Jayne still struggled with his breath as he went to stand next to Paul. Paul then whispered an order to Jayne to take his place.

Doug, Peter and Doctor Jensen appeared, also out of breath. The crowded room filled with laughter. After the three caught their breath, they joined in.

The joyous noise woke Hope. When she saw three men that she didn't recognize, she sucked in a nervous breath.

Jayne smacked the tallest one on the back with one hand and used the other hand to point at the doctor trying to breathe and laugh at the same time. The two were pleasantly laughing. The bold smiles on their faces seeped from an emotional overload as they descended from the rollercoaster ride they had been on for the last twenty-four hours.

Inhaling deeply, Hope relaxed her muscles and lowered her guard.

When the laughter ceased, Doctor Jensen faced his patient. "Hope, are you ready to go home?" His enticing eyes twinkled. "I think you would mend quicker if you were able to swim about freely in your tank. You'll get more rest if you feel safe. So how about it, do you want to go home now?"

Hope's lip quavered. She closed her despondent eyes. When no one vocalized her thoughts, she timidly nodded her head. Turning to Gabriella, the doctor beamed. "Would you join me for some paperwork? They will release Tyler under my care."

"Why," asked Gabriella.

"He has a high risk of an infection. So he's not out of the woods, yet."

Jayne reached out to help Gabriella up. Jayne's worried eyes never left Hope's direction as he stole Gabriella's place by Tyler.

"I'm happy that you're here… really happy." Hope closed her eyes and lowered her head. "I thought I had been dreaming when I saw you."

"He has been at your side since he got here," Tony interjected. His chin and shoulders pulled into each other. "If it hadn't been for him, you might not even be here with us today."

A wistful look and blank stare painted Hope's face. She laid her head back against Tyler.

Jayne sat his head back and stared dumbfounded at the ceiling, his imagination going wild.

{:-)-]~~{

Chapter 33

With Dr. Jensen's blessing, the hospital released the wounded, including Melista. Marshall remained MIA. Jayne's new companions helped the extended Sharp family back to the vacation house.

Relieved, Dolores stood in the open door greeting the convoy. Gabriella, surprised that her parents hadn't pushed on home, gladly smiled as she walked through the door. Without warning, nails dug into Gabriella's arms causing her to jump into a protective stance. Mary lost her balance and cried out in pain as her bottom struck the floor. Gabriella took Mary's hand in her own and guided her to a rocking chair in the tea room. She apologized over and over again.

Melista and Willetta joined Dolores and followed them into the feminine sanctuary. Mental exhaustion determined that they sit down in the floral chairs and fainting couches. The younger ones found comfortable squats on several fluffy white oval cushions far away from the brick fireplace.

Tyler walked into the house using two crutches. He waited while Kelly-He and Jerome helped Hope into the aquarium.

The confining world of wheelchairs disappeared for Hope. She looked up at Jayne. A weak grin crossed her lips. Jayne kindly returned it, but with a stronger genuine expression. The conservatory was filled with rejuvenating fresh oxygen that the plants generated. Moisture from the basins soothed her senses. The two central circular fountains played their beautiful broken record. Water used to be her enemy; it now sparkled with positive energy. Quick as a dolphin, Hope dove under the surface and twirled. The peaceful atmosphere lifted Hope on a spiritual cloud. The serenity of being in the water drowned out the trouble of the outside world. She allowed herself to settle on the bottom. With a soft smile, she fell asleep.

Tyler, Jayne, and Jayne's companions headed for the wooden room. Billy, William and Gabe followed. The men of the extended Sharp family joined them. Jerome opened the muddy brown curtains to let the room brighten. Kelly-He took the matchbox and lit the two huge candles on the mantel of the unlit fireplace. Everyone gathered around Tyler.

The two rooms buzzed with stories of the past two days. Confusion, anger, and fear poured from each storyteller. The attack at the zoo had made it clear that recent positive media coverage had not sufficiently quelled the general public's fears and misunderstanding of what had brought the H.E.C.C.'s into existence. The Sharp family had remained relatively isolated for the past year, caring for Hope, giving Gabriella time to heal, and seemingly waiting for direction in their lives. Now as comments were made and opinions interjected, they all wished to know the unexplored future. Before the zoo trip, Hope's hermit-like behavior restricted her to her small safe zone. Hope's first trip into the public blew up in their faces. This would not do, it could not be allowed to happen again.

Ideas bustled about to give her extra freedom around the house. But her survival commanded interaction beyond the family, without it, they ran the risk of losing her again.

In the wooden room, animated possibilities were discussed, but silence persisted in Doug, Paul, Tony, and Malcolm. They exchanged knowing glances as Tony attempted to light a cigarette. Satisfaction crossed Jayne's face as Jack politely stopped Tony. Jayne's lungs didn't appreciate the bitter stench of the commercial product. Jack offered their grateful guests cigars as his sons-in-law lit their homemade pipes one after the other. Awkward silence zipped everyone's mouths shut. Breathing and inhaling, sweet smoke spiraled in the air.

Standing in the middle of the room, Jayne opened his mouth several times. Doug raised his eyebrows, stopping Jayne from mentioning the plans for the city. Curling his lips in disgust, Jayne sat down in his chair. He lit a fruity charcoal on his hookah. Instead of spilling his guts, he calmed his mind with the sweet taste filtered through water.

Clifford and Kelly-He exchanged glances. A wide grin spread upon Kelly-He's face as he nodded. Clifford walked over to the wall sized mahogany bookcase. Reaching into one of the lower cabinets, he pulled out a navy blue gift-wrapped box. Next, he produced a pocket-sized redwood pine box.

"Gabe. Son," said Clifford. He handed the first gift to a wide-eyed Gabe.

"Uh, what's this for?" Gabe looked at each one dumbfounded.

"Call it an early birthday present." Kelly-He straightened his shoulders.

"But," Gabe protested, "my birthday isn't for 2 more months. It's in November. Remember?"

Jerome lifted his voice, "Yea, the 17th ...I know...Now, open it!"

"Yeah, open it!" Jeremy's eyes gleamed.

Gabe stammered, "But..."

"Son," Jack interrupted. "Do we need to have a talk about respecting your father and uncles?"

"Okay. Okay!" Gabe supported the box on the blue cast imprisoning his right hand. Pulling it into his chest, his splinted middle finger protruded. Clifford reached to help him, but Gabe pulled back scrunching his shoulders. With his bruised free hand, he tore off the neat wrapping paper. The scraps of paper fell to the floor revealing a white candy-sized box. Billy and William inched closer to Gabe to see him open the lid. Gabe's eyes widened, narrowed and then widened again. There in the box, laid a carved wooden pipe engraved with a pouncing wide-mouthed wolf for the end. Gabe's mouth trembled.

"You like it?" Kelly-He asked. His hands folded against his chest. Gently, he rubbed his right hand.

A tear welled in Gabe's left eye.

"You protected your cousins like a man." Clifford's firm voice didn't match his caring hand softly placed on his son's shoulder.

Oblivious to everything else, Gabe didn't see the approving looks and nods around the room.

"Now," said Clifford as he handed Gabe the pocket sized box. "You know, I won't tolerate cigarettes, but pipes are okay for occasional use."

Gabe nodded with a hard swallow and tightened lips. He startled his father as he snagged Clifford in a bear hug.

"Here you are boys," Kelly-He produced four giant chocolate cigars as a magician would portray cards. The men kept them for special occasions. "You deserve them." He tossed two at William and Billy.

Wickedly grinning, William greedily caught his. Billy dove and snatched his before it hit the floor.

William concentrated hard on ripping open the black foil when a second one hit him in the stomach.

Billy heard the thud and swiftly looked at Kelly-He. Confusion wrote lines on his forehead. "We never get seconds. Hmm? Always hard to get, second ones are. Yeessssssss... What's the..." his sentence was interrupted by fumbling the next one tossed at him.

"It's a special occasion. You boys deserve two this time," said Clifford as he helped Gabe fill his pipe. Jermoe helped him light it. Gabe incorrectly inhaled causing his face to turn green. The men guffawed and sniggered as Gabe was inducted into the circle of men.

A clanking sound turned all eyes to the closed door. The metal ring on the other side had been picked up and dropped twice.

Shrugging his shoulders, Tyler answered the door.

Mrs. Cook hesitantly said, "Some men are here... claiming to know Jayne."

"Let them in." Tyler answered with curiosity when Jayne shrugged his shoulders.

Joseph Vang pushed Mrs. Cook aside as he bulldozed his way in. The other investors trickled past only to find an unfamiliar crowd in the room.

Jayne stepped back from the door. The others followed his lead.

"Reconvene in bigger room. Please?" He bowed with his briefcase at his side. As Vang stood taller, his eyes remained focused on Jayne.

Hesitantly, Jayne looked at Jack and Tyler Sharp. Tyler motioned. Jayne volunteered, "Mr. Vang, let's meet in the dining room."

Playing the host, Marshall bolstered the door open for the investors that he had rounded up.

Gabe, Billy, and William spread out and turned on the audio system, knowing they weren't invited.

Jayne led the way down the hall. Making themselves at home, the investors looked at both sides of the hall. Tiny lights illuminated scenic paintings and portraits. One painting with a memorial plaque underneath portrayed a very young Mildred and her deceased twin sister, Angelica. One particular scene showing a sunrise over a mountain awed Jacqueline Hoge. She caught Derrick McKinney and then conversed about the financial avenues for selling Mildred Sharp's works. They trailed behind the crowd, pondering one further benefit of this investment.

Doug straightened his shoulders as he strode through the dining room door. Vang put his hand on Paul's chest causing a domino effect on Malcolm and Tony. Jayne motioned for them to pass. Nodding, Vang bounced aside. Jerking his hand out in front of him, Vang stopped Tyler with a little more strength than he intended.

"Hey," Tyler howled as he almost lost his balance.

"Mr. Vang," Jayne reprimanded, then raised his voice, "Sorry, Tyler." Shooting Vang a stern look of disapproval, Jayne wrinkled his nose. Vang shrugged his shoulders. Turning to Tyler, Jayne said, "After the investors meet, I'll let you guys in."

"Wait! What investors?"

"I'm sorry, you'll understand soon," concluded Jayne as he shut the door.

After introductions were made, the meeting started.

Slowly, Tyler knelt down and lay on the crimson carpet outside the door. He placed his crutches beside him. A musty smell tickled his nose. He jerked his head into his sleeve at the crook of his elbow and sneezed. Shadows and feet blocked the light under the crack in the door. He heard Jayne cough. The light totally disappeared. Startled, Tyler jerked back. He groaned. Jayne's brown eyes stared back at him with a glowing blue glint.

Cumbrously, Tyler tried to stand up. Jerome and Clifford helped him off his knees and onto his crutches. Tyler shivered. "Ugh."

"What?" whispered Jerome.

"Jayne's creepy catfish eyes. They glow in the dark," Tyler quietly hissed. "I got caught. His freakin' ears heard me."

A loud sneeze rang on the other side of the door.

Tyler and Jerome exchanged glances. Sighing, Tyler leaned against the wall until Kelly-He brought him the wheelchair. Tyler gratefully sat in it. Gently, he rubbed his bruises one by one. The snooping had overexerted him especially since every nerve in his body tingled. Tyler drifted off, softly snoring.

In the hall, Tyler's folks, his sisters, their husbands, and his in-laws gathered around. Zola excused herself to stay with the children.

An hour passed before Jayne opened the door. "Good. You're right here. Come in. Come in." He winked at the drowsy Tyler as the snooping hero entered. Jerome pushed Tyler out of the way, but as close to the action as possible. Kelly-He carried Tyler's crutches in and set them by the door.

Gabriella was the last one to enter. She dryly added, "So Marshall, how *much* money do you *need* this time?"

Marshall opened his mouth, but Derrick interrupted.

"Now, my dear, if you could just sit over here, we will discuss the future of your daughter."

Horrified at all the strange visitors and the possibility that they would take her daughter away from her, Gabriella flounced into a chair. Glaring, she crossed her arms. When all were seated, first names were called out clockwise to make everyone a little further ease.

Jayne stood up. He had waited what seemed forever for this moment. "I don't really remember how this all started, but to make a long story short, …Tyler, I didn't come up with any possibilities for Hope earlier in the wooden room, because I have already been working on a future for Hope. Everyone in this room has. They are trying to give Hope and the rest of the Heccs a new life. It is ready to become a reality. Doug, the projector please. Let's just show them first."

Proudly, Doug flipped on the projector while Jacqueline drew the curtains closed. The pictures that came into view were artists' renditions of the future enclosed city.

"I am proud to introduce to you, Center3arth Caverns." Jayne dramatically waved his arms. "It was an accident, originally with the 'e' as a '3', but we all like it." When they showed pictures of the ground breaking, Jayne continued. "As you see, we have already started construction. I'm afraid very little is paid for and well, like any project, we're a bit in debt. However, as word spreads, money will come in for the condos and much… much more. This will be a city fitted to both Heccs and humans. A place that is safe and comfortable, but also a place to learn and work and be alive in, not just to eke out a bare existence."

Blank looks still shot out from the Sharp household.

Marshall spoke up. "We're building the largest oceanarium in the world."

"Now, what exactly is an oceanarium?" Gabriella put out a feeler question. "And what does it have to do with my daughter?"

Jayne took over for Marshall as he briefly scanned all eyes on him. "Most of them are set up along the coasts. Think of the aquariums that you have here in your home." His eyes rested on Gabriella. Fear haunted her eyes while worry corrupted her peace. Shifting uncomfortably, Jayne focused solely on her. "An oceanarium is a saltwater aquarium that is giant-sized to house fish, mammals, marine animals and plants. They are mainly known as entertainment venues for the public with dolphin and whale shows. However, many people don't realize that a great deal of education and scientific study go on there." said Jayne as his eyes brightened. They briefly saddened as he cleared his throat. "The petshop was housed in-"

"Ours will be different," disrupted Marshall. "Ours is going to be ten times bigger than the current largest one. It's going to be an oceanarium and a small city all wrapped up into one! It's like killing two birds with one stone. A place for Heccs and their human families and friends to live."

"But, how are we going to maintain it?" interrupted Tyler.

"That's going to be the difficult part." Jayne's face saddened. "We already know that these types of facilities are more difficult to manage than freshwater aquariums, but ours is much larger than current oceanariums...so we are preparing for that. Temperature, acidity, and oxygen levels will all have to be closely monitored."

"Do I understand that there are going to be other creatures and mammals besides the Heccs," Clifford grilled. "Doesn't that defeat the purpose of keeping her safe?"

"A worldwide attraction keeping Heccs protected. We protect endangered species." Mr. Vang put his superiority complex into play. "We have dolphin, whale, manatee, sea turtle, and penguin. Small creature and garden of plant. Balance. YinYan. Aggressive species like shark be in separate aquariums, open to public like zoo."

"My daughter," Gabriella gasped.

"They won't be in the same body of water, and the Heccs won't be on display. They will just live and work there." Jayne soothed. "It will be like having an ocean in the middle of the desert, complete with entertainment and education."

Derrick interjected, "Jayne, the local universities are starting a volunteer program to help us with the upkeep. They are enthused about the prospect, as they have never been able to offer marine studies other than short-term off-site distance learning along one of the coasts." He snickered as he paused. "We are creating a whole new coast in the center of the country with an inland sea. Scholarships will be offered to the Heccs to continue their education with fees from outside students helping cover the cost."

Sighing like he was in heaven, Jayne smiled. This was indeed wonderful news. He turned toward the projector, but before he could explain the picture, Marshall interrupted.

"Jack, all you guys have to do is sell your properties, relocate the men's businesses and live in the provided condos! There will be enough room for all of you."

"I don't know about relocating my business." Jerome fearfully stated.

"We haven't even had a chance to discuss this." Jack hissed and his eyes slowly seized on Marshall.

"Why would we have to move?" Kelly-She stared in disbelief. Kelly-He put his hand on her shoulder.

"Why would the summer house have to be sold? Don't you have enough money invested, Marshall Harrison?" Gabriella was not amused at Marshall's involvement.

"If I could interrupt?" though annoyed, Jayne realized that such big news demanded time for thinking and digesting. When all eyes stopped glaring at Marshall and honed in on him, he continued. "This wasn't Marshall's idea. Most of these owners and investors are not here on Marshall's behalf. Let's focus back on the original goal that we are moving toward. The Heccs require a safe place to live. They need to be productive and lead healthier lives. They need and desire freedom." Jayne then spouted, "Remember, I am a Heccan, too! I might not have all the capabilities of the other Heccans, but I get stares and harassment, just the same." Distaste flew from his lips as his fists tightened at his sides. "If I get scowls, the others get worse. I am sorry to bring up the recent incident, but Hope needs a bigger and better place to live than this summer house! It might keep her safe from the radicals out there, but it is not fulfilling. Our project will protect the Heccs from violent bigots and provide a city where Hecc supporters can interact peacefully with them." With thanksgiving in his heart, he declared, "I am grateful for the summer house. It has provided me with a good home. So is Hope. However, it's time to look to the future."

Raising her hand for attention, Gabriella interrupted. "When I filled out papers at the hospital that released Hope, I was informed by several doctors that this incident might not have killed her, but it killed her desire to live outside this family. I will not have that! For her sake, she has to have other outlets and *outside* contacts besides living in a small tank with *whoever* is living or vacationing here at that moment. I think that this new place would be more than acceptable for her. However, shouldn't it just be Tyler, Mary, and I moving with Hope?"

"I'm afraid that we need every penny to make this a reality. The properties in the Sharp family combined will make a significant dent in what is needed for this to be built. Even with Paul, Malcolm, and Tony dropping in at the last minute, we still need your money to help make this happen. Some bills have to be paid upfront without credit."

Jack stood up. He looked around the room. All eyes fell on him. "I want everyone to leave the room except my family, Jayne, Doug, and one of the head investors." After everyone left the room, Jack put them through the wringer about the location and expenses involved. Derrick had been left in charge and answered Jack's hounding to the best of his ability. He showed them blueprints and expenses paid for and owed. Jerome, Clifford, Kelly-He, and Marvin hovered and pushed a bit to the center to see the papers spread before their father-in-law.

Tyler, wandering around on crutches, did a bit of his own clustering with the group until he decided he had seen enough. Before Tyler could escape the madness and walk out the closest door, Jack Sharp said, "Tyler, come back here. If you will excuse us, guys?"

Derrick and Doug took the hint and walked out while Jerome held the open door. He shut it.

"Now," Jack ordered. "I want all the couples to separate and discuss things themselves. Jayne, I want you to stay here at the table for any questions that might come up. Melista, I want you with your mother and me."

Everyone understood and nodded. Clifford and Marcy were already whispering back and forth before they even hit their corner.

Marvin and Beverly were hushed by Jack for being too loud as they reached their huddle. The two Kellys said but a few words. Jerome and Bonnie quickly conversed, shook their heads and pulled out chairs beside Jayne. Gabriella and Tyler didn't have a whole lot to discuss. Tyler kissed her forehead and walked over to Jack, tapped him on the shoulder and whispered, "We have no choice, no property, and I am leaving the room. The money we had saved up for our own place will go toward the city for Heccs."

Jayne saw Tyler opening the door and urged him. "Ty, please. Let me tell her first?" He pleaded with his eyes.

"You have my word." Tyler told him and awkwardly shut the door.

"Can we go in yet?" implored the investors.

"I *need* my phone!" Jacqueline whimpered.

Closing his eyes as he made his way through, Tyler shook his head. In relief, he sighed at the end of the hallway. Moisture and life filled his nostrils. He liked the conservatory. Sadness at the thought of leaving it changed his relief into a sheepish frown. He wondered if the new place would feel like a cage to the humans and enhanced freedom for the H.E.C.C.s. He shook his head and limped with his crutches and determination over to Hope's pond. A throbbing sensation reminded him that he needed a pain pill. When Tyler reached the encasement, he put his hands on the edge and stared at the surface of the water. When she didn't notice, he loudly rapped on the glass. He was not going away until they talked.

Hope surfaced, coughed and hissed, "Don't do that!"

"Hope…I need…you wanno…" Staring at her, Tyler only spoke in interrupted incoherent words and broken sentences. "Sorry…we need to talk now, please." When Kelly-He arrived to help him, Tyler turned around and sat down on the edge with his feet dangling.

Hope managed to maneuver herself onto the tank's edge. She splashed water all over the floor. Silence maintained itself.

"Sooo…" Hope didn't know what to say. She stared at him waiting for an answer. Wryly, she said, "You're a sight for sore eyes," looking at his damaged face.

Tyler sighed. He couldn't look at her. Bowing his head, he testified, "We went through a lot back there together."

"Yeah, we escaped the jaws of death!"

"You almost met the swirly gates."

Although Hope heard Tyler's feeble attempt to lighten the mood, she could not muster the emotional strength it took to lift the corners of her mouth.

Tyler tightened his jaw. "I felt so helpless when they knocked that reptile's door open and threw you in. Then, when they grabbed me." Rehashing the experience brought him to the verge of stinging tears. He placed his hands on his pulsing head. "My shin must have been bleeding from being pushed to the concrete when they took you away." He swallowed hard. "My only thought was to get you out. I didn't even see the croc when it bit me." Tyler reached down to gently touch his throbbing bandaged leg. "When I went after you, they tripped me. Thanks for saving me, by the way." He grimly smiled.

"That croc was after me until you started splashing around in the water." Hope stared with resentment at her fins. "He... she, I mean... I'm sorry she bit you. I got there as quick as I could."

"Hope," Tyler placed an affectionate hand on her shoulder. "You got there right on time. Your instinct powered up your electricity. The croc let go before she broke any bones or tore off a chunk."

Hope looked away. She placed her hands in her lap and shot daggers with her eyes at her silver nails.

"I was very lucky. I was able to catch my breath." Tyler reassured her. "That other croc was nowhere to be seen when I got out. I was just standing there feeling helpless. I didn't know what to do." Tyler's hand fell from her wet shoulder. "You were rolling with the crocodile. I couldn't see what all was going on. I was afraid it would kill you."

Hope rubbed her forearm. Leftover bite marks resembled bumpy flesh wounds. They were still healing from the inside out.

"They grabbed me from behind." Tyler continued as he stared at the floor. "When we got out of the water... everything... it just blurred. I couldn't push both men back at the same time."

"I blacked out. I've never released energy that powerful before. Agent Austin told me that I shocked the croc several times while she rolled me. He said that between me shocking her and using my gills to breathe, I killed it." Hope sharply inhaled. That's the last thing I remember before I heard Uncle Kelly yelling my name. I was so scared when I saw you on the ground. You weren't moving."

Tyler raised an eyebrow. "I can't say I remember either."

Hope lifted her voice in anger. "I was really gaining steam to shock those filthy humans. But you were so close. I didn't want to hurt you." Her tightened expressions turned to a deep longing.

"I'm human, Hope. I don't want to hurt you." Tyler reached out and took her hand in his.

"I was born human and now I'm not. I hate it."

"Not all humans are ready to wipe you off the face of the planet."

"I know," she said. It was Hope's turn to sigh.

"Maybe if I hadn't interfered, we could have escaped faster." Sadness filled Tyler's heart. "I just wanted to protect you."

"You did the right thing. You were right… If I had shocked them, I wouldn't have controlled it. I had so much anger built up that I would have killed them. I guess it would have been murder. They had no defense."

"I'm proud of you."

"But, I don't think I can control it next time. They hurt my cousins. I hate them."

"I'm new to this, but I don't think you controlled your emotions when you zapped the second crocodile. From what I hear, you knocked Uncle Kelly out too. Your mental hate affects your physical capabilities."

Hope rolled her eyes.

"To quote the wise Billy-Wan Kenobi, 'Once you swim into that trench, forever the darkness will dominate your destiny, consume you it will'."

A smirk lifted the right corner of Hope's mouth.

"It's very important for you to forgive those who hurt us."

"I will not pardon them." Hope raised her voice with spite.

"It's not your job to pardon them. It's okay to hate what they did. Terror gripped those people at the zoo and they snapped. They've worked themselves up over the last year. It was like a volcano ready to blow its top off. I bet they are fine folks, but they fell into the trap of mob mentality. They had a good enough upbringing to want to protect their families, just as you wanted to protect yours." Tyler patted her hand.

Hope sulked and blankly stared at the floor.

"When humans let fear and anger take over, it destroys them and those around them mentally. When Heccs let anger get out of control, it can kill immediately. With such an increased instinct and power implanted in you, you need to be fully aware of your circumstances and surroundings. How would a jury full of humans find you? Shocking someone could be considered more than just manslaughter. Your mother missed you so immeasurably before, I don't think she could handle you being sent off to prison or sentenced to death."

Their hands fell into their own laps.

Raising her eyebrows, Hope quipped, "What would they do? Put me in the electric chair?"

"That's not the point!"

Hope's face soured. An awkward silence fell on Tyler and Hope. Deep in thought, Tyler stared at the hallway. Hope tipped her head back to soak in Tyler's words.

Tyler laid his head back with his chin high in the air. His eyes portrayed his change of thought. "Why did you call for me in the hospital?" Hope started to answer, but was interrupted by Tyler. "Why did you call me your *dad*?" Tyler broke his words with confusion.

Hope couldn't take his confusion anymore. She interrupted him with enthusiasm. "You know. Well, you know, Dad." With her mischievous eyes, she watched him as his disappointed face turned into a gleeful smile. Hope's soul fed off Tyler's proud expression. "The last words I heard before I blacked out were *your* words. I remember hearing you yell at them not to touch your daughter. You called me your *daughter*. You fought heroically for your daughter. You didn't call me your little Heccwan, like my biological father does. You called me *your daughter*."

As Tyler listened, quick radical changes in Tyler's facial features were hard to keep track of. Hope saw happiness, fear, hesitation, longing, love, sadness and even anger. There were moods and emotions that showed faces that she yearned to laugh at, but she refrained from doing so.

"He really says that?" Tyler broke the eerie silence with a taut attitude.

"Yeah, it's okay. I guess he means no harm. But you are my stepdad, and even though I have accepted it. I haven't fully shown it. I also hadn't had an opportunity to see how much you loved me like your own daughter." Hope ended with a shrug. Then she became distracted. She saw Jayne step into the conservatory. He stood for a moment and then he took two steps toward her before pausing and stepping over to the wall. He leaned against it and slipped off his Crocs and sports pants.

Hope hesitated, "It is okay for me to have called you 'dad', isn't it?"

Taking no time to hesitate, Tyler said, "Of course it is!" He put an arm around her. I always wanted another child." Tyler elbowed her. "I just didn't know she'd be older than Mary." The two giggled.

Hope squealed. "So, do I get birthday presents for every year that you missed?"

Tyler answered her with shake of his head and the biggest grin he could muster. The two didn't notice Jayne had walked up until they heard the buttons on his shirt tap against the closet door.

Still laughing, they watched him sit down in front of them.

"I almost lost you." Jayne's face pouted.

"I know. I won't ever leave the house again." Hope put her hands on her chin.

"No!" Tyler and Jayne both protested loud enough to startle her into an upright position. "You are going out again!" Tyler proudly ordered. "No daughter of mine is going to hide from her fears! I will protect you again, anytime, anyplace! Yes, sir?"

Hope smiled. "Yes, sir!" She yawned and licked her lips.

"Hey, how 'bout we take a dip," teased Jayne.

"Sure." Hope's eyes glowed. She opened her arms.

"I need to talk to you, too." Jayne stood up and gave Tyler a hand down. He crawled in to wet his aching flesh. Hope slipped under the surface. Tyler crutched down the hall.

Jayne stood on the bottom and held his hands out toward her. Drifting to him slowly, Hope's lips twitched into a soothing smile. She let him pull her to him. After she rested her head on his shoulder, Jayne waltzed around the floor. Tender minutes passed, before Jayne jumped up and swam to the surface. A puzzled expression crossed her face as her lips tightened. She didn't want it to end. Jayne smiled. 'Trust me' he mouthed. Releasing her, Jayne popped his head above the surface. Hope joined him. The two coughed with the transition from gills to lungs. She stared into his eyes and her curiosity increased with his possum-eating-poop-grin. When she was ready to speak, the first words that came out of her mouth were, "Jayne. Tell me. Why are you smiling like you won the lottery?"

He laughed. Jayne then took her hands into his, before he elaborated. "Hope, you're not going to live here anymore. All the Sharps are going to move to a better place where you can be safe and interact with the public and meet nice people who like Heccs."

"Huh? What?" Hope looked unconvinced.

"I've been gone longer than I planned. I've been busy with tons of meetings. We're making a village for Heccs. There will be places for the Heccs to have businesses and eat and, well, expand their horizons so they can prosper and live. It will be like Venice, but in America, with water around all the buildings and in some of them. And there will be caverns and places to swim and live in an ocean, right in the middle of the plains! It will be a tourist trap! It will be a refuge! It will be our home and, maybe soon, our own country!"

Raising her eyebrows, Hope interrupted his enthusiasm. "What are you talking about, Jayne Flynn?"

"We're building an oceanarium city that we can live in! I never want to leave your side again. This will be a place where all the Heccs can live in a comfortable, water-filled community and still allow their human families to be close by."

"I don't know Jayne. I mean. I don't want to be around humans other than my family. I have plenty of social interaction with my cousins."

"I know that this wasn't the best time to break it to you. I've been working so hard on this. I want you to have a huge, beautiful, interesting, fun, safe place to live. With me and with your family and with the other Heccs. Instead of having us all living in fish tanks and swimming pools and bathtubs, fearing for our lives! The disaster at the zoo has made us realize, we're going to have to step things up a bit. Telling you, and your family, is one step. Now, the next step is getting the rest of the Heccs to agree to move in or all will be lost. They need to know that there is hope for all of us if we can work together on this. This is the best option we have been able to come up with that helps all the Heccs. I need your help making phone calls to the others."

"No, Jayne. I'm not calling the Heccwans or the Heccans. I'm *not* convinced that being in the public will make more people like us and keep us safe. I'm not even sure that I will be a Hecc the rest of my life."

"Oh, Hope! You don't mean that, do you? We can't change back and you know it!" Jayne paused. "There will be dry and wet condos were you can live with your mom and you will both have freedom. You can swim and your mom can walk!"

"So have you got pictures of this Utopian dream of yours that you speak of? How is it going to be a Hecctopia?"

Jayne swallowed at her sarcastic remark. "Gabriella," yelled Jayne.

"Right here!" Gabriella popped up and startled the two H.E.C.C.s. She had been waiting for them.

"Where's Tyler?"

"He's in the den... resting. Doctor Jensen arrived with home health. They're treating his wound."

"That's good. Well, hey. She's ready. Grab the wheelchair." The two helped Hope into the wheelchair and Jayne pushed her into the dining room.

Hope could feel all eyes on her. Hope's shoulders hunched and she scrunched her head into them. Most of the owners and investors stared, as they had never seen a full blooded H.E.C.C. up close before. When she peeked up, instead of hate, Hope saw caring looks from the strangers. Her aunts and uncles were ignoring her, poring over papers set before them. Relaxing her tense muscles, she slumped in the chair. Lifting her head, she saw her mother excusing herself through the crowd.

Gabriella walked up to Hope. "Oh, honey! It's beautiful. You'll love it! You're going to be so much happier!" She took her daughter's hand in her own and squeezed it.

Hope's anxious expression twitched into a nervous grin. Jayne took the lead and showed her blueprints and paintings of what the place would look like. Hope looked around the table while Jayne excitedly explained everything. Briefly she tuned out Jayne to listen in on her uncles' phone calls on their cells. Even her grandfather, Jeremiah, was deeply engaged making plans for moving on the portable house phone. *Evidently there's no time to waste*, Hope thought to herself. Continuing around the room, she picked up her aunts' conversation by focusing in their direction. Hope now appreciated her once horrid pointy ears. "Maybe," she betrayed her thoughts aloud. "I will learn more about myself if we move there."

"All the Heccs will be opening new doors to learning about our unidentified abilities," said Jayne kindly.

"Oh, did I say that out loud?" Hope looked up at Jayne. She mouthed, "I'm scared."

"Me, too." Jayne whispered under his breath and nodded.

The two reached out and clasped hands. They lost eye contact, overwhelmed by the thunder of words echoing in the dining room. Every owner reached new levels of vocalization to spout their glorious ideas with great pride. Moving from one voice to another caused a pounding sensation in both the H.E.C.C.'s heads. Sights and sounds drifted into a blur while the crowded room filled with one way conversations.

Chapter 34

Life at the Sharp vacation home mounted into chaos. The entire family ran around as though they were headless chickens. They would pause, yell in frustration, turn around and run in an entirely different direction. Hope's aunts and uncles made numerous trips back and forth to their own homes, occasionally leaving their children with Gabriella. Hope's new routine included a lengthy drive to the nearest indoor swimming pool once a week for the first six months. Sometimes she would swim with members from the Sharp family depending whether home school or work permitted. Jayne joined her when he wasn't on business trips. Hope enjoyed taking the Sharp females for a girly outing. When the trip once a week became twice a week, the second one rarely included a family member. Either Hope would swim alone or receive instructions from Dr. Jensen. Several times, the doctor brought different psychologists as part of their interview for the permanent position as the H.E.C.C. therapist. Hope had no more excuses; she now attended homeschool to finish her schooling.

Today's schedule reeked with deception since it was the third trip this week.

Gabriella hurried down the stairs and into the conservatory. Every step bounced the note in her voice as she loudly fretted, "Come on dear! We *needed* to be out the door 20 minutes ago! Doctor Jensen ordered you to get out of the house!"

Out of simple obedience, Hope popped her head up. She protested by making a fish face and dove to the depths of despair. She shook her head because she didn't want to see or talk to anyone. Her methodical circling of the tank was slow and precise.

Lonely boredom had consumed Hope's waking hours lately, while nightmares haunted her sleep. When she closed her eyes, distorted memories of paranoid fears mixed with partial truths forced her into sleeplessness. She dared not close her eyes longer than a blink. Several times, she considered telling someone, but tightened her mouth to keep her tongue from spilling her pain.

The water filtration system continuously voiced its opinion. Its humming added to Gabriella's aggravation while she briefly paused to inhale the fresh moist air. Focusing on organizing her purse relaxed her momentarily.

When Gabriella looked up, she did not see Hope getting ready. All Hope had to do was to hop her butt onto the edge and Gabriella would help her down. "Ugh!" After venting her frustration, she lifted her voice where her husband could hear her. "Tyler!" She sighed with little relief at the sight of Tyler running into the room.

Irritation stole Tyler's huge grin when he stopped in his tracks. He thought Gabriella and Hope were ready and waiting on him. He looked at his watch and shook his head. They were going to be late if Hope kept this up. "Come on, Hope. Do it for me. Please."

Hope hung her head as she surfaced, but coughing jerked her head up. Tyler caught her eye and winked. She managed a weak smile as she climbed onto the edge. Tyler helped her off the edge. Fiddling with the wheelchair, Gabriella made sure the brakes were on. Hope's mom and stepdad helped her into her wheelchair and covered her with thin wet blankets from the cooler next to them. They wheeled her out to the waiting car and helped her in. Tyler tossed the chair and cooler full of extra blankets into the trunk of his aging black sedan.

As Aunt Zola climbed into the back beside Hope, she sang, "Twenda! Let's go!"

With a flick of Tyler's wrist, the engine roared to life.

Gabriella opened the passenger door and peered in. She quipped, "Shotgun!"

Tyler shook his head with a grin as Gabriella settled in and slammed the door. He winced. In the rearview mirror, he saw Hope cross her arms and pout.

Pulling a damp blanket over her head, Hope tuned the world out. She fell asleep against the window. She softly snored. Tyler and Gabriella exchanged understanding smiles. Zola gently pulled Hope's head and shoulders into her lap. The young Heccwan's shoulders relaxed as she drifted into a deeper sleep.

A jolt from the car pulling into the parking lot startled her. Hope looked around. Vehicles of every size and color filled the huge parking lot.

"Wait," Hope exclaimed. "They were supposed to be closed." She gasped and crossed her arms as though she had been punched in the chest. "There are too many people here!"

"Let's stay calm, Hope," Zola soothed. "It's alright."

Tyler opened the rear passenger door. With his hand, he tested the air around her before he picked her up. Low heat. She might have been angry, but not enough to charge her electric organ. Hope clung onto him as he gently placed her in the wheelchair. Prying her fingers loose from him, he said, "Come on, Hope. We're late." Hurriedly, he wheeled her in.

"For what?" Hope angrily complained. She grabbed at passing doorways. On previous occasions, she was able to enjoy the view along the way before she reached her lonely session. Aunt Zola opened the door and they hurried down the hall. Hope crossed her arms with fire in her eyes. She scorned the times when she wasn't allowed to power the wheelchair.

Smiling, Zola quickly opened the door to the pool and braced it. Silly laughter and splashing echoed in the room. Immediately, Hope lowered her chin and placed her hands on the doorway. "I'm not going in," she hissed. "Dr. Jensen signed a contract saying that I was to be alone."

A gloom pulled at Zola's face and shoulders as she brushed past Hope causing her to lose her grip. "Hope. We're late."

Still focusing at her lap, Hope shook her head.

With a firm jaw, Tyler carefully pushed Hope over the slippery floor.

Laughter and splashes suddenly ceased. Lifting her head slowly, Hope's eyes widened. Brilliant silver and rainbow fins waved at her. They stood out like a 3D movie outlined by the dull white walls, floors, and greenish blue swimming pool. Hate left Hope's bones. A crooked grin formed on her face. The entire population of H.E.C.C.s stared at her, curious and smiling. Some floated, while others sat on the sides dangling their fins. Hope hadn't seen most of them since they were first rescued. Her widening expression froze. Worry lines developed. She had angrily hung up on Jayne and had not returned his phone calls the previous week. Searching every face for familiarity stole her smile.

A shrill whistle demanded her attention to the shallow end directly in front of her. When Aunt Zola picked up her coverings, Hope did not notice. Jayne's smiling face drew all of her attention.

"Come here, Sweeting." Jayne stood in the shallow end with open arms and hands. Tyler picked up the relieved young Heccwan and dropped her into Jayne's waiting embrace. He carried her as though crossing a threshold. Smiling, Hope placed her sassy arms around him. Her pupils dilated.

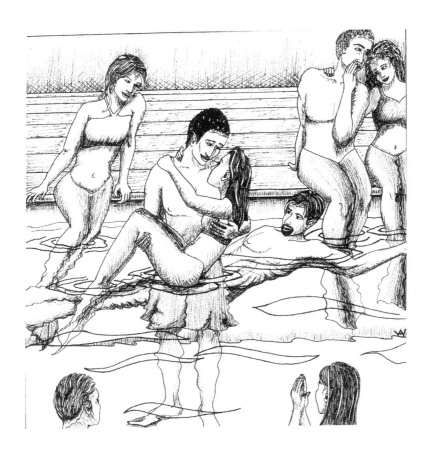

413

Once she had been safely settled in his arms, Jayne's eyes darted to stare at her fishy jewel dazzling on her forehead. Slowly, he allowed his face to be drawn to hers. Their hypnotized eyes met.

"Hey," breathed Jayne.

"Hi," said Hope warmly.

The heat from holding her bare thick skin lashed Jayne from head to toe. Their eyes focused on each other while their lips entangled with a gentle nibble on the other's lower lip. Hope's slippery fins and thighs gently fell from Jayne's arms. He modestly shifted his arms where his hands could hold her partially bare back. Their passionate kiss lingered momentarily.

Hope's head jerked back. "What about the ban?" Her fearful eyes pleaded.

Jayne frowned. "Our love will not hurt the landlubbers."

The couple cherished their locked lips again. Their mouths opened while their lips were still pressed tightly against each other, hiding their intertwining souls.

The H.E.C.C.s' whoops and hollers echoed in the room.

"Get a room!"

"Not a place to get jiggy with it!"

"Aw! Get a cave!"

"Get a tub."

"Whoohooo!"

"Gettin' fishy," blurted Jonathon next to the kissing couple.

A red hue brightened Jayne and Hope's burning faces. Jayne disentangled his lips. "It was just a kiss."

With their thickened skin, it was a huge blush for a H.E.C.C. Jayne's bulky diver's wristwatch snagged her purple bikini top making it difficult for him to covertly release her. With a bit of manipulating, he freed his watch. Grinning like a possum, he released Hope reluctantly, whispering, "Happy Hid!"

Hope's head inched away from him as she scoffed. "What?"

"You know, 'H.' 'I.' 'D.'....Hecc Independence Day! Well, it's a night early, but who's counting?"

"Why September 1st?"

"Well, the raid was August 31st ...and...it's been one year since your bad experience at the zoo..." Jayne hesitated. Hope showed no relapse in character so he continued, "...and exactly two years since we were rescued... so...it's..." Jayne paused and raised his voice as loud as he could. "Happy Independence Day!"

Everyone chanted the beautiful chorus with several rounds.

Before the song ended, Hope inched closer and said slightly above a whisper, "So this is why you couldn't come home to me?"

Thud. The door closed. Only the water settling from being sloshed could be heard in the entire room. Hope whirled about with sullen contempt.

"It's alright," assured Jayne as he placed a caring hand on her shoulder. "They went to go meet up with the other humans involved with the project."

"But... but..." Hope protested while she struggled against him.

"Hey! Hope! Look at me!"

"Okay," she raised her voice. "Okay." Hope looked at him.

"Everyone is here! Even your cousins came in the buses. Everyone who is involved is here. They just don't have access to the Hecc slumber party reunion. All sixty Heccs are here."

"You mean sixty-one?"

"No," said Jayne with dismay. "We lost that teenager. Remember?"

"Oh," Hope frowned. Her lips curled up before she screeched, "A Hecc slumber party!" Again, she shrieked with delight. With both hands, she swooped up water and splashed Jayne.

Shielding his face, Jayne inched closer to pick her up and toss her in the air.

Hope's arms shot out before landing in a belly-flopping splash. Her echolocation sonar tapped her head to attention and she chased all the Heccwans in close proximity to her. Hope raised her dolphin-like voice without realizing it. She came to a halt when she heard a return call. All the H.E.C.C.s lifted their voices in their own language. Jayne tracked her smell until he caught up to her. Gently, he grabbed

415

her arm, and pulled her along his side as they headed to the deep end. Their journey ended abruptly as commotion entered the room. Most ducked under the surface.

"It's just me!" Doug entered, wearing black slacks and a collared white short-sleeved dress shirt. When no one responded, he sang, "I've got fish."

Instantly heads bobbed up and the race to the edge was on with water splashing in all directions.

Following Doug, the twin's parents pushed carts precariously stacked with waterproof lunch boxes. Chaos ended as the H.E.C.C.s formed casual groups to sit in. Their lunches were passed around. When Doug handed Hope hers, she searched the room for Jayne. She yanked three times on Doug's pant leg as he handed another tray out. "Where's Jayne?"

"Oh." Doug looked around. "He must have left already." Giving Hope a wink, Doug soothed. "Don't worry, Hope. He'll be back a little later. He has ambassador work to do." Doug knowingly smiled and busied about so he could return to the conference.

Hope shrugged her shoulders. "Hmmm." There was so much catching up to do with the others. A sense of excitement filled her with anticipation for the Hecc party. She gobbled her food down without really tasting it. There would be plenty of jumping, gliding and tricks to try. She wanted to talk to the Heccwans who had been working at an oceanarium. She wanted to ask the diver about his job in the Bering Sea. And she wanted to visit with Jonathon since he knew Jayne so well.

One by one they finished eating and dove back into the pool. Many enjoyed the adventures of follow-the-leader. Marco Polo, a favorite, was played with their eyes closed exercising their advanced ears and echolocation. Beach ball volleyball, played without a net, or many rules, was fun and the lightweight ball bounced everywhere. The Heccan twins brought a modified football which didn't float for a game underwater.

{:-)-]~~{

Chapter 35

The formal dinner, provided by caterers, filled the room with the delicious smells of smoked brisket, baked chicken, mashed potatoes, corn, fresh rolls and salad. They understood that only casual conversations remained safe territory until the caterers left. After loading their plates with their choices, investors and owners piled in around the front tables.

Jayne brought his supper from the other room. He sat down at the head table as he scanned his surroundings. Jayne wrinkled his nose at the brisket on the plate next to his. His gleaming eyes fixated on the salmon sitting before him.

A waiter in a white shirt and black pants refilled Jayne's glass of water.

"Will you…" Jayne paused as he swallowed a bite. "…be able to gather up soon? We can clean up the disposable stuff. We want to start our meeting in seventeen minutes."

The waiter nodded, and stepped over to the closest waitress. The two hurried to the buffet tables without spilling their pitchers. While they dug under the table for boxes, Jayne leaned toward Derrick and said, "They'll be gone soon."

The people at the head table gobbled down their expensive meal without savoring any of it. The catering staff packed up, leaving the disposable baking dishes behind. The manager waved at Jayne before he too disappeared out the door.

Jayne stuffed bite after bite into his mouth while he watched the rest of the room eat at their leisure. After pulling the spoon out of his mouth, he spat a bite into a napkin, surprised. Bland mashed potatoes had gagged him. Once his favorite, the texture now offended him. An empty dish, sat before him; grilled salmon, salted kelp, pickled coconut, caviar, star fruit and capers were all gone. He had no mashed potatoes. Looking up, he noticed Derrick sitting sharp-eyed and displeased. Derrick's plate stood empty except for some mashed potatoes, yikes. Jayne sat back and quickly apologized for taking a bite off of Derrick's plate.

Derrick shrugged, rolled his eyes and pointed at the corner of Jayne's mouth oozing with salmon oil. Jayne stuck his long muscular tongue out and sucked it in.

Jacqueline gagged at Jayne's obnoxious manners. She pushed her plate away, covered it with a paper napkin, and cleared her throat. Still, her eyes politely followed Jayne as he stood up and walked to the podium.

Paul leaned forward. "What's wrong?"

Jacqueline shook her head. Derrick shrugged his shoulders and turned to watch Jayne.

Into the microphone, Jayne's voice rang out. "Welcome. Welcome. It's been quite an adventure. We are ahead of schedule with all the extra help from so many capable volunteers! Most of the main structures inside our 'Venice under glass' and the main ocean and canals will be done before we move in. However, the tourist attractions will still be under construction around us. The Grand Opening will be down the road, but our main focus is to provide a safe habitat for the H.E.C.C.s as soon as possible." He placed both hands in front of him on the dark stained wooden podium.

A loud cheer followed. Tyler and Gabriella sat on the edge of their chairs. They wanted to soak up every word. Gabriella felt as though she would burst. Excitement flowed through her veins. Beyond a shadow of a doubt, everything bubbled together toward a wonderful end product. Placing her attention on Jayne, she took in his every word.

"It is wonderful to have everyone gathered here tonight for Early H.I.D.!" Jayne outstretched his palms to the audience.

One-fourth of the crowd erupted again, while the confused majority remained silent. Jayne bounced both outstretched hands to gain control. "For those of you who didn't cheer, I want to explain: tonight we are starting a new tradition. Several families celebrated last year by themselves, but we will be celebrating this as a new nation from now on. I might be the only Hecc in this room, but each of you should also be celebrating. Two years ago today, on August 31st, your loved ones were rescued. Tomorrow is September 1st; the first day we stopped living as imprisoned Human Electric Cave Catfish. Some lived many years in unconscious captivity, but they have been returned home to you with life, health, and ..." Jayne paused. He lifted his voice and shouted, "Freedom... Happy H.I.D! Happy Hecc Independence Day!" This time everyone joined in the merriment.

The blank white wall behind Jayne lit up with the words, 'Center3arth Caverns'. Jayne pointed to it. Blueprints of the entire plan flashed across the screen for all to see. Gabriella watched the slide show with great interest especially the colorful illustrations of the finished city. A picture showed the foundations being set. She shuddered when she saw the construction workers setting the underground building anchors.

When Jayne started to talk about the foundations for·the over and underwater structures, Gabriella zoned out. The supporting piers lingered at the bottom of her bucket list. When the pictures of their new condo homes popped up, she would pay attention. The H.E.C.C.s might need water to survive, but Gabriella didn't want to wrinkle up from constantly being around water. The dry structures remained her concern, a place where she, Tyler and Mary could live. Guilt crept over Gabriella momentarily. She should be worried about the water structures since her eldest daughter, Marian 'Hope' Harrison would be spending most of her time in them.

Tyler paid close attention to the blueprints and the construction pictures. He certainly wanted to make sure that they would be living in a safe, well designed place. Frequently nodding, he thought it to be of sound construction for life in "Tornado Alley".

When the pictures portrayed the pillars inside the city disguised as rock cliffs, Tyler drifted in his thoughts. *Rock climbing might be an interesting new hobby. The city has lots of potential for adventure. Hmmm.* The next speaker's subject had exceedingly worried him since the day he found out about the city. Tyler's ears woke up when he heard Derrick rattle on about the provision of electricity from solar and wind power located on the property. He nodded his head in agreement about the candles, fire lit torches, and battery operated torches. The skylights would be a good addition, especially if they were made out of material that wouldn't shatter in a hail storm. He scratched his nose. When he saw the pictures portray the entire city as a cavern, he worried the decor would get old. Helping Hope didn't mean he had to be trapped or imprisoned himself.

"Electricity." Derrick raised his hand and tapped it in the air as if reassuring the audience. "I know you all are worried about how water and electricity will mix. Well, stop worrying. Most indoor buildings receive their electricity from the roof or waterproof cables in double-walled dry conduit. Everything is very well separated and grounded."

Gabriella yawned. Tired and bored, she slouched with her arms folded.

Tyler sat straight up for he feared that he would miss a detail. Nodding, he agreed with the way they handled the black water and its treatment. The information concerning the gray water piped through filtration tanks before pumped outside for irrigation satisfied a small portion of Tyler's curiosity.

Someone cleared their voice and interrupted. "Hey, um, (ahem)... Since the buildings are surrounded by water, how will fresh water for drinking, cooking and showers be pumped in?"

Derrick flipped through his notes. "Ah... yes... C3C will be pumping well water and recycling some gray water through our own treatment center. It will be piped in with high pressure water pipes with regulators at each service address." He paused to play with his index cards. "Trash in our 'Venice on the Prairie' will be kept to a minimum. The restaurants will not be using disposables and there will be a recycling station and hazardous materials drop-off. Trash in our 'ocean' will not be tolerated. What can't be recycled will be incinerated or composted."

Rolling her eyes, Gabriella made a face. She already believed that trash shouldn't be left to lie around. Straightening her back, she stretched her aching arms. Rearranging her tailbone, she gave the uncomfortable chairs a dirty look. Focusing on Derrick as he continued renewed her belief that all was progressing just as planned. Brine water from nearby natural gas exploration would be trucked in, treated and filtered, to fill the 'ocean' water to the desired depth.

Flashbacks captured Gabriella's mind of the times when her daughter, Marian, swore she was allergic to water. Shaking off the sense of loss, Gabriella intensely focused on the overhead projections of potted sea plants. The city under the city would look beautiful, but Gabriella was in no mood to do a lot of diving. A tear dripped down Gabriella's face while she thought about being separated from her daughter once again. A loud sharp hiccup escaped her lips. Her right hand flew to clamp her mouth shut. Sheepish wrinkles pulled at Gabriella's face as she scrunched her chin into her shoulders.

It didn't matter that Derrick was reassuring everyone that the H.E.C.C.s freedom was just around the corner. An unannounced tornado strike of nerves disheveled Tyler's mind. He thought, *Many times civilization has enjoyed stories which touched the distant horizon of possibility only to have technology suddenly allow that horizon to really be crossed without sufficient mental preparation. Books were written about space travel, walking on the moon…underwater exploration…* Reality wrapped its oppressive hands around Tyler's throat. He swallowed hard and shook his head; he could not change the sands of time. *Mermaids… Humanoids with the capability to harness electricity in the palm of their hands…* Cold chills shivered over Tyler from head to toe. *And I'm married to the mother of one of them. Who would have thought? We have definitely moved into the unknown. And now we are moving in with them…Wow. Looks like Venice…* Shifting to peer at Gabriella, Tyler wondered what crossed her mind. She looked stressed. Making a mental note to ask her later, Tyler turned back to pay attention to Derrick.

Derrick talked on and on about how paddleboats, rowboats, and Gondolas would be the main mode of transportation with a few authorized jet boats for emergency responders.

Life will change for all of us, thought Tyler. *What about us humans? A lot of focus has been on comforting the lives of the Heccs. Would constant exposure to water cause skin problems?* Tyler stared, but could not see past his nose. A sudden fear rooted him to his spot. The hair on his arms and the nape of his neck lifted. *What about Mary? She's still an untrained swimmer. Sure, she's dogpaddled in Hope's tank and has had a few lessons when she went with Marian to the pool, but in an ocean-like lake with currents? She's still inexperienced enough for drowning to be a serious concern.*

Focused on his hand gestures and notes in his hands, Derrick did not see any point in stopping. "The side tables located on the west side of the gymnasium are for filling out applications for employment in the city, those on the east for condos and school. Remember folks, the income looks extremely low, but you will not be paying bills on your condos since most of you paid for them when you sold your houses. A certain amount of food from the restaurants and the grocery store will be allotted to each home, based on numbers of individuals in the household, for the work you do around the city. Now if you choose to work in the mall after it's built, those companies will have normal wages and US taxes. But most will not be hiring until the month before the grand opening." Derrick's right hand gestured in circles at the crowd as he shifted his weight from his right foot to his left. "That's a few years from now." He firmly pointed at his toes. "This is the time to secure jobs as citizens of Center3arth Caverns working for Center3arth Caverns." He paused with an ornery grin. "Also, to the delight of the teenagers, there are jobs open for thirteen and up." There would have been a cheer from the thirteen through fifteen year olds, but they had escaped to a game room. However, the cheer from the sixteen and seventeen year olds made up for their absence.

A movement caught Tyler's eye. He saw his brother-in-law, Kelly-He, raise his hand. Tyler knew that money had always concerned him. Most of the families sold their houses, vehicles and any extra properties to be able to move into the city. Kelly-He had been the one in the family to make sure every detail was on the up and up. Tyler and Gabriella had helped with several H.E.C.C. fundraisers and also provided most all their savings to the giant, expensive project. This definitely had been a huge undertaking for everyone involved. Pride welled up in Tyler. The city would be making history in the construction of cities and buildings. It would be a big tourist attraction worldwide, too. Right now, no other country had H.E.C.C.s living in their society. It would be the first city in the USA built on piers and the first city built inside a giant oceanarium. Tyler glanced over at Kelly-He. What could possibly be his question? For the last two months, Tyler worried that Kelly-He and Kelly-She would back out of their decision to move with them. Tyler sighed with relief when he saw Kelly-He lower his hand.

"We feel it's necessary for the residents to step up as workers and volunteers for the H.E.C.C. museum and the Living Sea Hospital," said Derrick, but then he added, "...which we will own and run. The hospital will have a carefully vetted medical team, but we will want to add much of our own staff." Taking a deep breath, Derrick switched gears. "In our new city are beautiful places of worship for humans and Heccs alike. There are Protestant, Catholic and Jewish houses of worship. There is a multi-faith chapel that has smaller rooms for other religions. There is a watery access to the main floors and a few classrooms. Then there are lower underwater floors available for the Heccs and divers. Outside the city will be a coliseum with wheelchair access. I do believe a lot of you horse lovers want to start showing your horses again. It will also be nice to have concerts and other such large functions that will bring visitors." He smiled and took a deep breath before he continued. "There is room for young adults to move into their own places. Some shuffling and moving may have to take place in the future. Big families with larger lodgings, as time goes by and the family shrinks, may want to move to smaller accommodations. We will concentrate on building more condos after the initial move but they will not have front door boat access. This is not about making money from the citizens of C3C. You all are family to the Heccs, so this project is to try to keep you all together as you desire. Now, on to the subject of education; please give your attention to Mrs. Marcy Clark." He sat down and took his time to finish his glass of water.

Gabriella watched her sister-in-law walk to the front table and face the audience. She already knew what she was going to say, but she planned to pay attention out of love and respect.

Marcy cleared her voice before her announcement. "Education is very important for our human youth and it is extremely important for our Hecc youth. I am told that special touch screen computers will be placed in the wet classrooms where the Heccs will attend. Although C3C is responsible for the elementary and high school, the collaborating local university will be in charge of all college level education. Every room will be well equipped to allow the Heccs to fully participate in class activities. There will be a discount in cost for the further education of Heccs in the university and they will be treated like regular students. The Heccs will have a choice of publicly integrated or private classes. However, the private classes will still include our human youth that live in the condos with us. There will actually be Internet access in the whole city including classrooms. As for the school that we are running, it will be called the Private School of Sardines or Center3arth Elementary and High School when dealing with the outside world." A chuckle from the audience ended in a cheer.

While Marcy paused to wait for silence, she checked a small stack of three-by-five cards she had hidden behind her back.

Stealing a peek at Tyler, Gabriella inhaled deeply. *I can't wait,* she thought to herself. *Mary will love school. I can finally go back to work.* She sighed and her cheeks glowed with her radiant smile. She knew what topic Marcy was merrily approaching because she had helped her rehearse.

The room returned to silence and Marcy tucked the cards back before she continued. "Mothers will be encouraged to help with teaching a minimum of just one class so that they can be housewives. They will also have time for their own further education. The outside world understands that our school is a private school, but several local families have petitioned us to let their children attend. They will provide their own busing. They are also willing to pay extra money to participate in and help support our school. That situation will also apply to the University when it's up and running. The students who are taking classes are paying extra fees to attend our school because of the unique opportunities that will arise…" Marcy paused as she checked her notes.

Tyler leaned over to Gabriella. He placed her hand in his. She looked at him and batted her eyelashes.

"…and possibly to live in our city." Marcy hesitated. "The University has claimed a certain number of apartments for their local on-campus housing. Otherwise, students would have prolonged drives to participate in the few classes that are not available on their regular campus. I am told there are a couple of families that are moving here so that their children can participate in the high school and elementary school while their fathers will be working elsewhere. I'm sure the mothers or teens will have to find work in the mall in order to be able to support this more expensive locale. Please look for the education table for enrollment in the private elementary and high school. Even though the building for the university will be ready, it's going to take some time to coordinate staff and classes. The university is also waiting on the construction of the apartment building." Marcy dramatically paused. "Now, for a word from our sponsor…" Stifled giggling and acute curiosity as to the punch line of the joke caused silence. Marcy waited until Doctor Jensen walked up. Before returning to her seat, she shook his hand and whispered something.

Clearing his throat and shifting his weight a few times made Doctor Jensen's appearance seem uneasy to the audience. "Dads, moms, siblings and extended family, I have a heartbreaking announcement that needs to be made in preparation for this new adventure in your lives." He swallowed a few times. His left hand quickly crossed his chest and tightly held onto his elbow.

Doug politely smiled at Kelly-He sitting to his right. Hope's family had indeed earned his respect. Kelly-He acknowledged him.

The women started to mumble under their breaths. Their bodies were feeling agony boil all over their skin. They already had an idea of the developing topic.

"Family..." The doctor's voice cracked. "Remember, the Heccs are no longer human." His voice became stronger. "The young crave the guidance of the older Heccs. They will be seeking friendships within their new race. Their time will increase with Heccs and decrease with you. Your youth will have full freedom within the new city... and... well... that's the way it should be. Counselors will be provided during this difficult transition, for you and for them. Don't worry, they still love you and there are giant commons and retail areas where they will connect with you. You should understand that they probably won't want to sleep in bathtubs in your apartment anymore, but their apartments may adjoin yours if that is desired. You will not be at their beck and call, but neither will they be on yours. It is time that they start living to their full potential as separate entities, no longer dependent on humans to do every little thing." He paused and raised his hand and forefinger for dramatizing his conclusion. "For their sake."

No matter how hard Doug tried to pay attention to the meeting at hand, he could not. He had been to many previous meetings with Jayne. Everything felt repetitive and boring. Passing the time included squirming, yawning and stretching. Reaching into his pocket, his hand found his cell phone. Come to think about it, his phone had not received a text for several days.

Standing up, Derrick took the platform again. He introduced Jacqueline as the first retailer. Tyler and Gabriella eagerly clapped.

Jacqueline, clearly eager to express her joy, swiped the microphone before Derrick finished. "Oh, it's going to be so exciting.

'The Reef Cafe' is located on the main 'beach'. There will be a few tables on the beach and we will have waiters to deliver to people lying on towels on real beach sand that has been trucked in." She squealed with delight. "The skylights will provide plenty of sunshine while blocking those harmful UV rays. The best beach ever!! No sunscreen needed." Her girly hyper voice irritated a number of people in the audience. "There will also be tables where swimmers and Heccs may sit together. In fact, I will want to hire a few Heccwans to be waitresses in that area. There are cliffs next to the beach for the public to investigate, including a pirates' cave. The cave's sound system will pump ocean and whale sounds in to heighten the atmosphere. Anyway, I want to thank you for the opportunity to be part of this great community. This is so very exciting to be a part of such a new and brilliant tourist attraction." Jacqueline wrapped up and returned to her seat.

Out of the corner of Tyler's eye, he noticed Sonny <u>and</u> Albert stand up and snake their way through the tables to the front. They didn't wait for an introduction. Sonny took the microphone and started in. "I'm Sonny and this is my brother Albert Leddon. We are the owners of SeaSonAl Fish Farms. Our main product will be fish, providing it to restaurants and the Sea Floor Grocer. But we will also be in charge of the produce farm, orchard, and maintaining the stables there at C3C. We are looking for good strong lads to help out. Since I mentioned the grocery store, maybe I should ask Tommy O'Hayer to come up." Tyler only half listened. He was remembering what his father had told him. Jack was planning on working with Sonny and Albert to continue working with his hands. Tyler hoped the change of climate inside the city would not affect Jack's overall health.

Doug quickly pulled out his phone and opened it. The screen displayed an abstract black as blank as his mind. He zoned in on it and pondered the timing of firing it up.

Tyler admired Tommy's firm handshakes with the two Leddons as he approached the mic. Tommy immediately took the microphone.

"It's a great honor to have my grocery store in such a unique and attractive location. The pleasure is all mine. I look forward to seeing all of you and getting to know you all since I'll be your small town grocery man. Have any problems with the help and you just holler for good 'ol Tom, Thanks y'all for purchasing at the Sea Floor Grocer." Tommy gave a healthy wave and sat down. Tyler sat back with a wide grin. It was nicely panning out to be a small community where everyone knew each other and had something in common.

"The Office and Retail Complex is under our management." Paul Walkere had risen to the podium to speak. "Tony Smith and Malcolm Leeds, would you please come up?" He waited for a moment for them to join him before continuing. "There isn't much to tell, really. We have several corporations interested in having branch offices in the complex, mostly financial, insurance and consulting firms. Most, I'm sure, are looking at it as a good publicity move. Until the mall is built, several Heccs will have art studios and other businesses in the lower, more water-accessible spaces so that they can get started earning income. I will hand you back over to Derrick, unless Tony or Malcolm have anything to add?" He looked at them. They shook their heads. "No, well…" He looked back at the audience. "Here's Mr. McKinney."

A click and an ear piercing squeak echoed from the speakers as Derrick fiddled with a cordless microphone. His voice then filled the room. "Now, I would like to have Joseph Vang approach the podium." Sitting tall in his chair, he carefully set the microphone down on the table and focused his attention on Vang.

When Joseph Vang came forward, he made it clear that he did not enjoy speeches. However, he had an air of importance that followed and pounded his way into any room. "I have experts, including input from Jack Sharp. They design great Center3arth Caverns Hotel and Suite. It attract tourists. Luck follow you."

Vang left the audience, including Gabriella, with noses scrunched as if they had smelled something afoul. Tyler nodded. Mr. Vang was a good business man despite his gruff nature, but he knew that Mr. Vang rubbed Gabriella the wrong way, so he patted her hand on the table.

Derrick spoke clearly into his microphone, "The Hotel will be completely booked by construction crews, consultants, contractors and others working to complete the city. It won't be open to the public for quite a while. Joseph Vang will be sharing the profit from the hotel with the city for ten years. Face it folks, this is a very expensive project and we need all the extra income we can find to finish it. Now, we need to keep moving on." He paused with a sip of water. "Let's have the proprietors of the Movie Harbor speak next. Come on up."

The best friends, Gerald and Edward walked up. Gerald took the mic. "Hello, Ladies and gents! I'm Gerald Murphy and this is Edward Spleers." He glanced at a beaming Edward. "We have a spectacular design and it's coming along well. There are theater rooms with the same old design that you see around the world. Then we came along and reinvented that dry old drab theater. We have rooms that have half-dry and half-wet seating. Then there are the rooms that are fully wet with both free-floating and anchored furniture, no balconies." His excited facial features and body movements left the audience leaning forward, craving more. "There's a movie theatre under water for divers and Heccs. I hear the Heccs look forward to going to the movies again."

Doug knew who was up next so he positioned himself ready to turn on his phone.

"The decor gives the audience a comfortable cave experience. The balconies might look like hard rocks to sit on, but are actually quite comfortable. We'll even have waterproof stubs for the customers that can be reused." He had a very big grin on his face. "There's so much to tell you, but I guess you'll be experiencing it on your own soon enough. Thanks for believing in our idea." Gerald turned to Derrick. "Who do you want up next?"

"The outdoor swimming park," answered Derrick without batting an eyelash.

"Will the owners of the outdoor swimming park come up, please?"

Taking advantage of the excited applause of the crowd, Doug powered his phone on. After the annoying jingle announced activation, he switched the ringtone to silent mode. Immediately, the phone vibrated. Looking around the room, Doug noticed no one cared what he was doing.

Lee Biggs, Eric Fox, and Buddy Graham walked up and introduced themselves one at a time. Then Lee took over speaking. "Mer-folk Manor is, as you heard, an outdoor swimming park. However," he paused. His voice increased with enthusiasm. "We will also be building an indoor waterpark. We will be sharing the profits from the indoor park with the city to help defray the high maintenance costs of C3C. The swimming park will only be for the humans for the safety of everyone. Human tourists will come that wish to support the H.E.C.C.s and want to see the city but worry about swimming with them. This waterpark gives them an alternative."

"Thank you, Lee," noted Derrick as he commandeered the focus of the audience. "Since we are on the topic of tourist attractions... Perhaps, I should point out that I am honored to be the owner of the Treasure Islands Mall and the flea market after it's built." Derrick grinned from ear to ear. "Well, that closes the main business portion. Now we need to give you a reason why you will hear construction all around and a taste of what will be."

Several vibrating alerts stole Doug's complete attention. He could care less about the future, he was concentrating hard on the now. At the present time, he was involved in the gossip in the texts from people he knew.

Gabriella and Tyler watched the shy short man stand and walk to the mic. They had never seen him before so he fascinated them as he introduced himself. "Hi, I'm Frank Greenwood and I am in the process of turning a donated submarine into a restaurant. It's going to be really neat." The shy man started to sit down, but Derrick caught him and asked the name of the restaurant. Returning to the mic, Frank boasted, "The Sub Bar and Grill will bring a smile to your face and a fullness to your belly." He almost left the last word hanging as he hurried to sit back down. Tyler was happy to make note of the name so he could make reservations to take Gabriella there on their opening night.

A tall, skinny man approached the front of the audience. With his fist in the air, he yelled, "Yo ho ho! One more time! Yo ho ho!"

The audience cheered, "Yo ho ho!"

After scrolling through the rest of the text notifications, a number popped up that Doug did not recognize. He leaned in closer to see the screen on his phone as he opened the strange text.

"Ahoy, me Hearties! Avast Ye!" The man's voice lingered momentarily on his personal introduction. "I be Privateer Carl Stevenson, but ye can call me, Cap'n. Aye! Look ye for me Jolly Roger and scuttle yer ship and climb abawrd. Thar' be plenty of loot and plunder for grabs, if'n ye know how to find it." His chin tucked into his chest before he mischievously made eye contact with the audience. "Arr! Watch out for me Starfish Casino! Fun and activities'll be far ye seadogs and landlubbers alike."

The crowd straightened their postures, giggled and applauded.

After Doug read the text message, his face drained to ash white. It said, "Want a raise? Call weekly. Leave gossip on voicemail. Will deposit top pay." Doug snapped the phone closed and returned it to his pocket. His heart raced. Although a sudden fatigue feeling swept over him, his senses heightened to his surroundings. *I'm being watched*? Sweat dripped from his forehead and his toes curled. The men in the audience shifted in their chairs for they were ready to end this meeting. Doug shifted for a different reason. Boredom no longer overtook his every muscle, worry did. He could not hear anything but his own thoughts and even they betrayed him.

"We'll have private rooms for parties. Thar be fishin' abawrd ah big plank. Heccs'll fix booty to yar hooks. It be one of many Geocaches in the vast scavenger hunt all over de city. Treasure hunters from the 7 seas will gather in our secret sea far doubloons, and booty. T'other plank be far makin' stowaways walk and join

Davy's Locker! So come abawrd, me hearties: this be fer ye too. Not just landlubbers from faraway lands." Tossing his head back, Carl held his belly for his over-exaggerated laugh. "Har Har!" He paused, pointed a finger at the crowd, and sneered in character. "Weigh anchor and hoist the mizzen!" Carl punched the air and dramatically limped to his chair with his shoulder tucked into his chin.

"All right!" Tyler made a fist and pumped it next to his side. Before the cheers quieted down, he roughly sang a chorus from an episode of his daughter Mary's favorite cartoon. "Arr! A pirate...a pirate, a pirate says Arrrr!"

"Thank you, Carl." Another man took his place. "Evening', Stanley Jordan, at your service. After the Bay Apartments will be built, it will house some permanent residents and those who are just staying for college. Of course being a college town, we're going to require entertainment. How 'bout I get my good pal to come up and introduce his future business." He paused before teasing. "Percy Gillis, come on down." Stanley shook hands with his good friend, Percy.

Percy's toothy grin beamed as he waved hello at the audience. "I have entertainment for the young and old alike. There will be all sorts of music and styles of dancing under the stars in the Swabbed Deck Dance Hall. 'Course if there's too much rockin', don't come a-knockin'." He snorted at his own joke.

A few of the adults in the audience laughed.

Beads of sweat formed on Doug's forehead as he became a little light-headed. His chest tightened as his breathing became shallow. A numb feeling overcame him as all of his muscles tightened.

Percy said with a mischievous grin. "Seriously, folks, the boat will be docked so there won't be a problem. Aaaand there is an underwater dance hall for Heccs and divers who want to join them."

Gabriella and Tyler mimicked the rest of the audience with ooh's and aah's.

Doug focused his ghostly stare on Jayne while the rest of the audience clapped their approval after every speaker, but gave a little more oomph to the theater managers' finale. Grinning, Derrick waited for silence before he announced the next speaker. When he had the audience's attention, he called. "Mr. Purkey, Hunter, and Smith, would you please come forward?"

The young men looked barely out of college. The man in the middle spoke loudly in front of the microphone. "Yo, dudes and dudettes! Ma'name's Purkey. Dave Purkey. Ya need someone ta show you the ropes." His thumb on his right fist proudly poked at his heart several times. "I'm your man. Yaman! Me an ma'bros could totally use an extra paw or two at our companies. This," he patted him on the back, "is Allen Smith." Dave smacked the other man on his shoulder. "Over here, this is Brett Hunter. We-"

Brett gave Dave a nudge and completed his partner's thoughts without the added surfer lingo. "We own the Penguin Scuba Corp. and The Dolphin Express. We will be your guides for deep sea diving and interactions with the natives."

Dave sniggered. He and Brett exchanged glances, leaving the audience to ponder the unfamiliar inside joke. Straightening his shoulders, Brett quietly cleared his throat, but it echoed in the microphone. "Seriously, man, we will be exposing the public to marine life and will be seeing the Heccs a lot. Dave's old chum, Anthony, who you all call the Heccan Jonathon will be in charge of our Hecc help underwater. But as for human help, we are going to need a variety. We'll need a couple of strong men and delightful secretaries. Come look for our table."

Doug fidgeted. His knees shook with an agitated tick that would only be quenched by making a break for it. His ears could not comprehend any of the speakers. Staring around, he was numb and disassociated from reality. Heat rose behind his eyelids as the tingling in his stomach increased. The text message replayed in his mind like a broken record. He searched flashbacks to see if he could remember anything or anyone suspicious.

"Now, I think everything's covered...right?" Derrick paused, racking his brain. No one seemed to question his conclusion. "Oh, I remember. We will not be shutting down C3C to the public at any time; we will be open seven days a week. However, many of the shops will keep regular business hours according to their preferences. The security guards will have their hands full." Then he hurriedly dismissed them. "Thank you. Now, you shall be excused to check out the tables and for a thirty minute recess." After his announcement, Derrick charged away from the podium only to find himself surrounded by eager people who grilled him with question after question.

Absentmindedly, Doug scuttled out the door. His tongue seemed swollen and he could not swallow the huge lump in his throat. He located the farthest restroom in the building.

{:-)-]~~{

Chapter 36

The H.E.C.C.s families, investors, and speakers scattered in all directions. A few parents left the gym to nose around or check on the children. Others madly dashed over to the school sign up table. Adults and teens alike mingled and looked over the potential job market.

Tyler stood up, stretched, and followed the crowd heading for the employment tables. He turned his head to see Jerome, Marvin, Kelly-He, and Clifford coming to join him. When all had caught up with him, Tyler grinned from ear to ear. "Did you hear the names of the businesses?" He laughed as he placed his hand on Marvin's shoulder. "I should open a hecc of a pub where you can get heccuva burger for a heccuva price and have a heccuva good time."

Clifford, Marvin, and Kelly-He chuckled.

"Are you going to change careers and go into marketing," asked Marvin as he lifted his ice tea in Tyler's general direction.

"Naw, I don't think so." The mischievous sparkle in Tyler's pupils vanished. "Anyway..." He paused to clear his throat before he continued. "I wanted to thank you again for investing and moving with us."

"We're all in this together, little brother." Marvin slapped Tyler on the back.

Deep in thought, Kelly-He sighed while Clifford scratched and rubbed his new goatee.

A thundering of footsteps caused the men to whirl around to see the commotion. Gabe, Billy and William stampeded their fathers. Tyler jumped back to avoid being knocked over.

"Whoa, boys!" Kelly-He scolded.

The youthful boys couldn't respond because they were out of breath.

"What's so exciting, oh youth who are out of breath?" Marvin teased.

Gabe answered by waving a paper in front of his dad. "Guess what, dad! Guess what!" The other two jumped up and down and tried to catch their breath.

Tyler listened intently.

All three fathers laughed. They all repeated in between bouts of laughter, "What, what?"

"We got it!" All three young men hollered. "We got it!"

"Got what?" Clifford and Marvin asked in unison.

"I always knew you'd get chickenpox someday!" Kelly-He marveled. "Wow, I'm so proud of you."

"Wait, fellows. I know what this is about." Tyler chimed in. He tapped his finger three times on the side of his chin and pointed toward the ceiling.

The young pouted. "Ahhh," scoffed William.

"Wait! How'd you know?" Gabe popped the question as his shoulders dropped.

"No fair." William wailed.

"Ah. Very persuasive, the dark side is. Hmmmmmm," said Billy in his controlled sing song.

"I have my ways." Tyler grinned. He enjoyed pulling their chains.

"Yea," piped Kelly-He. "I heard about it at the last meeting."

It took a second for the boy's pouting to merge into distaste.

"Ahhh, dad!" William gave him a loving punch in the gut.

Kelly-He laughed so hard, he doubled over.

"Okay. Let's hear it. We don't really know. What's up, son?" Clifford put his arm around his son, Gabe.

"We got one of the boats!" Gabe stood a little taller. "It's not one of the glass bottom boats. They're cool, but we wanted the one that will bring in tips. It looks like one of those Gondolas."

William tried to run away before Kelly-He harassed him with a good squeeze, but, too late! William squirmed and pushed his way out of the strong grip.

"Hey," teased Marvin as he grabbed Billy. "Cool." He captured him in a giant bear hug, difficult as it was with Billy struggling to free himself.

"We're thinking of calling it, *Jumping Minnow*," joked Gabe. "It will be the only 'minnow' in an ocean! And with all the money that our family invested...I *own* it!"

"Will your tour be longer than three hours?" teased Clifford.

"Ah, dad," the boys simultaneously whined. Gabe, William, and Billy broke free, skipping away from their proud fathers. Their excitement never ceased as they raced to tell others of their fortunes.

"Hmmm." The forsaken sighed as they looked at each other. Their eyes followed a passing conversation.

"This is better than I expected!" One husky man said to a short skinny man.

"No kidding. It's like retiring early! I expected I would have to have three jobs instead of the two I had been working." The skinny man returned. "Now I will only have one and I will be able to take a class or two to improve my education!" He hooted with excitement.

The husky man looked over at Tyler and spoke up louder. "You better go sign up for your condo now before the good ones disappear!"

"Guess we should hurry!" Marvin scurried away from the group yelling over his shoulder, "Meet back here." He pointed to the floor in the middle of their circle.

Kelly-He, Jerome, Tyler, and Clifford split up.

Twenty minutes passed. Kelly-He and Clifford returned to the center of the blue carpeted room, deep in conversation. Smiling, Marvin was next.

With pursed lips, Tyler returned. "Sorry guys, I got stalled a few times on the way back by people who wanted my attention."

Marvin, Clifford, and Kelly-He nodded, sipping on coffee. Clifford spotted Jerome and waved him over.

"Hey, guys! This is cool! I will no longer complain about leaving the insurance business. I get to almost retire! Ha ha! This is so cool!" Jerome spiced up the glum looks. "No more faraway business trips or staying on the phone all day!"

Kelly-He perked up. "I couldn't move my landscaping businesses. I guess selling it to my manager wasn't so bad, but I still worry about the future. What happens if this bombs?"

"It can't bomb. Where would we move next? The coast? I mean in order for things to move on with the project, they needed all the income from our properties combined," said Marvin. Looking at Tyler, his eyes softened. "What were we going to do, say no? We're family. Jack's architectural firm is still one of the main contractors over-seeing the city design and construction. We will be moving the firm to the city and continue taking other jobs. Clifford's our accountant, but I think he is hoping to get a few more clients on the side. Jack is already retired, but I think he is still the big boss. There's no turning back. We are all moving into..."

Tyler interrupted, "But guys, Hope is my stepchild." Stress creased his forehead with worry wrinkles. "She isn't blood, so you didn't have to do it. You sold all your houses to help us provide an outstanding home for Hope. Dad handed the deed to the summer house over to the lawyer Martin so the Heccs could sell it or rent it out. If this doesn't work out, we are all going to be homeless."

Jerome put a hand on Tyler and looked him straight in the face. "We were there in the beginning and we're going to see this through. Hope is our family, too. We love her and that's that." He kindly smiled. "Things happen and we have a duty to help make sure Hope has the life that she needs. I wouldn't worry about it too much." He pulled his hand away and left Tyler to ponder.

"Well, I'm still hearing all the men talking about how much of a change this will be for them." Tyler decided to think on a positive note. "This is going to ease burdens on all of us." Tyler said and nodded approval. "We could even sell most of the vehicles since everything we'll need will be right there. It's going to be like living in a small town."

Clifford chimed in. "Hey, this will work. We have jobs lined up. There isn't a lot of maintenance for us to do. It is time to live life. Hey, we might even be able to meet up every week or maybe even every couple of days!"

Grins grew bright around the circle. They moved in closer to make a sharper circle and slapped each other on the backs.

Paul Walkere trotted up to them. "That's what I want to see, excitement."

"Hey, we could alternate things!" Clifford piped up. "Poker night, swimming, snorkeling..."

Tony and Malcolm arrived and said in unison. "Wow. Let us in, what's the word?"

"Guys' night." Tyler grinned while his mind was working. "I wonder if they will allow for some water skiing?"

"Did I hear someone say guys' night?" said Peter Austin as he and Bogey arrived in the circle next. "We're in."

The men joyfully conspired and brainstormed enough ideas to last a year or more.

{:-)-]~~{

As soon as Doug walked in to the restroom, the bright lights automatically switched on. He cringed; danger could be waiting for him anywhere. Gravity overwhelmed him as he stumbled to the white rectangular counter with two sinks. Fear reached around his neck and tightened its cold grip. He held his breath, waiting for the door to open behind him. *Nothing. There's no one.* He sucked in air before he passed out. Doug couldn't even focus on the spilled liquid soap on the counter or the paper on the floor. The muscles in his throat constricted the blood pumping to his head. "What do I do?" Drums beat his ears senseless as both his hands pulled at the mental rope around his neck. Bending over the sink, he shook his head. It rattled from a developing stress headache.

Doug slammed his tightened fists down. "Oh, God," he lifted his voice and chin to the ceiling. "What do I do?" Tears burst out of his ducts at an alarming rate. They fell down his reddening cheeks. *My world was just changing...finally for the better...right and wrong were no longer thrown together in a huge cement mixer.* His head dipped down. Fingerprints on the mirror blurred together, creating an abstract design. The more he exercised his weary pupils, the lower the expectation his eyes had for focusing on the world around him. A deafening silence thundered in his eardrums. *The I.V. Scissor King knows my phone number. Is Jayne working for him again?* His thoughts and muscles froze. *Nah, not possible.* Closing his eyes, Doug focused inwardly on the rhythm of his breathing.

After stretching his hands up high, Doug pushed his arms behind his ears. Suddenly, his upper limbs flew to his sides. His fists clenched and tightened. *Or is he?* He beat his thighs. *I need some cash...* Doug's arms and legs trembled. *But... I... don't want to work... for him... if Jayne isn't...* His knees buckled as he knelt to the floor. *All he wants is gossip...what harm? How do I approach Jayne? Do I approach him? Do I tell the FBI? What if Jayne is working for Doc? That would get him in trouble.* Pushing his hands roughly against the countertop, Doug stood up and stared at the door with his head cocked to the side. He opened his mouth and let fly as many foul words as he could utter. Staring at himself in the mirror, his eyes played tricks on him as the mirror waved away an appealing future. His mental image formed cracks which expanded into crevices and broke apart in small pieces. Reaching his right fist to his forehead, he mentally scrubbed the image away from his thoughts. *The mind is what people admire.* Since daily choices in life dictate character, Doug had quite a few big decisions to make. *Who do I want to be? Who do I want to choose? How do I make choices when the facts could be skewed? Who can I trust?*

{:-)-]~~{

Jacqueline made her presence known and signaled everyone to return to their seats to finish announcements. The men dispersed in the direction of friends or family.

Around the room, peace soaked in where fears had previously been hidden. Things were finally looking brighter for the H.E.C.C.s and their human families alike. This new city would be for H.E.C.C.s and those who loved them. After a few final announcements, the audience scattered to their pre-assigned cleaning duties. Bed was then welcomed by some, but most stayed up, chatting all night. Morning came and went and so did lunch. After lunch, everyone went back to their homes across the nation to prepare for moving day.

Jayne was floating on air, embracing a promise of a better future. Imprisonment in an oceanarium had been the beginning of this nightmare. Now, unrestrained access to an oceanarium would be the end of it. A brighter future than any could have hoped for just a few years ago, especially for Hope and Jayne.

{:-)-]~~{

THE END
(or is it the beginning…)

Glossary

*"It doesn't matter whether or not they were a menace to society.
The 'breath of life' leaving any body still leaves behind a corpse."*
- FBI SA Peter Austin

Biracial HECC - The 'mixed' breed has everything that a full-blooded H.E.C.C. has, but lack the chromosome that produces the tails.

Fermenting tanks - Liquid graves held the failed experiments of the I.V. Scissor King as a reminder of the complications. They were tall upright rectangular tanks. Each tank had 11x14 picture frames displaying the names, ages when kidnapped, pictures and complications. The evil scientist was clearly not prejudiced because the aquariums included every ethnic background, young and old alike.

Festar Ing and Yetchy Fungu Wounde (FesterIng & Itchy Fungu(s) Wound) - missed out on their bank robbing career.

Hamaan Dydeby Ropbourne (Hamaan Died-by Ropeburn) - Male murderer died by the incisions of the I.V. Scissor King

H.E.C.C - Human Electric Cave Catfish is a humanoid race which was created by the I.V. Scissor King. His experiments in regenerative medicine "succeeded" when he crossed Electric Cave Catfish's DNA with humans.

Hecc – Short pet name for H.E.C.C.s

Heccan - The male HECC lacks the fingerprint cranial 'jewel' and has normal chests like human males.

Heccwan - The female HECC has a fingerprint design that looks like a jewel located in the center of the cranial ridge. It drives Heccans crazy for love like the pheromones of a beautiful human woman would drive a human man crazy.

I.V. Scissor King - The nickname for the mysterious doctor who wore a disguise so that he could anonymously experiment with regenerative medicine and DNA splicing. He created the first new humanoid race that Earth has encountered in recent history. The term comes from the doctor's methods of experimentation, which included both I.V.'s and surgeries.

Juzte Donnet Tuche (Just Don't Touch) - A pedophile locked away in a fermented tank after the doctor's experiment failed.

Lucifer Israel Badde (Lucifer is-real Bad) - A serial killer who was kidnapped and died in early painful experiments by the I.V. Scissor King.

Oceanarium - A large aquarium to house and exhibit sea life.

Otto Hake Dick (OughtTo Hack Dick) - One of the pedophiles that bombed his chance in society. Justice was served by the I.V. Scissor King.

Regenerative medicine - The process of regenerating human cells, tissues or organs to restore or establish normal function.

Secret Code - A collection of underlined words inside this soft science fiction novel creating a fishy sentence revealing a possibility in the sequel. Example: A fortune inside a cookie, "Help. I'm an indentured worker at a cookie factory."

Zupid Lawz Zuckez (Stupid Laws Sucks) - A man marked as a sex offender simply because he urinated on the side of the road was also a victim of the I.V. Scissor King.

Nairobi Kipsigi and Amari Borane   Mary   and   Robert Sr Davis
(Daughter of Nairobi and Amari) Zola Kipsigi (son of Mary and Robert) Robert Jr
(D of Amari and Mary)   Mildred Davis And Jack Sharp

(Daughter of Jack and Mildred) Marcy Sharp and Clifford Clark
Gabriel Clark
Ella Clark
Blakie Clark
Identical Twins Henry and Sebastian Clark

(Daughter of Jack and Mildred) Beverly Sharp and Marvin Hart
Billy Hart
Frat Twins Charlene and Charlie Hart
Nick
Tannen

(Daughter of Jack and Mildred) Kelly-Sue Sharp and Kelly-ate Shaw
Frat Twins William and Willatta Shaw
Ashley Shaw
Identical Twins Mark and Tony Shaw
Lisa Shaw
Nina Shaw

(Daughter of Jack and Mildred) Bonnie Sharp and Jerome Burgess
Kenny Burgess
Vanessa
Identical Twins Hannah and Emma Burgess

Jeremy Cook and Delores Cook

(Son of Jack and Mildred) Tyler Sharp and Gabriella Cook and Marshall Harrison
(D of Tyler and Gabby) Mary Sharp   (Daughter of Gabby and Marshall) Marian Harrison

(Daughter of Jack and Mildred) Melista Sharp

List of Contributors

Artist:

During the birth of my creation, Ann Warren generously believed in me and my story. She promised to illustrate it when my chapters were each at least 20 pages long and only three chapters had been written. Wrapping up the book, I watched her breathe life into my characters by inking them on paper.

Editors:

Anita Siemer, Sara Hobson Jenlink, Robert Dyer, Patty Reddon, Theresa Walker, Kimberly Foster, Louise Pelzl, and Lori Brotz edited. They remained full of encouraging words, which provided me an endless supply of ink for my quills. Kristen corrected some special content which added truth to my work of fiction.

Photographer:

Neil Harmon is the photographer of my author picture, who captured my creative idea. Mermaids might be an old tale, but I have added new twists.

In my author picture for this book, I put a lot of thought behind it. Lying on the grass, I hold a quill above a laptop combining an extended past primitive writing style with the current technology. With a smile, I am garbed with a period overdress and a fantasy chemise. My literary creations are honored with silver nail polish and shiny jewelry.

Neil also filmed and edited the book trailer that I directed. It can be found online on my YouTube Channel. He performed visual editing on several illustrations and the Sharp family Genealogy chart.

Research:

Ben Harvey and his dad, Fred, held an open door policy at their diving shop. Their encouragement and information guided me along the way. Ben's enthusiasm about my new tale allowed me to see firsthand how enjoyable the world of diving is.

When I think of courage, the name, Rochelle Shaw, pops into my head. As I came across her during my research, she fought for my book. Although things didn't turn out like we expected, Rochelle's bravery inspired me throughout my journey. When I asked her about it, she said, "When you believe in something, you have to fight for it."

Dustin Hendricks, Murray Balk, Ned Marks, Tom Archer, and Jeff Davison helped me understand a bit of my research which wrapped up this book and will aide in my sequels.

David Sim showered me with his knowledge as an architect. Mike Eidem, Architect, has been helping me fix my designs for the Hecctopian city in the 'Tales From School' Series.

After contacting several companies dealing with Jet planes, I bumped into a kind soul, Kenny. I loved spreading my wings and learning more about how the world turns.

Web:

Check out the hard work of the web mistress, Alice Neville, on Jae's website: www.what-the-hecc.com

The Ink of an Octopus

Letter from Author

On our family vacation, we snuck a few minutes to enjoy swimming in the lake. While watching my little ones, I found myself feeling young, beautiful, and completely ornery. Lying on my stomach in the shallow water, I stated, "Look, I'm a beached whale!"

My first born laughed, but I could tell the joke zinged over his head. Still feeling chipper and cute, I held my thighs together while splashing my feet simultaneously in and out of the water. Batting my eyes and scrunching my shoulders, a thought hit me. Locating my husband soaking up the sun on the beach, I hollered. "Look, Honey! I'm a beached HECC."

With a crooked smirk, my husband groaned and snorted. Grinning like a possum, I got my satisfaction. The maniacal giggle that escaped my lips grew into hard laughter forcing me to stand up before I jerked my head underwater. The lightning thought of being born gill-less crossed my mind. My pondering led to considering how my first 'Tail' impacted my life, my immediate family, and friends.

As I think about the origin of this work of fiction, I am surprised to admit my journey started in my youth. Whenever life swallowed me whole, I escaped by drawing mermaids. Not long after, my lead based scribbles formed into words on paper. Keep navigating through these slippery pages and you will locate adventure, drama, and compassion. Perhaps on your journey, you will welcome these warm-blooded individuals as strangers, friends or foes. There will be times to rejoice that you are not the offspring of a tiger shark. If you desire to escape into a foo-foo fantasy world without trials, then you will be disappointed. Without tribulations, we humans do not remember that we claim each other.

Knowledge, values, and courage can be hidden throughout fiction. It's funny how I started this book to entertain. Yet along the way, I learned life lessons and furthered my education by researching books, educational movies, and the internet.

The science portion of my book lacked something until I found a program on the Science Channel describing almost every procedure I wanted to write about. The fact that scientists have attempted some worried me. Thank the Creator that not all the science has been perfected. Therefore, I beg scientists and doctors to stay away from DNA splicing, but hope they can perfect regenerative medicine.

Like most modern writers in this technologically advanced society, my journey took a different path when my computer died without a backup to turn to. My self-imposed challenge gave me a further headache when I changed Mildred to Melista and Melista to Mildred. That's completely confusing, disorienting my computer when I rearranged it. The final stages of my book included me chopping the book in half... twice. It has given me the start for at least three sequels.

This book has blessed me to be able to swim in the half full glass of optimism and enjoy its freedom. May my tale of freedom give you a boost to produce tails and swim.

Enjoy this tale as the first installment in the 'Tales From School' Series.

May your life be electrified.

Jae Byrd Wells

Bottom Dwellers

(The following disclaimer has been responsible for major controversy because a portion contains subtle humor. Several respected librarians and authors encouraged me to keep it.)

I am not responsible for injuries caused by falling off chairs, couches, tables, sofas, bridges, or other weird reading places.

I am not responsible for the idiots that do not put down their book to operate machinery. Blame them, but watch the road rage.

I am not responsible if someone old enough to pick up this book is not old enough to read it. I did not personally hand it to them.

I am not responsible for your taste in books. It was my cup of tea and I enjoyed devouring it. Thanks for politely trying a sip.

I am not responsible for you spilling any drink (whether cold or hot) while you were laughing or startled while reading this book.

I am not responsible for overlooked, scorned, and misplaced bedtimes by your offspring or parents. If they chose to use a flashlight to read the book after bedtime, ground them… but not from the book!

I am not responsible for anything you might wish to make up for a reason to sue me. There truly are too many stupid lawsuits that really have ruined this society. Do you know why I do not eat catfish? They are too closely related to lawyers.

I am responsible for writing this book. I am also responsible for making you reread the previous sentence. >;-) Mwahahahahahaa

Jae Byrd Wells

**No characters are based off friends, family or strangers. There are a few who have unique names with a hidden jab according to their stories. While reading the names aloud, one should be able to catch it. However, if not, search for the names in the Glossary.